PERILOUS CONFESSIONS

Book 1 of The Possession Chronicles

By

Carrie Dalby

For Angela Dalby,

thanks for all the "poison berry pies" when we were growing up.

And Martina McBride,
whose powerful voice on songs like
"When You Love Me," "Where I Used to Have a Heart,"
and "Cheap Whiskey"
helped bring greater depth to this story.

One

Adjusting the borrowed black caplet over her evening gown, Lucille Easton hoped to hide the unfashionable Victorian lines under the soft rabbit fur of her wrap the entire night. Lucy clung to her brother's arm as they followed their parents up the front walk of the Mellings' mansion. The pairs of ionic columns across the front porch draped with fresh evergreen swags were a festive welcome for the Christmas party.

Seeming to understand her distress, Edmund's gloved hand patted his sister's arm. "Don't fuss about it, Lucy. You look better in that dress than Susan did, and she wore it when she caught David's eye for the first time."

She groaned. "You speak of marrying me off when all I want to do is meet with Kate Stuart."

Edmund laughed and stroked his brown beard, which made him look like a Romanov Tsar—much too old for his twenty-two years. "As pretty as you are, I think the greatest challenge tonight will be keeping you safe from that gossip hound. Suitors are one thing, but Kate's talons are sharper than most. Don't be surprised if I pull you away from her."

Stopped in the advance of arriving guests, Lucy gazed in the nearest window at the lighted finery within the newly built mansion. A throng of society men and ladies roamed the front room with glasses in hand, trains and tails flowing behind, causing her to rethink the choice to opt for a new dress for a Mardi Gras ball rather than the Christmas party. Though the Easton family was far from poor, Lucy usually had no issues wearing hand-me-down dresses from her three older sisters because she'd rather spend her time writing than shopping. But tonight was a level of opulence she had never experienced outside of a masquerade.

When they reached the entry hall, Lucy paused, momentarily blinded by the electric lights reflecting off the gilded walls.

"Edmund, take Lucy's wrap so we can enter," Mrs. Easton urged her son as Mr. Easton handed her cloak to the help.

"Come on, Lucy," Edmund whispered. "Off with it."

To her delight, the silver embroidery at her waist and ruffled chest sparkled in the bright space. It helped her not feel dowdy in the dress she'd rescued from the attic. Though she didn't have a demi-train like the majority of the gowns in the house, her full, straight hem and elbow-length sleeves had a similar cut to others in attendance. As soon as they passed their outerwear to the staff, Mr. and Mrs. Easton disappeared into the parlor to pay their respects to the Mellings. Edmund led Lucy through the house to a rear morning room where most of the unmarried guests assembled.

Edmund went for the eggnog on the side table as Lucy stepped toward the corner, more comfortable to observe the room from afar than join in the conversations. Her brother, on the other hand, soon supplied drinks and laughter to several young ladies garbed in the peak of Edwardian fashion before he returned to his sister's side.

Edmund handed her a cup and took her elbow, leading her toward the sofa in the middle of the room. "Surely you'll forfeit your seat to my sister, Rupert," he informed his friend.

"Of course, Eddie." The plain-faced man stood from his snug spot on the couch and nodded to Lucy with a leering smile. "It would be my pleasure, Miss Easton."

Mortified, Lucy took the uncomfortable position between two brunettes in red and gold, ever aware of her blonde hair and pale dress. She sipped her drink and glared at her brother over the rim of her glass, to which he merely winked in return.

"That brother of yours," Judith McGowan said from her position to Lucy's right, "is he attached to anyone yet?"

"Not that I'm aware of."

"Even though he's running with the fast group now, he's still a great catch. Just look at him compared to Alexander Melling. It's like a man verses a boy, though the boy has a larger pocketbook."

The hosts' son had joined Edmund and Rupert in front of the fireplace. Alexander—the only one in the room with hair paler than Lucy's—stood out from the others, but blond hair on a man wasn't as unfashionable as for a woman. True, her brother's distinguished facial hair gave him a more mature look, but Lucy rather liked the impish smile of clean-shaven Alexander. She'd often admired him when he stopped by their house to collect Edmund for club meetings. After a few exchanged words with Alexander, Edmund returned to Lucy.

"Excuse us, ladies," Edmund addressed the women on either side of her, "but my sister is needed in the other room."

"Has Mother taken ill?" she asked as he set their cups on the table and brought her into the hall.

"Not at all." Edmund nodded to the person behind her. "She's at your service, though I hope I don't have to warn you about safeguarding her virtue."

"If you don't trust me, you're welcome to come with us, Eddie."

"That won't be necessary. I'll see you in a few minutes." Edmund took Lucy's hand and passed it to the man behind her.

Upon turning, Lucy met the piercing blue eyes of Alexander Melling. Her stomach quivered under his gaze and her cheeks warmed. "What's this about?"

Alexander tucked her hand under his arm and steered her toward the front of the house. "I'd like you to help my sister, but my first instinct was to save you from the discomfort Eddie carelessly placed you in." He angled his head toward hers. "A creative soul like you never wishes to be in the center of the room, surrounded by acquaintances. You need a cozy corner with a few intimate friends."

A glowing smile spread across her face. "Yes, exactly true. How did you know?"

He paused at the foot of the stairs. "I've watched you at gatherings and your brother has spoken to me of your writing talents. Knowing what I do about my own sister and her artist soul, I have empathy for someone like you."

"It's wonderful to be understood. I often feel isolated in social situations, especially with Grace Anne out of town. Thank you for freeing me."

Alexander led her up the staircase. "Your friend is touring Europe with her family, isn't she?"

"Yes, the Marleys were last in the south of France according to the postcard I received this week."

When they reached the middle landing, Lucy chanced a look at the main floor as they turned to the next half flight of stairs. The black clad figure of Kate Stuart disappeared down the side hall. Lucy wondered if the journalist had seen her going upstairs with Alexander. Though he took her to his sister, she wished Edmund had accompanied them. The last thing she needed was for Miss Stuart to think her overly bold with men when she sought employment at her magazine.

In the quiet of the upstairs hall, Alexander paused before a wall-mounted mirror. He pointed at the sprig of green hanging from the middle of the carved gold frame. "Does the mistletoe tradition work when it's above our reflection instead of us?"

Pleased with the look of her sparkling dress beside Alexander, Lucy couldn't stop the sly smile from curling at the corner of her lips as she turned to him. "I don't see why not."

Expecting him to quickly kiss her on the cheek, her heart fluttered when he took her hand from his arm and linked their fingers together. His other hand reached for her neck. Wanting to soak in every detail, Lucy kept her eyes open as he fingered her throat while he brought his face nearer. The excitement of the moment created more of a thrill than the hint of fear over being so close to a man she hardly knew. Closing her eyes in anticipation, his lips brushed her cheek on the way to her mouth. His kiss held a stronger taste of cognac and rum than the eggnog she'd drunk.

"I would have rescued you from a party long before tonight, but you were always inseparable from Grace Anne." With a warm exhale of breath, Alexander caressed her neck before lowering his hand. "Merry Christmas, Lucille."

The impetuous need to feel him under her lips once more took hold, and she planted a lingering kiss on his cheek. "Merry Christmas, Alexander. You can rescue me anytime."

"There are plenty of opportunities for that in the months ahead. I'll consider rescuing you at the pinnacle of Mobile's 1905 carnival season, if that's agreeable."

"Yes, very much so."

"Good. I'd like to see more of you." He held her gaze for several seconds and then examined her appreciatively. "You're a striking sight and I bet there's much cleverness and wit to be found in your company."

"I hold my own in a conversation, though I'd rather dazzle with my pen."

Still clasping her hand, Alexander tugged her closer as he searched her countenance with hungry eyes. "You dazzle me now, Lucille. If Eliza didn't need us, I'd dash out to the yard with you and hide ourselves within the camellia garden. They're just beginning to bloom and there's a snug bench nestled amid them. Promise me, if you feel overwhelmed tonight you'll escape there."

Lucy nodded, not trusting herself to speak as waves of emotions pounded her chest. If she could keep her hand within his the remainder of the party, she knew she'd have a lovely time. He led her to a closed door down the hallway. With a caressing touch, he released her hand and knocked.

"Eliza," he called through the door, "it's me."

"Come in."

Alexander turned the knob and placed his hand on the small of Lucy's back as they entered the bedroom. Never having been one to swoon after men, the rush of expectancy tingling throughout her body unnerved Lucy.

"I brought an angel to attend you when you make your obligatory rounds. You remember Miss Easton from cathedral functions, don't you?"

Enormous periwinkle eyes stared up at Lucy from the ruffled bed. Despite her raven hair, eighteen-year-old Eliza favored her older brother with the same haunted eyes and pale complexion. She sat cross-legged in the middle of the bedspread, her silvery gown fanned out around her.

"Yes, we helped the children with the three-legged race at the last picnic. I'm glad to see you in white, Miss Easton. I was afraid I'd stick out down there."

Though she didn't want to lose Alexander's touch, she stepped forward. "Please, call me Lucy, like my family and friends do. Only a few years ago I had the awkward experience of making the rounds when my parents hosted a party before my debut. I'd be happy to go about with you, if you'd like."

With a grasping lunge, Eliza threw herself at Lucy, burying her face in her puffed sleeve. "Thank you! I begged for them to allow this to be my debutante party, but they insisted it be all about the house and showcasing the beauty of Mr. Rogers's French Renaissance design. I have to wait until the New Year's Eve ball for my coming out like everyone else."

"You'll be the jewel of Mobile," Lucy said. "And turn some heads tonight as well."

"Anyone looking our way will be doing so to get a better view of you." Eliza released Lucy and stood. "Isn't she a breath of fresh air, Alex?"

"Yes, Lucille is like no other." The deep, calm way he spoke caused Lucy to shiver. "Let me escort you ladies downstairs."

Alexander parted the swarm of people in the front hall, allowing Lucy and Eliza to reach the parlor. Eliza went first to her parents, where she introduced Lucy to them.

"We spoke with your parents earlier," Mrs. Melling said as she pulled her lace shawl tighter around her green dress. "It's like you've blossomed into a full woman before our eyes these last years, don't you agree, George?"

Mr. Melling stroked his mustache, styled after President Roosevelt's, and studied her. "Yes, quite so, Ruth, though with the bevy of pleasant older sisters, one would expect no less. Be sure you see everything on the property before you leave tonight, Miss Easton. I would hate for you to miss anything we have to offer."

"Thank you, Mr. Melling. It's a lovely home."

Lucy followed a step behind Eliza as she made her way through the lower chambers. In the mahogany paneled dining room, Alexander met up with them.

"Eggnog, my beauties?" he asked.

Eliza happily accepted. Before passing it to her, he pulled a flask from his jacket and poured an extra splash of rum.

"You're a lifesaver, Alex!" She started on it right away.

"I thought you'd need a boost before hitting the singles' room."

When he turned to Lucy, she shook her head. "Nothing extra, thank you."

Alex caught Lucy's eye and smiled. "And you, Lucille, impressed our parents, which is no easy task. I was just informed to look after your well-being tonight."

"You needn't bother over me. Edmund has that charge."

Alexander laughed. "Come see how Eddie is otherwise engaged."

They were met with laughter and high spirits amid the young crowd. Edmund stood beyond the fireplace, half a dozen eager ladies and several men following his every word as he recounted the tale of what happened when one of their nephews tried to dress the Thanksgiving turkey last month.

"Oh, no!" Lucy blushed and turned away. "He would tell that story in mixed company."

"—and when Father fetched the platter, he brought it to the dining room with one of Lucy's petticoats trailing off the bird."

The laughter of the ladies and whistles from a few nearby men drove Lucy to seek a dark corner, even though it meant leaving Eliza. On the opposite side of the room she spied Kate Stuart, looking every bit a queen with her ostentatious brunette pompadour and sweetheart neckline, adorned with her signature gold watch she wore as a necklace. When their eyes met, Lucy felt the lady's talons her brother hinted at earlier, but she brushed aside the vision and approached her.

"Lucille Easton." Kate smiled, though the gesture didn't reach her shrewd, dark eyes. "I am glad you finally found the time to speak with me. You've been a busy girl since you arrived."

"I'm sorry for the delay, but I was asked to help—"

"I know what you've been up to. It's my business to know what everyone is doing at any given time."

Lucy held her breath, not knowing if the editor of the local gossip magazine would find fault in her behavior thus far, not to mention the story of a turkey wearing her underclothes.

"I know you're eager to write, but I am not keen on hiring someone whose behavior could fill several pages on their own accord."

"But I—"

Kate held up her gloved hand. "I know you mean well, but I am not sure you have thick enough skin to survive scandal or are self-deprecating enough to write about your own follies or those of your family and friends without fear of looking ridiculous. Writing fiction and poetry is one thing, real life is quite another cup of tea and not everyone is cut out for it."

Lucy clasped her hands in front of her churning stomach. "I understand your concern, but if you let me prove myself, I'm sure you'll be pleased."

Kate stood. The broad shoulders of the black velvet gown made Lucy feel small as she only reached the woman's nose.

"Tell me how you would write the incident of your brother's Thanksgiving story."

Lucy blanched. "The turkey wearing my—"

"That's exactly the type of story my readers expect, no matter who they happen to."

She bit her lip and gazed at the ceiling's plastered relief vines crisscrossing the room. "At the Mellings' lavish Christmas party, a certain Mr. E. was overheard sharing a humorous family story in which a young relation dressed their Thanksgiving turkey in his sister's petticoat. The festive bird was then presented at the table in the mentioned underclothes for undressing and carving. The status of the young lady's garment is still unknown."

Kate's smile reached her eyes. "Well done, Miss Easton. There might be hope for you yet. Look for a letter from me after the next edition is published. That's all I will tell you now."

Seeking relief from what she considered to be a disastrous interview, Lucy found the nearest exit to the back patio. A few couples milled about the shadowed areas, but she hurried beyond the lawn to the camellia garden. Her slippered feet were quiet on the oyster shell path between the mature bushes and she soon found the wrought iron bench. She sat and berated herself for having botched her prospects of securing a writing job.

"I'm glad you're able to find solace here." Alexander stripped the foliage from a white camellia, scattering the tear-shaped leaves on the path.

"I'm sorry. I should go back to Eliza." She went to step around him.

He caught her by the wrist. "No need. She's safely back in her room for the night. Thank you for helping. It meant so much to her—and me."

"I was happy to do it."

In the darkness, Alexander's eyes shone brightly. Finished with the stem, he ran his fingers over the opened petals and tucked the camellia behind Lucy's right ear. He trailed his fingers over her cheek as he lowered his hand. "It's not as soft and lovely as you, but you wear it well."

The familiar sensation of weakening under his touch returned. "I should get back inside."

"There's no need to run from me, but you do feel chilled. Please take my jacket." He slipped off his black tuxedo coat, revealing his coordinating vest over his white shirt. Laying his jacket around her shoulders, Alexander took the opportunity to lean close. "You look upset. Was it something to do with your conversation with Miss Stuart?"

Lucy returned to the bench and Alexander sat beside her, his leg touching the skirt of her gown. "It's supposed to be a secret because all the articles are anonymous, but I'm hoping to get on as a reporter for her magazine."

"Why would a brilliant mind like you want to write gossip that deserves to end up at the bottom of a canary cage?"

Lucy smiled, but a tear leaked out of the corner of her eye. "It's not my ideal profession, but I hope it will get the attention of her uncle. He's an editor at a publishing house in New York. I think it could be a boost in getting one of my manuscripts published."

He handed her a handkerchief from his pocket. "A boost from anonymous tidbits?"

"I'm willing to do anything that might help. I've been trying to publish my stories since I turned eighteen and all I have to show for two years' worth of effort are a few poems in the newspaper and a drawer full of rejection letters." She ran her thumb over his monogrammed initials on the handkerchief. "But I'm afraid I've ruined my chances. I assume Kate saw me go upstairs with you, and then Edmund's ridiculous story about my petticoat on the turkey was the topper. She probably knows we're here alone right now too. She thinks me more fit to write about than to do the writing."

"Then she's a fool." He lifted her chin. "But you can be assured no one knows I'm here with you. I exited the front and came through the back gate to join you. I can be discreet when it's needed."

She gazed at him intently—easy to do because they were within a fraction of an inch of being the same height. "You went through all that trouble for me?"

"I'd do all that and more, Lucy. May I call you that, like your beloved family and friends?" His fingers still supported her face.

"I wish you would." She tilted her head, lining herself up for a kiss.

"All artists need a spectacular love affair—something to power their work for years to come. I want to teach you what you can't learn from novels, Lucy." His mouth hovered over hers as he spoke the tantalizing words. "Will you allow me to open you to a world of passion?"

In response, she closed the space between their lips. Alexander's hands went to her waist and Lucy wrapped her arms around his neck, one hand clutching the handkerchief and the other tracing his collar. Just as she marveled how perfectly they fit together, the silence shattered.

"Lucy!" Edmund hollered from across the lawn. "Are you out here?"

Breathless, she pulled away from Alexander. He stood—bringing her with him—and took her in his arms for one last kiss. Then he deftly removed his coat from her shoulders and disappeared behind the camellia bushes toward the back of the property.

Lucy exhaled, shoved Alexander's handkerchief into the hidden pocket of her gown, and tried to calm her nerves before calling out to her brother. "I'm in the garden, Edmund!"

He found her sitting on the bench, hands in her lap, and the flower behind her ear. "Good. I was hoping you weren't out here with Alex. People were looking for him and I was afraid he'd tucked away with you."

She stood. "Would that be so bad? You were trying to marry me off earlier."

Edmund's teeth flashed white amid his beard as he laughed. "Not to one of my friends. I don't fancy hearing stories about my sister going around the smoking rooms, and some of them are the type to do just that."

"But you tell stories of my petticoat on the Thanksgiving turkey."

"Don't be sore, Lucy. I might have had one too many drinks, but I promise to behave the rest of the night." He removed the camellia from behind her ear and tossed it before taking her arm. "No need for you to return looking like a bohemian. Let's get back inside and find you a spot by the fireplace."

Two

The following morning, Lucy woke with a smile and threw open her curtains to allow the sun to filter through the windows. Clouds were blowing in from the north, but it didn't dampen her spirits. She removed Alexander's handkerchief from under her pillow and studied the scrolling red M flanked by an A and R and pondered his middle name. She craved deeper knowledge of him other than his flirtatious ways, wanting to understand him on all levels.

At one point the night before—after Edmund had secured her a spot by the fireplace—Alexander slipped her a tiny note when he passed her chair. She'd read, memorized, and tossed it into the fire to keep it from being seen.

Meet me on the south end of the portico fifteen minutes before the end of Mass.
I'll see you home.

Later, she'd caught Alexander's eye and nodded. Though she wasn't able to speak with him before leaving the party, she'd thought of him all night. Her mind replayed the feel of his hands on hers, the sandalwood scent that clung to his clothes, and how he tasted of rum and sensuality. She forgot about the reporting job, preferring to spend an hour before bed jotting down descriptions about Alexander in her journal. It brought an understanding to his words about a love affair fueling her work and she wanted more kindling for the fire.

Lucy dressed for church in another secondhand outfit, this one an icy blue that reminded her of Alexander's eyes. As a heavier winter dress, it rarely found use in the sub-tropical climate, and looked new though it was close to a decade old. The piping on the bodice narrowed at the waist in an attractive cut and the scalloped outer skirt of the wool fabric gave it a touch of elegance that made her feel like a princess.

Lucy settled in the backseat of the open-topped automobile between Edmund and their little sister, Opal. She smiled and tied a white scarf around her hat to keep it on as they motored to church for the final service.

"I don't see how you can look cheerful when we were out late." Edmund pulled his derby down, shading the tinge of red in the whites around his hazel eyes.

"And she was up later than you," Opal remarked, and Lucy scowled. "What? I could hear you scratching away with that pen of yours."

Edmund tugged Opal's blonde braid that hung under her wool hat. "Lucy's a serious writer. Don't complain when she's working."

"She could at least work somewhere else when she's up half the night. My bed's on the other side of the wall from her desk."

Opal's eyes were sharper than Lucy's mossy green, and they held the presence of a soul much older than her ten years. It felt like the girl could read the very thoughts within Lucy's mind and she didn't relish anyone being privy to her feelings toward Alexander when they were still fresh.

Lucy shuddered and crossed her arms. "You can't possibly hear me."

"I hear everything."

"Shall we call you a circus elephant because you have big ears?" Edmund joked, but neither sister smiled.

During awkward silences Lucy remembered her three siblings that went to early graves during the yellow fever epidemic in 1897. The five oldest siblings were already married or at finishing school when the disease struck the household. Opal was only three at the time, but the youngest sibling dangerously stared down her brothers and sisters after a fight over her toys. The next day, Peter, Aaron, Rebecca, and Lucy turned sickly, but Lucy was the only one left who'd witnessed the evil-eyed stare she felt had everything to do with their illnesses.

When the Eastons gathered on the front steps before ascending to the cathedral, Lucy took Edmund's elbow. "I'm in the mood to walk home today. If I'm not at the automobile afterward, don't wait for me."

"Plotting another story?" he asked.

She smiled, imagining the growing love story between her and Alexander. "Yes. Let me sit on the end in case I need to slip out early to write something down." She clutched the reticule to her chest as she climbed the steps to the massive portico.

While their parents and Opal made their way toward the front of the nave, Edmund and Lucy opted to sit near the back under the shadow of the organ balcony. It afforded a view of the two-story stained glass windows she was fond of daydreaming over, as well as the spectacular sight of the double row of Corinthian columns that stood like soldiers down the nave of the cathedral. The back location also allowed a glimpse of the Melling family—the parents along with Eliza's shiny black hair topped with a white lace mantilla.

Lucy knelt and stood throughout Mass, but her heart and mind were set on one person, and it wasn't the Lord. Toward the end of the service, she removed her notepad and pen from her reticule, fingering Alexander's handkerchief tucked inside. As reverently as possible, she made her way to the portico.

"Taking notes on my church attending habits?" Alexander, dressed in a smart grey suit with a coordinating derby, stepped out from between two of the monstrous Doric columns that flanked the front of the cathedral.

"More like the lack thereof." Lucy returned her items into her pouch and accepted Alexander's arm.

"I was there, Lucy." As they descended the steps, the smell of his sandalwood soap wafted over her like the first smell of peppermint at Christmas—delicious and invigorating. "I sat a few rows back, making sure you prayed when prompted, but I left twice as early to avoid any suspicion of us leaving together."

They exited the wrought iron gate that enclosed the church yard and paused on the sidewalk.

"And just how discreet is strolling through town?"

"It'll take the congregation a little while to catch up with our activities." Alexander winked. "Would you like me to walk you all the way home or bring you to my house where we can pick up an automobile?"

"I'm fine with the two-mile walk. It'll give us more time together, though I'm sorry we live so far out of the way. My parents wanted a bigger lot than those in the city for all of us to run around freely when we were young. But don't worry about me, I planned ahead." She stuck the toe of one of her sensible black boots out from the hem of her dress.

"I'm pleased to know you aren't a slave to fashion." They went around The Cathedral of the Immaculate Conception and headed west on the paved sidewalk on Dauphin Street.

"When dealing with clothes passed down from three sisters from the previous century, it's difficult to be picky."

"You always manage to look beautiful, though I've often wondered why you don't wear gloves like other ladies. Did your sisters wear them all out?"

Lucy's laughter rang like a silver bell. "I have several new pairs, but my mother gave up trying to force me to wear them when I turned eighteen. I need my fingers free to hold my pen."

Alexander smiled. "There's nothing less personal than the touch of a gloved hand. I liked being able to feel you last night." He placed his right hand on top of hers on his arm, allowing his fingers to briefly intertwine with hers. "I love how you shirk societal regulations, going to church gloveless and wearing old boots under a fine dress. Things like that shouldn't matter, though they are often all that are discussed by women in your social circle."

"My circle is smaller than most."

"And that's just the thing! It's refreshing to see that you don't fill your life with hollow relationships and cram your calendar with worthless events. Lucy, I'm honored you allowed my foot in the door of your cozy life."

If they weren't walking down the sidewalk midday, she would've kissed him. As it was, she waited until they passed another couple walking toward them, Alexander tipping his hat and nodding to them.

"Your whole self is invited into my world, Alexander," she whispered.

A mischievous smile lit his face as Lucy gave him a look that communicated she wanted more of the passion he'd spoken to her about. He brushed his thumb over her cheek. "Soon."

An automobile pulled along the curb of the dirt road, causing them both to stop.

"Davenport!" Alexander greeted the man in a dark suit with a black mourning band around his thick arm. "Did you skip out on church too?"

"Not at all. Trinity usually lets out before the cathedral."

Alexander turned to Lucy and winked. "I guess the Episcopalians will be the first ones privy to our doings." Gazing back to the man, he looked from him to Lucy. "Lucy, do you know Freddy Davenport?"

She extended her hand in greeting. "Yes, but it's been a while since I've seen you, Frederick. I'm sorry for your loss."

He removed his hat, sending a wave of rich brown hair over his forehead as he shook her hand. "Thank you, Miss Easton. I've missed my time with Eddie and your family. It's been too long since I last visited."

Alexander took Lucy's arm back in a way that communicated possession. "A widower can't hang around bachelors and debutantes. When does your sentence end?"

Lucy noticed Frederick tightening his square jaw. "Really, Alex, show a little compassion."

"Freddy knows how tactless I can be."

"I do remember your sharp tongue." Frederick cleared his throat. "New Year's marks the end of my eighteen months."

"I'll be sure you receive an invitation to the ball," Alexander said.

"I don't know if that would be my best choice for returning to society."

"Nonsense! My sister is coming out that night as well. Maybe you can give her a dance. She's determined no one will ask her."

"I might be able to do that, though you'd have to point her out to me." Frederick looked to Lucy, a sliver of hope in his brown eyes. "And maybe you'd honor me with a dance, Miss Easton. I remember spinning you around your parlor when you practiced for your first cotillion."

Her laughter caused the widower to smile. "Yes, your poor feet! I can assure you I'm much improved now."

Alexander placed his hand on hers and narrowed his eyes at Frederick. "I had no idea you two were such old chums."

"He was Edmund's closest friend during his school days," Lucy informed Alexander before turning her attention back to Frederick. "It is good to see you again. You must visit soon. Edmund will be home most of the week, and I'm sure our parents will be happy to receive you as well."

"I'd enjoy that. Thank you, Miss Easton."

"You can't refer to me as Miss Easton after alluding to our history of me stepping all over your feet. You must call me Lucy once again."

"Very well, Lucy. Warn your family and expect to see me this week. I'll see you later, Alex." He replaced his hat and pulled his automobile back into the street.

"Are you going to invite me over too, or should I be jealous?"

"You're welcome to visit, though Edmund seems to go out more often than he has visitors these days."

"I just might have to. I don't like the idea of another man seeing you socially." He reached into the front interior pocket of his suit, pulling out a hand-lettered invitation. "But I do want you to have this."

Lucy took the parchment with both hands. It was an invitation to the New Year's Eve ball hosted by one of the oldest Mardi Gras societies in Mobile, Order of Mayhem. Her father was a part of it, and she assumed Alexander's father was too since Eliza would come out at the ball—something she'd done herself a few years back. While she'd seen an invitation in Edmund's room, she'd had no desire to attend until that moment.

"You haven't already been invited by someone else, have you?"

"No, of course not." She tucked the invitation into her reticule between her notebook and his handkerchief. "For one who claims to have been watching me, you should know I've never arrived or left a party with an escort other than a relative."

He took her hand in his and replaced it on his arm. "That will change in the weeks ahead, but I need to be at the New Year's ball early. Have Eddie escort you, but let him know you have someone to see you home—without telling him it's one of his friends."

"You heard our conversation in the garden?"

"I may have stayed to listen." He grinned. "Some of us are cads, especially during carnival season, but I mean to treat our relationship proper."

"I should hope so. Edmund was a notable boxer in school and he wouldn't hesitate to defend my honor."

Alexander laughed. "Such wit and beauty should be a crime. Remember, you must be masked and gloved at the ball, no exceptions. Can you go one night without a pen in your hand?"

"Only if you occupy the space instead."

"I'll be there every moment I can." He hastily brought her hand to his lips and kissed the back of it. "Lucy, you have no idea the pleasure I feel at finally being next to you."

The back of her neck tingled at his words and touch. She squeezed his arm as they continued down the sidewalk. They walked the next blocks in silence, stealing quick caresses or coquettish glimpses.

"Will you be at midnight Mass next weekend?" he finally asked.

"Christmas Mass is something my family never misses. Even I enjoy the beauty of it."

"Are you disillusioned with church?"

"I'm going through the motions," she replied, "though I don't believe everything as I used to."

"I understand, but today I felt the joy of life bursting from my chest as I recited the words I've heard since childhood. Maybe it had something more to do with my view." Alexander stepped ahead, turning so he walked backward. "There was a stunning woman two rows up in a pale blue dress I couldn't take my eyes off of. The curve of her waist and her profile were my undoing."

Lucy blushed, and looked behind her to check if they had an audience. Seeing no one within their section of the block, she turned her attention back to Alexander's searching eyes.

"A hat covered her golden hair, but there was one tendril that seemed to tickle her neck. I wanted nothing more than to catch it between my fingers and feel what I believe to be its silkiness."

Lucy stopped walking and raised her hand to the back of her head. Sure enough, a lock of hair had escaped her chignon and trailed down her back.

"You have a way with words yourself, though I do believe you're a scoundrel." Her smile told him otherwise as she tucked the hair under her hat.

Back at her side, Alexander offered his arm and they continued their journey. She may have been gloveless and in old boots, but propriety kept Lucy from rushing down a side street with him. As it was, they walked in such a way that no daylight could slip between them and their hat brims bumped against each other when he leaned in to whisper.

The rumble of a familiar engine sounded behind them as they came to the end of the business district. Instinctively, Lucy placed a few inches between her and Alexander. Her family's automobile stopped along the opposite curb and Edmund jumped out before the Eastons continued home—Opal glaring at Lucy from her perch in the backseat as they pulled away.

Edmund weaseled his way between the two. "I suppose your writing ideas must have been awful for you to find a walk with this cad appealing."

"Your sister's a saint to put up with me and I can honestly say mine was the easier responsibility. But there's no need for you to take over now, I have her halfway home."

"Nonsense, I appreciate you looking after my sister, but you don't need to be late to Sunday dinner on her account."

"Yes," Lucy said, "I'm not worth missing pot roast."

Alexander and Edmund both laughed. Then Alexander held Lucy's gaze behind her brother's back for several seconds. She shrugged.

"You've convinced me to go home, Eddie, but would you like a ride to our meeting Thursday night? Father says I'm to have a new automobile before Christmas, and I think I'll have it by then."

"That'd be great."

"I'll swing by around seven thirty." Alexander tipped his hat and winked at Lucy. "And you have a wonderful week, Lucy."

"Thank you." She smiled in return, though it would be the longest four days of her life.

Three

Monday afternoon, Frederick Davenport paid a visit. Edmund was Christmas shopping with Opal, who was off from school work with her private tutor for the holidays. Mrs. Easton put Lucy in charge of entertaining him in the parlor until the others returned while she went over the Christmas menu with the cook. Lucy sat on an armchair adjacent to the matching green settee and poured tea for him.

"It was serendipitous running into you yesterday," Frederick remarked after he took his first sip. "Not until I saw you did I realize how much I've missed your family. This house was a fairyland to me. Some of my greatest childhood memories happened here."

"Fairyland or warrior kingdom? I remember Edmund collecting every boy within two miles to come over for battles in the yard."

"Yes, but pretending to be a knight was made real with a fair maiden like you taunting us from the tree fort." He paused, looking down at his cup before continuing. "I suppose it isn't proper of me to say while I'm still wearing my mourning band, but pretending to fight for your hand is what kept me on the winning side most battles."

Lucy's laughter turned her cheeks rosy, a striking look against her royal blue dress and bright hair. "There's no shame in that, it's just the fancy of a boy."

"Well…yes." He cleared his throat. "Are you out with Alex much?"

"Yesterday was the first time. He found me on the portico after I slipped out of church early and offered to see me home. Just a few blocks after we spoke with you, my family passed and Edmund joined us. He sent Alex on his way and walked me home himself."

"I suppose your brother wasn't pleased to see him with you."

Lucy tilted her head. "Why would you say that? They're close friends these days."

"It's not something I'd normally speak of in the company of a lady, but I'll call on the liberties of having grown up together to do so." Frederick cleared his throat again. "There have been stories about Alex passed around men's clubs and smoking rooms for years. Now, whether they're personal accounts bolstered to make him appear more commanding or rumors grown too large or even the truth, I don't know. But he's not someone I'd be comfortable with around my sister."

"Edmund did immediately squeeze between us and called him a cad."

"It's good to know his head is still on straight, even if he's surrounding himself with men like Alex."

Her heart wrote double time, but she didn't know if from fear or jealousy. "What sort of stories do the men talk of in their private rooms?"

"Most of it's political, business, or finance related, but after a few drinks, the subjects can swing to women and the like."

"Such as what?" She sat on the edge of her seat, leaning toward him.

Frederick shook his head. "I won't be accused of tainting your ears."

"It can't be that bad, otherwise why would refined gentlemen discuss them?"

"When a group of men are gathered together for drinks, they cease to be gentlemen and become rowdy boys. I've been glad to escape that sort of thing these past eighteen months of mourning." He paused and swallowed hard. "Well, that didn't sound right."

Lucy put her cup on the table and took Frederick's closest hand. "I know what you mean. I detest parties. Your poor, broken heart."

His face colored as he gazed into her eyes. "I'm mending well, but thank you for your tenderness, Lucy. It means the world to me."

In that moment, Frederick wasn't the childhood friend of her brother, but a man—broad, athletic shoulders, a noble nose, and tender brown eyes that had seen love and loss in his life. Lucy read the warmth in his eyes to be for her and withdrew her hand.

"Well," she said as she straightened in her chair, "perhaps you can reform the men. Show them how a true gentleman conducts himself when you return to society."

His smile turned down at the corners. "I'm hardly someone the upper crust would follow. I'm a mere accountant while the others are lawyers and the like."

"Your father started the best accounting firm in the city and now you run it. That's nothing to be shy about. If they can accept Edmund as the youngest living son of an import salesman, I see no reason for them to look down on you."

"Eddie's charismatic, always ready to charm his audience with wild stories and daring adventures."

"That and his troupe of older sisters. I remember him collecting pennies from his friends to peer in the window when Susan, Cora, or Emma had suitors over. When the twins both had a man over, he collected double."

Frederick laughed, nearly upsetting his cup. "I'd forgotten about that. I was in charge of keeping the boys in line. He paid me five cents for my efforts."

"Yet he calls his friends scoundrels. What could be worse than profiting from spying on your sisters?"

"What's this you speak of?" Edmund crossed the room and pulled Frederick from his seat, embracing him with a slap on the back. "I told you I wouldn't charge you to look, Freddy, but you never took me up on my offer. How are you, old friend?"

"As well as can be expected, thank you. It's good to be here. Lucy's been a marvelous hostess this past half hour."

Edmund sat beside Frederick and narrowed his eyes at his sister. "She seems set on taking over all my friends lately."

"That's because she's selfish!" Opal, standing in the doorway clutching a parcel, glared at Lucy as the malicious tone of her words settled around the room in uneasy fragments.

Used to the outbursts, Lucy ignored her.

Edmund pointed a finger. "There's no reason to disrespect your sister in front of company."

"Everyone fawns over her, but they'll know the truth soon enough." Opal stomped up the stairs and slammed her bedroom door.

"Sorry about that." Edmund lifted his eyebrows in exasperation. "I guess she's bigger and crankier than the last time you were here. I love Opal to pieces, but I can't help but think that with all the older siblings, the family used up every bit of pleasantries available to us before she was born."

Lucy hid her discomfort behind a teacup.

"She was always an odd bird," Frederick remarked. "Why does she have a private tutor instead of attending school?"

Edmund looked to Lucy as if to gage if they would take Frederick into their confidence as he used to be, but she looked away. *If he wants to tell about Opal breaking desks and beating up a boy at school, that's his affair, because if Mother finds out, she'll be furious the incident with her baby is out of the bag after keeping it hidden a year.*

"She's a sensitive child, as mother likes to say," Edmund explained. "The crowds and noises at school are hard on her nervous system."

"That's understandable," Frederick said. "But what of Lucy accused of being fawned over? Is that because Alex had her in his sights yesterday? He was quite possessive of her when I stopped to chat."

Edmund shook his head. "I made the mistake at the Mellings' Christmas party of allowing Alex to bring Lucy to his sister to help make her rounds as Lucy had years of practice with that. Eliza Melling's coming out this season, if you didn't know."

"Yes, I've all but promised to dance with her if I make it to the New Year's ball."

"I hope you come. I could use another set of eyes to keep track of Lucy. She informed me she received an invitation and asked me to accompany her there."

"I'd be happy to help."

"Times like this I miss Peter." Edmund's voice sounded far away. "He would've been eighteen this year and more than willing to help keep an eye on Lucy, and probably take a dance or two with Eliza."

"Really!" Lucy sighed in annoyance. "I'm not a bud out in her first season. I'm twenty and quite capable of conducting myself properly at a ball. I grew up between two strapping boys who taught me a thing or two about survival. How do you expect me to get and keep a suitor if you're going to track my every move?"

"Lucy, you're a peach. It's not you I'm worried about, it's the men. You've avoided Mardi Gras balls most of the time and haven't seen how wild they can get. New Year's is mild compared to most because all of high society is there, including the budding beauties, but I have half a mind to take you to mine this season so you can see firsthand what the bachelors around town are really like."

Edmund had joined a society the previous year, but as memberships were kept secret, she didn't know what group. Whichever one it was, she expected Alexander a member as well because they attended many meetings and social events together.

A gleam sparked in her eyes. "I think it would be very enlightening for me. What date should I mark on my calendar?"

"Really, I didn't mean I would—"

"No, Freddy is our witness. You said you had half a mind to make me go, and I'm telling your other half it's a good idea."

"I'm afraid you walked into that trap." Frederick laughed.

"Well then, you must join the society too. I know I'll need more eyes on her at the Mystics of Dardenne masquerade."

Lucy gasped.

"I'm afraid I'd never fit in with a group like that." Frederick straightened his cuffs.

"We aren't as bad as the newspaper made us out to be, but you can see why I don't enjoy the thought of my sister being there."

"Indeed, I don't see how you could even entertain it!" Frederick clenched his fists. "Respecting Lucy as I do, I feel obligated to attend for her safety, though I have no desire to join your ranks. No offense to you, Eddie."

"What the papers printed last year about the immoral behavior was grossly exaggerated."

"So there weren't any women of a certain profession in attendance?" Lucy pointedly asked her brother as she remembered the articles recounting the raid that ended with prostitutes and revelers being arrested.

"Well…" His cheeks blushed under his beard as he stared at his hands. "I can't say there wasn't, but you can be assured I had nothing to do with inviting them."

"I have a good guess for a culprit," Frederick muttered, casting a shadow in Lucy's heart.

"But the happenings weren't done in full display like the reports hinted at," Edmund hastened on. "And every last one of the members was at confession and penitent all Lent."

"And that makes the behavior okay?" Lucy reddened herself, covering her eyes in an attempt to darken the vision that had come to her of a drunken Alexander consorting with painted women. Not to mention the shame her parents would have if they discovered to which group Edmund belonged.

"Look what you've done to your sister. It's no place for a lady, or a true gentleman for that matter."

Lucy sat straight and returned her hands to her lap. "But I must go! Don't you see? That's exactly the type of thing I need to witness in order to bring my stories to life."

"And just what type of novels do you plan on writing?" Edmund demanded.

"Nothing like that, you can be sure. It's the vision of the debauchery of the upper class that brings out the worst in characters. Do you not see the potential for irony? The glorious opportunity for romantic interludes?" Her eyes shined as she imagined the words she would write after attending a bachelor's ball for the first time. "Now, what date do I put on my calendar?"

Edmund sighed and exchanged weary glances with Frederick. "January twenty-seventh. I'll secure invitations for you both, but, Freddy, you must be the one to bring her."

Four

After Frederick's visit Monday afternoon, the hours crawled by for Lucy. Anxiety over Alexander's true character were heavy in her chest while the rush of emotions she'd felt during her moments with him over the weekend dulled to a distant memory. She spent more time at her desk than in bed each night. By the time Thursday evening approached, she had smudges under her eyes.

"You need fresh air, dear," her mother told her at the supper table. Mrs. Easton's face, set with a few rows of fine lines and crowned with gray, was still pleasant at fifty. "Sit out on the porch after you eat, but be sure to bundle up. It's already in the forties."

"It's her ridiculous obsession keeping her awake at night," Opal muttered.

"What's that?" Mr. Easton asked as he wiped his mouth with a linen napkin. His gray hair appeared silvery in the gas lights. "Our Lucy is possessed?"

"No, *ob*sessed. With writing, if you haven't noticed, James," Mrs. Easton replied. "The side of her right palm is constantly stained with ink these days. If that's not a good reason to wear gloves in public, I don't know what is."

"Mother," Edmund said, "Lucy doesn't need to be pecked over while eating. Save it for the parlor."

"Nevertheless, I want you on the porch when you finish here."

"Yes, Mother."

A few days before, Lucy would have jumped at the chance to be the one to welcome Alexander when he arrived. Now she sat uneasily in one of the wicker rocking chairs on the porch of the Queen Anne home. The parlor window backlit her as she rocked to calm her nerves. She wore her grandmother's red cloak over her skirt and blouse, tucking her hands under her arms for added warmth.

Lucy caught her breath when headlights pierced the darkness on Catherine Street. Alexander pulled into the driveway behind Mr. Easton's automobile, the brass trim gleaming on his new vehicle. He jumped out of the door-less driver's seat. The arched fret work and railing around the porch framed the shadowed yard in white like an eerie painting Alexander crossed through.

"I thought that was you out here." He removed his goggles, ran his hand over his blond hair, and sat on the railing across from Lucy. "I hoped to see you, especially after our time was cut short Sunday."

Her heart pounded at the sight of his angelic face, bringing to the forefront all the emotions she'd first experienced at the party. He stretched his leg out and tapped the tip of his loafer against her boot when she didn't respond.

"Edmund means well, but he can be a pain." She stood and pulled the cloak tighter around her.

Alexander reached out, but let his arm fall to his side because the front door opened.

"Is that a Model B Touring?" Edmund pulled the door closed behind him.

"Sure is. Want to take it around the block?" Alexander tossed him the goggles.

"Yes!" Edmund leapt off the porch, then spun back to catch Lucy's attention. "Mother wants you back inside when I leave, young lady."

Lucy saluted her brother and he ran for the Ford. After cranking it, he drove in an arc across the front yard and turned toward Dauphin Street.

Shadowed from the front window by her standing before him, Alexander fingered her right pinky as he smiled. "You shouldn't be waiting for me in the cold."

"I wasn't technically waiting for you. Mother sent me out for fresh air after supper."

"I don't ever want to think of you waiting for me. I should be the one with baited breath, waiting to catch a glimpse of you. Even in this dim light I can tell you look ravishing in red."

"Then you'll be pleased to see me in my new Christmas dress." She gave him a flirtatious smile.

He raised his hand as if he were going to stroke her cheek, but clenched it in a fist as he lowered it. "I'm learning to put aside the natural man, Lucy. Like I told you Sunday, I want to treat you right and not rush things."

In that moment, no matter what he'd done in the past, he was hers for the present—and hopefully the future. "But don't go too slow. You also promised me a love affair."

Alexander closed his eyes. When he opened them, the yearning in his gaze nearly brought her to her knees. "Thirty minutes after Edmund gets home, meet me inside the gazebo."

A tapping sound struck the parlor window and she turned. Opal peered out with her calculating eyes. Lucy turned back to Alexander. "I'll be there, but I have to go inside now."

He touched his hand to his heart. "I'll be waiting for you."

She couldn't hide her smile when she went inside. Hoping it would melt away so her giddiness wouldn't be too obvious, she took her time hanging the cloak in the entry way before joining Opal and their mother in the parlor.

"Lucille was on the porch with a man—alone." Opal ran a finger over the tall Chinese vase their father brought home from a shipment last year.

"Don't make it out to sound like more than it was," Lucy said as Mrs. Easton turned from her needlework. "Alexander Melling got a new automobile and let Edmund drive it around the block. I chatted with him for a minute before coming in."

"You were very kind to his sister at the Christmas party. She looked petrified with those giant eyes, but she moved and spoke with grace. Hopefully, this season will acquaint her with the confidence she needs in adult social situations. She's pretty enough to keep a full calendar."

"People only like the Mellings because they're rich." Opal sneered. "I bet whoever fancies Alexander is only after his father's fortune."

"Opal! Discussing money is not something a lady does. You need to learn to control your mouth before it gets you into trouble." Mrs. Easton went back to her embroidery. "I don't know what's gotten into you lately."

"I'm tired because Lucille keeps me awake half the night with her scribbling."

"I know you are a sensitive child," Mrs. Easton said, "but your sister is quiet."

"Her desk is right against the wall by my bed and it keeps me up! Even if no one believes me, I know it's true." The furrowed brow over her emerald eyes made her look like a villain out of a fairytale.

"Lucy, dear," their mother said. "Is there any possible way to rearrange your room so your desk is against another wall?"

She crossed her arms and sighed, all joy from her moment with Alexander gone. "I think it would fit in the space where my dresser is."

"Have Eddie help you switch them around tomorrow, and for tonight, please take your writing time in here. Now we're all settled and I don't want another word about it. And, Opal, since you're tired from your lack of sleep this week, ready yourself for bed. I'll be up at eight thirty to tuck you in."

The smile left Opal's face and Lucy could tell she bit the inside of her cheek to stop from saying anything sassy.

"Yes, Mother," she muttered. "Good night, Lucille."

"Go on and fetch your pen and paper while she's changing. We can have a bit of quiet time before I see to her."

Lucy, with the threat of her little sister done for the day, reflected once again on Alexander. Opal's bedroom overlooked the front of the house, leaving no fear of being seen in the backyard from her. Edmund's room was across from Lucy's and stood watch over the backyard, as did her parents' suite, but they weren't ones to peer out windows at night.

Not knowing when to expect the meeting to take place, Lucy sat at her dressing table to fix herself up a bit. With the cold night, she needed to wear the cloak's hood over her head. She didn't like the way it fit with her hair up, so she pulled the pins out of her pompadour and brushed the blonde waves. She used her tortoiseshell combs to pull the sides back so her hair wouldn't fall over her face while writing. As she gathered her journal and pen, Opal poked her head in the open door.

"Since when do you have to fix your hair to write?"

"Since I've been exiled from my own room and Edmund is out for the evening. I'm forced to look presentable in case a guest should return with him while I'm in the parlor. I'll even need to keep my boots on, and I find it next to impossible to write while wearing shoes."

Opal glared up at her. "You don't fool me. I've seen you write everywhere, with and without shoes."

"And you'd better get to bed before Mother catches you running around. Your tired routine doesn't fool me."

"I haven't seen your hair down in ages," Mrs. Easton remarked when Lucy entered the parlor. "And I think the fresh air did you good. There's color in your cheeks. I know things have been difficult between you and Opal lately, but do try to enjoy yourself this season. You're not getting any younger and the eligible men will be snatched up before you know it."

"Mother!" Lucy dropped her things on the secretary hutch in the corner and turned to her in shock. She'd never been one to push marriage.

"You need to get out more this season. Last year, you only attended the New Year's ball."

"I'm planning on going out more, Mother. I even secured my own invitation for the Mayhem's ball, as well as a smaller masquerade at the end of January."

"Such wonderful news, Lucy! I don't know why it took these men so long to open their eyes to you, but I'm delighted. With at least two balls to attend, and most likely more invitations to follow, you'll need more than one new gown this season. Shall we go into town tomorrow to shop?"

Lucy laughed and joined her mother on the settee. "Let me see how long it takes to redo my room first."

"When Susan and her family come for Christmas, Opal will be sent home with her for a month. Susan could use the help with her three littles now that there is another on the way, and I think being the oldest will be a good experience for Opal. She's alone too much of the time since the others are no longer with us." Mrs. Easton crossed herself. "Bless their souls, my dear Peter, Aaron, and Rebecca."

Lucy swallowed the lump in her throat that always came at the mention of her deceased brothers and sister. "That might be just the thing for Opal."

Susan—the oldest sister, second in age to Maxwell—moved to Grand Bay after marriage. Mother brought the girls out for a few weeks each summer, but other than that, only the occasional Easter or Christmas visit unless Susan came to town for shopping or to attend a special event, rare happenings when she was in the family way.

"Your father and I will take the train out the last weekend of January and collect her."

The weekend of the Mystics of Dardenne ball! Lucy couldn't believe her luck. "That sounds like a great plan."

"Yes, and it will give you time to focus on your social engagements without worrying about her sour moods. I know you've been lonely with Grace Anne in Europe this past month. Maybe you and Edmund can host a small party some evening there's not a ball. Be sure to let him know the invitation to entertain is open."

Mrs. Easton piled her needlework into the sewing basket and stood. "I need to see to Opal, and then ready myself for bed. Make sure the lights are out if you're the last one up." She kissed her daughter's forehead and ran her hand over her hair. "I had forgotten how much Opal's hair is like yours. I wish women's fashion was for it to be worn down. You'd be sure to put all these brunettes to shame with your hair."

"Thank you, Mother. Good night." Lucy stretched the length of the settee, wrapped her arms around herself, imaged a different set of arms enfolding her, and dozed into a sleep-deprived slumber.

Five

"Are you dead?"

Edmund's voice startled Lucy awake. With a gasp, she sat up straight, swinging her feet to the floor.

"Easy there, Lucy. I don't want you fainting because you got up too quickly."

She rubbed her forehead, grateful to see her brother alone. "You know I'm not delicate. What time is it?"

"Almost eleven. Why are you sleeping in the parlor?" Edmund sat across the coffee table from her.

"I was kicked out of my room because of my noisy writing habits, but dozed off after Mother went to bed. Tomorrow, you have to help me move my desk so it's not against Opal's wall. But that's not the only news." She leaned toward him to whisper over the top of the hothouse flower arrangement. "Mother's sending Opal home with Susan at Christmas and she's to stay with her for a month."

"A full month?"

"Yes, and we're allowed to entertain whenever we want. Plus, Mother and Father are going to take the train out the last weekend of January to get her."

Edmund stroked his beard and raised his eyebrows. "The last weekend, as in Friday the twenty-seventh?"

"They'll take the train out that morning!"

"That's a load off me. I began thinking if they saw us leave for a ball on the night my society was known to be hosting, they wouldn't let us out of the house. You won't tell them which I joined, will you?"

"Of course not." She sat back. "I have my night out to think of too. Maybe by then I'll have my own date and you won't need to send Frederick with me."

"If you have a date, we'll really need Frederick's eyes on you." He laughed. "You know, I always though the two of you got along brilliantly when we were growing up. I remember telling him once if he waited another season he could have a chance with you. But the next thing I knew he was escorting that little twig around town and they were married just before your debut. I guess her Yankee blood couldn't handle that summer's heat, but she never did look healthy."

"Really, Edmund! I hope you don't talk to him in such a way."

"Never. The poor chap has had it rough as it is, but he's my only friend I'd trust with you." He stood and covered a yawn. "Want me to get the lights?"

"No, thank you. Now that I'm awake, I'm going to work for a while."

"You're a slave to your art, but I'll be sure to help you with your desk in the morning. Good night, Lucy."

"Good night. And thank you."

She crossed to her supplies and sat before a clean page in her journal. Opening her fountain pen, she jotted down her first thoughts from the evening thus far.

> *Bright days are coming ahead*
> *Without the threat of storm clouds*
> *You played your last trick*
> *Took your last stab*
> *Now it's time for me to shine*
> *With you no longer around*

Lucy reread her words, embarrassment creeping in because it came across harsh. She loved Opal, but she didn't like her. Leaving her pen on the open hutch, she stashed her journal under the cushion of a rarely used chair in the corner. In the event she couldn't slip back in the parlor before going to bed, she wanted it squirreled away until the morning. She shut off the gaslights in the parlor and hall. With ten minutes remaining before she met Alexander, Lucy stopped before the foyer mirror and finger-combed her hair where it had been ruffled from sleep. With cloak and hood on, she made her way to the back door.

Surprised to see the lawn brighter than the interior of the house, she gazed heavenward. The brisk night air sparkled with stars and the white glow of a full moon above the tree line that divided the yard from Catherine Street. Standing in amazement, Lucy soaked in the details to aid the description she would later write.

The white-domed gazebo stood in the shade of an ancient magnolia in the back half of the yard, partially hidden by azalea bushes. Lucy crossed the silver lawn, her breath steaming out like fog in a magical forest. Alexander stood in the far shadows of the wrought iron structure, wearing a black overcoat that he didn't have on earlier. He met her in the middle, took her hands in his, and leaned until their noses were almost touching.

"I feared you wouldn't come." Alexander's minty breath warmed her face.

"And I thought you came to me in a dream."

His hand went to her cheek, his thumb tracing her lower lip. "May I kiss you, Lucy?"

"Yes, now and whenever you want. You needn't ask again."

After their kiss in the camellia garden, she should have been prepared for the intensity of the intimate exchange, but passion poured over her like spilled ink and sent her head swimming. His coat smelled of cigarettes but his kiss was fresh, like it was only for her. Her hands went to his shoulders and around his neck while his went under her cloak, pressing their bodies together as he tasted her mouth as though famished. His lips moved down to her jaw. Then he nibbled at her neck, along the high collar of her blouse, as his hand deftly went at the buttons at her neck. Startled, she pulled away.

"Sorry, Lucy. I'm afraid that was more love affair than courtship, but you did want some of that too."

"So I did." Feeling the lingering heat from their bodies, she lowered her hood to cool her face.

Alexander wasted no time in pulling her hair free from the confines of her cloak. Running his fingers through the length of it, he arranged it to tumble over her shoulders. "So help me, it's as silky as I imaged. You know what this means, don't you?"

"No, what?" She mimicked his quiet tone as he took her by the waist once more.

He nudged her back until she was against the iron bars on the far side of the gazebo.

"It means we're living in an enchanted story. You're the cloaked girl in the forest and I'm the prowling wolf who can't keep away from that which looks and smells amazing." He buried his head in the curve of her neck, taking in the scent and texture of her hair as he melted against her. "You needn't fear me, Lucy. I do care for you, even when my passions rule, but you must be stronger than me. Don't ever let me take advantage of you."

A brew of fear and fantasy wrestled within her body. While she craved more of him, the distress of what Alexander was capable of doing—of how much she would go along with him—held her back. She lifted his head off her shoulder and waited until he focused on her.

"I'll have to learn my own limits and you must control yourself. I'll not be responsible for your actions. But keep in mind, if you do cross a line, my brother will be after you."

He kissed her cheek. "I've behaved poorly in the past, but I want this to be respectable, even if we sometimes meet in hidden gardens in the middle of the night." He pulled her cloak closed at the front, fingering the tasseled knot at her throat that held it secure. "Propriety with a dash of scandal for your artist's soul. How does that sound?"

"Delightful." She kissed him. "The most glorious words come out of your mouth."

"Because I'm looking at the wonder that is you, Lucille Easton," he said as he ran a fingertip along her lips.

"Are these rehearsed lines you use on all the women you call upon, a seducer's script to pave the way to a lady's ruination?"

"You've heard some stories about me?" He sighed when she nodded. "My past is no secret, though some things have been exaggerated. But aren't the colorful characters with a past always the most interesting in novels?"

She smiled. "Yes, they are."

"Knowing that I'm not perfect doesn't affect your feelings for me?"

"I knew that much before you spoke to me at the party."

"But you've learned more about me since then, haven't you? Does Eddie suspect?"

Not knowing if her brother had told him about getting roped into inviting both her and Frederick to their society's ball—and knowing there were penalties for disclosing membership information—she spoke her words with care.

"I don't think so, but he did call you a cad and sent you home when he caught us walking together. More things were hinted at when Frederick visited the other afternoon. He accused you of being possessive toward me, for one thing."

Alexander gripped the iron bars of the gazebo on either side of her shoulders and leaned closer. "I've seen the way Freddy looks at you. He fancied you in childhood, but saw you clearly for the first time as a woman. He's nearly free to act upon his feelings and he'd be a good catch. With Davenport, you'd have security, a quiet life, and no lingering scandals to haunt your relationship, unless there's something sinister about his dead wife."

"The things you and Edmund say about—"

"He married quickly and young for a man of his standing, but I'm not one to point fingers. If I started, there'd be a line two miles long down Government Street of people waiting to accuse me of misdeeds or confess in shared vices. I've been spoiled and rash, never thinking of the future. But with you, I finally see beyond the next party, the next season, the next year. I see my future and it's nothing without you beside me." He cradled her face in his hands. "I want to rediscover everything with you, Lucy. See what I've already spurned as naught through your fresh eyes and fall in love with life. And your lips, softer than flower petals, I'd never want for the touch of another woman all my days."

He kissed her, slow but firm, and released her.

"What you'll get with me is the possible ruination of your good character, coupled with my experience and passion, with devotion like I never thought I'd feel in my lifetime. And you'd go down in history as the first woman to change the heart of a Melling. Do you think you can handle all that, or do you want to play it safe and walk away?"

She wrapped her arms around his middle and snuggled into his shoulder as he enveloped her in return. "We'll be the most remarkable love story this city has ever seen."

He kissed her forehead and smoothed her hair. "I knew you had to feel the same way. Come, I have something for you." Holding her hand, he led her across the shadowed space to one of the benches. In a shaft of moonlight lay two gift boxes the perfect size for a man's necktie. "I might not be able to see you until the ball except at church, so I wanted to bring your Christmas present tonight."

"Alex, you didn't need—"

He silenced her with a kiss. "I've been thinking of you all week. When I went shopping for Eliza, half the things in the stores reminded me of you, but when I saw these I couldn't help myself.

Open this first." He held the narrow, diamond patterned box before her.

With a slight tremor in her hand, she lifted the lid free. He took it from her and she pushed aside the foil-stamped tissue. Lifting up the black material, she gasped. Held in the moonlight, the intricate lace evening gloves looked like a black spider's web. But not just any gloves, they were fingerless.

"I'm not sure what you plan on wearing, but I thought these would be good for the ball." He put the box on the bench and reached for her arm. Undoing her cuff, he rolled up her right sleeve. "Let's see how you like it. And if you do, the other box has a shorter pair in white, which might work well for church. That should make your mother happy."

"Oh, Alex!" She slipped on one of the black gloves. It sat halfway up her fingers and reached the upper arm. "It's beautiful. I've never had a more thoughtful gift."

He linked his fingers through hers. "And we can still touch. But more importantly, you'll still be able to write."

She laid her cheek against his. "Thank you."

"I might be a scoundrel with a dark past, but I'll have you know you're the first woman outside my family I've ever bought a gift for. None of them ever meant anything to me, Lucy. You're the one—the only one for me."

His hands were in her hair again as they kissed, but it ended too soon.

Hugging her to him, he spoke into her ear. "It must be going on midnight and you need to get out of the cold. We can do this again if you'd like. I'll figure a way to make it work if moments like this are agreeable to you."

"I'll take whatever time with you I can get."

Alexander helped her repack the gloves and tucked her hair into her cloak. Then he pulled the hood over her head and gave her a final kiss before handing her the gift boxes, his gaze focused on her in such a way that laid her own passions bare. "Merry Christmas, Lucy, my love, my joy."

"Merry Christmas, Alex. And thank you again."

She dashed through the cold moonlight to escape the yearnings his presence created. An hour later, her heart still raced with the sensation of his touch and kisses as she lay in bed trying to think of the right words to describe her night.

Six

Lucy stumbled out of bed when the sound of
maids' voices in the hallway woke her. Not wishing to be in the way
as linens and laundry were collected in her room, Lucy gathered fresh
clothing. She glanced at the gift boxes on her desk and slipped them
into a drawer to be safe from curious eyes. Lucy crossed the hall to
the bathroom while Naomi and Sharon cleaned Edmund's room.
When she changed, she remembered Alexander's handkerchief still
tucked under her pillow. Not wishing for it to go through with the
family laundry, she hurriedly buttoned her pigeon-front blouse and
smoothed her skirt over her petticoat.

Naomi Joyner, the cook's niece who helped three days a
week, shoved the rest of Lucy's bedding into a sack.

"Naomi, I'm afraid I'm going to have to go through all that.
There's something I might have misplaced—"

"Under the pillow, Miss Lucy?" Her right eye, blind from
birth, was several shades lighter than her keen left one.

"Yes, exactly so."

"Check the corner of your desk, Miss Lucy." Her brown
hands quickly pulled the strings closed on the sack.

Lucy retrieved the neatly folded square that sat
monogrammed side up. Folding it once more, she slipped it into her
skirt pocket. "Did anyone else happen to be in here when you
stripped the bed?"

"No, Miss Lucy. That's a fine quality piece of fabric, but your
secret's safe with me."

"Thank you, Naomi." Lucy placed her hand on the young
lady's shoulder, remembering the quiet times they shared together
through the years. "The world—especially my family—isn't ready for
this news yet, but hopefully after New Year's."

"I hear the holidays are always happier with a beau."

Lucy smiled as she arranged her hair in a loose pompadour. "It's starting to feel that way."

After seeing to her hair, Lucy joined her mother, Edmund, and Opal in the dining room. A low fire burned in the hearth to aid their comfort in the chilly morning.

"Good morning, everyone," she said as she took her seat next to Opal.

"Lucy, you look positively glowing this morning," her mother said.

Opal only sneered, but Edmund looked up from the newspaper. "So you do. As soon as I'm done with this, I'll help you with the furniture."

"Do you plan on being home today?" Mrs. Easton asked her son. "I was hoping to take Lucy into town for a quick shopping trip if you can keep an ear out for Opal."

"I'd be happy to. I'm off to the Aethelwulf Club after supper, but I'm at your disposal until then, Mother."

"You're such a dear."

"Only when he wants to borrow the automobile," Opal grumbled.

"I'll have you know I'm riding with a friend tonight. You can take your bitter mood and—"

"Edmund, that's quite enough." Mrs. Easton's teacup clattered on its saucer. "I know everything has been tense around here lately, but this bickering has to stop. Never between the ten of you children has there been such contention. I'm too old for this!"

Edmund spoke first. "I'm sorry, Mother."

"I'll try to be more pleasant," Lucy said.

All eyes fell to Opal. She pushed her last piece of French toast around her plate with a knife. "I guess I can do better."

"And I expect a separation after Christmas will be good for all of you." Mrs. Easton stood, causing Edmund to rise to his feet.

"Mother," he said as she turned toward the door. "Would it be okay if I invite Freddy for Christmas dinner if he has no other plans?"

Her hand went to her heart. "Yes, the poor boy lost his father and his wife all within a year."

"And now his mother lives in Atlanta with his sister and her family. If he's staying in town, he's likely to be alone."

"We can't have that after all the time he spent here when he was younger. Invite him, even if you have to go out of your way to extend the invitation. I should have thought of that myself when he was over the other day."

After their mother left, Opal made a gagging sound. "More opportunities for Lucille to be fawned over. You should have seen the way she was with Alexander Melling on the front porch last night. Of course, Mother believed Lucille when she told her she'd only kept him company when you went for your ride."

Edmund crumpled the paper as he lowered it. "And just what were they doing?"

Opal stared at her toast. "Well, I couldn't be sure because Lucille stood directly in front of him, but I imagine there was something not right going on."

"So Lucy was *standing* across from a person she spoke to and you *imagined* something was going on. I see your game now, Opal." Edmund raised the paper to show he was done with the conversation.

Opal stomped out of the room and the parlor's double pocket doors crashed together. Remembering her journal, Lucy rushed from the table. She caught Opal reaching under the seat cushion.

"That's mine!" Lucy snatched it out of her hand.

"You're too late. Before breakfast, I read all about your joy over me leaving and some glowing lines about a man who sounds an awful lot like the one you were entertaining on the porch last night."

Refusing to allow Opal to know she'd discovered the truth, Lucy threw out a haughty attitude rather than anger. "Well, that shows how much you know—which is nothing! This is my plotting journal for character sketches and emotional conflicts in my stories."

"Does that make Alexander Melling your muse?"

"A writer never uses one person to base a character on. There might be some physical characteristics in common, but it's not him."

"But that 'pale hair in the moonlight' and 'glowing blue—'"

"Don't make yourself ridiculous. You're getting too old for these fancies." Grabbing her pen from the hutch, Lucy walked out of the room with her head high, though inwardly shaking.

"Lucy," Edmund called as she passed the dining room, "aren't you going to eat?"

"I'm not hungry."

After Edmund and Lucy made quick work of rearranging her room, she stashed her journal in her stocking drawer and met her mother downstairs. Lucy opted for a simple black wool capelet, and her mother a fur stole over her gray afternoon dress. They walked to Dauphin Street and took the streetcar heading to the business district.

"Today, we're starting at the top," Mrs. Easton informed her as they sat on the wooden trolley bench. "We're going to that new Parisian dress shop."

"Mother," Lucy whispered, "are you sure?" She knew better than to mention money in public and already there were a few ladies across the car glancing at her and whispering.

"James secured several crates for the proprietress when he placed bulk orders from France last month. I'm sure she'll be pleased for our business."

That meant her mother expected the owner to come down on the prices for her since Mr. Easton saved her money on shipping costs.

Across the way, the ladies continued to stare, and when Lucy and her mother stood to exit, one of them said to the other, "It has to be her. Mary Margaret and Judith were at the party and heard Edmund tell the story themselves."

Another lady made a gobbling sound as Lucy stepped off the trolley. She turned to stare at them. The one closest the window waved a copy of Kate Stuart's *Snitch* magazine as the streetcar pulled away.

"Lucy, you've gone pale. What is it?" Mrs. Easton took her arm.

"I forgot to eat breakfast."

"Let's stop in the bakery, then."

Lucy went to the newsstand and purchased a copy of *Snitch* while her mother went on to buy her something to eat. The salesman gave her a funny smirk when she bought it.

"I already know, thank you kindly."

"It's been the talk of the town all morning." He tipped his cap to her. "Enjoy the extra attention, Miss Easton."

She slumped to the nearest empty bench and stared at the cover, mulling over the option of *not* looking inside. Needing to know what others were talking about, she opened the booklet. Beyond the full-page ad for skin care cream, Kate's letter from the editor announced holiday hijinks and Mardi Gras insight ahead. On the next page, leading the "Holiday Recap, So Far…" was the turkey in the petticoat story as Lucy had recited it to Miss Stuart at the party. Heat bloomed across her face and the thought of ripping her own talons into Kate Stuart for stealing her words rushed through her veins.

"Oh, Lucy, now you're redder than a magnolia seed." Mrs. Easton handed her daughter a muffin after she sat.

"Did you know Edmund told the story of Gilbert dressing our turkey at the Mellings' party?"

"Goodness, did he?"

"Yes, and now it's in *Snitch* for all to read. I've already been talked about on the trolley and joked over at the newsstand. And those ladies over by the fountain are probably discussing it right now."

"It can't be that big of news."

"Mother, it's the lead story! I'll never be able to go to the New Year's ball now." She took a mouthful of the cranberry muffin without trying to be dainty.

"We need to get you the most opulent gown. The right dress will quiet any lingering jests over the story."

"It's not that easy these days, Mother. Word of mouth is one thing, but when something's printed it adds a new life to it."

"I'm old-fashioned in my belief that the perfect dress can solve any problem. Everything will be back to normal in no time."

Mademoiselle Bisset at the dress shop was more than willing to part with an exquisite gown at a fair price, but Lucy needed to be persuaded into accepting it.

"Miss Easton, you will do me a favor by choosing this ensemble. I am new in town and did not know most women in mourning would not attend the balls during carnival season, and there is simply no interest. But you, with your youth and beauty, coupled with the perfect gold mask, will be able to wear this gown splendidly."

"It's not too morbid to wear a stylized lily print when I'm not in mourning?" Lucy asked her mother.

Mrs. Easton fingered the fine gold threads that created the scrolling vines over the black silk. "More than half the people there won't know the difference, and besides, isn't that the sort of thing carnival is all about—the dark and light, the symbolism of life and death?"

Lucy rather liked that idea. The deep cut of the heart-shaped neckline of the first bodice made her look every bit a woman flaunting herself at Death. Besides coming with two coordinating bodice pieces and the full, court-length trained skirt, the gown had a full-length removable train.

"If you would do me the honor of purchasing it, I will throw in a bonus." The shopkeeper straightened. "I am going to New Orleans to visit friends over Christmas. I know an artist there who does the most delicate Venetian masks. I shall commission a gold one especially for you and this gown, if you will but purchase this from me today. I will also have my seamstress alter the removable train into two different length coverings for you. A cape and stole will get much more use than a train, especially when this gown already as a lovely one on its skirt."

Mrs. Easton looked back at her daughter and sighed. "You're too used to second-hand gowns, Lucy. You deserve to dazzle, and I do think this one would be the better choice for New Year's Eve compared to your new blue one."

Lucy fingered the gold embellishments on the sheer, bell-shaped sleeves on both bodices. The gloves from Alexander would be a perfect fit with them. "We'll never be able to manage the dress boxes on the street car, but I do think it's beautiful."

Mademoiselle Bisset clapped her hands. "I will send my delivery boy to your house with them before closing and can bill Mr. Easton at his office. The mask and wraps will come next week."

With the help of an assistant, Lucy changed out of the gown and back into her blue suit while her mother completed the transaction. They were soon amid the lunch hour pedestrians on the sidewalk.

"Let's see if there's a table available at the hotel and have dinner before heading home," Mrs. Easton said.

Wanting nothing more than to get out of view from all the stares and giggles the city handed her that day, Lucy inwardly groaned.

"We hardly get out together, Lucy. And I think I see Freddy Davenport at the corner."

Mrs. Easton elbowed her way through the crowd like someone half her age, leaving Lucy struggling to keep up through the mass of jeering faces. By the time she reached Frederick and her mother, Mrs. Easton had talked him into taking dinner with them as well as coming over on Sunday afternoon for Christmas dinner.

"Let's hurry. I'd rather not end up at some lunch counter if the hotel fills up before we get there."

Frederick offered his arm to Mrs. Easton.

"No, thank you, Freddy, but do take Lucy. She's prone to dawdle."

Lucy sighed, but offered a half-smile to Frederick as she took his arm. The whispers and stares continued to taunt Lucy, but Frederick didn't mention anything out of the ordinary until a turkey call yodeled over the other noises.

"Are people acting a little strange today or is it me?" he asked.

"No, it's me, or rather it was Edmund." She proceeded to tell the story of Edmund at the party and the write up in *Snitch* that very morning.

Frederick, to Lucy's pleasure, didn't laugh. "The Easton house is always full of mischief, but Edmund should know better than to tell tales outside the walls. Shall I trounce him for you?"

"I wish you would," Lucy said as she entered the Trellis Room behind her mother.

"I'd be happy to avenge you to him or that magazine," he whispered to her as they waited to be shown to a table. "They were unflattering toward Harriet and it afforded her little help in meeting new friends. They said, 'The new Mrs. D. is a tiny mite of a Yankee, not half the woman we expected for our sporting Mr. D.' or something like it."

Feeling sorry for Frederick, Lucy placed a hand on his forearm. "I would have friended her but you didn't visit after marriage. Why did you never bring her to us?"

His cheeks grew red and he stammered over his words. "Your house was always one of youth and adventure. It didn't seem right bringing Harriet there when I…when—"

"Our table is ready," Mrs. Easton said.

Lucy felt uneasy over what Frederick left unsaid, though they were shown to a cozy corner table half hidden by potted palms. She dropped the topic of his deceased wife and did her best to follow the examples of the other two by not paying mind to the smirks and mutterings happening around her.

"Relax, Lucy," Mrs. Easton said after tea was served. "All will be well by the ball. Freddy, are you attending New Year's Eve?"

"Eddie talked me into it. It will be my first time without my mourning band, but I'm afraid I'm too out of practice to be of much service at a party."

"Nonsense. Lucy will be happy to share a dance or two with you to break the ice, I'm sure of it. Why, you practically taught her to waltz, didn't you?"

"Yes, and his toes are permanently damaged from my abuse." Lucy stirred a scoop of sugar into her tea and looked to Frederick with a teasing smile. "We need at least one dance together so I can prove I retained the lessons, though I might need to practice dancing in the new gown. The train is longer than anything I've previously worn."

"I'd be happy to assist you when I'm over for Christmas, if you'd like." Frederick gazed at Lucy with hope. "It would be like old times."

"So it would," Mrs. Easton interrupted. "It will be a wonderful day."

That night, while Edmund and Alexander were at the men's club, Lucy sat at her desk and stared at a blank sheet of paper as she tapped the end of her pen against her teeth. She planned on seeing Alexander at church the next night and wanted to slip him her Christmas present—a poem she'd yet to write for him. Lucy closed her eyes, listened to the rain pattering on the roof, and imagined Alexander coming to her through the darkness—the way his hands on her waist made her feel and the taste of his kisses. Then her pen moved across the parchment with the precision only someone secure in their words could master.

Love Affair

You come to me in winter
With the heat of summer rain
Touching, we melt together
In the forge of love
That burns brighter than the azure of your eyes

The pounding in my chest
Is only for you
At your touch, the sound of your voice
I come alive
Like a lily before Easter

White and pure
Until you touched me with your soul
Now I'm pink with desire
Cravings for you flooding
As I wait for the red your touch will bring

When Lucy reread what she'd written, she colored under the weight of the words. Never would she have dreamed of penning such passion. Alexander proved to be her greatest inspiration. The final stanza could be considered scandalous, but she rationalized that it might refer to any point in their future—like their wedding night. But she wasn't sure it would be appropriate to give it to him, especially at the cathedral. After the third reading she understood each word held truth and he deserved to know her feelings. He had declared her his love and joy the night before, and she was certain she'd one day give him her all.

Seven

Saturday afternoon, warmer than the days previous, brought ominous clouds and rain. The weather postponed Susan's family from driving into town, so the house stayed quiet while Mrs. Easton and the help did their final Christmas preparations. Lucy, tired of being in confined quarters with Opal, retreated to the front porch with her well-loved copy of *Northanger Abbey*. Alexander's envelope—concealing a fresh copy of the poem on her scalloped-trimmed stationery—was tucked within the pages. After transferring the poem to the gift paper, she'd burned the original in her fireplace, determined no one else would read it.

Lucy tucked her legs under her skirt on the three-person swing outside the dining room window. Not long after she settled, a courier peddled up to the front step and shook the rain off his arms before opening his satchel.

"Miss Lucille Easton?" he asked.

"Yes."

"Special delivery." He handed her an unmarked envelope.

"Let me step inside and get something for you." She stood.

"No need. I was well paid. Merry Christmas!" He hopped back on his bike and cut through the rain before Lucy sat back down.

Believing it a letter from Alexander, the decidedly feminine script and a coin attached to the bottom corner caused her heart to sink.

> *Dear Miss Easton,*
> *By now you know that I printed your tidbit about your brother telling your family's Thanksgiving joke. I have enclosed a quarter for your contribution and you will be pleased to know that, on a trial basis, I will be happy to print at least*

"Who does she think she is?" Lucy muttered.

"What's that, bad news from one of your admirers?" Opal
asked through the screen of the dining room window.

"It's a letter from a female, so you can stop looking for
trouble."

At supper, Lucy did her fair share of being moody, which
brought a smile to Opal's face.

"It's Christmas Eve, Lucy," Edmund said as they finished the
meal. "Try to enjoy yourself." He drank the last splash of wine from
his goblet and held it toward his father, who guarded the bottle.

"Not until the ladies finish their glasses," Mr. Easton said.

Edmund frowned at his mother's half-full glass and shook his
head at Lucy's full one across from him. Taking pity on her closest
sibling, Lucy raised the crystal in a toast before bringing it to her lips
and chugging like she imagined the men did in their smoking rooms.

"Lucille Amelia Easton!" Her mother's hand went to her heart.

But Mr. Easton laughed and Edmund cheered.

"Merry Christmas, Lucy!" He hurried to his sister. Taking her by the hand, Edmund spun her around the room like they were at a country dance.

Mrs. Easton finally caught the laughter and drank the remainder of her wine—with a little less flourish than her daughter. "Refill them all and we'll gather in the parlor to sing."

After an hour of singing carols, accompanied by Mrs. Easton on the piano, the family quieted to listen to Mr. Easton read the story of the first Christmas while Mrs. Easton crocheted a red stocking. Lucy chanced a look at Opal, who snuggled against their father's side on the settee, but she glared at her in return.

After the reading, the family went to their separate rooms to dress for church. Lucy, pleased with the warmer weather because she wouldn't need to cover her wool dress with a wrap, buttoned her dainty white boots before tightening her corset strings. Then she pulled on the flowing red skirt with a wide swag of white lace circling it two-thirds of the way down. The matching red blouse had wreaths of white lace details on the arms and bust. She pulled the white gloves up her forearms and then fastened the cuffs.

She opted to bring her mantilla rather than wear a hat, allowing the motif of white lace to grace the ensemble from head to toe. Lucy placed the folded head covering in her reticule between Alexander's present and her notebook. A wave of guilt over the impure feelings she'd written tugged at her, but for the first time in her life, courtship was real and desirable.

The ride to church was punctuated with exclamations from Mrs. Easton of the novelty and beauty of Lucy's gloves from an admirer she refused to name.

"I don't know why I never thought of it myself." Mrs. Easton patted Lucy's lacey hand with her silk gloved one as they walked to the cathedral from their parking spot. "Whoever he is, he has my approval. He's gotten you to do the respectable thing that I've been unable to persuade you toward for years."

As they neared the cathedral, Lucy nudged her father and mother together and fell in behind Edmund and Opal in the gathering crowd of Christmas well-wishers. Carolers singing "The First Noel" in the park across the street brought gooseflesh to her arms as she spotted Alexander's pale hair in the throng of people ascending the portico. The urge to rush to him surged through her body. Alexander stepped to the side when he reached the top, securing a spot next to a column. He leaned against it as though bored, but Lucy smiled to herself as he actively scanned the crowd while his arms were crossed in a way that projected he'd rather not be there. When his eyes met Lucy's, a grin lighted his face. In response, she raised a gloved hand in greeting and brought it to her heart as he'd signaled to her the other day.

At the top of the steps, Edmund handed Opal off to their father and turned to Lucy. "We're sitting with the family tonight," he said when he had her on his arm.

"That's fine, but I'd like to listen to the carolers for a few minutes. Feel free to mingle while you wait for me."

Edmund brought her to a spot between the towering columns to the far left and crossed over to greet Alexander. Then he moved on to several young women adorned in festive dresses trimmed in fur and new hats. As soon as Edmund passed him, Alexander skimmed through the crowd and stopped just shy of Lucy.

"Merry Christmas, Lucy." His eyes were more vivid than ever with a blue bowtie at his neck and a coordinating silk handkerchief peeking out of the breast pocket of his dove gray suit.

"Merry Christmas, Alex." She felt their mutual attraction as cords binding them together.

"Your dress is heavenly, if you don't mind me saying so." He reached out and brushed her hand with his. "And those gloves are just the thing to compliment the ensemble."

"Mother informed me she approves of the admirer who gave them, whoever he is."

"That's a lucky man who can find favor in the eyes of his lady's mother."

Heart pounding at the nearness of him, Lucy removed the tatted reticule from her wrist. "Would you mind holding this while I place my mantilla?"

"Not at all." He appeared amused at her formality, but played along.

When he had the ends of the drawstrings in hand, Lucy slid open the pouch and removed the mantilla and the envelope, placing the latter against his palm until he closed his fingers around it. He slipped it into his coat pocket. Smiling, she placed the mantilla atop her head.

"How's this?" she asked.

"Crooked as always." Edmund elbowed past Alexander and straighten the head covering before his friend could move. "I can no longer leave you unattended unless I wish you to be set upon by the likes of him. Like a moth to flame, he always flocks to the prettiest women."

"I think that's you chasing Judith and Mary Margaret." Lucy retrieved her bag from Alexander with a smile. "Thank you. I hope you find the words tonight comforting."

He patted his pocket. "I'm sure they'll be agreeable."

Edmund took his sister's arm. "Let's go find our seats. See you later, Alex."

"Merry Christmas, Eddie. Lucy." He winked at her as they left.

Edmund and Lucy were taken along with the last of the crowd trying to enter the sanctuary. The parishioners in front of her had come to a standstill and the interior climate, heated by hundreds of bodies in unnecessarily thick winter clothing, rushed through the doorway to escape. Her hands trembled and she clasped them together over her brother's arm, trying to steady them before Edmund noticed.

After several deep breaths, Lucy chanced a look behind her. Beyond the shifting bulk of people, Alexander leaned his head back, eyes closed, paper clutched to his chest. A few seconds later, his eyes reopened and went immediately back to the stationery. He appeared to reread the poem, and then he folded and returned it to his pocket while sporting the biggest grin Lucy had ever seen. Content that she'd seen his joy, she turned back toward the door. Then she lost all feeling in her legs and the world seemed to dim.

"Edmund," she gasped. "I can't breathe."

Eight

Edmund placed his arm around Lucy and pressed their way through the crowd to get to the edge of the portico for more air.

Alexander met them on the steps, concern prominently displayed on his face. "What happened? She was fine moments ago."

Edmund lowered himself to the top step with Lucy beside him, her head resting on his shoulder. "I don't know. She's always been the sturdy one. It was the twins who were prone to fainting. She felt a little shaky and gasped that she couldn't breathe."

"Corset might be too tight." Alexander dropped to his knees and reached for her waist, but Edmund knocked his hand away. "What? I've seen it with my sister."

"It's not my corset, but thank you for your concern." She turned to Edmund. "I won't be able to go in, but I'll stay out here and listen."

"I'm not leaving you alone or with him. Let me tell Mother you took ill so she won't worry about us." Standing, Edmund peered down at Alexander kneeling on the step in front of Lucy. "And you keep your hands off her. 'Her corset's too tight' doesn't work with my sister, nor do any of your other games, do you understand?"

"I have no intentions of playing games with Lucy, but I'll stay with her until you return."

Edmund stepped toward the door, looking back twice before he disappeared into the cathedral. Lucy straightened her skirt and crossed her legs at the ankles, her limbs no longer numb. Alexander shifted to a seated position on the step aligned with her knees, resting his hand there for a moment.

"It scared me to see you weaken. What happened?"

Lucy gazed across the park. Only one couple remained on a bench on the far side of the square. "I turned back and there was a crowd of people between us and even more people in front of me. And then the heat of the church struck and I felt powerless. I thought I was going to die right there on the threshold of the cathedral. Maybe it was the lustful thoughts I had when writing the poem. Maybe I'll never be able to walk into a church again because my desires have been stirred. How do you sit there calmly while my body is tremoring with want?"

He ran his hand down her arm. "I have years of practicing this stony façade, but I can assure you my body and soul are anything but calm at this moment. Your words, Lucy…your sweet, honest, sensual words made me want to climb the highest spire and shout to the world that you love me at least half as much as I do you. Knowing that you long for me, that you look forward to what's to come in our relationship—I can hardly breathe at the thought of it. If we were anywhere else than on the steps of this church when I read those words, Eddie would be pounding me into the ground by now. Do you understand me?"

She nodded and brought her lace-covered hand to his cheek. He responded by quickly kissing her palm.

"I won't be able to wait until the ball to see you again. And my sentiments are too strong to hide from Eddie. Will you be brave with me, Lucy?"

"Yes, I can do anything knowing you're by my side." She lowered her hand and fingered her reticule that lay on her lap—white on red, which reminded her of what she'd penned.

Seeming to read her mind, he asked, "Would you write me another poem?"

Lucy's slow spreading smile radiated from her heart. "Perhaps, if you behave."

Alexander groaned and clenched his fists. "'Restraint' will be my new middle name."

"Then what does the R stand for? I've been curious since you gave me your handkerchief."

"Randolph, but only use it if I'm in trouble."

"Then I'm sure the name is quite worn out by now."

He laughed and the thundering roll of the organ notes followed Edmund out of the cathedral. Without speaking, he cut around Alexander and helped his sister stand. When they were halfway down the steps, he turned back.

"You may come with us."

Alexander rushed to close the distance. Edmund led them across the street to the nearest bench. After Lucy settled, he motioned Alexander to sit beside her. The organ cords rumbled in the distance like the lowing of animals.

"Please tell me my worst nightmare isn't coming true," Edmund said.

"And what would that be, Eddie?"

"You know damn well what I mean!" He towered over his friend.

With his words, Lucy understood why Edmund moved from the cathedral steps—and that Opal wasn't the only one with a venomous tongue. Fear drove her heart back to racing as she held her breath to see how Alexander would respond. She wouldn't blame him if he lied—she'd never seen her brother that upset.

Alexander stared at Edmund. "I'm not here to play your sister. I respect you both too much for that."

Edmund turned to Lucy. "Was this weakening spell a ruse to get out here with him?"

"No, I can assure you I haven't felt that awful since I came down with yellow fever. Maybe it was the evil eye Opal gave me before she entered church that set it in motion."

"Now you're going to blame our sister for your flirtations?"

Alexander stood before Edmund, hands clenched. "Lucy's not a flirt and you know it! I came to her when she looked unwell because I have—"

"Dear God, don't let him speak it!" Edmund groaned. "Of all the ladies in this city, why must it be my sister?"

"I've been watching from afar, but between you and Grace Anne always being around, I've had no opportunity to get to know her."

"And I was worried about Kate Stuart—and for good reason after she printed that bit—but I should have been wary of you. I stupidly placed her in your hands at the party like bringing a lamb to slaughter."

"There's no sacrifice, Edmund," Lucy said. "The feelings are reciprocated."

"I've taught you better than this! I've warned you time and time again against my friends with one exception. And do you think our parents will be pleased? I'm sure they know tales about Alex to some degree."

"Mother told me she approves of my admirer based on his gift." She raised her hands.

Red faced, Edmund snatched Alexander by his collar and displayed his knuckles inches from his nose. "Just how far have you gone with my sister to buy her gifts the first week?"

He didn't flinch. "It's not for a gentleman to speak of."

Edmund brought his fist back, ready to strike.

"But I may speak of it," Lucy rushed the words as her brother turned to her. "We've only kissed a few times, Edmund. Nothing's happened—not like you're thinking."

"And do you know why I'm thinking this way, Lucy? I'm not joking when I call him a cad. He's not worthy of you."

"Yes, and I know it." Alexander stepped between the siblings. "But I'm changing my life, Eddie. Think of how I was at the meeting Thursday and Aethelwulf Club last night. Was I different than my old self?"

Edmund's face calmed. "You didn't get drunk, but maybe that was because you had the new automobile and didn't wish to wreck it. But you also didn't throw out any hair-brained schemes in reference to our masquerade like you did last year, and told no tales of your weekly conquests." He shuddered as he turned back to Alexander. "And so help me God, if there are *ever* any tales—"

"I would never, Eddie." Alexander placed a steady hand on his shoulder. "She possesses my heart—the heart I didn't know I had. Everything else until this point was nothingness. Lucy is the only one for me."

He knocked Alexander's hand off his shoulder. "No. No. No. No. No!" Edmund stomped until his laps took him further away.

Alexander sat back on the bench and took Lucy's hand in his. "This is going better than I expected. I figured I'd have a black eye by now. For that deliverance I thank you for speaking when you did." He raised her hand to his lips and kissed her knuckles. "Thank you."

Lucy wanted to taste him once more but settled on squeezing his hand. They didn't release their linked fingers when Edmund stopped before them.

"Did you meet my sister in the garden during your party?"

"I did," Alexander said. "I saw she was miserable in the crowd earlier and told her about the quiet space if she wanted to escape for a while. She didn't go there to meet me. I followed her to see if she needed anything."

"One of your snares."

"I thought it was a game at first, but there's no shaking this free."

"Did you do anything to her on the front porch when you came to pick me up Thursday?"

"I think I touched her hand once, but nothing else. I wanted to do more—any man would—but I'm overcoming my weaknesses. I'll do right by Lucy, I promise. I wouldn't be able to live with myself any more than you would be able to let me live."

Edmund kicked the yellowing winter grass. "I want to believe you, and God knows I want my sister to have happiness, but it's wrong, though you're a striking pair. I've never seen either of you with such a peace. Still, it makes me ill to think of it! I've heard too much out of your mouth—witnessed too much firsthand—to ever be comfortable with my sister on your arm."

"Fortunately, you're not my judge," Alexander said. "I went to confession this weekend and laid bare everything I'd held back during my empty confessions since I came of age. Father Quinn was quite shocked and my knees were sore from the time I spent in prayer, but it was all worth it to be able to stand before Lucy and not be burdened by my past. It's there as a haunting reminder, but each day it will slip further away." He placed his other hand on top of the one holding Lucy's. "She's precious to me, Eddie. I'm sorry I was a fool all this time, but I mean to make things right."

Edmund stroked his beard. "How did you get the gloves to her?"

"I met her in your backyard after I dropped you off Thursday night."

Edmund pushed a finger into his chest. "You're not to be alone with her, do you hear me? No more sneaking around! I'll not have my sister made out to be the type to do such things, even if she has a weakness for romance novels."

"Then allow me to court her openly. Act as chaperone that we might meet often. I beg you, Eddie, and you know this is by far the noblest thing I've ever asked for your help with."

"It's no contest, but…I don't know."

"Give me two opportunities to see her this week and then the ball Saturday night. If I'm not a different man, you may strike me down."

"Come over with Eliza Tuesday afternoon for tea and we'll decide on the next date then, if you keep in line." Edmund popped his knuckles. "And if not, it'll be the shortest courtship in history and you'll need an undertaker."

Nine

Lucy sat on the settee in the parlor with Susan and her youngest, Ava, when the doorbell rang at a quarter to one Christmas afternoon. The resemblances between the three females were evident in their well-defined chins and fair hair—though Susan's had darkened to an ash blonde. When Edmund came in with Frederick, Susan heaved her pregnant self to her feet.

"The Terror Twins are back together! Eddie and Freddy were always sure to trick the neighborhood boys out of their coins and embarrass the Easton sisters in the process."

The adults in the room laughed and Frederick blushed as he accepted Susan's hug.

Turning to her husband in the corner chair, Susan introduced the new arrival. "David, this is who you've been hearing about all these years, Freddy Davenport. Freddy, my husband, David Shepard. We can't tell a story about Eddie's younger years without Freddy being involved. Oh, the horrors they inflicted on Emma and Cora and me, it was beastly! Lucy, you've quite been spared the troubles we went through."

"I wouldn't say that. Nowadays the jokes end up in gossip magazines." All eyes turned to Opal, who was on the floor with two of her nephews. "I, on the other hand, am practically an only child I'm so ignored, which is fine because it keeps my petticoat from ending up on a turkey and being printed about in magazines."

Maxwell's wife, Lottie, giggled, but the rest of group remained silent. Lucy kissed Ava on the head and left the room. The train of her red Christmas dress chased her like the bitter words from her sister.

Lucy ignored her mother putting the finishing touches on the platters of food and crossed the kitchen to the back porch. The thick air and gray sky with the threat of more rain was as unwelcoming as her sister. She held her skirt up to her knees to keep the wet grass from staining the hem as her white boots avoided the mud. When the door opened and shut behind her, she didn't look back.

A moment after she settled on the iron bench in the gazebo, Frederick came to the archway. "May I join you?"

"Of course."

He crossed to her and hesitated before the bench.

"You can sit. I haven't been known to bite since I was four."

Frederick went for his cufflinks as he sat. "Yes, and I think I still have a scar on my forearm from that. Would you care to see?"

Lucy backhanded him playfully on his biceps, surprised at the firmness. "Did you come here to tease me, Frederick? I thought I was escaping that."

"I'd never tease you in a room full of people, but I must ask, why don't you call me Freddy like everyone else but you insist I call you Lucy?"

"Probably the same reason I stopped calling Edmund 'Eddie.' He was no longer Eddie without you when you went your separate way for college. You're both your own men now, and you a good deal more mature than my brother can ever hope to be."

"But why are you still Lucy when you're no longer a girl?"

"Because I prefer it. Lucille sounds too refined. And while we're at it, I've heard three other sisters referred to as *Miss Easton* and have trouble thinking of myself with that title."

"You take words seriously. Are you still writing?"

"Every day. It's my hope to have a novel published before long. I have four different manuscripts, but I can't find the right publisher."

"As a numbers man, I'm afraid I'm no help there."

Warmed by his concern, Lucy gave him an appreciative smile. "Just stay pleasant company and you'll be as helpful as anything."

"I'm glad you're all right. I came out here expecting to comfort you from hurt feelings, but you're as plucky as ever." He stood and paced in front of her a few times. "I know it's silly of me, but I was planning on giving you my handkerchief if you were teary eyed. Now I'm disappointed because you aren't. How awful is that?"

Her first instinct was to laugh, but that would be as tactless as her sister-in-law. Then she noticed the bold lettering on the handkerchief he'd removed from his pocket. The blue D, flanked by F and L made her think of the initiation Kate Stuart had given her as a challenge. With Alexander now a part of her life, she wasn't sure she'd go through with it. But the second monogrammed handkerchief within her reach was too good of an opportunity to pass in case she decided to play along with Kate's game.

"It's a handsome square of fabric and I'd be happy to take it for a while if it would help you feel better."

"You would?"

The boyish eagerness in his brown eyes reminded her of the time when she was thirteen and she'd fallen off Edmund's bicycle. Frederick had rushed to help while Edmund continued lounging on the porch with his magazine, only concerned if she'd scratched his bike. Frederick carried her into the house because she'd scraped her knee bloody on the oyster shell drive.

"Anything to help a friend feel better."

"Keep it as long as you'd like. I trust you with it."

The way he said it made her think he spoke of his heart. "Frederick, it's not—"

"Lucy, Freddy! Dinner!" Edmund shouted from the backdoor.

"He knew you came out here?" she asked.

"Yes, I thought he was coming with me, but he stopped to help your mother." Frederick offered his arm when she stood.

"Let me gather my skirt first. I need to keep it off the grass." Lacking a pocket in her Christmas dress, she shoved his handkerchief up her right sleeve before lifting the hem of her skirt. "How close behind me were you when I came outside?"

He colored. "Your skirt is longer in the back. There wasn't much to see from where I walked."

"So you did look! And Edmund thinks you the most respectable of his friends."

"Some things can't be helped, Goosy." His old name for her slipped out and he covered his mouth.

Lucy eyes widened and then a laugh erupted. "That will keep me young forever! Let's be utterly ridiculous together." She turned her back to him and glanced over her shoulder. "Carry my train for me."

It was Frederick's turn to laugh. "You're serious, aren't you?"

"Always."

Frederick lifted the hem of her red train off the stone floor of the gazebo and Lucy carried the front a few inches off the ground to keep it dry. When they came around the azalea bushes, Edmund laughed as she dropped into a curtsy.

"My dignified sister," Edmund teased as he held the door for her. He slapped his friend on the back when he passed through. "And her humble servant. You can drop it now, Freddy."

When Lucy sat across the dinner table from Frederick and their eyes met, she knew the last few minutes of mirth had been a terrible mistake.

***

To help keep the Sabbath more subdued even though it was Christmas, the Eastons opted to exchange gifts that evening. Maxwell and his family had returned to their home in town, but Susan's family remained for the night. They all settled in the parlor, along with Frederick, who'd been invited to stay. Mrs. Easton handed out the stockings that had been magically filled while they ate a supper of leftovers from their dinner. Frederick, on the floor to the side of Lucy's chair, appeared touched as Mrs. Easton handed him a filled stocking as though part of the family.

Lucy put a hand on his shoulder. "She made it especially for you yesterday, hoping you'd stay," she whispered.

Frederick placed his hand atop hers and the warmth seized Lucy's heart. She didn't want to stop being kind to Frederick, but she seemed to be doing everything wrong. Or perhaps he read too much into it because every action appeared to evoke a tender response. How much more would he respond when he was out of mourning? Lucy knew he'd have to be told she was spoken for by Alexander.

After everyone had exclaimed over the perfection of their oranges, chocolates, and trinkets lovingly customized for the individual by the lady of the house, Mr. Easton distributed the larger gifts to each person, starting with the youngest. Susan's Ava had help opening a new Teddy bear named after the president and the two boys had a new set of blocks and a hobby horse crowned with real horsehair. Mr. Easton rolled in a shiny blue bicycle for Opal and she unwrapped a cycling outfit with a split skirt and a sporty sailor top for which she seemed genuinely pleased.

Then all eyes were on Lucy as her father placed a large, square box on her lap, which caused her to groan from the weight. Mr. Easton placed a hand on his daughter's cheek. "For that obsession of yours, sweetie," he said with a wink.

Lucy tore into the paper like an eager child. It was too heavy for her to lift out of the box from her position so she shredded the packaging until it was free—a handsome black and gold Underwood 5 typewriter. She squealed and hugged it before tapping at the keys.

"As if I don't have enough trouble sleeping as it is!" Opal complained.

"There will be set hours of operation for that beast, Opal," Mr. Easton said. "And if you want some typing help, Lucy, I'll have one of the secretaries in my office give you lessons after the first of the year."

Lucy ran her fingers over the keys of the typewriter and watched as Edmund—younger than Frederick by three months—opened a box containing a new tuxedo. Then Frederick received a purple silk bowtie set, which Lucy looked forward to seeing him wear during carnival season.

After the other gifts were distributed, Frederick turned to Lucy. "That has to be heavy. May I carry it to your desk?"

"That's all right. I'm sure Edmund can do it for me."

"No," Edmund said, "let Freddy. He's stronger so it will take him less effort. Besides, I need to get this tuxedo hung up."

While the younger children were being prepared for bed, the three oldest went upstairs with the gifts. Lucy stepped ahead of Frederick to clear space for the typewriter.

Frederick placed it on her desk. "It looks nice."

"It's amazing!" Lucy smiled at the Underwood and ran her fingers over the keys once more. "Too bad I can't use it right now. Opal would have a fit. I think I'll bring my writing to the parlor tonight."

"Do you need anything else, Lucy?"

"No, thank you." She smiled briefly, not wanting to hold his gaze too long. "I'll be down in a minute."

Before returning to the parlor, Lucy removed her boots and stockings and let down her hair. When she undid her cuffs, Frederick's handkerchief fell from her sleeve and she tucked it into the drawer of her nightstand.

While she only wanted to get comfortable to work, when Frederick stared at her rather than paying attention to the chess game between him and Edmund, Lucy had second thoughts of her choice to alter her dress standards. She had run loose-haired and barefoot with him as recent as four years ago, but she needed to remember they were both adults now.

"You look mesmerized, Freddy." Edmund punched his arm. "It's just Lucy."

He turned back to the game on the coffee table, Lucy watching him this time. She noted the red rising to his cheeks as he leaned forward to whisper to her brother. "The way her hair tumbles over her shoulder and the confident movements of her hand across the page is captivating."

"How many glasses of wine did you have with supper?" Edmund looked at his sister and raised his eyebrows.

"Only one, but it's getting late. We'll call it a night when this game is over." Frederick, still flushed, turned to Lucile. "That is, unless you want to practice dancing in that new gown."

"Not tonight, but thank you. It's kind of you to remember." Lucy finished her journal entry about the typewriter and readied to leave before there could be any awkward goodbye from their guest on his terms.

"It's been a splendid day, Merry Christmas." She kissed Edmund lightly on the forehead while rubbing her knuckles into his scalp—something she'd learned from him. So he wouldn't feel left out, she did the same to Frederick.

"Merry Christmas, Lucy," they said in unison.

She laughed. "Susan was right. The Terror Twins are back in action."

When she came out of the upstairs bathroom in her nightgown and robe, Edmund followed her into her room.

"It's not too late, you know."

"What's not?" she asked.

"To change your mind about Alex." Edmund sat at her desk before her typewriter.

"Why would I do that?" She poked his back. "Don't think about touching the Underwood."

"Freddy was absolutely smitten with you today. I think he'd be yours for the taking come next week. He's always been sweet with you, but today there was something new behind his gaze."

"If you think he has feelings for me, it wasn't proper for you to send him into my bedroom."

He stood and went toward the door. "I told you, I trust him. That stands no matter what his feelings are or where he is. Unlike Alex, Freddy has never done anything that makes me uncomfortable for you to be around him, even if he is an experienced widower." He stepped back to her, tossed an arm around her neck, and rubbed his knuckles into her scalp. "Think about it, Lucy."

She ducked out of his reach. "I don't need to. I've already given Alex my heart."

"Then let's hope he proves worthy."

Ten

Susan and David set off for Grand Bay with their children and Opal Monday morning, her new bicycle strapped to the back of their automobile. Even with Lucy banging away on the Underwood, the household was remarkably peaceful, though it took twenty-four hours for Lucy to stop tiptoeing around the house. Being afraid of awakening the wrath of Opal was what she'd dealt with for the better part of a year and her sister still haunted her while no longer there.

Tuesday at noon, Lucy and her mother took a simple meal in the breakfast nook on the back porch. Mrs. Easton, pleased that Alexander and Eliza Melling were coming to tea, had the cook baking a hearty selection of treats and Sharon and Naomi scrubbing the parlor.

"It's wonderful that Eliza is getting to know you better before her debut. I'm sure you'll be a great help to her. It's such a blessing Alexander and Eddie are friends. And Freddy's been very attentive to you this past week as well." Her mother's raised eyebrows reminded Lucy of Edmund's teasing expression.

"Mother, he's always been like that, but people forgot how he doted on me. Think of all the scraped knees he carried me in for, all the broken toys he fixed to quiet my tears. He even beat Edmund that time he stole my journal. That's Frederick—it's his nature to be protective."

"Don't discount someone because he's overly familiar."

After eating, Lucy went up to change into a tea gown. With the weather holding in the high sixties the past few days, she opted for one that was new to her in the spring of 1903. As she rarely dressed for tea, it was in mint condition. The periwinkle under layer cast a pretty background for the off-white lace topper. Once dressed, her stomach felt jumpy—in a good way, like when riding the roller coaster at Monroe Park. With still an hour to go, she pulled out her hairpins and plopped on the bed with her old slate and a piece of paper on top of it to jot down her feelings.

I've Waited

I've waited for you
Years it seems
But it was only last week
You said my name
In such a way
That moved my soul
And made me yours forever

I've waited
Two and a half days
To see your smile
To feel your hand on mine
As we go through the motions
Society deems necessary for us to progress

I've waited
And will continue to wait
Until we make our escape
Free to explore everything
With sight, touch, and taste
Only then will we belong to each other

Lucy reread the words and chose a piece of the stationery she'd used for the Christmas poem, copying it on the fresh page.

"Lucy!" Edmund stuck his head in her room. "Did you not hear the doorbell? I barely made it in before they were at the door."

"I'll be right down."

With trembling hands, she shoved the poem into an envelope and shut the original in her top dresser drawer because there wasn't time to burn it. Unsure how she would present the poem to Alexander, she tucked it into the wide periwinkle sash at her middle and hurried down the stairs. When she stopped in the parlor doorway, her mother looked at her with disbelief. Realizing what she'd done, Lucy's hand went to her loose hair and her eyes went to the floor as she rocked back on her feet.

"At least I remembered to put on my shoes."

Everyone laughed except Mrs. Easton and the men both stood.

"That's an absent-minded writer for you." Edmund patted their mother's shoulder. "Now that our hostess is here, even if somewhat disheveled, you can go rest."

"Really, Lucy!" Mrs. Easton hissed when they passed each other.

Lucy raked her fingers through her hair and made a hasty braid that she threw over her shoulder. Then she chanced a full look at Alexander. Amusement shone in his eyes, looking more gray than blue in his dark, pinstriped suit.

"You look radiant, Lucy," he told her as she took the armchair on Eliza's end of the settee. Alexander had the far end and Edmund the armchair adjacent him—within striking distance. They both returned to their seats once Lucy settled.

Eliza giggled. "I often do the same thing when I've been painting and time gets away from me."

"I'm glad to hear it." Lucy smiled at her, somewhat unnerved by the girl's luminous eyes. "I apologize in advance. I'm not used to being hostess, and I'm sure my manners are lacking in some regards. If I forget to offer something, don't be afraid to ask. And if my conversation is dull, please yawn."

Eliza threw her head back and laughed. "Alex, why have you not brought me here before? Lucy is truly the life of the party."

"No," Lucy cut in. "I'm only animated among friends. You'll never see my wit at a party. I believe my intelligence drops when I'm surrounded by too many people."

"That's exactly how I feel, Lucy. We're kindred spirits, to be sure."

The next quarter hour, Edmund stayed mostly quiet. After several attempts to involve him in the conversation, the three others went on without asking his opinions until Naomi brought in the trays.

Lucy served Eliza while Edmund gazed up at the ceiling as though bored. She took the opportunity to pull the envelope from her sash and tucked it under Alexander's saucer.

"One sugar, please, Lucy," he said with a wink.

That brought Edmund back to attention. "Sorry I'm poor company today. I think last night was my first decent night's sleep in four days but I'm still feeling it today. I'll take three sugars and cream when it's my turn."

"I'll pour tea but I draw the line at dishing up food for everyone," Lucy remarked. She pointed to the plates on the coffee table between all of them. "Everyone can help themselves whenever they want."

"Scandalous! I like it." Alexander flashed his impish grin.

"Yes, our mother would disown her if she heard her say that." Edmund turned to the Mellings. "Don't let the fact that Lucille Easton doesn't serve a proper tea leave this room."

"I'll keep all Lucy's secrets," Alexander said, which earned him a narrow-eyed stare from Edmund.

"I think this is how it should be." Eliza took a plate and helped herself to several petit fours. "As if we women have nothing else to do with our time, our hands."

As Edmund gave Eliza his quizzical stare, Lucy passed Alexander his tea. He caressed her fingers for half a second and then deftly slipped the envelope into his coat pocket as he took the cup and saucer with his other hand.

While everyone ate, Alexander excused himself, patting his pocket as he passed Lucy. He returned with his suit coat removed. With the jacket off, his white shirt and red necktie brightened his eyes. Or maybe it was his thoughts about what he'd read that had him glowing.

"It's grown a bit warm, where shall I put this?"

Lucy was up in a flash, guiding him to the hooks in the foyer. As soon as they were around the corner, he slipped the envelope into her sash. A gasp of surprise escaped her lips at his touch. Then Edmund came, hands full with his tea and food because he didn't take the time to set them down.

Lucy took Alexander's jacket. "Edmund, do you wish your coat off too?"

"Might as well since this is the most unconventional tea I've ever attended. You're like Alice, playing at her first grown-up tea party in Wonderland."

"And you, dear brother, are the joker in the queen's deck of cards."

Alexander laughed at the siblings' sparring and helped Lucy hold Edmund's dishes while he removed his tweed jacket. When

Lucy returned Edmund's tea, he took Alexander by the arm and marched him back to the parlor, giving Lucy the opportunity to see what Alexander had given her.

The envelope was empty of paper, but on the inside of it he'd written a note.

The sight of you fills me with joy
Your touch is the reason I breathe
I crave to taste your sweet lips again

She returned to the parlor on wings of delight. When the conversation got around to Christmas, Edmund made a point of letting their guests know that Frederick had stayed with the family all afternoon and evening.

"Yes, he's like another brother or cousin around here." The annoyance in Alexander's voice clearly on display.

"Maybe once upon a time, but I wouldn't say that now," Edmund goaded Alexander.

"I saw Alex's automobile last week, but what did you receive for Christmas, Eliza?" Lucy asked in an attempt to change the subject.

"Mostly dresses and fluff, but Alex was kind enough to get me a new box of pastels and a table-top easel. I hope to buy a few canvases this week that will be a good size to work with on it. I think I'll find what I need with a trip to Luscher's, but I detest shopping with my mother."

"I'd be happy to go with you. I'll need to pick up a few ink ribbons myself. My parents gave me an Underwood 5."

"How exciting for you!" Eliza beamed. "May I see it?"

"Of course." The men stood when the ladies did. "Everyone is welcome, though I'm sure Edmund is bored with it by now."

"I'm over the *clickity-clacking*. Yesterday was constant, as was the cursing over her mistakes."

"I did no such thing!" Lucy exclaimed.

"But you were thinking it," he countered.

"So I was."

Everyone laughed as they moved to the hall. Alexander reached for Lucy's hand but Edmund blocked him. "You're not to step a toe into her bedroom."

"I could skip out of the office early tomorrow and take you ladies shopping," Alexander told them on their way up the stairs.

"Everything is slow this week. I was glad to only stay a half day today."

"That would be wonderful," Eliza said. "Could you make it tomorrow, Lucy?"

"My schedule's free. What time can I expect you to pick me up?"

"Is two agreeable?" Alexander asked.

"Certainly. I appreciate you including me with your plans."

As soon as Lucy showed Eliza into her room, she glanced behind her. Edmund had Alexander by the throat. She wound a fresh sheet of paper into the typewriter and let Eliza have a turn with it before going to the doorway.

"Edmund, let him go!" she spoke with a quiet fierceness.

"The deal was two social calls with me in attendance." He gave Alexander's shoulders a shake before shoving him away. "He purposely invited you when he knew I'd be working!"

"Eliza invited me. Alex only offered to drive us. I'll be in public with his sister the whole time in the middle of the afternoon. Remember, I'm not a child, Edmund."

With fists clenched, Edmund went to his bedroom and punched the pillows on his bed.

"He's just letting off steam," Alexander whispered. He took Lucy's hand and walked two steps backward, where they couldn't be seen from either open doorway. Alexander gave her a quick kiss as he caressed the hand he still held. "Thank you for the poem. And yes, the taste of you is worth the risk of a clobbering."

Lucy wanted to lean in for another, but the typing ceased. She hurried to her room. Eliza handed her a typed note thanking the hostess for the tea.

"You're much better than I! Tell me you've had practice so I don't feel bad."

Eliza laughed. "I used to play at being secretary in my father's law office, but I'm happy to say I've outgrown that phase of my life. I think all the typing worked up my appetite, though. I could use another cup of tea and more sweets."

Lucy linked her arm through Eliza's and they met Alexander in the hall.

"Are you coming, Edmund?" Lucy called into his room.

"I'll be down in a minute."

Eliza stopped in the half bath in the downstairs hall, so Alexander and Lucy entered the parlor without chaperones. Knowing how best to leverage the moment, Alexander pulled her into the corner and took her into his arms. His kiss was warm and filled with the sweetness of cakes. He pulled away before anyone returned and escorted Lucy to her chair. Then he took his sister's seat, affording him the chance to hold Lucy's hand while they waited.

"I should have stayed away because now I want nothing more than to kiss and hold you."

"Come to me tonight," she whispered. "Edmund won't expect you to try seeing me the same day. Meet me in the gazebo at eleven."

"Seeking that love affair, are we?" He kissed her hand as the hint of a blush warmed her cheeks.

Eliza returned and Alexander moved down to his old place on the settee. The three then helped themselves to more cake while Lucy refilled their teacups. The doorbell rang at the same time Edmund came down the stairs.

"Special delivery for Miss Lucille Easton from Mademoiselle Bisset," Edmund announced as he entered the room.

"You can place it on the side table, thank you."

"But don't you want to open it?" Eliza asked.

"Yes, but I was told it's rude to open mail when guests are over."

"And you're going to start abiding by the rules of etiquette after shirking them while serving tea?" Alexander teased.

"Well, when you put it that way…but really, I know what it is. I'm not sure I should show everyone."

"What is it?" Eliza set down her plate.

"My mask for the New Year's Eve ball. The shop keeper picked one out for me when she was in New Orleans over Christmas. Apparently, she has an artisan friend there who makes Venetian masks."

"Venetian masks are the most beautiful." Eliza sighed.

"You must show us," Alexander said. "It would be rude to deny your guest her satisfaction."

That earned him a glare from Edmund as he retrieved a letter opener from the hutch for Lucy to cut through the twine around the package. "Just open it, Lucy."

At some of the masquerades, like the Mystics of Dardenne, anonymity and full head masks for the members were the norm. But the New Year's Eve ball was about recognition, making Colombina style masks—which only covered the eyes—the standard for men and women. When Lucy opened the parcel and removed the mask from its cocoon of protection, Eliza gasped. The edge was trimmed in gold braiding and the background mostly black, with gold scrolling lily vines encircling the eyes in an asymmetrical flow. The left side—with less detailing—blended from black to gold. A tasteful grouping of black ostrich and cockerel feathers burst from the top corner.

"The workmanship is divine!" Eliza exclaimed. "How the artisan can paint uniformly around curves is a wonder. Are those lily vines?"

"Yes," Lucy replied. "It mimics the pattern on my dress perfectly."

"Are you going to model it for us?" Alexander took another sip of tea.

"I need to save something for a surprise at the ball."

"We haven't seen the dress, so that can be it," he countered.

"She said no," Edmund barked. "Respect her limits!"

"Of course, Eddie. I was only teasing. You know that, don't you, Lucy?"

"Yes. Lighten up, Edmund. You're much too cranky for guests."

"We'll be leaving soon." Eliza set down her empty teacup.

A few minutes later, everyone headed to the foyer. With the others crowded around the front door, Edmund said his goodbyes and retreated upstairs.

"This is the most fun I've had in months. Thank you for having us. You'll have to come to us next time." Eliza embraced her.

"I'd enjoy that."

With her arm around Lucy, Eliza whispered, "I think Alex likes you."

"I might like him too," she whispered back.

Eliza stepped away, giggling.

"What's this?" Alexander asked as he slipped on his coat.

"Just the fancy of young ladies." Eliza exited the door her brother held open and stepped to the side, turning away as if giving the couple privacy.

Alexander took the moment to intertwine his fingers with Lucy's and leaned toward her ear. "Eliza's the opposite of your brother. She's very accommodating. Tea at our house will be quite different. I'll see you tonight, my queen."

Eleven

At ten fifty-five that night, Lucy tied on her new mask over her loose hair. She still wore the cream-colored tea dress but was now barefoot. Masked and cloaked, she made her way across the yard, holding her gown up to protect it from the damp grass. Alexander rushed to her in the doorway of the gazebo.

"Do you not know how you tempt me, Lucy?" He took her hands still holding her skirt, tugging the fabric higher until it caught between them as they pressed together. He no longer had a visual of her bare legs, but he rubbed his knee against hers in a way that left her wanting more.

Lucy hugged him and kissed the corner of his mouth as she wrapped her leg around his. "We played at courtship this afternoon. I'd like a taste of the love affair now."

He held his position as she ran her hands over his pinstriped jacket, but his mischievous smile appeared pained as he traced the outline of her black and gold mask. "I'm not sure I know how to moderate myself to only give a taste."

"Then let me lead." She brought her lips to his for a deep kiss.

Seconds later, his hands were under her cloak, gripping at the lace gown on her hips and dominating their osculation. After a minute of fervor, he nudged her away, her gown settling around her ankles.

"I'll never live to see the new year if we keep this up. And it's for purely selfish reasons I must leave. I don't want Eddie to kill me until the city sees you on my arm at the ball." He kept one hand on her waist but brought his other to the mask. "And you're stunning in that. It makes me want to stare at those petal-soft lips of yours. Well,

---

more than stare. It gives you an erotic allure I don't think you're aware of. Why did you wear it tonight?"

"You asked me to model it this afternoon, and while I didn't want to do it in front of Edmund and Eliza, I wanted to show you. I want to give you everything you ask of me, Alex."

Alexander embraced her. "Do you understand what you're saying?"

"Yes," she whispered. "I think so."

"Oh, Lucy." He lowered her hood and tugged her hair free. "Your virginal innocence evokes sexuality without trying. Eddie accuses me of playing, but if he knew how you've unknowingly performed the part of seductress, I think I might earn some sympathy."

Lucy blushed and gazed at the ground. "I know a little from books, but I'm listening to what my body says. How can something I feel so strongly be wrong?"

"It's wrong tonight, Lucy. Trust me." He planted kisses around her mask as if he consecrated her as his own. "There will be a glorious time for us at some point in the future, but for now, run from me. I'll see you tomorrow afternoon."

∗∗∗

Lucy delighted to see the way Alexander doted on her and Eliza while shopping. Every bit the charming gentleman, he fetched things around the stores, carried parcels, and held doors. And when no one watched, there were winks and secret smiles.

When the Mellings dropped her off at home, Alexander held Lucy's hand while walking to the porch, which put a giddy smile on her face that didn't fall when Edmund opened the door scowling.

"Hello, Eddie. Rough day at the office?" Alexander grinned in a way that dared his friend to attempt to take away his pleasure.

"Because your sister is looking on, I won't put you in a headlock."

"We didn't go about town like this. That's just now, and only because no neighbors are in sight."

"It's the ones you don't see you have to be careful of," Edmund muttered. "Go home. I don't want to see you again until the ball."

"What about the meeting tomorrow night? Want to ride in with me, again?"

Edmund frowned. "Only if you swear not to meet my sister afterward."

"I promise there will be no covert meetings with Lucy tomorrow." Alexander brought Lucy's hand to his lips. "Thank you for making the afternoon enjoyable. I'll see you at the ball, unless I happen to see you when driving Eddie tomorrow."

She took her parcel with the extra typewriter ribbons from him. "Thank you, Alex."

Edmund followed her to her room. "Did he behave himself?"

"Don't be an ass, of course he did."

"I can't help but be concerned."

"Is that what you call grabbing a man by the throat, shaking him, and beating on your pillows? I've never seen such violence, Edmund. I'm beginning to worry about *you.*"

"So am I, but only because you're pushing my sanity to its limits by going out with Alex."

"It's been a week and I'm still in one piece. You need to relax and let me handle the relationship for myself. Believe me, Edmund, if I need you, I'll not hesitate to ask for help."

"All right, Lucy. I'll try to back off."

But Edmund's version of backing off was different than Lucy's. At supper on Thursday, he let it be known that he accidentally invited Freddy over when he would be gone to his meeting with Alexander.

"Do you think you could give my apologies and entertain him for a bit, Mother?"

"Of course. Freddy is always welcome here, isn't he, Lucy?" Mrs. Easton said.

"Frederick is, but Edmund's *mistakes* are not."

After dinner, Edmund grabbed his coat and hat and waited at the end of the driveway for Alexander so he wouldn't have an excuse to come in the house. Several minutes after he left, Frederick rang the bell.

Mr. Easton sat him in the parlor, discussing the trouble going on in Russia for over half an hour. He served everyone an after dinner drink which made Lucy's head spin, but seemed to give Frederick a boost of confidence.

"Since I'm here and we didn't get that practice dance in on Christmas, shall we try it tonight?"

"Yes, that's a splendid idea." Mrs. Easton smiled. "Lucy can go change while you help James push the dining furniture to the side.

Bring the gramophone in as well. A Strauss waltz should do nicely, I think."

Lucy knew she needed practice with the longer train and didn't protest. When changing upstairs, she took the time to re-pin her hair. Her mother came in and fastened the back of the sweetheart neckline bodice.

"I almost forgot my gloves." Lucy removed the gift box from her drawer and pulled out the black full-length pair.

"My stars, Lucy! Those are fine! Are they from the same admirer as the church pair?"

"Yes, I received two pairs for Christmas." Lucy couldn't help smiling at the memory of Alexander in the gazebo.

"And you won't tell me who?"

"You watch at the ball and see who I dance with the most."

"So mysterious, Lucy. Do you want to wear your mask?"

"No, I want it to be a surprise."

Mrs. Easton showed her daughter where to hold her skirt when walking on stairs with the extra weight and length she wasn't used to.

"Can you imagine trying all this with Opal staring on?" her mother asked as she attached Lucy's wrist loop to the designated hook on the side of her gown, sweeping it off the floor for dancing.

Imagining her sister's cold stare, she shivered. "No, not ever."

"Go on," Mrs. Easton motioned her toward the dining room as the parlor clock struck nine. "I'll give you both a few minutes."

Frederick arranged the last of the chairs to the side of the room when she entered.

"Sorry for the trouble. Mother is just as anxious about my dancing in this thing as I am."

"It's no trouble." He turned to her and stared.

"Have I grown a second nose?"

He ran a hand over his face and appeared as though he could use another drink. "I suddenly feel like a little boy peering in the window at one of Edmund's sisters."

Lucy laughed. "I thought you never looked."

"I didn't, but I image it felt a lot like this—unworthy to ever share the same space with such loveliness."

"Oh, stop, Frederick. It's just a dress."

He turned on the gramophone and the soft, reedy sound of "The Blue Danube" began. "Miss Easton, would you care to dance?" He bowed before her.

She raised her right hand, which fanned her gathered train to the side in a shimmer of black and gold. "I'd be delighted, Mr. Davenport."

Their waltz started as the music swelled. After a few missteps, the rhythm of the patterned dance became second nature. Lucy's arm fatigued halfway through the dance. Without missing a beat, Frederick adjusted his grip on her hand to support the weight of the train for her.

"Don't feel you need to carry the burden alone. Any partner worth having will be mindful of the gown's weight on your arm and compensate for you because it's an honor to hold a lady's train."

"Is that what you told yourself on Christmas when we paraded across the yard?"

He laughed, his eyes crinkling at the corners. "Yes, Goosy, I thought of my noble deed to keep your skirt dry the whole time."

"Anything to keep your mind off peeking at my legs."

Frederick tried to hide his embarrassment, but a few splotchy areas crept up to his cheeks. "I told you I didn't see much."

"You're the only person I know who's easier to tease than I am." She straightened her posture and readjusted her hand on his shoulder.

He in turn adjusted his hand at her waist, another whisper of a blush reaching his cheeks. "How's your arm holding up?"

"It's perfectly fine since you took over." She slid her hand from his shoulder to his biceps. "What are you doing these days? I tend to think you could support me all evening without weakening."

"After Harriet and my father passed, I joined a gym. It's better to have somewhere to go in the evenings rather than an empty house. I prefer the rowing machine and boxing most days. It's a good balance for me. Eddie was always the better boxer, but I think I could take him now. He looks like he's gone soft along with his high society friends."

"I have no doubt you could." She moved her hand back to its proper place as her parents came to the doorway.

"They make a striking pair, don't they, James?" Mrs. Easton asked her husband.

"Yes, indeed. That's the gown from Mademoiselle Bisset?"

"Half of it," Mrs. Easton replied. "There is another bodice, and the matching cape and stole were delivered this afternoon. She gave us quite the deal, you know."

"So you keep telling me, Evelyn. But no worries. Our Lucy deserves to be spoiled every once in a while. Now tell me good night. I have to meet a ship first thing in the morning."

The song ended and Frederick brought Lucy to a stop. Offering his arm, he walked her to her parents.

"Good night, Father." She kissed his cheek. "Thank you again for the gown. Are you staying, Mother?"

"No, but you take your time. If Eddie makes it back before you leave, could you help him return the furniture, Freddy?"

"Of course, Mrs. Easton. Thank you for having me this evening."

"Help yourselves to whatever you need. I know dancing makes one thirsty."

After the Eastons went upstairs, Lucy and Frederick took seats on the misplaced dining chairs to rest for a few minutes. Then they danced to "The Blue Danube" once more, chatting quietly about nothing in particular while they moved around the room. Afterward, Frederick found their glasses in the parlor and refilled them with brandy, though they sat mostly untouched on the edge of the dining table. He put a collection of Vivaldi string quartets on the gramophone and danced Lucy around the room once more.

Lucy felt his intense gaze, and though he didn't say anything, he communicated his feelings clearly. There was no doubt in her mind he was more than fond of her, but she cared for him too much to break any bad news before he had the opportunity to express himself. He'd be mortified to know his intentions were easy to read, especially when wearing his mourning band.

The two were thus engaged in a waltz of cloistered emotions when the front door opened.

"Mother? Lucy?" Edmund called.

Footsteps went toward the parlor. Then Alexander's voice rang out. "That's Freddy's automobile out there. Where the hell are they?"

Lucy's eyes widened.

"They'll find us soon enough." Frederick tightened his hold on her waist and danced her exuberantly around the room.

Edmund and Alexander opened the dining room door.

"Thank you for inviting me tonight, Eddie," Frederick called as he led Lucy through the steps. "Your parents and Lucy have been most hospitable."

Alexander's eyes narrowed as he crossed the dining room, tapping Frederick's shoulder to cut in on the dance.

"Pardon me, Freddy." His hands were on Lucy before Frederick could step away.

"Her train is quite heavy and you need to help support—"

"I'm well-versed in holding a lady's arm. I've dance with numerous Mardi Gras court members over the years, if you haven't noticed."

"Perhaps he questions your stamina as you aren't as athletic as he is." Lucy teased as she placed her left hand on Alexander's shoulder.

"I've never had complaints over my stamina or anything else for that matter." With one hand low and firm at the small of Lucy's back and the other supporting her burdened arm, Alexander spun her away from a red-faced Frederick.

"You're exquisite, Lucy. Every bit a woman in control of her destiny in this dress. And once again, the gloves are a perfect match."

The Vivaldi—which was nearing the end when Alexander interrupted—finished.

"Do you have any Tchaikovsky? Something from 'Swan Lake'?" Alexander asked Edmund as he stayed poised with Lucy, awaiting the return of music. "I insist on a full dance before leaving."

"It's in the other room." Edmund stomped to the parlor.

"And how did you know I prefer Tchaikovsky?" Lucy asked.

"I figured his scores would be just the thing for a writer who enjoys a good romance."

A genuine smile graced her face. "You know me well. Would you bring me to my drink while we wait?" She motioned to the corner of the dining table and he brought her there.

"Brandy?" Alexander looked across the room at Frederick. "I expected you to be the wine or champagne type."

Frederick shrugged. "It's what Mr. Easton offered us earlier. I merely refilled them."

"Eddie," Alexander said when he returned with the Tchaikovsky recording, "did you know that besides being unchaperoned, Freddy was trying to get Lucy drunk?"

"Your accusations are irrelevant because of Freddy's trustworthy character."

Alexander crossed his arms. "So even if I'm falsely accused, I'm immediately found guilty?"

"That's about right," Edmund replied as he set the song going.

"You must remember, Eddie, that we're all innocent until proven guilty." Alexander took the half-empty glass from Lucy and downed the rest of it before setting the tumbler on the table. He took back her hand and resettled his other at the curve of her waist with the opening swell of "Swan Lake."

Alexander's upbringing had trained him well for social situations. While he followed the foundations of the box step, his movements were anything but traditional. Lucy glided on a cloud as she held Alexander's azure gaze. The room around them blurred into a swirl of green and oak as he shared with her his passion through each flowing step and the pressure of his well-placed hands.

As the waltz built to the crescendo, he tilted his head toward her ear. "I love you more than ever for having shared this moment. Saturday can't come soon enough."

Her body hummed to its core. When the waltz ended, the urge to press against him and move to a primitive dance she instinctively knew overwhelmed her. Instead of listening to her wants, she stepped back and let her hand fall from his shoulder.

"Lucy, I feel it too," he whispered as he released her hand.

The two other men must have as well. Edmund took his sister's arm and Frederick stood guard beside Alexander.

"You look utterly peaked, little sister. It's time you went to bed."

Knowing things could only grow heated, Lucy nodded. "Thank you for helping, Frederick. And, Alex, you dance divinely." She unhooked her wrist loop, allowing the court-length train to fan out behind her as she made her way to the stairs.

Twelve

Not long after Mr. Easton and Edmund left for work Friday morning, the telephone rang. Mrs. Easton allowed Naomi to answer, but made her way to the hallway in expectation of being asked for.

"It's Miss Susan," Naomi said as Mrs. Easton reached the hall.

Lucy drank the rest of her coffee and prepared to return to her room to practice typing.

"Good heavens! She's never been as bad as that!" Mrs. Easton put a hand to her forehead.

Concerned, Lucy paused at the bottom of the stairs as her mother tapped her fingers on the phone box while listening to her oldest daughter.

"Yes, yes. Have David bring her home at once. I'm sorry for this extra stress, dear. It was meant to be a help to you. If he leaves within the hour he should be able to get back to you by dark, even if he rests a moment here to eat." Mrs. Easton paused. "Don't worry yourself any more, dear. We'll deal with her when she gets here. Have your housekeeper watch the littles and get yourself a nap."

She hung up the receiver with a sigh and turned to Lucy. "God knows what I'm going to do with that girl when she gets home."

"What happened?" Lucy put a comforting hand on her mother's arm.

"Gilbert apparently got a hold of Opal's bike and crashed it into the tree at the end of their lane this morning. Opal had one of her episodes and started throwing rocks. One almost hit Ava and another went right through the parlor window. Fortunately, David hadn't left for work and was able to confine her. She's on her way to us now."

Lucy's face fell. All her plans for the month were in jeopardy. "But the ball—"

"Don't you worry, Lucy. You'll go to the ball. We all will. I'll see if Cook can watch Opal for the evening. Father and I can come home early if needed." Mrs. Easton hugged her daughter. "This is your season. Don't let your sister ruin it for you."

The morning was a loss for typing. While grateful to have had the previous night of dancing practice free of those evil green eyes, Lucy couldn't help but think of dressing and leaving for the ball under Opal's eerie glare.

When she heard an automobile outside midday, she watched from her window as Opal stormed across the front yard and into the house. The wall shook from the force of her bedroom door slamming. Brother-in-law David, a gentleman to the core, calmly untied Opal's bicycle from the back of his vehicle and wheeled it to the porch. Mrs. Easton welcomed him when he carried Opal's luggage to the house and Lucy joined them for dinner.

The three ate with little pleasantries, all keeping a watch on the doorway. No one knew if Opal listened or would make an appearance. After eating, Lucy stood on the porch to wave David off with her mother.

Mrs. Easton sighed. "We'll still try to visit Susan at the end of January. Maybe Opal will be settled by then."

Lucy uttered a silent prayer that the family would still go the weekend of the Mystics of Dardenne ball. If Opal took that away, she'd not forgive her. "I'm sure all will be well, Mother."

"We can only hope."

Lucy climbed the stairs, daydreaming about dancing with Alexander in the black lily gown. She waltzed into her room and balked at the sight of Opal digging through her dresser.

"There you are," Opal's voice was sharp as a blade. "I've waited for you, years it seems."

"Why you little fink!" Lucy took Opal by the shoulders and shoved her out the door.

Playing theatrics, Opal dropped to the floor. "Mother, Lucy pushed me!"

Mrs. Easton climbed the stairs and helped Opal stand. Lucy went through her top drawer to check that her gloves and papers were all still there, and then stood in her doorway clutching the original draft of the poem with one hand.

"Mother, she has to stay out of my room! She has no respect for my private things and it has to stop!"

"Lucille's writing love poems, Mother." Opal sneered from their mother's arms. "She wants to taste and touch a man. How vile is that?"

Lucy roared, as much at herself for her folly in not already having burned the poem as at Opal. She slammed her door and turned to the fireplace. Her morning fire was mostly ash, but she laid the poem in and poked it under until the heat coiled the page. After adding more fuel, she opened her window to the chilly day, curled atop her bed, and cried in frustration.

***

Mr. and Mrs. Easton left for the ball at six thirty Saturday evening in a hired car, leaving the automobile for Edmund and Lucy. The masquerade started early because the committee had promised to shut down by half past midnight as New Year's Day was the Sabbath.

At a quarter to seven, Edmund knocked on her door. "I don't want to be too late."

"Come in." She sat at her dressing table, holding the mask to her face. "Will I look a fool tonight?"

"Only when you're with Alex." He seemed to have a change of heart when she frowned. "Come on, Lucy. You look amazing. Thursday night you had two grown men fighting over you because of the way you look in that dress."

"I hope I'm liked for more than my looks."

"Of course you are. It even appears Alex appreciates your wit and mind."

"You won't embarrass me tonight, will you?"

"As long as Alex behaves himself I won't. I'll give Freddy permission to punch him if needs be too."

"You wouldn't!" she cried.

"Just try me." He smiled. "May I tie on your mask?"

"All right. Mind my hair, though."

She watched Edmund in the mirror. His black matte Colombina mask was a classic choice, but the smart lines of his new tuxedo would set him apart from the pack, as would his gold bowtie and vest. Opal peeked around her door.

"You stay out of here," Lucy warned.

"I've no need to come in tonight. I've already discovered your secrets for the week." A smile creeped upon her impertinent face.

"Opal," Edmund warned, "be a dear and don't provoke your sister. Yesterday's exhibition was enough to last until the New Year."

He'd missed her being caught in in the act of raiding Lucy's room, but Opal had recited a few lines from the poem at the supper table, causing Edmund to redden and stirring Mrs. Easton to give Lucy a private talk about acceptable courting behavior for young ladies.

Opal slipped away with a smirk, knowing she'd won.

Lucy looked at Edmund's reflection. "Is there a certain someone you're looking forward to dancing with tonight? One of the ladies you entertained with your turkey story perhaps?"

"I'm sure you'll be too busy charming the room to notice me."

"I've no need to charm a room. I already have the heart I'm set on."

Finished tying her mask, he placed his hands on her shoulders. "Lucy, look in that mirror and tell me what you see."

"I see a girl playing at being a grownup. Like you told me at tea this week, I'm not a proper adult. I'm playing in a looking glass world and throwing the norms of society to the wind."

"I tease you, dear sister, in an attempt to keep you level-headed. Your absence of beaus through the years has more to do with me than you lacking any attractive qualities. I may have threatened too many boys along the journey who I saw looking at you a certain way. All the way back through my teen years I've warned my friends from trying anything with you—all except one. I realize I took the protective brother thing too far because the ones who don't listen are exactly the type I wanted to keep away to begin with."

"Edmund, really—"

"I'm sorry that I did you wrong, but I can't back down when the threat to your virtue is the greatest."

"Leave me be, Edmund. You and I are the middle children out of ten. I helped raise the younger ones until they were taken from us." Her voice cracked. "You don't need to protect me as you do. I can handle things."

"Don't start crying, Lucy. It should be a joyous night. Let me get your cape. It's already close to freezing out there. I'll try to give you some space, okay?" Edmund draped the cover around her shoulder. "I'll get the motor started while you finish up."

Lucy fastened the cape closed with the heavy gold chain and then hooked her skirt to the wrist loop to easier navigate the stairs. She tucked both Alexander's and Frederick's handkerchiefs into her black beaded reticule along with her invitation.

By the time they drove downtown, no parking could be found near The Battle House Hotel. On his second pass around the block, Edmund dropped Lucy at the front door. She entered the grand lobby where she checked her cape at the coat counter, slipped the ticket into her reticule, and removed her invitation. After pausing under the massive chandelier in the lobby, Lucy released her skirt from the loop.

Two masked men sat in nearby chairs. "She knows how to make an entrance," one remarked.

The second man crossed to her with confidence. "Miss, would you save a dance for me?"

She couldn't help the shy smile from coming to her masked face. "You're welcome to ask me once we're both inside."

"Are you crazy? Don't you know who that is?" the other man asked his friend when he returned. "Easton will box your ears if you make a move on his sister."

Lucy believed Edmund had exaggerated his claims, but the words spoken by the man left no doubt. She took a deep breath and crossed into the chandelier-lit ballroom. Her parents were deep in conversation with another couple, and she purposely avoided them on her way to the perfect spot to re-hook her skirt—an alcove partially obscured by potted palms along the back wall.

Halfway to her destination, Lucy met Kate Stuart, who wore a violet plumed mask. The magazine editor appeared sewn into an obscenely tight purple gown and the watch chain swayed across her bosom as she moved with mincing steps.

"Do you have a moment, Miss Stuart?" Lucy asked.

"Lucille Easton, I would recognize that hair of yours anywhere. I assume you received your payment and letter."

"Yes. Thank you for considering me. I accept your offer and would like to begin tonight by showing you these in confidence." She opened the clasp on her bag and pulled out the handkerchiefs monogrammed side up.

"Miss Easton, you've had a busy Christmas week! And from two of the most unlikely men. It usually takes initiates weeks to secure the first one." She tilted her head and sneered down at Lucy. "But remember that final rule about behavior unbecoming of a lady."

"Yes, of course." Lucy tucked the handkerchiefs back into her reticule and tried to keep from blushing. "Have a lovely evening and a Happy New Year."

Before she could take a seat to secure her train, the man from the lobby approached her. "May I have the pleasure of a dance?"

"Even after the warning from your friend?"

"Some things are worth the risk." His smile revealed a chipped front tooth, something Lucy had seen before, but couldn't place the name of the owner.

"Then how can I refuse? I just need to sit a moment to secure my train."

She sat in the nearest chair, removed her black satin bracelet from her bag, and hung both loop and bag from her right arm. She found the expertly hidden button on the side of the gown and attached it to the hook. Then the gentleman led her to the middle of the floor as the orchestra played the next song. Halfway through the movement, her mystery partner received a tap on his shoulder and he stepped aside.

"Spunner, you old dog." Edmund slapped the guy's back. "Just keep your hands where they're supposed to be."

Sean Spunner smiled at Lucy as they continued their dance. "Guess I lucked out."

Before they could walk her off the floor, they were greeted by another unknown suitor asking to dance. Lucy accepted and relaxed under the light steps, not caring if she ever knew the names of all the men she'd dance with in her lifetime because she would only care for one of them. *Maybe Edmund did me a favor by keeping all the suitors away. I needed to save my heart for the one who really matters.*

Disappointment over the next interruption soured her mood until the sight of Frederick caused her heart to flutter. He wore a handsome black tuxedo with his new purple bowtie and coordinating mask and gloves

"You look dashing tonight, Frederick."

"And you are a vision." His hands were positioned the same as the other partners, but his felt firmer on her body. "That mask is just the thing for the dress."

"Thank you." Lucy smiled, but looked away when his brown eyes seemed to turn serious.

Behind Frederick, Alexander wove through the dancers as he made his way to Lucy. Her previous smile doubled and she turned her head to keep his gaze as they waltzed further away. The lines of his tails were even finer than Edmund's, and his white gloves, bowtie, mask, and vest were striking in the sea of darker colors.

Frederick followed her stare. "I'll bring you around to him."

"Thank you, Frederick."

As good as his word, their next pass around the floor brought her directly before Alexander. Without being asked, Frederick gave Lucy's hand to him and stepped away. "If you would point out your sister, Alex, I'd be happy to dance with her."

"You're a good chap, Freddy. Black hair, mask, and dress, all trimmed with pearls. Check near the refreshments. She has a sweet tooth."

Then they were off, Alexander's right hand low and snug on her waist and his left thumb caressing her palm as they glided around the room.

"I wasn't able to speak of it the other night, but that dress is perfection. It displays your flawless skin and curves like nothing I've ever seen." She didn't mind when his gaze went to her neckline. "If there was a secret garden nearby, I'd rush there with you right now and cover you with a thousand kisses. Would you go with me?"

"You know I would, Alex."

"Then I'll have to think of something." His smile brought her to the edge of euphoria with the idea of escaping the pretense of the ball with him.

When the lull between songs dispersed the other dancers, Alexander kept her in his arms in the middle of the floor. During the next song a tap came to his shoulder and the man asked permission to cut in.

"Sorry, not now," Alex replied.

The second man was met with, "I don't wish to share this vision of beauty."

The third time it happened was Edmund with a warning. "You've made your point, Alex. Quit acting like you own her."

After her brother walked away, Alexander tightened his hold.

"You do own me," she whispered. "You possess me, body, heart, and soul."

During the next dance, the tap on Alexander's shoulder made him scowl but Lucy smiled at the gray-haired intruder.

Alexander turned and immediately stepped away. "Mr. Easton, sir."

Not being one for dancing, Mr. Easton got right to the point as he waltzed his daughter around the room. "Your mother wishes to know if Alexander Melling is the one who gave you the gloves."

"He is."

"Then I expect you to present him to us at some point this evening."

"I'd be happy to, Father."

"You look like you could use a rest after all those dances." He brought her to the far side of the room and sat her where there were two free chairs. "And, Lucy, dear, be careful."

"I will. Thank you, Father." She kissed his cheek and he left to report his finds to her mother.

Four different men wishing to dance with her inquired but Lucy declined them all, claiming she needed to rest. Gratitude washed over her when Alexander came with drinks.

"It's getting ridiculous," she remarked. "I don't even think I've collectively danced as many times at parties since I came out as I've been approached tonight and it's just the first hour."

Alexander swallowed half his punch in one movement and leaned to her ear. "I told you that dress showcases you in a new light. Dance with them if you must. It's pleasurable to watch you from afar, to see the way the gown sways from your hips and the swell of your chest when you've danced too much." He ran a finger down the sheer glove on her arm in between them. "But I might change my mind about that if there's a leering man clumsily leading you around."

"And if it gets too painful, you can always cut in and rescue us both."

"Exactly right, my queen." He kissed her ear before straightening.

Electricity coursed through her from the brief touch of his lips. Seeking to cool herself, Lucy took her first sip and nearly spit it out. "What did they do to it?"

"Some of the Mystics of Dardenne brothers added too much gin to the punch, but I can assure you it wasn't me this year."

She tried one more sip and handed it back. "I'll need something else."

He drained her cup in one gulp. "And I'll need to stay away from anything more for an hour. They did ruin it, but I'm not one to let alcohol go to waste."

For each of the next two dances Lucy started with Alexander but ended with a mystery partner. The third dance began with a new young man, stumbling drunk. Before she could think how to handle the situation, Frederick cut in. Without waiting for the man to reply, he took Lucy's hand and spun away from him.

"Thank you. I was beginning to fear for my toes and dress. He looked a little green."

"The poor chap must have gotten a hold of that punch."

"Yes, it was quite undrinkable. Alex is going to find something more suitable for me."

"That's good of him. Eliza is a pleasant young woman. I've danced with her twice, though I won't take any more lest she get the wrong idea."

"I've seen glimpses, but have yet to speak with her."

"You both seem to be admired dance partners tonight." Frederick's hand on her waist pressed into her slightly.

"I quite feel like a bud myself today."

"You've blossomed into your own woman, Lucy. The men are just waking up to it, though Alex seems to be the quickest on his feet. He's waiting for you now with a beverage."

"He's watching our every move, is he? Hold me closer if you wish and we'll see what his tolerance level is with my dancing partners." A beguiling smile lit her face as she closed the distance between them.

"I don't want part of any games, Lucy."

He tried to pull away, but she held him firm. "No game, Freddy. It's research for a sweeping romance I aim to write."

"Well, in that case, and since you called me Freddy like an old friend…" He shifted his hand to her hip and increased the flourish of their movements in such a way that it rivaled Alexander.

Lucy's gasp turned to a laugh midway up her throat. "You're always so helpful."

They danced in silence for a minute and then Frederick moved them toward the edge of the floor.

"I see I need to increase my efforts to keep up with Davenport," Alexander said when they came to him. "I just hope Eddie caught that display so I won't be accused of improper advances when I do likewise."

Lucy laughed and Frederick excused himself.

"Wait a moment." She turned away from Alexander and opened her reticule. She pressed Frederick's handkerchief into his hand. "Thank you for your help, today and always."

Frederick frowned before forcing a smile. "Anything for you, Lucy."

When she turned back, Alexander offered her a glass of champagne and placed his white gloved hand on the small of her back when she accepted. "Is that more to your taste, Lucy?"

"Yes, thank you."

He leaned into her side. "And I shall like to taste of it from your lips. Your teasing smile coupled with that mask is my undoing. I must rush you away from here."

"My parents want a formal introduction. We need to see to that before escaping."

"Then let's get to your parents and play at those courtship rules so we can move on to our love affair." He fingered her cheek. "You'll find me most accommodating in that regard tonight."

A thrill of expectancy raced through her body. She took his arm and walked beside him while fantasizing of his kisses.

"Lucille!" Mrs. Easton said when they reached her parents' table. They were seated with Maxwell and Lottie, as well as two other couples Lucy didn't recognize with their masks on. "You were positively radiant on the dance floor, and with so many suitors! Didn't I tell you the perfect dress would cure everything?"

She took her mother's hand and kissed her cheek below her gold mask. "Yes, Mother, you did. You remember Alexander Melling, don't you?"

"Of course." She offered her hand and he kissed the back of her silk glove.

"It's a pleasure as always, Mrs. Easton."

"I figured you were a charmer, Alexander, but those gloves show a depth of understanding I didn't expect from you." Mrs. Easton, having already married off three daughters, was well versed in tactful hints to suitors without fully disclosing her approval or condemnation of the beau.

Not missing a step, Alexander countered. "I've matured much this year and the mere presence of your daughter is enlightening."

"She's the brightest of my girls."

"If I may be bold, Mr. Easton," Alexander turned to him, "I'd like to ask permission to see Lucy home after the ball. I would have her back by a quarter to one, or earlier if that time is unacceptable."

Mr. Easton wasn't as subtle as his wife. "I can't say I'm comfortable with that as you wrecked your last automobile after a late night of revelry not too long ago."

Alexander humbly bowed his head. "I've made my share of mistakes, but have learned from each one. The accident you refer to helped me understand my limits. But to be on the safe side, as Lucy is most precious to me, I've secured a cab for the ride home."

Mrs. Easton took her husband's hand and squeezed it twice, which meant she approved of something. Mr. Easton, however, wasn't in a hurry to give his consent.

"If twelve or another time is more agreeable, I'm happy to oblige for the honor of escorting Lucy home. I'm at your mercy, Mr. Easton." Alexander tenderly took Lucy's hand and tucked it around his arm to show he wasn't backing down.

Mr. Easton stared at him another half a minute. "Twelve thirty should give you enough time to stay for the countdown and then make it to our house."

"Thank you, Mr. Easton. Mrs. Easton." He bowed to them. "I'm sure we'll see you again."

Thirteen

After leaving her parents, Alexander collected
a selection of finger foods for them to share before securing a fresh
glass of champagne for each of them. They wove through the room
to the far alcove, an intimate space with already a few couples in the
oversized armchairs.

Lucy sat and released her wrist loop, placing it in her bag on
the side table. Alexander handed her a glass and then cozied in beside
her. The feel of him snug against her aroused Lucy's focus to the
cravings of her body in a new way.

"Would you care for a chocolate dipped strawberry or should
we save the sweets for last?" Alexander's grin was the tiniest bit
naughty as he removed his white gloves.

"Let's save it."

He held the plate before her and she took a tea sandwich.
While she ate, she studied the three other couples in the alcove. One
pair she recognized as newlyweds who attended the cathedral. The
bride sat with her head curled on her husband's shoulder and her legs
over his lap. He absentmindedly caressed her knee in between drinks.
The dreamy smile on her lips created the first burning jealousy Lucy
experienced because of another woman's relationship. The second
couple was deep in conversation, their masked faces inches apart as
they whispered. And the third—involved in a shameless display of
necking—pricked her cravings as she imagined the feel of
Alexander's mouth on her collar bones and lower.

Alexander's hand on the bare skin of her upper back made
her gasp. He kneaded the base of her neck. "I wish we were doing
that too," he whispered. "But we'll have our moment soon, I
promise."

"How can you be sure?" She took another sandwich from the plate to keep her mouth busy.

"Let's just say that some of my brothers are planning a little mayhem for the Order of Mayhem ball, to remind the gentlemen they aren't living up to their name like they used to." He quickly kissed below her ear and checked the clock on the wall opposite them. "Just be sure you're close to me at ten thirty."

"Then I'll stay these last few minutes, though I can't get any closer to you than I am now."

"But we can get much closer." He kissed the corner of her lips and leaned his forehead against hers. "Lucy, if you knew the battle going on inside me right now, I fear you'd run from me forever."

She gripped his knee. "It can't be more than what I'm feeling."

"We need to finish the food and then we'll have our time." He held a chocolate dipped strawberry in front of her mouth. "Take a bite."

Having read scenes in novels about the sensual flavors of fruits and chocolates, Lucy played coy. She took a tiny nibble of the tip of the berry then gave him a provocative smile. "Teach me how it's done."

Alexander placed her fingers on the stem and brought it to his mouth, covering the whole berry. His lips brushed her fingertips as he positioned his mouth to bite the fruit. With the snap of his teeth, the stem dangled from her hand. Lucy continued to watch his lips, mesmerized by the allure she felt toward him.

Picking the other berry from the plate, Alexander motioned for Lucy to place the empty dish on the side table. "Now it's your turn."

He tapped her lips with the strawberry and she took the moment to inhale the scents. When the smooth chocolate touched her the next time, she clamped around it and took her bite. A half an inch of fruit remained on the stem.

"You can't leave any part untouched. You must taste it all and allow all to be tasted. Do you understand what those images of pink turning to red in your first poem mean to me?" He lifted her chin with a fingertip and searched the shadow of her mask to seek the truth in her eyes.

She held his gaze, knowing he'd see the fire within as she replied. "Yes, and when the time comes, I won't be afraid."

His smile was both terrible and beautiful in that moment. Lucy's heart raced until his hand caressed her neck. "Do you know where my mind went when you wrote of waiting to explore everything in your last poem?"

She relished the feel of his hand at her jawline. "That's when we'll truly belong to each other, when we're free to share everything. I want nothing more than to learn everything about you, for you to know me as no one ever has."

"Your desire ignites my passions in a way that I'm afraid will burn you when our moment comes."

His words sparked unquenchable lust from the depths of her loins just as the ballroom fell into complete darkness. The music came to a halt and several women screamed. A shifting of the crowd moved in the blackness and then everything quieted like a muted summer shower.

Alexander caressed her neck. "It's okay. This is what the Dardennes are doing, but it will only last a few minutes," he whispered.

"Then don't waste our privacy." She moved onto his lap.

Immediately, he caressed the skin exposed by her gown while he found her lips. He tasted of chocolate-berry-champagne and she couldn't get enough.

"Sounds like some people are enjoying the dark," a man whispered.

"And why aren't we?" a female replied. There were a few giggles and sounds of others kissing.

Embarrassed, Lucy pulled away. Alexander's mouth tickled her ear, fingers caressing her décolletage.

"It's okay, Lucy. It's carnival season. But even if it wasn't, I'd still feel this way for you. Look, it's starting."

Lucy snuggled beside Alexander, resting her head on his shoulder, but her heart still raced. His right arm went around her waist and she took his other hand in hers. On the far side of the room, a dozen lanterns in groups of two wound their way through the maze of people. The lanterns were carried by men in black body suits with skeletons painted on them, their heads covered with skull masks. Lucy's hand tightened around Alexander's.

"Don't worry. They're here to promote our party." He hugged her closer and kissed her cheek.

After the lantern bearers congregated in the center of the room, one of them climbed on the backs of two of the others.

"Now hear this!" he shouted in a booming voice. "The Mystics of Dardenne are disappointed in this drowsy ball. We invite those who wish to enjoy the merrymaking of the carnival season to its fullest to join us as we lead a dance. Those having the most fun will earn an invitation to our Flights of Fantasy masquerade! Powers that be, the lights! Musicians, at the ready with something lively, please!"

The room returned to its crystal-lit glory. The Dardenne skeletons were all covered from head to foot in matching clothes, shoes, and gloves, leaving nothing exposed that could disclose their identities. After floundering with their sheet music, the conductor started the orchestra into a peppy Strauss waltz. Costumed skeletons dispersed, dancing with ladies and gentlemen alike as they tried to rowdy the crowd. The dance floor cleared of the mature set, leaving mostly those under of the age of twenty-five to entertain—and offend—the other guests.

"Is that Eliza with one of them?" Lucy pointed across the room. Alexander's sister was led around the floor in a swaying, suggestive dance.

"Dear God, it is!"

Alexander pushed his way through the crowd to get to Eliza. Taking her arm, he pulled her away without bothering to cut in respectfully. He started walking away, but a gloved hand was on his shoulder and the skull leaned closer to tell him something.

Eliza, all smiles when her brother brought her to Lucy, collapsed beside her. The flounces of her matte black ruffles covered Lucy's shimmering lily print.

"That was the most fun of the whole ball! I wish to dance with him all night. And he even gave me an invitation." She patted her reticule.

Alex crossed his arms. "You won't be going!"

"It's my invitation and I aim to go." She turned to Lucy. "Go out and dance with one of them and secure your own."

Two of the skeletons galloped into the alcove, pretending to fawn over the couples in the other chairs.

"We need more young lovelies at our masquerade!" one of them cried. "And what better place to spy them than the lovers' corner?"

The other skeleton went straight for Eliza and pulled her to her feet, but Alexander shoved him aside. The man pranced around the back of the chair and dangled an invitation in front of Lucy.

"For the pretty lady with poor taste in men." Even though Edmund disguised his voice, he didn't fool Lucy.

She took the card from him and slipped it into her bag. "Thank you."

With the sudden motion of a leaping cat, Eliza clung to Edmund's glove as he danced away. Alexander turned to get her, but Lucy took his arm.

"Alex, let her dance."

"She's just eighteen. It's her first ball." The fear in his voice was more telling than anything he could have confessed.

Lucy wrapped her arms around his neck, her reticule hanging from her wrist. "And you know firsthand what masked revelers are like on nights like this, don't you?"

His hands went to her waist, pulling her against him. "All too well, I'm afraid."

"Edmund is just trying to get you to understand where he's coming from in regards to me."

"How do you know it's him?"

"He can't disguise his voice enough, but when I saw him stop you when you took Eliza, I knew. While I don't agree with everything he does, I understand why he feels the need to do it."

"You and Eliza are entirely different situations. She's a bud and you're a full woman."

"Edmund wouldn't hurt her."

"He's no saint, Lucy. He's been at my side during more than a couple shenanigans this past year." As though he sensed the concern and disappointment, Alexander moved his hands to her hips to refocus her attention. "Why do you think he worries for you so much? It's not just the stories, as I know he claims. He's been on the front lines of sin too."

Dread pooled in her gut. "But he wouldn't—"

"No, I don't think he would." Alexander wrapped his arms around her. "But it's still a rotten thing to drag Eliza into this feud of his."

"Agreed."

He held Lucy closer. "Let's dance. I feel the need to outdo Freddy's last spin with you."

Lucy hooked her wrist loop while Alexander pulled his gloves on. Eliza danced with a new partner, so Lucy didn't entertain the thought that Edmund whisked her away when the skeletons left.

Instead, she absorbed the emotions of the Tchaikovsky score and the blue of Alexander's eyes.

"I think I'm losing my good name, like you warned me," Lucy told Alexander when she returned from the ladies' room. "Usually, I'm ignored or spoken to in passing. Now I'm positively frowned upon."

"Oh, Lucy, I am sorry." He stroked her cheek.

"None of that matters when you look at me. When you speak to me, I forget every wrong. And when you touch me, I'm invincible. I'll go on forever as long as you don't let go."

When the clock inched toward midnight, Alexander positioned them closer to the doors. "Give me your coat ticket. I plan to be out the door with the last word of 'Auld Lang Syne.'"

"You want to have me home early to impress my father?" She retrieved her number from her reticule.

He leaned in to whisper with a smile that set her insides quivering. "No, I want the longest carriage ride with you possible."

With the striking of midnight and the traditional song sung, Alexander collected their wraps. Under the great chandelier in the lobby, he helped Lucy into her cape. Once he had his black overcoat on, he took her arm and led her into the freezing night.

"Your carriage awaits, my queen."

In the first spot in front of the hotel, a shiny black carriage pulled by two horses waited. A uniformed man stood at attention.

"Master Melling, Miss Easton." The words came off his dark face in silvery puffs. He opened the door for them and Alexander held Lucy's elbow as she stepped in.

"You know the address," Alexander said to him. "I don't want us there a minute before twelve twenty-five, but no later than twelve-thirty or my lady will be in trouble."

"Yes, sir."

Once on the padded bench beside her, Alexander immediately removed his mask, coat, and gloves, tossing them onto the bench across from them. As the carriage pulled away from the curb, they fell into semi-darkness. The only windows not curtained were the ones adjacent to the front bench. When they passed under a street lamp, the glow softly illuminated the space.

He opened the buttons on his tuxedo jacket. "Do you want your cape off, Lucy? I'll keep you warm."

Her hands went to the gold clasp. "And what are your intentions for the ride?"

"To hold you until my love soaks into your soul." He knelt before her, swaying with the motion of the carriage. The lines from his mask were etched into his skin around his eyes but his hands were warm as he took the cape's clasp from her and slid the covering off her shoulders. With a teasing smile, he added, "And kissing, lots of kissing."

Alexander reached behind her head and untied the ribbon securing her Venetian mask. He placed it carefully beside her cape on the other bench. With his thumbs, he gently massaged her mask lines and trailed kisses around her eyes.

"Does that feel better?"

"Yes." She touched his cheek with her black, lacey hand.

Alexander slid onto the seat and pulled her into his lap. With arms around her, he rested his head against hers and breathed deeply several times. The rhythmic motion of the carriage coupled with the feeling of his warm arms swaddling her body stirred Lucy's yearning for more.

"Touch me, Alex. Touch me like you did in the dark." She arched against his arm supporting her and leaned her head back, exposing her neck and décolletage to him.

He danced his fingers across the sweeping expanse of her porcelain skin, down the curving lines of her gown's neckline. "You're magnificent. May I kiss you?"

"I told you there's no need for you to ever ask. I'm yours."

"This will be quite different." Eyes intent, he continued to caress her skin. "After this, no ordinary contact will be fulfilling. The craving for more will be intense. Once we start down this path, there'll be no turning back."

"Do you truly love me?"

"More than life itself."

"Then taste of me, Alex." Her words begged to be fulfilled.

He went for her lips to start. Then he nibbled down her neck as she clung to his vest. When his mouth reached the hollow of her collar bones she moaned in pleasure and arched anew. Alexander went to her décolletage, pulling aside the neckline of her gown enough to leave a passion mark where it wouldn't be seen. Lucy's body coursed with new sensations while Alexander's attentions returned to her mouth. His fingers touched wetness on her cheek.

"Tears, Lucy?" his voice broke.

She lay limp in his arms. "I never thought it would be this beautiful, feel this good."

Alexander hugged her to him and buried his head into the curve of her neck. "There's so much more, but this is by far the most beauty I've ever experienced. All the rest of my days, I only want to share this with you. Moments like this and more."

"I could stay like this forever. I love you, Alex."

A few of his tears dripped onto her breast, and with their moisture, her love bloomed more. Their next kiss, flavored with the salt of their joy, was tender and deep.

Three sharp strikes sounded on the roof of the carriage.

"What was that?" Lucy pulled away.

Alexander stroked her arm. "That's our five-minute warning."

"You think of everything." Her smile faded.

"What is it, Lucy?" He took her chin in his hand but she wouldn't look at him. "Don't spare my feelings. Tell me what's bothering you."

"I can't help but think that this isn't your first time with a woman, that I'll never live up to your previous encounters though you're my everything."

Gently, he kissed her cheek. "You've already surpassed everything, my queen. You'll be my first for many things and my last for all."

Gooseflesh prickled her arms.

"I've failed you." Alexander retrieved her cape and placed it around her shoulders and fastened it at her chest. "I'd hold you all night if I could. Someday we'll be able to, but tonight we must think of your parents." Alexander buttoned his suit jacket and coat before tying open the curtains.

Their time drew to a close as the carriage pulled in front of the Eastons' turreted home. The automobile was still gone, but Mr. and Mrs. Easton could be seen through the window.

Alexander paused before opening the front door and kissed her ear. "You were my first carriage ride."

Then he ushered her into the parlor with her parents. Alexander helped her remove her cape and stood with it on one arm, holding her hand with the other.

"You appeared to have a lovely time from what I saw of you," Mrs. Easton said.

"Yes, Mother. Everything was wonderful."

Mrs. Easton turned to her husband. "And see, Alexander got her home a few minutes early. You needn't have worried. Would anyone like coffee or tea?"

"No, thank you," Alexander said. "But I would enjoy that another time. I think I've kept Lucy up long enough. I hope to see you all at ten thirty Mass, and if it would be agreeable, I would like to sit with Lucy and see her home afterward in my automobile. No lengthy walk in this cold, though I hear it is expected to warm up tomorrow."

"You're welcome to sit with us, Alexander," Mr. Easton said.

"It will be my pleasure, sir, and Happy New Year, Mr. and Mrs. Easton."

Fourteen

Lucy sat at the vanity in her underclothes before dressing for Mass, marveling over the passion mark Alexander left on her heart. Her mind wrestled with impassioned dreams during her slumber and her body still felt the ghost of his touch on her skin, but shame seeped in. She blushed at the fact that she experienced no guilt during their moments of indulgence and realized she was lost without Grace Anne. If her friend wasn't touring Europe, she'd have someone to discuss things with because she had more experience with men than Lucy ever wished to have. Two weeks of seeing Alexander Melling a handful of times and she'd let him touch and kiss her in ways she'd never imagined before marriage. Alexander walked into her life and threw open all the doors to her heart, body, and soul. True, she'd seen him around for years, and even admired his cool stare and style, but she never believed she would be anything more in his eyes than Eddie's little sister. Now Alexander held her future in his hands, whether for good or ill Lucy didn't know, but she prayed in that moment—one hand on the mark over her heart—that what she had with him was true.

Excitement over seeing Alexander at church already replaced the negative feelings. Lucy slipped into the pale blue dress she'd worn the day after the Mellings' Christmas party and met her family in the dining room. Her parents discussed the morning newspaper and Opal moped in the corner. Edmund, in his robe, had his head over a cup of coffee.

"You look lovely today, Lucy," Mrs. Easton said as Lucy poured herself coffee at the sideboard. "Isn't that the dress you wore the other week when Alexander walked you home?"

"*Tried* to walk me home, Mother. Edmund joined us, if you recall, and sent Alex on his way."

"Really, Eddie." Mrs. Easton frowned. "Your sister is finally getting attention from eligible suitors and you're trying to chase them away. Now isn't the time to baby your sister. I know it must be difficult to see your friends having interest in Lucy, but there's nothing wrong with it. Cora's Charles was good friends with Maxwell and he didn't try to run him off. If Maxwell could tolerate a man six years his sister's senior to come calling, I see no reason for you to despair over a few years difference between Lucy and Alexander."

"It's not the age difference I'm concerned about, Mother."

Lucy sipped her coffee and picked at a biscuit.

"He was a bit of a rascal growing up from what I've heard, but he seems to be settling down, and if it's with our Lucy he means to settle with, I see no problem. He's been a gentleman with his lovely Christmas gifts and asking your father for permission to see her home last night. And when he got her home, before curfew mind you, he asked to sit with Lucy during Mass today."

"Don't be blinded by his riches, Mother," Opal said in a cold voice from the corner.

Edmund's laugh was bitter. "Out of the mouths of babes."

"Eddie and Opal," Mr. Easton said as he dropped his newspaper, "you must not speak to your mother in that tone."

"I'm sorry, Mother." He drained the rest of his cup. "I think I'll make it to church after all. Please excuse me."

Lucy looked to her mother with pleading eyes. "Please don't let him sit by Alexander."

Mrs. Easton patted her daughter's hand. "I'll do my best, Lucy."

Edmund's seating arrangement was worse than Lucy imagined. Rather than trying to sit beside them, her brother went to the pew directly behind the couple. She sat between Alexander and Opal, with Edmund breathing down their necks. When Alexander's rich tenor rang out during the hymns, warmth spread in her chest. Lucy wanted only one thing more than elbowing Edmund in the stomach, but it was even less appropriate behavior to engage in the cathedral than violence. Her mind further strayed when she caught sight of the newlyweds from the alcove at the ball a few rows over. Alexander's touch loomed large in her memory. The passion mark burned at her breast and a flush of remembrance heated her cheeks as she shifted uncomfortably.

Looking sideways at her, Alexander opened her hand and drew a question mark with the tip of his finger on her lace-covered palm. Moved that he'd noticed the change in her demeanor, a smile lit her face as she opened his hand and drew a curving heart with her finger. He clasped her hand, and with a deliberate movement, brought it to his lips. It was more like a pressing of his lips to her knuckles than a kiss, but it elicited a jab from Edmund.

At the close of Mass, Lucy wanted to rush out the door, but Alexander said his goodbyes to her parents and then made conversation about it being the coldest New Year's Day to the people in the next pew. When Eliza made her way up the aisle, Lucy understood he'd been stalling.

"Lucy!" Eliza's mantilla slipped near the edge of her glossy dark hair. She squeezed into the emptying pew in front of them. Alexander adjusted her head covering as she knelt on the bench. The church emptied, leaving the foursome an island in a sea of pews. "Tea at our house this week. What day is better for you, Tuesday or Thursday?"

"Tuesday, and thank you for the invitation."

Eliza put her hands at her narrow waist—her black silk gloves a striking contrast to the emerald dress—and lifted her chin to motion to the sentinel behind Lucy. "You're invited as well, Edmund. It would be good to see you again, especially after those dances we shared last night."

"Whatever can you mean? The time I tried to cut in, your partner wouldn't allow it."

"You know perfectly well, *Mr. Bones.*" Her eyebrows arched over her luminous blue-violet eyes and she lifted her shoulder in a way that was both innocent and suggestive at the same time.

Edmund stammered. "Well, I just…don't think I can make it Tuesday."

"You know I'll expect another dance at your masquerade." Eliza leaned over the pew and lowered her voice. "What were those moves? Something with a Latin flair, I believe. Do you think Mobile is ready for the Tango?"

Alexander put both hands on her shoulders and nudged her to return to the other side of the pew. "Remember where we are, Sister."

She gazed heavenward and crossed herself, then went back to making eyes at Edmund.

He held her stare. "How did you know it was me?"

"I'm an artist and my favorite subject is the human form. When I meet someone, I study their structure, and not just that of their face."

"That's more than enough information," Alexander stated.

But she continued. "I've been sizing you up for years, Edmund. I would know you anywhere, no matter what you're wearing. If you ever want to model, I'd be more than happy to draw you. Your shoulders are perfection."

Edmund adjusted his stiff collar and went a little red under his beard. "Uh, thank you, Miss Melling. I need to be going now." He practically ran out of the sanctuary.

Alexander laughed. "That was a little heavy handed, Eliza, even for you."

Lucy's hand went to her heart as she looked between the siblings.

Noticing her confusion, Eliza took pity. "Alex asked me to invite Edmund to tea in such a way he would be sure to refuse, but everything I said was true."

"And people think you shy!" Lucy exclaimed.

"I'm like you, Lucy. Not one to prattle on for the sake of small talk, but fully animated within a small gathering. I told you at your tea we were kindred spirits."

"Yes," Alexander said, "you are both burning with passion and creativity, but you must stay away from Edmund. You may admire his features from afar, but he would not be a good match for you. Let me see you to Father and Mother so I can bring Lucy home."

Alexander took Eliza on one arm and Lucy on the other.

"Why is he not a good match for me, Alex?" Eliza asked as they walked down the nave.

"He's as boring as they come in regards to the affairs of the heart and needs to be spoon-fed anything beyond bringing flowers to show affection."

Eliza frowned and sighed. "Well, I can still look."

"And that's all."

On the portico, the three were much stared at and whispers seemed to circle them like vultures. After both ladies removed their mantillas, Alexander led them down the wide steps to the sidewalk where his parents waited.

"There's a striking group. Alex, always remember a man is only as handsome as the woman on his arm is beautiful. That makes you very handsome indeed for the moment." Mr. Melling winked at Lucy.

"That was a lovely gown last night, Lucille," Mrs. Melling said. "It was nice to see you in something current for a change."

"Lucy has classic taste, Mother. I find it refreshing." Alexander placed his free hand atop Lucy's on his arm.

"When I was young, they were simply called second-hand, but in Lucille's case, I suppose it would be third or fourth. Having three older sisters must be difficult, dear."

"I'm not one for shopping, so it simplifies things." The stares and whispers from strangers were one thing, but to be criticized by a woman she might call mother-in-law someday was too much.

"She's like Eliza, Mother. She cares more for her work than what she wears."

"And I suppose after raising all those children, Mrs. Easton can't be bothered to check that one of her younger daughters is properly attired. The poor woman must be overworked with a household that size. Next time Eliza and I go shopping, we will send for you. I would love to help dress you, Lucille."

After the stories she heard about shopping with her mother from Eliza, the idea was nauseating, but she managed a polite smile. "Thank you, Mrs. Melling. That's very kind."

"Lucy will be over for tea on Tuesday afternoon," Eliza said. "Maybe we can plan something then."

"I will be at the D.A.R. tea that afternoon, which I had hoped you would attend with me, but we can discuss it later." Mrs. Melling studied Alexander and Lucy a moment. "Are you seeing her home?"

"Yes, Mother," Alexander said, "but I'll return soon."

After they said their goodbyes, Alexander led Lucy around the corner to his Model B and helped her in.

"I've never ridden in an automobile without a door beside me." She put her hands on the short, padded sides of the leather seat. "It's comfortable enough sitting still, though."

"I won't let you fall out, Lucy." Alexander stopped in the front to crank the motor before climbing in. He pulled on his goggles. "But if you get scared, feel free to hang on to me."

The motor chugged along like it wasn't in a hurry and Alexander placed his hand on her knee. "This drive home will be much different than last night's. I hope you won't be disappointed."

"No time spent with you could be a disappointment." She removed his hand from her knee and laced their fingers together.

"Though you were right about there being no going back. I ache for your touch, Alex."

He slid his hand free from hers and took the next corner with both hands on the wheel. "Sorry, bad timing on my part. The ride isn't too dusty for you, is it? I'm trying to keep it slow."

"It's fine and I feel perfectly safe."

"I didn't want to let you go—last night or just now." Alex chanced a quick glance at her and smiled.

"Last night was magical," she whispered.

"I want to take care of you." He grabbed the nearest canopy support bar. "I'm going to buy my own vehicle next time. I'd like it to be fully enclosed, no matter the expense. This is fine in pleasant weather, but I don't think it will be much fun in heavy rain. I'd have to tuck you away in the backseat to keep you dry. There's a blanket back there if you need something on your lap to keep warm right now."

"I'm good, really I am. There's no need to fuss over me."

"You're the first lady I've sat with in church, and left church with for that matter. I told you there's much new territory for us to cover. Memories that only you and I share will abound. Tell me, how is your typing going?"

"Slow. I'll have to get to my father's office this week for lessons. I'm practicing for hours a day, but I'm afraid my approach is all wrong. I still hand write everything for now."

"There's nothing as lovely as a handwritten poem."

Lucy blushed. "There might be another one soon."

Alexander sighed. "But for now, our time comes to an end."

"Tuesday isn't far away." Lucy tried to convince herself by saying it aloud.

"Then you're stronger than me because I don't know if I can make it two days without gazing upon you." Alexander pulled into the driveway behind Mr. Easton's automobile and pounded the steering wheel. "That's it!"

Lucy leaned away, unsure what to think. Alexander ran around to help her out. Rather than taking her hand or elbow, her took her by the waist with both hands and lifted her out with a flourish.

"Alex! What is it?"

He was too busy grinning to speak until she had both feet on the ground. He brought a hand to her cheek and leaned toward her until their foreheads nearly touched. "You can sit for a picture with Eliza, and then I can gaze upon your likeness every day."

"I've never sat for a portrait before."

"A painting would be nice, but I'm just talking a sketch. Eliza's drawings are better than Charles Dana Gibson or anything you see in print these days. We'll save the official portrait for the engagement. Would you do that for me?"

Lucy's mind froze at the mention of engagement. "Would I…"

"Sit for Eliza to draw you! She might even be able to do it when you come for tea. She's fast with her sketches, but her details are amazing." He placed her arm around his and started across the lawn for the front porch. "You will, won't you?"

She clung to his arm as they climbed the steps. "Yes, but only because it's for you."

Edmund stood in the parlor window, so Lucy brought Alexander to the turret side of the porch. Seeing that she gave them a pocket of privacy, Alexander leaned in for a kiss. Lucy pressed her body against his, and then the squeal of the front door broke the silence.

"Tuesday," he whispered as her took her arm.

Edmund leered at the couple. "If you ruin my sister, I'll be forced to kill you."

"You're the one who's ruined things for me, Edmund, and you know it."

"That's hardly fair of you to say." Her brother crossed his arms.

"What's this about?" Alexander asked.

"You know damn well!" Edmund glared at him.

"Apparently, he's been threatening men for half a decade if they even looked at me. Dateless years, balls without dancing—it's all his doing."

"Then I must thank you, Eddie. You've kept her pure for me all this time so she can be the one to show me everything I've missed in my life until this point."

"You cad! It was all to keep her from men like you!"

"Men like us, Eddie?"

Edmund looked ready to throw a punch. Lucy tucked herself against Alexander's chest and he immediately put his arms around her.

"Get out of the way, Lucy. Let me teach him a lesson!"

"No, Edmund. You've done enough damage." Tears spilled over her cheeks, but she tried to hide them against Alexander's jacket.

"I don't mean to hurt you, Lucy. I only want what's best because I know how this world really is and you deserve more."

"Let her decide what's best for her life," Alexander said. "That's all she wants, to be in control of her own destiny."

Edmund muttered something that sounded like "free to ruin it" but he went back into the house and shut the door.

Alexander nudged Lucy's chin up with one hand and removed a handkerchief from his pocket with his other. He dried her face and kissed her forehead. "I won't let him stand between us."

Fifteen

On Tuesday morning, Lucy rode into work with her father and Edmund, happy to be free of Opal for the day. She wore her red cloak over a cream-colored blouse, beige skirt, and sensible brown boots because she wasn't sure if she'd be walking to or from the Mellings' house for tea.

Edmund slumped to a small, cluttered desk in the corner of the main office and Mr. Easton reminded his son of his promise. "Settle down with a wife and partnership and a private office are yours."

Lucy followed her father into his office and plopped herself in the leather chair behind his massive desk. "Are you ready to retire, Father?"

"More than I'd like to admit." He shuffled through a stack of papers. "I think I've earned the right to take as long as I wish with the morning paper. Not to mention your mother's been hinting at travel. I'm at the age when I need to rest after excursions, not hurry back to the office."

"Do you think your trip to Grand Bay at the end of the month will satisfy Mother?"

"One can only hope it will be enough to get her through carnival season. Maybe Edmund will find the right girl by then. It appears love is in the air this winter." He put a hand on his daughter's shoulder. "Are you happy, Lucy?"

"Yes, very much." She couldn't help the smile that sprouted on her face.

"Does Alexander treat you well? And I'm not talking about buying you fancy gloves."

"Yes, Father. He's respectful and romantic, everything I could ask for. He even likes that I write, and that isn't the easiest thing for a man to tolerate."

"You deserve someone who does more than tolerate what you love."

"And he does! He bought those gloves for me so I could still hold a pen, took me to buy more ribbon for the Underwood, and cherishes what I write for him."

"My little Lucy, writing poetry for a man. I hope you keep poems like Opal found to yourself." Mr. Easton turned back to his papers, looking weary. "If he comes to me to ask for more than this courtship, shall I give him my blessing?"

"Yes, Father, thank you! Please don't listen to Edmund over this."

"I know Eddie means well, but this is your affair, not his."

"Thank you. It means the world to me." She rose and kissed his cheek.

"I'm glad to see you happy, Lucy. Now go report to Miss Sandra for typing lessons."

Maxwell arrived when she was on her way to the secretary.

"Lucy!" He hugged his sister. "I didn't get to speak with you at the ball. You were quite occupied with Alexander Melling. Lottie was shocked when Father gave him permission to bring you home. She thinks it's scandalous and you're embarrassing the whole family. She's quite ashamed of her last name at the moment."

Lucy stared into his hazel eyes, much like Edmund's, but with gold flecks like their father's. "And what do you think? I hope you aren't letting your dear wife dictate your feelings."

"Never. We Eastons are free thinkers." He straightened his stiff collar in mock respectability.

"But it looks like she's giving you gray hair, right there." She poked at the gray at his brown hairline and laughed. "I think I see a few in your mustache too."

Maxwell smoothed his facial hair. "She's a bit testy lately, with her not feeling good all the time, but she means well."

"I was surprised to see her at the ball with her in the family way again."

"It will most likely be our only ball this season. She'll begin showing more each week."

"Yes, but you still haven't told me what *you* think about Alex and me."

Seeing Edmund watching them, he took Lucy by the elbow into his office. While his brother was still a junior partner earning a modest salary at Easton & Sons, Maxwell was a full partner with financial benefits and a private office.

"I personally think Lottie is jealous you're out with a man higher than our family on the social ladder, even with his horrendous reputation. But with what I know of Alexander, I think he's a good match personality wise for you. You need his vibrant, outgoing spirit to balance your quiet introspect. But at the same time, you have a curiosity about life and he's adventurous and wealthy enough to support you in that. Well played, Lucy."

"I didn't go chasing him. He found me, much to Edmund's distaste."

"He was always jealous when his friends had just as much fun playing with you as they did him. Is he still threatening them to stay away from you?"

Lucy nodded. "He's being most unreasonable to Alex though he's been as close of a friend to him the past year as Frederick was to him growing up. He's taking things too far, like sitting behind us in the cathedral of all places, as if Alex would try something in the middle of Mass!"

"I'll talk to him. How long are you in the office? Do we need to change the sign to 'Easton & Sons & Daughter'?"

She laughed. "Only until dinner. I'm here for typing lessons. Father and Edmund are going to drop me off and eat at home today. I have an invitation to tea I need to be at for two o'clock."

"You're taking tea out of the house?"

"Eliza Melling invited me over."

"Convenient. She's one of the buds this year, isn't she?"

"Yes, and she got swept up with those Dardenne skeletons at the ball. Alex was horrified." Lucy left out the information that it was Edmund who danced her away and Alexander was part of the society too.

Maxwell laughed. "And Lottie thought Alexander was going to pull you out to the dance floor during that display of Dardenne disorder. Oh, it's good to see you, Lucy. Why don't I take you to dinner? We can go to one of those luncheon counters Mother detests and then I'll bring you to the Mellings' house in time for tea."

"You want to take me out?"

"Of course. As Mother said, you're the most intelligent of my sisters, though I think Opal will give you a good race one day. I don't think I could handle a meal with Cora or Emma without someone else to balance the conversation from frills and fans, or whatever it is they're talking about these days. Susan, on the other hand, she and I were closest growing up. I'd tolerate her companionship over a sandwich."

"I'd love that, Maxwell. Thank you."

"Be ready by twelve thirty," he told her on the way out of his office.

"Complaining to big brother, are you?" Edmund asked when she made her way to the secretary.

"Someone needs to keep you in check."

Edmund cut in front of Lucy's path. "Everyone else is blinded by the fact that you finally have a beau. I'm the only one who understands the danger he possesses."

Lucy held his stare. "Is that because you hold the same danger to other ladies?"

"Don't allow him to turn you against me."

"You're doing that yourself, Edmund."

***

Miss Sandra proved an excellent tutor, demonstrating the proper hand positioning on the typewriter keys and showing Lucy how to remember which keys were where. After several hours of typing nursery rhymes, Lucy showed marked progress and dinner with her brother felt like a celebration of mastering the typewriter. Maxwell and Lucy laughed through their meal at a luncheon counter near the corner of Royal Street and then he drove them west to the Mellings' house.

"Are you sure you don't want to change first?" Maxwell asked as he pulled into the driveway and replaced his derby. "You're dressed for a day at the office, not tea at a house like this."

"Eliza's an artist and understands my drive to write. She won't be offended by my clothes. Her mother, on the other hand, I don't think I'd wear this if she was here, but she's supposed to be at a D.A.R. meeting."

"It's good you found yourself another unconventional friend. Allow me to walk you to the door."

Expecting a servant to answer, Eliza in a deep purple tea gown with black hair veiling her shoulders, surprised the Eastons.

"Lucy, come in!" Her eyes settled on Maxwell and went wide as she smiled. "I forgot there was another brother."

Eliza stepped onto the porch, bare feet peeking out from under the bottom ruffle as she circled his form in the plain black business suit. She pointed to his red necktie.

"Green would be a better choice for you. Or blue. You need earthy hues. Same goes with the suit, a brown one would bring out your undertones best. But those shoulders! Surely there's no shortage of strength and virility in the Easton men!" As if noticing the surprised look on his face, Eliza stepped back into the house. "Don't mind me, Mr. Easton. I can't help but think of painting a person when I first meet them. I mean no harm."

Lucy laughed. "Eliza, my brother and oldest sibling, Maxwell Easton. Maxwell, Eliza Melling."

"I must confess I feel odd offering my hand after being thoroughly examined." Maxwell grinned and shook Eliza's hand. "I have to get back to work, but you ladies enjoy your tea."

"Thank you, Maxwell." Lucy gave him a quick hug. "I'll see you soon, I hope."

"It's nice to meet another member of Lucy's family," Eliza said. "Especially another brother with such strong characteristics."

"The pleasure was mine, Miss Melling." He tipped his hat.

Eliza ushered Lucy into the foyer and motioned to take her reticule and cloak. She handed over her bag and then Alexander appeared.

"Allow me." Dressed in navy slacks and a crisp white shirt, he untied the tassel at her throat. With hands on the shoulders of her cloak, he leaned in for a kiss. "I've missed you, Lucy."

"I missed you as well."

After removing her cloak, a hand went around Lucy's waist and the other to her neck as he kissed her again. This time he lingered and teased, though he kept it subdued.

"That's a proper hello kiss." Alexander switched from holding her waist to her hand. "Where are we taking tea, Eliza?"

When no answer came, they both turned to Eliza. She stared at them with an odd half-smile. "The angle of your faces—the way your jaws moved…was there tongue involved?"

Lucy's face grew warm and Alexander squeezed her hand. "It's not something you ask, and a gentleman is never supposed to tell."

"Then you may speak freely, I'm sure."

He laughed at his sister's remark. "The joys of younger sisters are many, but one who's an artist beats every other horror imaginable."

"I only want to understand what I saw. Lucy's neck was maidenly at that angle, even with the high collar. And the way you both tilt your heads to fit together is poetry."

"Would you prefer to draw our kiss than a portrait of Lucy?"

Eliza clapped her hands together. "I would do both! How long can you hold the pose?"

Lucy laughed nervously. "I really don't know about this."

"But now I'm curious about what we look like together." Alex wrapped his arms around Lucy and nuzzled into her neck. "And posing for a picture is a great excuse to keep on like this."

"Give me three minutes to get the base lines down and then you'll be able to move. Tea, by the way, will be in the morning room. The light in there will be perfect for drawing." Eliza put a hand on each of their shoulders and nudged them toward the back hall. "Pick any spot near one of the windows and get comfortable. I need to fetch my supplies."

In the room Lucy suffered mortification at the hands of Edmund and Kate Stuart during the Christmas party, Alexander closed the door behind them.

"She doesn't mean to be nosy," he said. "She's just overly concerned with the workings of the human body. But I did hold back because she watched us."

"I know, and thank you."

He pulled her close, a hand caressing an arm through her sleeve and his mouth hovering over hers. "Is our tea just as unconventional as yours?"

"More than mine ever could be with Edmund breathing down our necks."

"He's not here now." Alexander's lips brushed her lower one and then his hands went to her hips and pulled her against him in a way that made her gasp. "We fit well together. It's a crime to stay apart."

Not able to restrain herself, she pressed her hungry mouth to his, tasting the playful kisses while aware of the undulating movements of their bodies. Then the sofa pressed behind her legs and Alexander urged her down.

"Alex, what are we doing?"

His blue eyes widened when he seemed to notice he had her beneath him on the sofa. With sorrowful eyes, he stroked her cheek. "It's that love affair trying to take over. I'm sorry, Lucy."

"Don't apologize. You make me feel loved and beautiful beyond anything I ever imagined."

Alexander pulled her up and she ran her hands over his chest, the fine cloth of his shirt smooth under her touch. She undid his top buttons and kissed the hollow of his throat. In response his hands went around her waist as his mouth roamed hers.

A knock sounded, followed by Eliza's voice. "I hope you two are practicing for the picture, but I could use help."

Alexander held Lucy close another moment, leaving her with a kiss that made her forget why she was there while he went for the door.

Eliza brought her sketch book and a jar of pencils to the sofa. "Did you decide on a location?"

"No." Lucy gave her a shy smile. "We were too busy practicing."

"I don't blame you. Once I find my perfect specimen, I doubt I'll get much else accomplished. That's why I'm working hard to understand everything before then. I'm not sure how much time I would have for learning after I meet my muse."

"To an artist," Alexander said as he ran a hand down Lucy's arm, "the person is a muse. To everyone else, the person is a lover. Which am I to you, Lucy?"

"Both." She settled into an arm chair with a dreamy smile.

"That's not going to work," Eliza told her. "If you want that location, and the light is good there, Alex is going to have to hold you in his lap. That is, unless you want him in yours. I suppose he could straddle the chair and—"

"Sister"—Alexander took Eliza by the hand—"why don't Lucy and I get settled while you watch. Quietly. When we're in a good position, you ask us to stop."

"I suppose that will be more natural rather than a forced pose." She stuck a pencil behind her ear and took another in her hand. "Have fun, but keep it civilized."

"Really, Eliza! You might as well be laughing over there."

"Oh, no, Lucy. I take my work seriously. And I do want you to enjoy yourself. I'm hostess after all, and sitting for a portrait should be fun." Eliza settled cross-legged in a chair she'd pulled closer to them.

"Pretend she isn't here," Alexander whispered in Lucy's ear. "It's just you and me and we've been waiting days to spend this time together. May I hold you in my arms, my queen?"

Lucy nodded. Alexander carefully sat with her in the designated armchair. Her legs draped over one of the armrests, and both his hands went to her neck as he undid the top few buttons of her blouse.

"Just to make it easier to see your lines," Alexander whispered as he tucked the neck of the shirt under itself. "Your elegant lines, Lucy. I can't wait until I can see and taste of them daily."

He kissed his way around and up her neck while caressing her back. Though they were being observed, Lucy couldn't help the sighs that escaped as Alexander expressed his desires. When his lips completed their journey to hers, she accepted his kiss without inhibitions. She shifted into him, a hand gently skimming around his neck and her other on his shoulder. The tips of his fingers slightly raised her chin as their kiss deepened.

"There!" Eliza's pencil immediately scratched across the page.

They held their overall position as best they could, but didn't stop kissing. To still her lips meant Lucy would have to think about the other set of eyes on her, and she did not wish to dwell on Eliza while involved in such an intimate situation with Alexander. She was sorry she'd agreed to it, but she loved him enough to do things she never would have entertained before.

"Move now if you must," Eliza said, "but if you can at least keep those sides of your faces to me, it will be helpful."

Lucy pulled away first, gasping. Alexander leaned his forehead to hers to keep their profiles inline.

"Are you all right?" he asked.

"I'm light-headed."

"You've made her swoon, Brother." Eliza kept drawing, but smirked. "It did look like quite a kiss."

"It was wonderful, though I would have preferred to have been free to move about and change positions," Lucy whispered. "We might have ended up on the sofa, again."

"You have no idea how close you are to the truth." Alexander's puckish smile and trailing fingers across her neck were her defeat.

She brought her cheek to his. "I'm yours, Alex. We'll belong fully to each other soon."

He brought their lips together and pulled her into a tighter embrace. "When you speak like that, the love affair wants to take over, and I know that's not what we need right now."

"But the feeling of need is stronger than anything else," her breathy voice whispered.

"The natural man is a titan compared to the voice of reason."

"I wrote you another poem. This one is different, though. You might not like it."

"There's no question whether I'll like it or not. It comes from your soul, which I love as much as your body."

"I'll give it to you to read while I sit for the other portrait."

"If you two are going to have such lengthy conversations," Eliza said, "speak louder so I'm privy to them."

"Just because you're drawing us like this," Alexander told her, "doesn't mean you get to see and hear everything. Don't let this shared intimacy go to your head."

Eliza huffed. "Fine. Kiss once more and I'll check my sketch before sending for the tea tray." They did, and after making a few more marks, she pronounced the picture complete. She handed her book to Alexander and left the room.

Sixteen

Lucy, still in Alexander's lap, studied the gentle sweep of their bodies on the page. "It's perfection!"

"I told you she was brilliant." He followed the curve of Lucy's face down to her shoulder on the page. "But her subject is exquisite."

Eliza returned to find them kissing in the chair. "We'll have company in a moment when the tray is brought."

"Clear the sofa, Eliza." Alexander, still holding Lucy, stood.

"I can walk."

He kissed her lips. "But I never want to let you down. I want to cherish you always and be the type of man you deserve."

"Then you may start safeguarding my reputation by not allowing the help to see us so familiar with each other."

"Father tends to only employ the most loyal of workers who would never tell stories about what goes on in our houses."

"Houses?" Lucy asked as she settled herself at the end of the sofa closest to Eliza's chair.

"This one and Seacliff Cottage, near Montrose." Alexander sat beside her, inches closer than socially acceptable. "The staff here is from the old house, with a few new additions since the move to help with the larger space, and the workers across the bay have been with the family for years, the coachman for more than a generation. None would betray what goes on within the Mellings' walls."

"You should bring Lucy to Seacliff sometime. The house is on Ecor Rouge, the highest waterfront between Texas and Maine, and the view of the bay is amazing. I have a rock on the cliff I like to draw at, but it would make a good writing spot as well. When I find my muse, that's where we'll meet. Amid the wild beauty in the secluded house." Eliza's gaze seemed to flit away into an imaginary world.

"Would you like to go one Saturday?" Alexander took Lucy's hand into his. "We could take the ferry over in the morning and stay the day, picnicking on the beach and anything else you'd like."

"That sounds lovely."

"I'll plan for us."

"And Alex's bedroom there is—" Alexander's cold stare quieted Eliza a moment. "I was just going to say how dark and romantic—"

"It's not something to discuss, even if you think the company is all the parties involved."

Eliza, looking embarrassed for the first time, focused on her guest. "I beg your pardon, Lucy. I assumed since you were so free with your affections that you had already…"

Lucy's hands went to her warm cheeks. "Is that what people think of me?"

"No, of course not." Eliza leaned over and took her hands. "It's just me, having been privy to your affections. There's nothing to worry about, I'm sure," Eliza patted her hand before letting go.

"I warned you about your character being called into question if you were to be seen with me." Alexander placed a hand on her back. "Do you regret your choice?"

"No." Lucy turned and kissed him quickly on the lips. "It's just a shock to hear things vocalized the first time. I've received the stares and a few whispered remarks, but I've never been confronted with the words."

"I meant nothing bad about you," Eliza said. "I know how things are in regards to love—at least I like to think I do, as my time has not yet come. But not everyone is pious because they attend church. They teach us we are all sinners and some of us live up to that more often than not."

"Should I be offended?" Alexander asked with a teasing smile.

"Always, Brother."

The refreshments arrived and the three settled in with a comfortable lull in the conversation, as if they were old friends not needing to fill the void with prattle. Alexander often put his hand on Lucy's knee or back, reminding her of all the places he'd touched in the past few weeks. *Eliza thinks I've lain with him, and Edmund believes* that's all he wants me for. But maybe I am mad because that's half of what I think of when our skin meets.

Eliza finished off the petit fours and turned to her brother. "How do you want the portrait? Lucy's face, profile, full body? Dressed how she is, wrapped in sheets, nude?"

"Do you ever want to have tea with her again?" Alexander set down his cup with a clatter. "And people think me the wild one."

"You're both scandalous. The way Eliza hunted my brothers this week tops it all. Edmund running out of the cathedral like a scared cat and circling Maxwell today like a shark."

"Greater than our time in the carriage?" he murmured in her ear.

She turned to him, losing herself in the liquid depth of his eyes. "That wasn't shameful, that was beautiful. And I still have your lingering kiss right here." She touched above her breast.

"Lucy…" He took her face in his hands and brought their lips together with conviction.

Eliza gave them a moment and then clapped her hands. "Focus! Our time is running slim if you want me to complete my sketch before Mother gets home. Alex, where and how do you want Lucy posed? And I mean for the picture, so wipe that smirk off your face."

Alexander looked exasperated. "I wasn't—"

"I know, but your expression right there was worth it. And yes, I am the naughty one, Lucy. All this passion and zest for life and art screams to break loose, but I only set it free before a select group of people."

"I don't know if I should be flattered or shocked," Lucy said.

"Both," Eliza giggled.

She posed Lucy sitting sideways in an armchair, her arms folded on the back of the seat, with her chin resting on them.

When Alexander went to retrieve the poem from Lucy's reticule, Eliza unpinned her blonde hair. "I've never seen Alex this happy before. His friends often teased him for being cold-hearted, but since the Christmas party he's warm and caring."

"He's awoken a place in my soul I didn't know was there."

"Lucy, whenever you are ready to be with him, I'll help any way I can. I'll clear the location of bystanders, travel with you so it doesn't look like you're alone, whatever you need." Eliza finished arranging Lucy's hair and then stepped back. "Now you look like an artist. A painter of words with love's bright flame."

Eliza resettled in the chair across from Lucy, cross-legged with her sketchbook on a pillow in her lap.

Alexander slipped into the room. "You're even lovelier with your hair down."

"Don't make her move," Eliza admonished. "She's in the perfect position. And don't touch her hair either."

Alexander clasped his hand behind his back and leaned down to plant a simple kiss on Lucy's forehead. "You're a vision of all that is good in this world and I trust my sister to capture that on page."

"Capture your heart on paper. Now there's a worthy request. If you would remove yourself from standing in front of her, I could get started."

"I love you, Lucille Easton," he said before retreating to the sofa.

The smile created by his words lit Lucy's face with a warm glow.

"Hold that thought!" Eliza nearly shouted as she tackled the paper. "Don't move until I get your lips drawn. I can't see you, Alex, but I know you're looking. Any excuse to gaze at or touch her lips, am I right?"

"You know me well."

"Suffered through eighteen years of your moods and mischief. When will you take my brother off my hands, Lucy? No, don't answer me yet. You must hold your pose."

Eliza worked in silence while Alexander opened the poem. "May I read it aloud, Lucy?"

His sister growled. "She's not to move."

"Blink twice for yes," he said.

She gave the approval. It wasn't an overly sweet or intimate poem, though it still held her passion and opinions. As he read, Eliza's hand slowed as she listened to the words.

Arms of Love

I used to believe
All I was taught
And then I grew to question
Everything
Everyone
There was no constant
In my sea of life

Each day brought new storms
Each hour new waves

Lost without an anchor
I drifted into you
Your compass gave me direction
Your rudder steered me straight
Into the arms of love

I can sit with you before God
But it is our fellow man who disagrees with
Who we love
How we love
Where we love
No matter if we know it is true
For ourselves

My love for you is constant
Through the storms
And the waves
I sail on
Your arms around me
Your lips upon mine
Our bodies cleaving ever closer
Until the break of day

"Permission to cleave unto the model?" Alexander asked.

"No!" Eliza shook her pencil at him. "I'm behind as it is."

"Permission to whisper in the model's ear?"

"Give me a few minutes." Eliza refocused on the page.

Lucy, though stoically holding her position, fluttered inside. Hearing Alexander read her words gave them new meaning. She hadn't realized how sensual it could be taken, and she reflected on the other two poems, how they must be saturated with sexual undertones she hadn't been fully aware of. Pink, red, touch, taste, and cleaving bodies. How much did she want for those images to fill her writing?

"The light in your eyes changed. Go back to happier thoughts," Eliza demanded. "Don't make me send Alex over."

She couldn't help the laugh that shook her shoulders, jostling her hair and causing her to shift her pose.

"Alex, to the rescue." Eliza motioned to Lucy. "I need her back the way she was, without too much fondling in the process."

"Don't be vulgar, Eliza. Lucy isn't merchandise, she's my queen."

He took hold of Lucy's hair and brushed it all back with his fingers. Then he rubbed her arms and shoulders to rid her of any stiffness. Leaning over her, he kissed her a few times and brought her hair back around her face and shoulders.

Alexander paused with his mouth by her ear. "Your poems all end with me wanting to carry you to bed. Is that your intention?"

"Quite possibly." She gave him a secretive smile.

"Hold there! Just a few minutes more. Whatever you told her, Alex, you did well."

"I only hope I do as well when it comes to fruition."

Lucy chanced a look at him. Alexander held his hand over his heart and her body tingled with expectations she didn't know how to fulfill.

When Lucy could relax, she spoke to Eliza. "As soon as he asks me."

"What's that?" Eliza looked up from the page.

"The answer to your question because I couldn't move earlier."

Eliza's head tilted to the side and then the smile hit her face when she remembered asking when she'd take Alexander off her hands. "Well, for all of our sakes, I hope it's soon."

"I'd leave with you for an elopement in a heartbeat, Lucy, but it wouldn't help our situation with our families. Not counting Edmund, I don't think your father's keen on me and my mother can't abide your fashion choices. I think I need to take you on a few more dates—and get you home on time—and you should survive a shopping trip with Mother first."

"If you love her, you wouldn't ask that. Whatever you do, Lucy, don't let her lace your corset."

"And now I'm frightened."

"Don't be. I'll be with you," Eliza said. "I'll try to talk Mother into shopping soon so you can get it out of the way. But whatever happens, don't let her in your dressing room."

"You're perfection the way you are." Alexander crossed the room to her. "Permission to handle the model?"

"If you must." Eliza waved them away with one hand as she kept working.

Alexander pulled Lucy into his arms. Resting her head on his shoulder, he hugged her tighter, burying his head in her loose hair. "You're my everything, Lucy. I don't want to make a mistake that could cost us our future together."

"I love you. Someday, everyone will see that what we have is true."

In those tender minutes Alexander held her, Lucy's heart further joined his.

"Finished!" Eliza clutched her sketchbook to her body. "You have as many admirable lines as your brothers. Not the same ones, of course, but your structure is just as sound. That Easton chin is as fine on you as them. While they have their shoulders, you have the curve of your neck and graceful arms."

"And do we get to see it?" Alexander asked, still hugging Lucy.

"Let me go cut the page out properly."

"And the other picture?"

"I did that for me, but I suppose I'll turn it over as well." She gathered her supplies. "I'll be back in a minute."

Alexander brought Lucy to the sofa, where her poem lay on the cushion. "Please tuck it away, Alex. If your mother saw it—"

He silenced her with a kiss but folded and placed it in his pocket. "You needn't be ashamed of your feelings."

"I'm not, I just don't fancy baring my heart to those who won't appreciate it." She sank to a seated position and he sat beside her.

"How will you survive as a writer? Not everyone who picks up one of your books will enjoy it. What will you do then?" His fingers brushed her hair from her face and trailed down her cheek.

"Quite possibly cry on your shoulder for a while, but the sting won't be as bad because I'd have accomplished my goal of publishing, which no one could take away from me. But you and I…we're vulnerable right now. You can be taken away from me and I don't want to risk it, especially at the hand of your mother."

"Nor do I, but in the end, it isn't Mother we need to be worried about. You're all that's precious to me in this world, Lucy. I'll fight until my dying breath for you."

She fingered the row of buttons on his shirt, the top ones undone from her earlier efforts. "I want to be safe, but sometimes emotions of pure recklessness surge through me and I would risk it all for an hour alone with you."

"I'll need more than an hour, Lucy." His hands kneaded down her back as he kissed her searchingly. "I might need to lock us away for a week to treat you to every pleasure you deserve, to explore everything I want to share with you."

"I can't leave you two alone for a minute without you going at each other like there's no tomorrow." Eliza took her seat adjacent to the sofa.

When Alexander and Lucy untangled themselves, Eliza presented both pictures at the same time.

"You didn't need to make me up to look so pretty, but it's lovely."

"She captured you flawlessly, no embellishments. The curl of your lips, the wave of your hair, the spark in your eyes…Eliza, you outdid yourself, thank you."

"Lucy's an easy subject. I'd be happy to capture her again, but our time is up."

"May I drive you home?" Alexander asked.

"All this sitting still has me ready to move. The day's warmed nicely. I'll be quite comfortable walking."

"Then I'll walk you home, I insist." He collected his pictures and left the room.

Eliza took Lucy's arm and brought her to the foyer. "Remember what I told you earlier. The offer stands indefinitely. You two are positively dripping with passion. It hurts me to think you're denying yourself anything."

"It's not denying, just delaying." It wasn't the sort of conversation she ever expected to have with Eliza—she had trouble even thinking about bringing it up with Grace Anne. "But I do appreciate your willingness to help. And your talent is great."

"You'll have to see my paintings next time."

Alexander descended the stairs. He'd tied a robin egg blue cravat at his neck and pulled on a navy jacket that coordinated with his slacks.

"And there's a man who knows how to choose the right colors for his complexion," Eliza said.

Alexander smiled. "And, of course, it was done without any help from my sister."

Lucy leaned against him. His scent of sandalwood was stronger, like his jacket had been hanging with a sachet of it. She slipped her arms under his open suit and hugged him.

"We might as well say our goodbyes here, while we're sure of a relative amount of privacy," he said.

Eliza stepped forward. "Let me excuse myself. It's been fun, Lucy. I hope I didn't scare you or Maxwell too badly, but your family's the handsomest in town. I'm sure he's used to it."

"An old, married man like him?" Lucy laughed. "He probably went back to work with a spring in his step because a young lady made eyes at him."

"That was more than eyes," Alexander said. "I believe I overheard the word 'virility.'"

"Well," Eliza said as she tilted her head and pursed her lips, "you know me. I can't help myself."

Seventeen

The rest of the week Lucy practiced typing for several hours a day with nursery rhymes and sought ideas for tidbits to send in to Kate Stuart for the next edition of *Snitch*, all while avoiding Opal's vigilant eyes. Edmund didn't ride to his Thursday meeting with Alexander, so it wasn't until Sunday that Alexander and Lucy were together. Alexander sat with the Eastons once again, but Edmund sat on the far side of his parents, virtually ignoring his sister and friend.

After Mass, Maxwell made a point to properly introduce himself to Alexander.

"I met your sister Tuesday when I brought Lucy to tea, but I wanted to make your acquaintance." They shook hands, but before he could introduce Lottie, she hurried up the aisle with their two children, refusing to make eye contact. "Excuse my wife. She has her hands full with the children. I should go help."

Alexander nodded. "Of course, thank you for stopping."

Maxwell leaned in. "I know you've heard some rough things from Edmund, but all threats are the same from me if you hurt our sister." Then he winked and slapped Alexander on the shoulder.

"I think those brothers of yours could do with a little less virility." Alexander rubbed the spot where Maxwell's hand landed.

Lucy laughed and took Alexander's arm on their way out of the cathedral. "At least he means well."

On their way across the portico, Lucy noticed Edmund talking with Mary Margaret Fitzgerald. His charm was on full display—dazzling smile and hand gestures usually seen on the stage rather than up close—as he told her a tale. Lucy hoped it wasn't one at her expense like he shared at the Christmas party.

"That's exactly what Eddie needs." Alexander held her arm as they descended the steps. "He needs a girl of his own to keep his mind off us."

"I just want him to be happy."

Alexander helped her into his automobile. "I'm happy enough for the world, though this week was incredibly long without seeing you every few days. I'd been spoiled until now. I didn't realize how much I looked forward to catching a glimpse of you through the window when I'd pick up Eddie." He cranked the motor and hopped in. "I need to be more proactive in planning for us. Do you enjoy Monroe Park, operas, plays, concerts?"

"Yes, all those things, and anything else, as long as they're with you."

"Would you want to go to another ball before mine? One I can pick you up for and take you home afterward, because you know I won't be able to collect you on the Dardenne night. I'll hire a carriage to pick you up because we'll need a ride home." He laughed as he drove. "I've been staying sober lately, but I'm not sure how I'll do at that party. There's usually not a safe drink to be had in our place. Lucy, if you can love me after seeing my behavior when I'm crocked, I'll know you're mine forever."

"I can't help wanting to kiss you when you talk like that."

"Why's that?" He rolled the automobile to a stop in the middle of the road.

"Because it sounds like you don't believe I truly love you and I want to prove that I do."

"I don't mean it like that, but you'll have no complaints if you want to prove something." He gazed around the street. "It's just us for the moment."

Lucy took the initiative.

"You take my breath away," Alexander said as he pulled back after several seconds. "But I don't trust myself to sit in the middle of Ann Street kissing you any longer."

He hurried her home and pulled in front of the house, keeping the driveway clear because her family hadn't returned.

"Is this the part of the story when the handsome prince carries the young maiden into the empty castle and—" He fell upon her lips.

Lucy leaned away. "We aren't stepping a foot inside the door unchaperoned, and you know it. You may escort me to the porch swing."

"I like my idea better." His hand caressed her cheek.

"So do I, but you're trying to stay on my father's good side, remember? Not to mention my two older brothers waiting to beat you soundly."

"The perils of love." He sighed, and then hopped out of the automobile. Lucy watched him unabashedly, studying the confident way he sauntered to her. Alexander took her hand and kissed the back of it as she stepped out. "What has you captivated?"

She grabbed his red silk tie and pulled him to her. "You, and the fact that we unintentionally coordinated our clothing today. Not to mention you walk to me with such purpose I can't help but feel awed when your hand touches mine."

"You're my destiny, and I'd hoped you would wear the red dress again." He eyes roamed from her bright eyes to her full lips. "You have me, now what are you going to do to me?"

She let the silk of his tie glide between her fingers, tugging it out of his suit as her hand went to the end of it. When it slipped free, Lucy grabbed the lapels of his jacket and stared into his clear blue eyes. "I'm going to kiss you, Alexander Randolph Melling, in hopes that you'll secure many dates for us in the days ahead."

"*Many dates?* You better make this amazing." He gave her a teasing smile as she wrapped her arms around his shoulders and leaned in.

They kissed and held each other until the sound of an approaching motor warned them their solitude within the tree-lined yard came to an end. Without speaking they transitioned to strolling arm-in-arm to the porch. The automobile continued down the street without pausing.

"Do I merit a few dates?" Lucy asked when she settled on the swing against his side.

"You've earned a lifetime of devotion with those lips." He kissed her temple and leaned his head atop hers.

Lucy closed her eyes and focused on the sensation of being in Alexander's arms. His lean strength and warmth coupled with his scent was usually her defeat, but she focused on the peace rather than the lust. Both were there, but if she was going to make it to their wedding, she needed to focus less on the physical and more on how Alexander affected her mind and spirit.

"I love you, Alex. Even after reading all those novels, I never thought it was possible to feel like this about someone." She placed her hand on his knee, the white lace of the gloves a stark contrast against the dark suit. "It's thrilling, but I'm scared too."

"Don't be." He pulled her closer and covered her glove on his knee with his free hand. "I have love enough to see us through anything."

"Even Edmund?" Lucy asked as the Eastons' automobile pulled in, but neither of them moved. She could feel his smile though she couldn't see it from her position.

"Yes, even both your brothers."

"Aren't you two a sweet sight." Mrs. Easton beamed. "But you should have gone in and started dinner preparations, Lucy."

Alexander stood, causing Lucy to straighten. "We were only concerned about going inside without someone with us."

Edmund walked by and choked back a laugh.

"Indeed, Alex." Mrs. Easton took his hand. "But we've kept you waiting this long. You must be half-starved. Stay for dinner with us. We do a cold luncheon of leftovers on Sundays, but in the winter, we leave a pot of soup simmering so there's something to warm the belly as well."

"Thank you, Mrs. Easton. That's most kind of you. I gladly accept."

"Splendid! Wait with the men while we get the table ready."

"This is my first Sunday dinner with a lady," Alexander whispered as he escorted Lucy inside.

"Give us ten minutes!" Mrs. Easton hollered before ushering Lucy and Opal into the kitchen. Lucy set the dining room while her mother and sister prepared the food.

At dinner, Edmund seemed to try his best to ignore Lucy and Alexander across the table from him, and Lucy ignored Edmund and Opal.

"It's nice to be in a house without help," Alexander remarked.

"Oh, we have help, Alexander. We aren't bad off, you know."

"I meant no offense, Mrs. Easton. God-fearing folk like yourselves are thoughtful enough to provide the Sabbath off for your help. My parents keep a minimum of two in the house at any given time, the poor souls."

"Our cook will be back for supper this evening, but the maids are only part time during the week. I've often told my children if they can't make their own bed a few days a week, they aren't fit for society."

"It's a logical choice and you run a lovely household."

"Lucy," Mr. Easton said, "is your typing continuing to improve?"

"Yes, Father. The nursery rhymes were the key. Typing what I have memorized is much easier than copy work or thinking up something fresh, though I hope to type up my—some of my original shorts this week. And if that goes well, I'll begin typing one of my novels. Maybe a typed submission will get the attention of an editor better than a hand-written one."

"I'm sure you'll do well, Lucy. You have a good head on your shoulders."

"Thank you, Father."

"Clever and beautiful," Alexander murmured.

Mr. Easton looked across the table to his wife. "It appears Lucy will be attending another ball. I'll see there are ample funds for a gown this week."

Opal scowled and crossed her arms.

"That's not necessary, Father, but thank you. My black gown has another bodice and I can use that."

"But there's also the opera coming up." Mr. Easton nodded to Alexander. "Your beau laid out plenty of social events for you to attend with him in the weeks ahead and I gave my permission to all."

"More balls and the opera! Alexander will spoil you for sure." Mrs. Easton dabbed her mouth with her linen napkin. "Save the other gown combination for the opera, Lucy. You get something else for this next ball."

"Lucy gets everything she wants!" Opal stomped out of the room.

After an awkward silence, Alexander turned to Mrs. Easton. "My mother and Eliza have wanted to plan a shopping trip with Lucy. I'm not sure how things work between women, but if it's not too improper a thing for a mother to share, perhaps they might be invited to attend Lucy when she shops for the new gown."

"That would be lovely. Everyone in town knows Mrs. Melling has exquisite taste. They would both be welcomed."

"I'll let them know." Alexander took Lucy's hand in his and looked across the table. "Edmund, I was thinking about going to Monroe Park Friday night if the weather is agreeable. Would you like to join us, maybe invite a young lady along? I could collect you and Lucy and whoever else after supper."

To Lucy's surprise, Edmund appeared to consider the offer. She watched her brother with eagerness, hoping to mend the rift that pulled Edmund away and separated him from his friend.

"I'll let you know Thursday evening for sure." Edmund excused himself from the table. When he passed behind Lucy, he whispered, "Still doesn't mean I approve of you and him."

***

The shopping excursion was set for Wednesday. The Mellings' driver collected Lucy and her mother at precisely eleven in the morning. The Lyman limousine was one of the only partially enclosed vehicles in Mobile and Mrs. Melling seemed quite proud of it.

"Eliza, be a dear and sit in the front with the driver so our guests can ride snug in the back with me."

"No, Mrs. Melling," Mrs. Easton said. "Please allow the girls to ride with you to keep their hair fresh. I have no objection to riding with the driver. I ride with my husband upfront without the luxury of one of these windshields several times a week."

"Very well." Mrs. Melling motioned to Lucy. "Come in, Lucille."

Lucy squeezed in beside Eliza, her ecru muslin dull next to Eliza's tailored ensemble.

"Another ball invitation for you, Lucy!" Eliza's gloved hand took Lucy's bare one in a friendly embrace. "The Revelry Makers are posh from what I understand. You'll need something striking for this Gilded Age party."

Mrs. Melling clasped her leather gloves in her lap. "That's why I'm here, dear, to be sure Lucille choses something that won't embarrass the family. Alexander asked me to see to it himself."

Lucy reddened and was grateful her mother didn't hear the remark.

"He did no such thing," Eliza whispered to Lucy. "She's trying to wear you down so you'll do exactly what she says."

They started at the Parisian boutique and Mrs. Melling seemed impressed Mademoiselle Bisset was pleased to see Lucy and her mother. The ladies left the shop empty handed, followed by three other stores without purchases. Mrs. Easton did her best not to be annoyed that everything she suggested wasn't good enough for Mrs.

Melling's standards, but Lucy could hear the strain in her mother's voice.

"Redfern is a completely respectable design company. They aren't House of Worth, but they've been designing quality clothes for two generations," Mrs. Easton debated. "My wedding suit was a Redfern."

"I am not saying they are not respectable. What they design special for the European royalty are divine, but their store-bought items are not to my liking." Mrs. Melling lifted her chin and turned away.

Eliza rolled her eyes and grabbed the nearest sales girl. "Do you have any chocolates or peppermints? I'm about to faint."

"Right away, Miss Melling."

Eliza smiled and planted herself on the nearest chair, behind a display of skirts. "It works every time," she whispered to Lucy. "It's the only way I survive shopping with my mother."

Lucy smiled and wandered toward the front of the store. Looking in from the sidewalk was one of Mademoiselle Bisset's shop girls. She motioned to Lucy and she slipped out the door.

"Pardon the interruption, Miss Easton, but Mademoiselle Bisset sent me to find you. She just received a special delivery from a friend in Paris and thinks it's what you're looking for."

"Thank you! I'll be right over." Lucy rushed back in and told Eliza.

"You go ahead and try it on. I'll bring them in a few minutes."

Lucy rushed out the door and straight into a suited gentleman.

"Oh, I beg your—"

"Lucy!" Frederick took her arm to steady her. "Whatever has you in such a hurry?"

She laughed. "Would you believe if I told you I was rushing to see a dress?"

"On the surface, no, but I believe your reason to see the dress in question would be the true matter of you running me down."

"You know me too well, Frederick." Without thinking, she took his arm and started walking. "I'm in pursuit of a gown to wear to the Revelry Makers ball next Monday. I'm going with Alex and I've been out shopping with our mothers and Eliza the past two hours trying to find a gown that suits everybody, or more specifically, Mrs. Melling."

"Shopping with the family? That's quite a step. But why should Alex's mother care what dress you chose?"

"Apparently, she's all about fashion and is about to drive Mother batty."

"Poor Mrs. E."

"The two have been debating different designers and Eliza and I are ready to scream. She gave me a head start so I can try on the dress before her mother can interrupt." She clung to his arm and looked up at him. "What are you doing on this side of town?"

"I was going back to the office after my dinner hour, headed that way." He pointed behind them. "But some bright-eyed young woman took hold of my arm and pulled me away with her."

Lucy dropped his arm. "Forgive me, I wasn't thinking. I merely saw your friendly face and wanted to bring you along on my adventure."

"I don't mind, it's good to see you again. I'll be at the ball too. I hope you'll save a dance for me even though Alex will be at the forefront of your attentions."

"It's the least I can do after dragging you to the dress shop." She stopped before the door. "Would you like to come in?"

"It wouldn't be proper, but I look forward to seeing you Monday. Take care not to run down any other unsuspecting men before then, Goosy."

She laughed. "I'll try not to, Frederick. Thank you for escorting me."

"The pleasure was mine." He smiled at her in a way that made her want to hug him, but she slipped through the door he opened for her instead.

Wearing her dress corset under her regular clothes through all the previous drudgery finally paid off. The gold taffeta, satin, and plissé chiffon adorned with roses made from beaded pewter lace were breath-taking and the train was a manageable length.

"You are the most fun to dress, Miss Easton. You look lovely in most colors and you are easy to please." Mademoiselle Bisset took her arm. "Come, I will show you a mask that will go wonderfully with this while we wait for your dear mother and the Mellings. I now carry a selection of my friend's Venetian masks for the season."

In the dressing room, Lucy tied on a Colombina with a crackled gold base and silvery lace trim around the edges. To the left side a chocolate rosette and tall feathers in brown, gold, and silver blossomed.

"Do you need help, Miss Easton?" the shop girl who had fetched her asked.

"No, thank you. I'll be out in a moment."

When she emerged from the dressing room, Eliza spun her around. "Perfection!"

"Lucy, it's lovely," Mrs. Easton agreed.

Mrs. Melling peered down her nose. "Those fluttery sleeves look like they belong on a negligée."

Mademoiselle Bisset stepped in to smooth things over. "The gown was a summer one from this past year. A dear friend's event fell through and she didn't have the heart to wear it anywhere else so it's here on consignment."

"The mask is perfection with it. Isn't it beautiful together, Mother?" Eliza asked.

"It is, but I do not see how it would work, this summer gown in January."

"Balls are always warm inside and Miss Easton has a stole and cape that would go well with this. She will be prepared in any weather." Mademoiselle Bisset smiled kindly at Mrs. Melling.

"Mother, it's gorgeous and you know it," Eliza whined.

"Before I agree to this gown," Mrs. Melling said, "I need to ask Lucille who the gentleman was outside the other store."

"That was only Frederick. I accidently ran into him when I rushed out the door."

"You appeared overly familiar with him and you left on his arm."

"Really, Mrs. Melling!" Mrs. Easton huffed. "Freddy Davenport has known her since she toddled around the house in diapers. He's practically family."

"Pay me no mind," Mrs. Melling said calmly. "I am overprotective of my children. I would hate for Alex to have his heart broken over some misunderstanding. It would be best to limit your time with other men, Lucille. Think how you would feel if Alex walked down the street with a young lady on his arm."

"Yes, of course." Lucy was glad the mask shadowed her eyes, which were on the verge of tears.

"But the gown, Mother," Eliza said.

Mrs. Melling waved her hand as if she dismissed the whole thing. "It will work just as well as any other. I'll have the automobile waiting out front."

Eighteen

Friday evening came, and though Lucy survived shopping and tea with Mrs. Melling and Eliza two days before, she was eager to hear the report from Alexander. As soon as the lights from his automobile shone through the parlor window, she went to the porch with her black capelet in hand.

"There she is, my lady of the golden gown!" Alexander crossed the yard, handsome in his charcoal suit, derby, and blue bowtie. He had her in his arms as soon as he mounted the steps. "Eliza told me all about the dress, how your hips are the focal point of the ensemble and that I wouldn't be able to take my eyes or hands off them when I see you."

"And that's all the news you have for me? Nothing of what your mother reported?"

"She complained about the French woman who sold you the dress after having one of her girls run you down in another shop to get your business. Also, the tea at the hotel was cold, and the sandwiches dry. But other than that, she only mentioned that you were the loveliest creature in the city—beside Eliza—and that she could finally see why I love you, despite your lack of fashion sense and proper upbringing, which she blames your mother for."

"Is that all?" Lucy waved her hand and held her chin high in perfect mimicry of Mrs. Melling.

Alexander laughed and took her in his arms again. "Lucy, you naughty thing. Don't let her catch you doing that." He kissed her ear as Edmund came out of the house.

"Ready? Or are you going to stay on the porch and neck all night?"

"Is that an option?" Lucy's eyebrows rose with interest.

Edmund gave her the evil eye like Opal often did, but Alexander laughed anew.

"She's joking, Eddie. Lighten up. Just because it's Friday the thirteenth doesn't mean you have to go around with a frown." He took Lucy's capelet and fastened it around the shoulders of her pink walking suit.

"It's not the best day for a first outing. I should have thought of that before asking Mary Margaret to accompany us."

"But you went through the trouble of tracking her down at Wednesday Mass. I'm sure she'd be disappointed if you cancelled." Lucy took Alexander's arm and they all went to the automobile.

"Yes, but she wasn't sold on this being a group outing when she learned it was with you two. Please behave yourselves."

"We will, Eddie," Alexander promised. "How would you like to drive tonight?"

"That'd be swell."

Edmund settled in the driver's seat and Alexander helped Lucy into the back, making sure she was comfortable. When they pulled up in front of the Fitzgerald's Antebellum home, Alexander waited for Edmund to start up the front walk before planting himself beside Lucy.

"You're simply luscious in pink." He threaded their fingers together and rested their hands on his leg. With a wink he added, "But I'll try to behave myself like Eddie asked."

"Good, because I don't think he'd want to pound you in front of his date."

When Edmund disappeared between the columns of the front porch, Alexander used their privacy for a lingering kiss.

"I don't need the amusements at Monroe Park. Your body gives me all the thrills I could ever want. I'd stay like this with you all night if I could."

Her hands went to his, which roamed her waist. "Alex, I think we'd better stop."

He straightened and smoothed over her wool skirt before taking her hand back. "You're the one for me, Lucy. Always and forever, the keeper of my heart."

She gave him a firm kiss and then leaned against his shoulder. "I never thought I'd look forward to balls and parties, but knowing you're bringing me on Monday, I can hardly wait for the day to come."

"I look forward to arriving with you on my arm, holding you all night, and chasing the other men away from you."

"Not all. I've promised a dance to Frederick."

"You don't need to torture the poor man any more than necessary. Dancing with Freddy at every ball will do him more harm than good."

"He was kind enough to see me to the dress shop when I ran into him Wednesday. If he asks me, you mustn't deny him."

"I've seen the longing in his eyes when he looks at you. It wounds me when you dance with a man who looks upon you that way."

"Alex…" She touched her hand to his cheek and sweetly kissed him. "I'll promise no more dances after this, but I'll not go back on what I've already said. I chose you. Read my poems again if you doubt my heart."

Alexander leaned over her with hunger in his eyes. "The day can't come soon enough. I want you—all of you."

The yearning tugged at her middle and her chest burned with want. She shifted her leg toward him and he gripped her knee, his hand rubbing over the soft skirt. "I want you too, Alex. Make it so as soon as you can."

He gazed into her pleading eyes and traced her lower lip with a fingertip. "I'm doing my best, but I don't want to spoil it for us. Timing is important. Do you trust me?"

"Yes."

"Then be patient."

He pulled her to his side as the front door of the house opened. Mary Margaret wore a red velvet hat that matched her winter suit with a white rabbit fur stole and muff.

"I'm sure your mother would approve of Mary Margaret's style. Should I have worn a hat?"

"I see no need for you to cover that glorious mane of yours. And to hell with what my mother thinks of style."

Lucy replaced her head on his shoulder, still holding hands. Edmund, with Mary Margaret on his arm, paused beside the automobile. Anger burned in his eyes, but it was his date who spoke.

"Don't you two look…*cozy* back there."

"Quite so, Mary Margaret." Alexander smiled. "Please forgive me for not standing to greet you properly."

She rolled her dark eyes and then fixed her gaze on Lucy, who raised her head from Alexander's shoulder.

"It's good to see you, Mary Margaret. I'm sure we'll all have a splendid time this evening."

"That remains to be seen."

Edmund helped her into the front passenger seat and readied to leave. The drive took them south of the city to the bay front park.

"There's no need to stumble around together," Edmund said. "Let's meet at the carousel at ten."

"Sounds like a plan. You two have fun." Alexander clapped him on the shoulder then steered Lucy toward the electric lights of the wooden roller coaster. "Be sure to cling to me if you get scared."

"You might regret that." Her smile brought an even bigger grin to Alexander's face.

"The only regret I have in regards to you is not speaking to you sooner."

As they stood in line for the ride, Lucy's hand migrated from Alexander's arm to his hand. She leaned against his side, hands linked, unashamed of their love amid the Friday night crowd. When they reached the front, they were given their choice of rows and Alexander opted for the back. Once seated snugly in the rear car, he removed his hat and put his left arm around Lucy. She gripped the bar in front of them as the ride began.

Alexander kissed her at the peak of the first hill. They sat motionless atop the world for a glorious moment before the momentum of the other cars plunged them into the valley. She screamed and leaned into Alexander for support. Up and down and around curve after curve, Lucy clutched his leg with one hand and squeezed her eyes shut against the jerking motions.

As they clattered to a stop, she opened her eyes. "I don't remember it being that terrifying, but I've never been in the back before. It's quite a different experience."

"Everything with you is a new experience." He donned his hat and helped Lucy out, bringing her to the shadows of the coaster just beyond the exit stairs. His hands went to her face, his mouth inches away. "I'm afraid your hair is in tatters. May I fix it?"

Not trusting herself to speak, she nodded. He dropped her hairpins into her reticule and brought the loose waves first around her face, then tucked them behind her ears as another group of riders roared overhead. Studying her with an impish gleam, he took the hat from his head and placed it on her at a jaunty angle.

"You're gorgeous, Lucy. There'll be no doubt where my heart lies when people look upon you."

After another kiss, he purchased two hot chocolates at the café. They sat at a table at the edge of the sidewalk and Alexander was greeted warmly by several people, but Lucy was ignored.

When it happened the third time, Alexander called the couple out on it. "You know Miss Easton, don't you, Mr. and Mrs. Powell?"

"Of course," Mrs. Powell stammered as she eyed Alexander's hat and Lucy's loose hair. "I went to school with Emma and Cora. How do you do?"

"Fine, thank you. I made the mistake of riding the roller coaster with my hair too lose and it pulled everything out. Alex was kind enough to loan me his hat to hide the damages."

"Quite untraditional, Melling, but if anyone can pull off that look, it's Miss Easton here." Mr. Powell gave Alexander a sly smile before his wife turned to him.

When they parted ways, Alexander kissed Lucy's cheek. "Did you catch that devilish remark right under his wife's nose? Women have worn their hair down many times through the centuries. Just because present fashion dictates otherwise, don't let it get to you when people look down at you in passing. They're jealous of how beautiful you are."

When they were done with their drinks, they strolled beyond the yacht club pier where the pedestrian traffic was less and settled on a secluded bench under a sycamore tree.

"Are you warm enough?" He took her hands in his.

"Yes, but it's such a wonderful evening I could be half frozen and not care."

"I'd just have to heat you up like I did in the carriage on New Year's." He tugged her closer and they kissed with intensity until the sound of footsteps crunching across the oyster shell path jarred them back to the reality of their public location. Alexander checked his wristwatch. "We should head back."

"That would be nice, but I like this as well."

He pulled her to her feet and hugged her to him with a force that knocked the hat from her head. Burying his face in her loose hair, he kissed below her ear. "We need to leave or God help the next people who walk by."

"Alex…" She rested in his arms. "I'm yours forever."

A primeval groan escaped Alexander's throat. With a groping touch, his hands slid down her back. "Lucy, you sweet creature, you have no idea the dangerous situations you place yourself in. I can't trust myself here with you another moment."

"Then save me."

"Yes, my queen." He kissed her once more then retrieved his hat from the ground. After slapping it against his leg to clear it of any debris, he replaced it on her head. "Your royal crown."

They got in line to ride the carousel.

"You choose where to sit, Lucy. I bet you have a favorite horse."

"The brown one with black hair and the garland of purple flowers. I always thought it looked noble."

Alexander lifted her onto the horse sidesaddle and took the white horse beside her. "Do you ride? Real horses, I mean," he said.

"We kept two carriage horses before the automobile, but only the boys were allowed to ride them occasionally. I rode a few times growing up with my friends who had horses, but it's been years."

"I love to ride and was on polo teams during my school years. When we got the automobiles, our horses were sent to Seacliff Cottage. I try to make it there a few times a month, but the stable hand takes good care of them. We still have carriage horses there as well. The roads aren't good enough to merit purchasing an automobile for that side of the bay yet."

The tinkling music grew louder, signaling the ride about to begin. Lucy clutched the pole with one arm. "What's your horse's name?"

"Janus. Eliza's is Flora. When we make it over there, we'll go for a ride. There's nothing like riding along the bay. Flora's a gentle girl and would give you no trouble."

When the carousel came to a stop, Alexander hopped off his horse and lifted Lucy from hers, his hands staying at her waist longer than necessary. They exited the carousel hand in hand and were met by a frowning Edmund and a sour-faced Mary Margaret.

"I need to get Mary Margaret home and it looks like you two have had more than enough fun. Whatever happened to your hair, Lucy?"

"We rode the roller coast first and my hair didn't survive the experience."

"Couldn't you have fixed it?" Mary Margaret asked.

"Possibly, but Alex offered his hat. I figured it just as fine as any other option. But I suppose I can fix it now, seeing as how it shames those in my company."

"It's too late for that, Lucy." Edmund started toward the parking area with Mary Margaret.

Nineteen

On Saturday, Lucy delivered three typed gossip tidbits to Kate Stuart's house, pleased to have accomplished her monthly task. Sunday marked the third week Alexander sat with the Eastons at the cathedral. Lucy enjoyed his warm tenor during the hymns and his presence at her side more than ever as she looked forward to attending the ball with him the next night.

Monday evening, Lucy braided her hair and wrapped it into a bun atop her head to do something different from the traditional pompadour. The new gown was a natural fitting one. No petticoats were worn under the golden dress, but it had an extra layer of silk lining it. The tapering at the waist was done with hidden darts, so the single piece gown flowed seamlessly from her chest to her waist and over her hips to the ruffled edge.

Lucy waited until the front door opened to make her grand descent of the stairs. Her train trailed behind and her mother's silver beaded reticule hung at her gloved wrist. On her face she wore the plumed mask and a smile—which grew as Alexander's amazed expression gazed over her body. He didn't yet wear his mask and there was no questioning his thoughts.

Edmund looked from Alexander to Lucy and then laid his forearm across Alexander's windpipe. "You keep your hands off her, do you understand?"

Alexander brushed aside Edmund and stepped forward to take Lucy's arm. He kissed her cheek and murmured, "I forgot how to breathe."

She fingered his gold bowtie and the satin lapel of his tuxedo jacket. "You're dashing yourself. Did Eliza coordinate for you?"

"Yes. Shall we say goodbye to your parents?"

She nodded and they walked into the parlor together.

"Oh my stars! You two are the most handsome couple I've ever seen! Don't you agree, James?" Mrs. Easton turned to her husband.

Mr. Easton studied his daughter and sniffled. "Yes, they look well and happy together. There's no doubt Lucy is all grown up now." He changed his focus to Alexander. "Twelve thirty should be ample time to enjoy the ball. Safeguard my daughter, do you hear?"

"Yes, Mr. Easton, with my life."

Opal glared from behind a book in the far armchair. "You'll have to wait for those tastes and touches."

"Opal!" Mrs. Easton's face displayed her shock.

Alexander blanched and glanced sideways at Lucy.

"Opal," Mr. Easton said, "do you need a reminder of what is appropriate conversation for company?"

"No, Father."

Alexander and Lucy retreated, stopping in the foyer for her black cape. Before he picked it up, his hands went to her hips. She caught her breath at his touch through the thin gown, and her green eyes widened.

"God help me tonight," he whispered as he pulled her to him. "You're a walking fantasy." He brought the cape around her shoulders and hurried them out the door.

"Another carriage?"

"I thought with the weather being colder you'd be more comfortable. And I didn't think you'd object to having more privacy either." He smiled at her as they crossed the yard. "But after seeing you, I'm afraid this ride could prove our undoing."

The same driver who'd brought them home for the New Year's ball stood by the opened door. Alexander helped her in and then told the driver to take the long way and give the warning.

Alexander removed her cape and reticule before she settled fully into her seat and laid them beside his coat, gloves, and mask. When the carriage took the first corner Alexander untied both sets of curtains and they fell into privacy.

"Lucy, I don't want to wrinkle you, but I must have something to tide me over until afterward." He kneeled before her and his mouth went to hers.

At first, he kept their bodies apart, but as the kissing intensified, he wrapped her in his arms as they moved together in the rhythm of their passion.

"Alex, I fear I'll be unfit to enter the ball at this rate."

"Forgive me. My hunger is stirred and it's getting more difficult to satisfy it with each encounter." He settled beside her on the cushioned seat and straightened her gown across her lap. Then he lifted a fluttery sleeve and kissed her shoulder.

"I don't want to stop either, Alex. I'd ride around all night in your arms if it wasn't for the fact that my parents would hear if we don't make an appearance at the ball."

"Let's leave early." He kissed her neck.

"But we haven't even arrived yet."

"That doesn't mean we can't plan ahead."

She arched against the velvet upholstered backrest to showcase her décolletage.

His gaze lowered from her mask to her chest. "Do you know how beautiful it is that you trust me enough to display your own cravings?"

"I let my heart lead and what it wants is you."

His intense stare bore into her soul as he fingered the pewter lace flowers along her neckline. "And does your heart crave a new passion mark? Is that what this gorgeous display is about?"

"Your kiss and touch, always."

Three sharp raps sounded on the roof and Alexander leaned back with a sigh as he closed his eyes. "We'll have more time when we leave. Lucy, you're the first lady I've escorted to a ball of my own accord."

Alexander tied open the curtains and put on his finishing touches. That night he wore black gloves and a gold Colombina mask trimmed in black satin, like his tuxedo jacket. He helped Lucy into her cape before he pulled on his own coat, and then she patted her hair to make sure it still sat well.

They pulled to a stop directly in front of Temperance Hall on St. Joseph Street. When the driver opened the door, Alexander slipped him several dollars and whispered to be ready for them at eleven. Lucy had never been to a ball without at least one member of her family in attendance. The feeling of aloneness overwhelmed her as they entered the three-story building. She clung to Alexander for comfort and he held her arm in a show of possession. They checked their outerwear and became the focal point of the ballroom. Amid a room of numerous other metallic outfits, Lucy's and Alexander's golden hair set them apart from the other masqueraders.

The first two dances were for members of the Revelry Makers and their dates. Alexander found Lucy a seat along the far wall and went in search of drinks. Without companionship in a room of unfriendly faces, Lucy trembled. The overwhelming terror that besieged her in the doorway of the cathedral on Christmas Eve returned. She clasped her hands in prayer and shut her eyes against the swirl of gowns on the dancefloor.

"Lucy, are you all right? You look pale," Frederick's low, kind voice washed over her.

She grabbed his gloved hand, needing something familiar to help disperse the dread threatening to take away her joy. "I grew weak and awful feeling, but I'm all right. Do you see Alex? I'll be fine once he gets back."

Frederick inspected the room. "I don't see him, but would you like me to check upstairs? I think the refreshments are on the second floor."

"No, don't leave me, Freddy." She tightened her grip.

His smile under his traditional black mask helped her relax into the chair. "I'll stay as long as you need me."

"I can't ask that much of you. What will your date think?"

He gazed upon Lucy with affection. "I came alone, again."

"It's good to see you out, but you should bring a date."

"It's all right coming like this. I'm able to dance with whatever pretty lady strikes my fancy."

Lucy laughed, further clearing her head. "That sounds more like Edmund's style than yours."

"No need to worry about me, Lucy, I'm getting along fine. You're as lovely as ever tonight, and you'll be pleased to know Alex is on his way over."

Remembering the sobering words from Mrs. Melling on the shopping trip, Lucy squeezed Frederick's hand and let it go. "Thank you, and I'll be happy to dance with you soon."

Alexander came with two champagne glasses and a slightly annoyed expression. "Good evening, Freddy. Thank you for keeping Lucy company." He handed Lucy her drink.

"I saw her looking pale and came to check on her."

Alexander's hand went to her cheek. "Are you all right?"

She took a sip. "Better now, thank you."

"Still," Alexander said, "we might want to leave early so you aren't out too late. You've been working long hours on your typing, I'm sure you need your rest."

"Yes, that's a good idea." Lucy smiled over his cleverness.

"I'll let you rest a bit more, but I'll be back for that dance." Frederick left with a smile.

Alexander pulled a chair closer and sat with an arm draped over the back of her seat. "Did you really go pale?"

"Yes, I had trembles and went faint like I did outside church Christmas Eve. I wasn't in danger because I was already sitting, but that sense of doom—like I was trapped and dying—was the same."

"I won't leave you again." He brushed her cheek with his fingers and leaned to her ear. "Do you know what tomorrow is?"

"Tuesday."

"Yes, the seventeenth." He kissed her temple. "One month since that fateful Christmas party that brought us together and changed me forever. One month of your sweet kisses, your soft skin, and your passion. My life didn't start until that night. I was nothing until I had you in my arms. Dance with me now or I fear I'll fall upon you with a thousand kisses."

"Save that for the ride home," she murmured as they stood.

The orchestra was the same that performed at the Order of Mayhem's ball and they played many familiar tunes. Lucy's arm didn't fatigue with the light fabric and Alexander was such an accomplished dancer, she felt like they'd just begun when they'd completed three scores. With the opening notes of "The Blue Danube," a hand landed on Alexander's shoulder.

"I believe this is our song," Frederick said.

Lucy laughed. "Yes, our practice tune."

Alexander bowed. "You may share it one final time."

Frederick kept their bodies at a respectable distance but his movements were fluid. "I'm glad you're feeling better. You seem happy with Alex."

"I am, Frederick. I know you and Edmund were worried at first, but he's been a perfect gentleman. He loves and respects me. Don't feel like you have to protect me from him."

"I'm still going to the Dardenne ball to watch over you. Even if he behaves himself, the rest of them might not. I'll keep my distance, but know that if something happens, or you look distressed, I'm liable to swoop in and carry you away like I did when you'd scrape your knees."

"I appreciate your concern."

They danced the last minute in silence. Lucy, feeling the mood of the song, drifted along to Frederick's lead with a dreamy smile. As he had at the last ball, Frederick ended the dance before Alexander and gallantly gave Lucy's hand to him.

"I hope you appreciate her, Alex."

His arm went around her waist. "I do, Freddy. Every moment of every day."

Frederick gave a hollow smile and walked away.

"I actually feel sorry for him," Alexander said as he switched from his arm being around her to holding her hand. "Would you like to go upstairs and get something to eat or continue dancing?"

"I want to be in your arms, Alex."

They danced several more songs and then climbed the stairs for a drink and a bite to eat. When they returned to the main floor, it was quarter to eleven.

"One more, then we'll slip away." He pulled her close, his hand low on her back.

"Keep it respectable, Mr. Melling," she teased. "We don't want to draw attention because people will notice us leaving."

"You have a wicked mind, Miss Easton."

"I'm used to plotting, just not for my own benefit."

They settled into a respectable pose and danced around the floor. When the Vivaldi ended, they casually strolled to the lobby and Alexander collected their things from the coat check.

"Give us an hour," Alexander told the driver as he helped Lucy in.

When they were a block away, Alexander released the curtains and removed his gloves, mask, coat, tuxedo jacket, and vest.

"Even the vest, Alex?" Lucy laid her cape and mask on her lap.

He reached for her hand. "We have more time and I want to be comfortable. Would you like to get my tie?"

Lucy handed him her accessories to put on the other bench and undid his gold bowtie. She tossed it onto his clothing pile and opened the top two buttons of his shirt. After pulling off her black lace gloves, she wrapped her bare arms around his neck. "Now what?"

His face was in the shadows, but his eyes were still the brightest spot. "Those thousand kisses I keep threatening you with— I'll start with covering your arms."

Alexander took her right hand from around his neck and kissed the back of it before trailing up to her shoulder. When he'd repeated the same with the other arm he lowered her onto the bench and started in on her neck as he gently tugged down her gown.

Lucy grasped his waistband and pulled him against her. "Alex, is tonight the night?"

He sat up halfway, seeming to take in all the details: his hand at her chest, the slight gyrating movement of her pelvis below him, and the hunger burning in her eyes—and shook his head. "No, Lucy. You need more than a quick romp in a carriage. You deserve complete comfort and time. Not to mention respectability."

Her hands fell away from him and her body stilled, except for the pounding of her heart. She willed the tears to stay inside so she wouldn't look a fool.

"Lucy, I don't deny you, I'm only postponing until the time is right. I want to give you pleasure, but doing what you think you want right now wouldn't bring you joy in the morning." He kissed her lips, but when she didn't respond, he pulled her into his arms. "I love you too much, but I understand your frustration. The cravings of the body are some of the most potent in the world. I'm battling myself right now and that losing side is loud."

"Am I no longer respectable?" Her lower lip trembled. "Do you think less of me?"

"Never, my queen. Knowing you desire me as much as I do you makes me love you even more. We'll share this passion soon, I promise. There are a few more things that must happen first. Will you continue to trust me?"

"Yes, Alex. Always."

With great tenderness Alexander kissed across the exposed skin, lowering his efforts until he reached her décolletage. He hesitated, but Lucy pulled the hem down until the top of her corset showed. The aching need inside her wanted to scream as they stared at each other.

"You're perfection, Lucy, and I can't help but think I'm not right for you." She caught her breath before he continued. "But I feel completely at peace in your arms and I know we're meant for each other."

She arched in rapture as his mouth played along her body. Alexander gave her the passion mark and then kissed and touched until he stopped her hands at his shirt buttons.

"We need to slow down. There'll be no broken hearts tonight."

Lucy settled in his lap, resting her head against his shoulder as his arms enveloped her. "I love you," she whispered. "No one understands how good you are to me."

"You make it easier to put aside my old ways. Being with you is its own reward."

Twenty

Lucy stayed busy typing her most promising manuscript, *Azalea Blossom*. She tried not to worry about which—if any—of her three stories Kate Stuart would choose to include in the next edition of *Snitch* because the magazine didn't release until the morning of the Mystics of Dardenne ball the following week.

On Wednesday, Eliza telephoned. Knowing their privacy was limited on the public wire, Lucy invited her over for tea the next day. Lucy, in a white lace tea gown, and Eliza in a blue one, sat in matching chairs before the parlor fire on the cold afternoon. The pocket doors were closed against Opal's prying senses, and the two women leaned close.

"Alex is planning something," Eliza said after eating a lemon cookie. "He's stayed at the office all day this week, and he never does that unless he's deep in thought. It keeps Mother out of his business and Father is less likely to pester him if he appears actively engaged at the firm. Yesterday, before he left for work, he came to my room and asked me to invite you to Seacliff Cottage for a week from Saturday. He was most distressed at supper when I told him I hadn't asked you yet. Naturally, he calmed when I told him I was taking tea here today. I wouldn't be surprised if he picks me up afterward."

"He's welcome anytime."

"I'm sure he is." Eliza winked. "I don't know what he was thinking with planning a trip across the bay the day after his ball when we'll have to be at the docks early to catch the ferry. He's usually passed out drunk after the masquerade for twelve hours or more—once he makes it home, which usually isn't until the next afternoon."

Lucy leaned forward and dropped her voice. "Maybe he chose that day because my parents are supposed to be out of town."

Eliza's smiled wickedly. "Then maybe that's the day…it would be the perfect place."

Her face grew warm. "I think he means to wait for marriage."

"My brother?" Eliza laughed. "He's changed, but I don't know if he's capable of that much restraint. Oh, don't be mad at me, Lucy. You know how I am."

"He loves and respects me."

Eliza took her hand. "I know, and I'm happy for you both."

Lucy did her best to keep their conversation away from Alexander after that. When it was time for Eliza to leave, Lucy helped her into her black fur cape, hat, and muff and donned the red cloak for herself. "I'll see you to Government Street."

When they were halfway down the road, Alexander pulled to a stop in front of them.

"I hoped to meet you at the Eastons', Eliza." Alexander dropped his goggles around his neck and hopped out. He took Lucy's hand and kissed her cheek. "Good afternoon, Lucy. You look as lovely as ever."

"Thank you, Alex." She fingered the brim of his black hat. "You look great yourself."

"I just had good news. Is there more good news, about what you were supposed to inquire, Eliza?"

She turned to Lucy. "I don't think she ever said if she would accept or not. Did you?"

"No, I didn't." Her mouth momentarily turned down. "I'm worried about the schedule, with the ball the night before, and if we'll be rested enough to enjoy the outing."

"Catching the ferry shouldn't be a problem. We'll pick you up before eight thirty. If we get home by two in the morning, we'll still have several hours of sleep before then. And the day itself will be a vacation—riding on the beach, a picnic, and maybe a bonfire before catching the ferry back home."

"Or we could make it even easier and stay the weekend," Eliza said. "What, Brother? There *is* a guest room."

"Edmund would kill you, Alex," Lucy said. "The day trip is pressing things enough."

"Agreed." He kissed her forehead. "A day trip is all. I'll send word to Seacliff for preparations."

"How exciting!" Eliza hugged Lucy. "It'll be a magical day."

Alexander placed his hands on Lucy's shoulders and leaned in for a kiss. "I'll pick you up at seven Saturday night for the opera."

***

After the lightness of the gold gown, Lucy felt strange in the heavy brocade of the black lily. The second bodice was much more open across the chest. At first, she feared the lingering passion mark would show, but it was just below the broad neckline. The evening was chilly, but warmer than other nights. She opted for her stole for the first time and placed it in the foyer with her black reticule before pulling on her lace gloves and joining her parents in the parlor.

"You're such a grown woman now, Lucy," her mother remarked.

"A woman, never a lady," Opal muttered.

"You, Opal, will hold your tongue tonight." Mrs. Easton's gaze cut as sharp as anything the young girl could give.

When Alexander rang the bell, Mr. Easton led him in with a hand clasped on his shoulder like he'd just given him a talking to. Alexander seemed subdued in his black tuxedo, bowtie, and top hat compared to the pop of bright color he wore to the balls.

"You're looking well this evening, Mrs. Easton." He removed his hat and kissed her hand.

"Not as well as Lucy, but I manage at my age."

With a dashing smile, he turned to Lucy and offered his hand. "You never cease to amaze me, Lucy. Are you ready?"

"Yes, I've been looking forward to this all week. I've never seen *Carmen* before, but I've heard some of the score on the phonograph. There's much passion within those songs."

"So there is." Alexander tucked her arm around his and stopped before Mr. Easton's chair. "What time shall I return with her?"

"Back by eleven. We'll be waiting."

Lucy, shaken over her father's odd behavior, stumbled on the runner in the hall. "Has he been listening to Edmund?"

"No, Lucy." Alexander held her stole open and she turned her back to him. He kissed each shoulder in the cutout area between the lace. Hugging her before him, he brought the wrap around her. "He just realizes you aren't his little girl anymore and he's hanging on as long as possible."

When they got to the bottom of the front steps, Alexander paused. "We have a few minutes before we need to head out. Would you like to go to the gazebo?"

"We haven't been out there since our first week together. Will you help me with this train or should I get my wrist loop?"

"There's no need." Alexander scooped her into his arms and carried her to the backyard.

"Alex! What if my parents see us out the window?"

"Then they'll know I'm the one who swept you off your feet."

He set her down gently on the bench and knelt before her on one knee. From his pocket he brought forth a velvet box and opened it to showcase a European-cut diamond engagement ring. Lucy caught her breath, a hand going to her open mouth.

"Lucille Amelia Easton, you own my heart and I don't want to live without you by my side. Will you marry me and seal my fate as the happiest man on Earth?"

Before he could slip the ring on her finger, she was at the edge of the bench with her arms around his neck. "You know I will, Alex. I've considered myself yours since our first kiss by the mistletoe."

"It was that good?" His mischievous smile brightened his face even in the dusky night.

"Your touch is all I'll ever need to survive this world." She went in for a kiss but he insisted on placing the ring on her finger first. Then they shared a kiss deeper than any before.

Alexander sat beside Lucy and took her left hand into his, fingering the engagement ring. "It's rose gold, which reminded me of your lips and hair, but if you don't like it, I'll buy you whatever you want, Lucy."

"It's lovely, Alex. You're more than generous." She touched the large, round solitaire diamond. "I'd no sooner ask for another than walk away from you."

"You deserve the best, and my parents will need to see something substantial to understand how serious I am about you."

"Parents! My father—"

"I went to Easton & Sons Thursday afternoon to ask your father's permission—which he surprisingly agreed to without hesitation. When I arrived today, he asked me at the door if I'd propose tonight. That's why he wants you home early. I think he means to keep us out of trouble, especially after your talk of the passionate opera music." A finger trailed along her décolletage.

She closed her eyes and smiled. "Promise me you won't make me wait too long. I don't need a lengthy engagement or parties in my honor. I just need you and the fulfillment of those poems."

"We'll talk to your parents tonight and mine after church tomorrow. I would choose Saint Valentine's Day, which would give us over three weeks to plan something modest and find a house. You don't need anything large to start off with, do you?"

"You know I'll be happy wherever you come home to me. Just give me a little space for my typewriter and—"

"A bed." He pulled her to her feet and kissed her neck. "A bed fit for my queen."

Her arms were around his neck and she rested her head on his chest. "Thank you for stopping me the other night. You're right, I would have been miserable the next day. I can wait for your full touch a few more weeks."

He picked her up and started toward his automobile. "It will be worth it, Lucy."

***

Alexander and Lucy returned at a quarter to eleven. Mr. and Mrs. Easton were in the parlor, listening to Mozart on the gramophone. Lucy, in too much of a hurry to remove her stole, flung her arms around her father and kissed his cheek.

"Thank you, Father!"

"I spoke to you about it the other week, and an Easton always honors his word."

"Let me see, Lucy." Mrs. Easton set down her needlework.

Lucy collapsed on the settee beside her mother and held out her hand. "We had box seats at the opera, Mother."

"Alexander, you'll spoil her rotten!"

"I'll treasure her always, Mrs. Easton, and see that she's properly cared for, but I don't think Lucy is one to spoil. To spoil there must be a hint of bad to begin with, and Lucy's character is pure."

"Come here, Alexander." Mrs. Easton held out her hands and took his into her own. "Sit. Right there on the table."

Alexander smiled and perched on the edge of the coffee table across from his future mother-in-law. "Yes, Mrs. Easton."

"I always knew it would be a special man who would make the perfect match for our Lucy. Now that you've signed on for that role, see that you fill the position properly. Live in such a way that would bring no shame to you, Lucy, or God."

"I'll do all I can, Mrs. Easton. You may be sure of that."

She released his hands and patted his cheek. "You two will make the handsomest grandchildren yet."

"Mother!" Lucy went red.

Alexander laughed and took Lucy's stole.

"Take your jacket off if you'd like, Alexander." Mr. Easton stood. "I'm going to get some wine for a toast."

"Allow me help you." Alexander left the room with Lucy's father.

"Lucy, you're blessed for life with that one," her mother said once they were alone. "He can take a joke and an admonishing in stride. Besides that, he loves you and his position with his father's law firm is as secure as they come. But God help you with that woman for a mother-in-law! No one will envy you that."

"Mother, be nice."

"I will, as long as I never again have to shop with Ruth Melling."

Lucy ignored the remark and folded her gloves neatly on the table. Then she crossed the room to the gramophone and put on the "Swan Lake" recording, returning to her usual corner of the settee. Once the men returned, the red wine was poured and the glasses distributed.

Mr. Easton's toast was simple. "To Lucy and Alex, may their love never end."

"When do you want the wedding?" Mrs. Easton asked them.

"I'm hoping for Saint Valentine's Day," Alexander replied, "but we'll wait to see if that's agreeable to both sets of parents."

"I think it would be lovely, don't you?" Mrs. Easton asked her husband.

"Yes, I was never a fan of lengthy engagements."

Edmund returned from his evening out and looked to his parents with red-rimmed eyes. "I didn't expect to see you still up."

"Grab a glass, Edmund." Mr. Easton pointed to the wine bottle. "We've toasted your sister's engagement."

He raked his fingers through his brown beard while his narrowed eyes stared at Alexander.

"Congratulations." His voice was low, deliberate. Then he turned his cold gaze on his sister, but what he saw seemed to soften him. He came to her side and kissed her cheek. "You'll be a lovely bride, Lucy."

Mr. and Mrs. Easton stood, followed by Alexander.

"It's way past our normal hour to retire." Mr. Easton shook Alexander's hand. "Edmund can chaperone. You're welcome to stay as long as he's about."

"Welcome to the family, Alexander." Mrs. Easton kissed his cheek. "I hope your parents will be as pleased as we are."

Twenty-One

Lucy believed the half hour with Edmund staring over her and Alexander the night before was the worst of her life, but when she found herself sitting in the Mellings' parlor after Mass Sunday afternoon, she understood she hadn't experienced terrible yet. She studied her clasped hands on the lap of her mint green Sunday dress from the previous Christmas season. Eliza, not formally invited to sit in on the meeting, paced the marble foyer.

"I see the ring." Mrs. Melling's tone was cold. "Go ahead and say it."

Mr. Melling lowered his newspaper.

Alexander squeezed Lucy's knee. "I've asked Mr. Easton's permission and Lucy has accepted my proposal. The Eastons toasted us last night when we returned from the opera, and I hope you'll share in our joy as well."

Eliza clapped her hands and danced about the doorway in her bare feet.

"Of course *they* are overjoyed. It is practically a match in a higher social class for this girl. But for me it is just as shocking as when Lottie Godwin married Maxwell Easton, but at least he is the oldest and not some younger son like that one you run around with. Is this his doing? Did he trap you with his sister?"

"Eddie doesn't think me good enough for Lucy, and I quite agree with him. It's I who's to marry up, not her."

"I see no problem, Ruth," Mr. Melling said. "They make a striking couple, and her older sisters have kept their looks after marriage and children. Miss Easton is an asset to Alex."

Lucy's face heated.

"She's not an asset or someone seeking to climb the society ladder!" Eliza stomped into the room. "Lucy's her own self and a wonderful, talented person!"

"This doesn't concern you, Eliza." Mrs. Melling glared at her daughter. "You may go to your room."

"It does too! Lucy's my friend and she'll be a fine sister-in-law. Her family is every bit as good as ours, if not more so because they wouldn't say such things in front of a guest."

"That's quite enough, Eliza. You may go to your room as your mother said." Mr. Melling's piercing stare shot first to his daughter and then to Lucy. "Miss Easton surely understands your mother's valid concerns."

"They aren't valid." Alexander moved to the edge of the sofa, holding Lucy's hand. "We don't need your permission, but I'm willing to hear input. We'd like to be married on Saint Valentine's Day and—"

"Absolutely not!" Mrs. Melling cried. "Marriages during carnival season are always overshadowed by the other festivities, and that is too soon to plan things properly to begin with. You must wait until after carnival, and Lent for that matter. June would do well."

"Mother, this isn't your affair. The bride's family plans the wedding and we don't want all the parties and fuss to begin with."

"If money is the issue, we'd be happy to help with a proper recep—"

"Stop with the money!" Alexander let go of Lucy's hand and clinched his fists. "The Eastons are perfectly well off, they just don't flaunt their earnings."

"Watch your tone of voice, Alexander," Mr. Melling warned.

Alexander stood, knuckles white and face red. "None of this is about money! It's about Lucy and me and how we want to begin our life together as soon as possible."

Mrs. Melling's hand went to her heart. "The girl isn't in trouble, is she? This isn't to be some rushed wedding because—"

"You've gone too far! I'll not stay here and allow you to insult my future wife!"

Alexander yanked Lucy by her arm, running for the backyard. Too afraid to speak, Lucy stumbled after him. When he reached the bench in the center of the camellia garden, he looked from his violent grip on her wrist to her eyes brimming with unshed tears.

"Did I hurt you? My God, if I've hurt you—"

"I'm fine." The pooling of her tears spilled over the corner of her right eye and streaked down her face.

"You're frightened and upset, and for good reason. I behaved monstrously and my parents were abominable." He tenderly ran his hand down her arm and kissed her wrist. After helping her sit, he fell to his knees before her, looking like a frightful boy afraid of a reprimand. "I'm sorry, sorry for treating you harshly and for bringing you with me to tell them. I knew they wouldn't be as kind as your parents, but I should have known better than to trust them with our happiness."

Alexander collapsed against her knees and wept on her lap.

Unsure if he would be remorseful for falling apart, she kept her hands at her sides. He had cried beautiful, happy tears on their carriage ride home from the New Year's ball, but this display of raw emotions strangled the witness. When Lucy could no longer sit while his heart broke before her, she ran her fingers through his hair in hopes of soothing him.

"Alex, I'm here. I love you and I'm not going anywhere without you." Her fingers trailed down his scalp to his neck and massaged the tension in his muscles there. "I need you."

He lifted his head a few inches from her lap and wiped his face with the sleeve of his jacket before ripping it off and throwing it on the oyster shell path beside him. The agony in his cloudy eyes was intense as he stood. "You'd get along fine in this life without me. You're strong, smart, and brave. It's me who needs you. I'm weak, impulsive, and cowardly."

"We need each other." She stood before him and placed her hands just above his belt buckle. Running her hands up his chest, she reached around his neck to pull him to her.

Alexander tasted of love and humility. Their kisses grew longer and deeper. She pressed her body to his in hopes of healing him with her touch. In response, he moved against her in a way that made her gasp.

"Alex, I need you, your touch, your love. You promised me we'd share absolute passion soon. Don't take that away from me."

His lips were on hers in a desperate plea for forgiveness and his hands moved up her back in undulating movements. "I won't forsake you, Lucy. I'd carry you to my bed right now if I thought it would help things."

"Plan for us. You know my heart. It's you whose opinion I treasure."

He hugged her to him. "Have your mother send the paper our engagement announcement stating that the wedding will happen at a soon to be determined date. Let the word get out and maybe my mother will have a change of heart."

***

Lucy spent most of the next two days hunched over the Underwood. It kept her mind off of the Mellings' words and the engagement notice that ran in the society page of *The Mobile Register* that morning. The phone rang several times, followed by her mother's laughter and Opal's stomping feet. Coupled with the three pages she'd managed last week, she painstakingly finished typing the first chapter of *Azalea Blossom* before supper Tuesday.

At five fifteen, after stacking the crisp pages in a new manuscript box her father brought home for her the day before, Lucy brushed through her hair and put it in a simple braid. She hurried downstairs and flopped onto the settee in the parlor.

"Lucy!" Her mother sat straighter in the side chair. "Are you forgetting Alex is coming for supper? Where are your stockings and shoes? And your hair and posture! You need to start practicing being the lady of the house. Do you ever see me barefoot and loafing around?"

"No, but I bet you'd like to." The merriment was obvious in her eyes, and in response a smile hinted at the corner of her mother's lips.

The doorbell rang and Lucy jumped up.

"Don't you dare open the door!"

After seeing Alexander out the front window, nothing could stop Lucy from rushing to the foyer. She swung the door open and he momentarily gawked. After his pause, he stepped in and pulled her into a hug that lifted her off the floor.

"Really, the two of you!" Mrs. Easton came up behind them. "Shut the door before the neighbors see you, and then Lucy needs to go finish getting dressed."

"She's lovely the way she is, Mrs. Easton. I'll be a happy man to come home to her like this every day. This is the look of an accomplished writer: shoeless, natural hair, and comfortable clothes." He kissed Lucy's cheek. "Have you had much progress this week?"

"I finished typing the first chapter minutes ago!"

He kissed her again, his arms still about her waist. "We'll have to celebrate tonight, right, Mrs. Easton?"

She looked somewhat bewildered. "Yes, of course."

"I've had nothing but congratulations all day from the office staff, clients, and random people on the streets during my lunch hour." Alexander closed the door and removed his black coat and suit jacket before leading Lucy to the parlor. "Who all have you spoken to, Lucy?"

"I've been typing since breakfast. Mother had to force me downstairs for dinner. If I hadn't finished that chapter, I'd be up there now."

Alexander stopped in the middle of the parlor, placed his hands where Lucy's white shirtwaist tucked into her skirt, and kissed her fully on the mouth. "I love you even more for your dedication to your story."

It was a brief kiss, but when Lucy saw her mother's face over Alexander's shoulder, she couldn't help but blush.

Mrs. Easton shook her head and smiled. "It's been too long since I've witnessed young love. She's soon to be your wife, Alex. Do you wish her to finish dressing properly for supper?"

"I'll never order her to wear what she doesn't wish to. If Lucy's comfortable, so am I." Alexander led her to the settee and waited for Mrs. Easton to sit in a chair of her own before joining his fiancée. He sat against Lucy and draped his arm around her.

In response, she tucked her feet underneath herself and rested her head on his shoulder, fingering his blue necktie. "I'm very comfortable," she murmured.

"And now I better understand my husband's preference for a short engagement. We've received dozens of telephone calls from friends wishing Lucy and you the best, but as our girl was hard at work, I fielded them all. There's a list by the telephone if you wish to see everyone who's sent their regards."

"I'd be pleased to look at it before I leave." Alexander poked Lucy's knee. "We should look it over together."

Lucy snatched his hand and brought it to her lips, kissing his fingers before nestling their joined hands between their laps. "I'd be happy to."

"Freddy was one of the callers," Mrs. Easton said. "I told him Alexander would be here for supper and to stop in for a drink afterward so he could congratulate you both in person. It took some convincing, but he finally accepted the offer, the dear boy. I wish I had another eligible daughter for him, but Opal is much too young and Rebecca would have been too. Excuse me."

Mrs. Easton left the room sniffling.

"Who's Rebecca?" Alexander whispered.

"My second youngest sister—she would have been fourteen this spring. Yellow Fever took the three children between me and Opal when it last struck the city. Rebecca was only six, Aaron nine, and Peter eleven. I was deathly ill too, but pulled through when the others couldn't."

"I'm sorry, Lucy. I vaguely remember all the deaths within the congregation. I'm afraid I was a young man concerned only with myself those years of my youth." He kissed her forehead and held her closer.

Mrs. Easton returned to her previous seat. "It does me a world of good to witness your feelings for each other. While I was shocked to see you lift her off her feet when you walked in the door, I now understand it for what it is—complete adoration. I'm glad to know you're more than a charmer. I do believe my Lucy will be safe with you, despite my previous concerns."

"I'm honored, Mrs. Easton. I wish my mother could see our relationship as you do."

"It's harder with the boys. A mother knows her daughter is still her daughter when she marries, but a son is pulled along with his wife's family, even though she takes his name. I hardly see Maxwell or his children and he lives two miles away. But Susan, Cora, and Emma are as close to me as ever though they live out of town."

Alexander nodded his understanding. "I'll give them a few days more before approaching the wedding subject again."

"Don't wait too long, Alex." Lucy squeezed his hand.

"I won't." He leaned down and kissed her forehead just as Mr. Easton walked in.

"What's this? Lovebirds cuddled in the parlor with mother hen watching?"

"James, they have a beautiful relationship and understanding not often witnessed." Mrs. Easton took her husband's hand and he paused to kiss her cheek. "Welcome home."

Edmund, his stiff collar gone and shirt opened at the neck, slunk to the far armchair.

"Really! Both my grown children appear in varying stages of undress on a night we have a supper guest."

"But Alex is no longer a guest, Mother," Edmund said. "He's practically family."

"Freddy is coming after supper and he's not," Mrs. Easton said with authority.

"But he is, Mother, more so than Alex. Freddy's logged more time here than any of our cousins."

"Very well, though I don't imagine Freddy showing up without wearing a suit."

"I'm sure he'll be more than happy to remove his jacket when he arrives," Edmund remarked.

When the clock struck six thirty, they made their way to the dining room and Edmund was sent in search of Opal. Mr. Easton stopped in the front hall to remove his jacket.

"James, the example you set—"

"I'm following theirs, dear. Tonight is for Lucy and Alexander."

After supper, they all settled in the parlor. The doorbell rang and Edmund answered it. He returned with Frederick, without a jacket or tie.

"See, Mother? Freddy was more than willing to relax this evening," Edmund announced.

"I'm glad you came, Freddy." Mrs. Easton kissed his cheek when he leaned down to hug her. "James and I are only staying long enough to toast, then we'll send Opal to bed and turn the parlor over to all of you."

"Thank you for insisting I come, Mrs. E. It's good to be here." He turned to the settee and gazed wistfully at Lucy cozied under Alexander's arm. "Lucy, you know I wish you the best."

She offered a hand and he took it in both of his and brought it to his lips.

"You'll be a lovely bride."

Alexander narrowed his eyes, but forced a smile for him. They shook hands with what appeared to be more force than necessary.

"You're a lucky man, Alex. I've never seen her happier. I wish you both the best."

"That's good of you, Freddy."

Frederick made his way toward the chair in the far corner.

"No, Frederick, you can sit here. There's plenty of room." Lucy patted the settee beside her.

"Plenty of room because you're practically in Alexander's lap," Opal sneered.

Frederick sat as close to the armrest as he could. "Your parents are aware of how they're sitting, Opal. I'm sure if it was improper they would have been asked to move. It's only natural they display more affection with their engagement announced. There are certain liberties—"

Edmund got to his feet and pointed at Alexander while staring Frederick down. "He's to take no liberties with my sister!"

"Do something," Lucy whispered to Alexander.

Alexander raised his hands in surrender. "Why don't we have this conversation later? This is supposed to be a joyful occasion, let's not ruin it for the ladies."

"Well said." Frederick gave Alexander an approving nod.

Edmund settled back, arms crossed and frowning, but he was more than eager to take his tumbler of brandy when his mother carried the tray around the room.

"For Alex and Lucy, and their happily ever after." Mr. Easton raised his glass. After everyone took their first drink, he gazed around the room. "And just to be clear, as the four of you are the ones most likely to be involved, Eddie and Lucy cannot entertain while their mother and I are gone this weekend. No guests inside the house. Is that clear?"

"Father, why can't I have Freddy in for a drink if I want?" Edmund asked.

"It's easier to just say no to everyone than make exceptions for one or the other of you. This is a sensitive time for your sister and I'm sure you won't mind helping safeguard her for the weekend."

"Of course, Father."

"Good, I expect you to hold each other accountable, and for Alexander and Freddy to keep watch as well."

"Yes, sir," the two men said at the same time.

"Now enjoy the evening." Mr. Easton took his wife's arm and nudged Opal along, shutting the pocket doors on their way out.

Edmund poured himself another glass and waved the bottle as a way of asking if anyone else wanted more. Frederick declined.

Alexander pointed to Lucy's full glass. "I think I'll be finishing hers."

"Unless you want to see me tipsy," she said.

"Might not be a bad idea to find out what type of drunk you are before marriage." Alexander winked.

"I'm sure she'll have a chance to see you plastered Friday night." Edmund smirked.

Alexander rested his head on Lucy's shoulder. "I'm not like I used to be."

"If you do one-tenth of what you did at last year's ball, I'll have to dispose of you for my sister's sake." The two stared at each other, seeming to dare the other to start in on details.

Alexander looked away and took a sip from his glass. "I'm not the same man I was last year, and if you cherish your sister, you'll speak no more of it unless you want *your* stories told."

As though seeking to end the tension between the friends, Frederick turned to Edmund. "Do you still need me to bring Lucy Friday night?"

Alexander straightened. "Like hell you're bringing my fiancée to the masquerade! Where'd you get that idea?"

"We arranged it the week of Christmas. Lucy tricked Eddie into inviting her and when I found out what society it was, I insisted on coming to watch over her."

"I thought she received the invitation New Year's Eve like my sister, who, no thanks to Eddie, thinks she's going too."

Edmund stared into his glass. "Like Freddy said, she tricked me into inviting her before she knew which one it was. I told her I'd get her an invitation, so I did…on New Year's Eve."

Alexander pulled away from Lucy. "And you never thought to tell me?"

"I didn't think it would matter how I got there, but now that we're engaged, I see it does."

He hugged her to his side. "Would you want to see me escorting another woman to the ball?"

"Of course not."

"Then why would I feel any different about Freddy bringing you, especially with your shared history of dance lessons and everything?"

"Yeah," Edmund said with a smile, "he's probably the first guy to put his hands on Lucy's waist. That's big, like 'first kiss' big."

"That's enough, Eddie." Frederick paced the room a few times before settling in the armchair Mrs. Easton had vacated. "You're a mean drunk, everyone knows it."

"That you are, friend. At least I'm a passionate one." Alexander set his empty tumbler on the coffee table and kissed Lucy's ear, causing her to giggle.

Edmund stood and glared down at Alexander. "Do you have to sit there with her and rub it in? Yes, you won. I couldn't chase you away! You somehow charmed my parents, and in the end, you're riding away with my sister. But it's more like you stole the prize because everyone knows you don't deserve her."

Frederick was at his side before he finished speaking. "Come on, let's go to the kitchen and make some coffee."

He knocked his arm away. "I don't know how to make coffee."

"Well, I do, and you're coming with me." Frederick got behind and nudged him forward.

"It should be you sitting beside her, yet you keep the peace."

"I do it for Lucy," Frederick said as he steered him out.

Lucy shivered. "I've never seen Edmund like this."

"Consider yourself lucky." Alexander pulled her legs over his lap and hooked his arm around her back. "At our parties, I'd come up with the ideas and he'd beat down anyone who stood in our way from making them happen. We were quite the formidable pair."

"Alex, you're still wearing your tie." She touched the knot at his throat, admiring the way the ring on her hand looked against the blue silk. "Would you like me to loosen it?"

"I better keep it on this time, but will you allow me an indulgence?"

"I belong to you, body, heart, and soul."

Lucy tilted her head back, hoping he'd kiss her neck. Instead, his fingers on the top of her foot caressed like a million tiny feathers. He teased around her ankle and then, with a smoldering gaze, his hand went under her skirt as he followed the curve of her calf to the back of her knee. With a sigh, she brought her hand to his collar, pulling his face close enough for her to kiss. He trailed kisses around her neck and then carefully moved her back to her previous position beside him, smoothing her skirt and kissing her once more on the lips.

"Allow me to come home from work every day and pleasure you once we're married."

"You're an angel sent to teach me all that love has to offer." Her arms went around his middle as she rested her cheek on his chest.

"I'm just a man, and a flawed one at that. Don't set me too high on a shelf. I'm bound to fall from your grace if you do."

Twenty-Two

Friday morning was bone-chilling. All the occupied rooms had fires in their hearths, and after a hot breakfast and goodbyes to Lucy, Edmund drove their parents and Opal to the train station on his way to work. Lucy settled at her typewriter as soon as they were gone. When the phone rang downstairs, she kept typing.

Naomi stopped in her open doorway. "Telephone, Miss Lucy."

Curious, because she hadn't had a phone call since Grace Anne left town, she hurried downstairs.

"This is Lucy."

"I told you to stay away from that gossip hound at the Christmas party! She had you in her sights and now me!" Edmund's voice shook with indignation.

"What is it?"

"No good is what it is! All the secretaries are talking about it, and I won't be able to take dinner out today. I'll be home by noon." Then the line went dead.

Lucy hastily put on wool stockings, another petticoat, and boots under her skirt to protect herself from the freezing temperature.

"Naomi," she said as she cinched her reticule on her wrist, "I need to stop in town to pick something up. Please let your aunt know Edmund will be here for dinner."

Lucy snatched the red cloak from the foyer and ran down the front steps as she tied it around her neck. When she reached the front yard, a blast of northerly wind took the breath from her. The faces of the other passengers on the streetcar were closed and irritable. Only those having to get out were roaming town in the twenty-degree weather, which meant no housewives or chatty young ladies were there to witness Lucy flying to the nearest magazine outlet to purchase a copy of *Snitch*.

Lucy tucked it under her cloak and crossed the street to catch the next west bound trolley. She didn't dare open the magazine until locked in her bedroom. After pulling off her boots, she sat cross-legged on the rug before the fireplace. Edmund's pain was on the first page.

> *Mr. E. and Miss F. enjoyed their first date to Monroe Park on Friday the thirteenth.*
> *Hopefully, it isn't a bad omen for the budding relationship.*
> *Though Mr. E. is fetching, he's been unlucky in love thus far.*
> *All the best with Miss F.*

The first two lines were what Lucy had sent to Kate Stuart, but the additional closing remarks turned the tone from humorous to humiliating. She tossed the magazine on the floor and covered her face with her hands. She allowed herself to be miserable a few minutes before picking it back up. Scanning through the gossip tidbits and advertisements, her eyes fell upon the following on page five:

> *Previously shy Miss E. seems to have had a bumper Holiday season.*
> *Before the clock struck twelve on New Year's Eve,*
> *she'd collected not one but TWO handkerchiefs*
> *from some of our city's most handsome men:*
> *A.R.M. and F.L.D.*
> *Both of whom she was seen dancing zealously with at the Order of Mayhem's ball.*
> *Well played, Miss E!*

"Well played" didn't describe what Lucy had done—it was Kate Stuart's game that won her readers while it cost "Miss E." even more of her good name than dating Alexander. The fact that Kate Stuart purposely set her at doing things only to create stories for her magazine soured Lucy's stomach. Lucy had been warned by those she loved most but was too intent on being published, no matter the cost. The only relief she had was the fact that there were no other reports about her family or friends in that edition. She tossed the magazine into the fire, where the papers curled and smoked until they burned to ash.

Lucy paced the parlor as Edmund stomped in from his half-day at the office. He flopped into their father's chair and rang the bell for help.

"Fetch me the bottle of brandy, no glass, just the bottle," he barked at Naomi.

Mortified, Lucy followed Naomi and took it from her so she wouldn't be subject to Edmund's rudeness again. "Thank you. I'm sorry, but Edmund's having a bad day."

"Ain't your fault, Miss Lucy," she said as she handed the bottle over.

"But it is."

Fortunately, after the drinks everyone shared the other night, the bottle of brandy only had a cup of liquor in it.

Lucy shoved it at her brother. "Next time, get it yourself. You're not king of the castle. You've no right to ring for the help when Mother and Father never do."

"I'm king here this weekend. Speak nice to me or be sent to the tower. And don't get any lofty ideas about a prince coming to save you. After that write up in *Snitch*, I doubt Alex will be on speaking terms with you." He took a swig of the brandy. "Might as well kiss that engagement goodbye."

"But it's not like it said, same as what it said about you! Kate Stuart takes a grain of truth and crushes it until it resembles what she wants it to. You haven't been unlucky in love, you just haven't wanted to settle down."

Edmund took another drink. "I know that, and you know that, but do Mary Margaret or any other lady I might turn my eye to in the future know the truth? To all of them, I'll be the unlucky suitor, cursed in love."

"If Mary Margaret really likes you, that fluff won't matter. It's not like they said you were stringing along two women."

Edmund laughed. "And where's the truth in that bit about you and the handkerchiefs? You did dance with both of them on New Year's Eve—and the Revelry Makers ball from what I heard. Are you in possession of both of their handkerchiefs?"

"Not any more. I only have Alex's, and I've had it since his Christmas party. He gave it to me in the garden, when I was upset by my conversation with Kate Stuart." She took a heaving sigh and clinched her fists. "I should have known it would all end badly!"

"And what happened to Freddy's?"

"I gave it back to him when I was done with it."

Edmund laughed. "A used hanky? That's rather tacky, even for you."

Lucy plopped onto the settee. "I didn't use it in that sense. I used it for another purpose. One I fully regret."

He leaned forward. "Lucy, what did you do?"

"I set my own goal ahead of the well-being of my family and friends."

Edmund paled. "Did you write—"

"No. Yes. I don't know anymore! I'd have to tell you everything from the beginning for you to understand."

He crossed his arms and sat back in the chair. "I'm here and listening."

She told him how she sent Kate Stuart a letter asking for a reporting job, her appointment to speak to her at the Christmas party, Alex's harsh words in the garden when she told him about her reasoning for trying for the job, and the letter of acceptance upon initiation.

"I'm glad Alex saw through her. It sounds like she looked to pad her magazine at your expense. All except that Wragg Swamp deal. That's just plain stupid. I hope you know better than to go in there."

"I know better, but my brain was ready to do it. The whole scheme makes sense to me now, I just didn't see the signs. I was too busy thinking about her uncle at that New York publishing company. I already had Alex's handkerchief and then Frederick offered his to me in the gazebo on Christmas, and being the fool I am, I took it so I'd have it to show Kate. I showed her both at the New Year's ball in what I believed was confidence, and then gave Frederick his back after I danced with him because I didn't want him to think I was being sentimental."

"That's a harsh brush off, Lucy. You know he likes you and that was his first day out of mourning."

"He's too kind! I can't tell when he's implying more and when he's just being Freddy."

"He cares for you enough to take sides with Alex against me in your defense. Tread carefully with him tonight."

"I will, if he even wants to speak with me."

"Freddy won't turn his back on you, but why did you even think about working with Kate after she ran that piece about the turkey last month?"

"That was my piece," she whispered.

"What?"

"Kate wanted to know if I could report a story even if it was embarrassing to me or my family."

"And that didn't tip you off? You're too naïve for your own good!"

"I had no idea she was going to print it! I got that letter from her after the magazine came out along with twenty-five cents for my story."

"You're a goose!" Then Edmund's mood sobered and he leaned forward. "Did you write any of the stories in today's edition?"

She stared into his hazel eyes, but didn't want to say the words. "Not as it's printed. I only sent in the first two lines about your date, which were humorous. Kate added the rest and turned it into a mockery. I'm sorry, Edmund. I didn't know what she was like."

He stormed out of the room and returned with a glass of rum.

"Edmund, please don't get drunk. You have your ball tonight and—"

"What do you think I'm going to do at the ball? I'll get drunk there anyway!"

"But your date? Is Mary Mar—"

"I'm not fool enough to bring a girl to this party. She'd hate me and my friends within an hour. Not that I'd be able to talk with her or anything. Our costumes this year are cumbersome."

"Those skeleton things?"

He laughed. "If only! Those were a breeze compared to what we have tonight."

"What is it and how will I know which one is Alex?"

"You'll see when you get there. He's picking me up at six because we all have to meet to dress before it starts. Maybe you can figure out a secret handshake or something. That is, if he's speaking to you."

Lucy clutched her stomach. "Can you explain things to him? Help him understand?"

He swallowed the remainder of the rum. "You'll have to do your own groveling."

***

Lucy huddled on the front porch swing in her cloak. A hired carriage pulled up at a quarter to six and Alexander emerged in a black wool trench coat, hat, and gloves. He rushed to her, his skin pale and eyes shadowed in the dimness of the porch.

"I told you never to wait for me, especially in the cold." His breathe smelled of woodsy sweetness, and his grabbing hands went under her cloak, pulling her to him with a thrusting motion. "You've disobeyed me in more ways than one. How shall I punish you?"

She flinched away from him. "You've been drinking."

"'Tis the Dardenne way of revelry. Well, the first step of it. As this will be my last ball with them, I want to do it properly."

"Your last ball?" Her eyes widened.

"You're no longer a member once you marry. Strictly bachelors, like the old groups used to be." He kissed her mouth and down her jaw. "My bride, you're simply naughty for waiting for me out here and for collecting handkerchiefs."

"I only have yours, Alex." She squirmed in his grasp, trying to move her torso away from his to keep the dizzying sensation of his body from overpowering her better judgement. "I made the mistake of trying to work with Kate Stuart, and it all built into this mess of half-lies against Edmund and me. I'm sorry yours and Frederick's names got pulled into it."

"Calling me out as one of the handsomest men in the city is no shame, it's having my fiancée's name linked with a second man's that the disgrace. Mother was livid and told me she saw you on Freddy's arm when you were out shopping. Now she's insisting that we wait until summer before she agrees to our marriage. She thinks I need to make sure you're totally committed to me and Father agreed, though he still thinks you're a great catch." He pinched her backside—but with his gloves it was more like a sharp grab—before groping his way up her middle.

"Alex!" Hurt and disappointment crowded her voice. "But you told them we didn't need their permission to marry."

"We don't, but this whole experience has given me something to consider. But right now I can't think straight. I can only focus on your lips, the feel of your body against mine." His tongue probed mercilessly as he lowered her to the swing.

Edmund came out the front door and—to Lucy's horror—laughed rather than pulled Alex off her. "He's drunk already? That's the Alex I know and tried to warn you away from. How do you like him now, Lucy?"

She struggled against Alex's roaming hands as he tried to feel every inch of her. Lucy caught her breath and tried to speak as she squirmed out from under him. "Alex, you need to stop before you hurt me."

His smile chilled her more than the temperature. "Hard and fast is your punishment, naughty Lucy."

Edmund grabbed him by the collar. "Drunk or not, that's my sister you're talking to!" He rattled him by the shoulders and turned to Lucy. "Do you want to slap him or shall I box him on the nose?"

Lucy stood and pulled the cloak around her to cover her rumpled skirt and blouse. "Just let me fix him some coffee."

"Won't do him a lick of good. He'll drink even more to get the buzz back." Edmund shook Alexander by the neck of his coat. "Can you apologize to your fiancée for attempting to defile her on the front porch?"

Alexander's eyes crossed and it took him a moment to focus. "Did I get too excitable?"

Edmund huffed. "To say the least."

Alexander took Lucy into his arms and kissed her. "I'm sorry. It's been a rough day."

Images of Dr. Jekyll and Mr. Hyde swarmed in Lucy's mind at the change of her beloved from monster back to man as she tried to quiet her quaking hands under her cloak.

"Try not to drink anymore." She leaned on his shoulder to whisper to him. "You need to be sober for our trip in the morning."

He kissed her cheek. "I'll try to remember. The driver is coming for you at eight thirty. The first dance is at nine and I expect you there."

"How will I know which one you are?"

"By my gentle touch if I'm sober. Otherwise by my steadfast desires and tendency to beat away all the other men."

"That's nothing for me to go on."

He kissed her hard. "It's all I can tell you. Welcome to the Mystics of Dardenne Masquerade!"

Twenty-Three

Twice in the next hour, Lucy dry heaved into the bathroom sink. Never had she been alone in the house so long, and the experience on the porch with Alexander brought fear to the surface. She lay in her underclothes in front of the fireplace, trying to erase the dreadful memory of fighting off Alexander. A few tears fell when she remembered his words about having things to consider and the looming possibility of postponing the wedding for months.

When the mantel clock struck seven, she stumbled to the bathroom to wash. She took great care dressing, wanting to be perfect for Alexander, hoping he would understand her devotion to him. Her gown, a solid navy silk accentuated with velvet panels, had a demi train plus lace and sequin overlays on the bodice. At the center of the chest she'd added a butterfly detail in peacock colors to go with the "Flights of Fantasy" theme. The neckline was a simple U-cut, but lower than all the others gowns. She was grateful the last passion mark had faded, for it would have been visible. Next, she worked her hair into a tight twist atop her head and secured a navy turban that completely covered her hair. The front of the silk turban held a peacock broach from whence a dozen wispy feathers sprouted in an arch. Her mask was leather cut into the shape of a butterfly—an eye hole in each upper wing—painted to match the peacock on her breast.

Before going downstairs, she brought out her jar of lip stain she'd bought on a whim last summer. She painted her lips the color of fuchsia azaleas and hurried to her parents' room to borrow her mother's navy opera gloves, gold reticule, and black velvet dress cape.

Her ride arrived at precisely eight thirty.

"Good evening, Miss Easton," the driver said as he helped her into the carriage.

"Lucy, you're divine."

"Eliza!" She sat beside the young lady in bright blue with a blue jay mask. "Alex forbid you from coming."

"He did, but even if I only last an hour, I want to see the festivities." She linked her arm through Lucy's. "I wish I'd thought to conceal my hair. And your lips! Lucy, you're glowing with sensuality. Is tonight going to be your night?"

"Alex was drunk when he stopped to get Edmund and practically tried to take me on the front porch. That's not how I want my…experience to go."

Eliza nodded in understanding. "He's a completely different person when drunk."

"I'm glad you're here and I won't have to enter alone. From what Edmund told me, I won't be able to tell any of the members apart. Maybe you can help me distinguish Alex out of the lot."

"I'd be happy to."

Despite the freezing temperatures, Temperance Hall was surrounded by curious bystanders and a smattering of police, as if they expected trouble. When the carriage door opened, Lucy stepped out first. A murmur swept the crowd, speculating on who she was, but she kept her eyes fixed on the walkway.

The lobby of the rental building was draped with greenery to make it look like a tropical forest, a gilded cage housing half a dozen parrots in the center. Lining a red carpet from just beyond the coat check to the ballroom door stood the Mystic of Dardenne members like creepy soldiers standing guard. They were dressed in medieval raven-beaked plague masks with mesh-covered eye holes, baggy dark clothes, and topped with hooded gray cloaks.

Eliza gripped Lucy's gloved arm while they waited in line at the coat check. "How absolutely thrilling!"

"It's morbid! Much worse than the skeletons." Lucy tried to keep the tremor out of her voice.

"A few of them are turned this way, but I can't tell anything from here with their costumes cut the way they are."

They slipped their tickets for their capes into their reticules and turned to face the gauntlet of masked men. When the couple in front of them walked the carpet, Dardenne members reached out to the lady, trailing their gloved hands down an arm or touching a cheek while murmuring to her.

Eliza, electrified by the power-play the members exhibited over their guests, stepped ahead to walk the carpet alone. Each of the men toward the front of the gauntlet touched her. Lucy could hear hissing voices that sounded like "pretty lady" and "we have you now, sweet girl" and took a step back.

From the middle of the row, one of the Dardenne members rushed forward and took Eliza by the elbow. *Alex!* Lucy tried to memorize each detail on his mask, but realized while there were several variations of the raven mask, half a dozen of the exact same ones were shared between the members. As Alexander marched his sister toward the ballroom, none of his brethren dared touch her.

Wanting to wait until Alexander returned—in hopes that he would escort her as well—Lucy stepped to the side to allow the couple behind her to pass. A hand went to her back and a man in a black tuxedo leaned over her shoulder. "It's overwhelming, isn't it?"

"Frederick!" His name escaped her lips with relief. His warm smile below his purple mask a beacon amid her fear. "I'm glad it's you."

"You're flawless, Lucy." His hand went to her arm, running his own gloved fingers over hers. "May I escort you in?"

She hesitated and then pulled her arm free. "No, Alex didn't want me arriving with anyone else."

"He should have prepared you for this walk. Do you think he'll come get you as he did his sister?"

"I only know I can't walk with you, especially after that article. I'm sorry your name got brought into the magazine again. Forgive me."

Frederick touched her quivering chin, his glove soft on her face. "Don't worry about me, Lucy. I'll be fine. You go ahead. I'll be close behind in case these Dardennes get any ideas."

"I'll never be able to repay you, Frederick." She briefly squeezed his arm and then turned her attention back to the carpet.

After taking a deep breath—and praying she wouldn't faint— she started her journey. Hands pawed at her, coupled with shocking words spoken eerily through the curving, beaked masks.

"Painted lips are more fun to kiss."

"You should know better than to come alone."

"Those are some wings I'd like to spread." The man who said that received an elbow to his gut from the guy next to him. *Edmund?* Lucy prayed her brother was sober enough to watch over her.

At the door to the ballroom stood a member in a similar plague costume, but this one all black. "Invitation, please, though we make exceptions for beautiful women." He leaned on Lucy's arm as she pulled the card out of her bag. She couldn't tell if it was from drunken necessity or flirtation but she hurriedly left him behind.

Suspended from the ceiling of the ballroom were dozens of giant paper birds, and a few real scarlet macaws swooped through the air. The perimeter of the room had at least a hundred potted plants, creating dozens of intimate alcoves for the guests to enjoy. Every twenty feet were punch tables with glasses at the ready. Positioned at the foot of the dance floor stood a huge golden birdcage housing a stage and a nervous-looking string quartet.

Lucy easily spotted Eliza's black hair and blue dress across the room, gazing into one of the palm trees at a macaw.

"I always wanted a parrot, but they're too noisy for Mother. She only keeps canaries, but they're no fun to play with or draw."

Not wanting to discuss Mrs. Melling, Lucy changed the subject. "Where should we wait? Alex is expecting me for the first dance, so I can't hide in a corner."

"You mustn't hide tonight, Lucy. You're the most beautiful thing here. No going into dark corners, unless it's with my brother." She giggled.

"He might not even come for me. I think he saw me with Frederick when he got back from bringing in you in. That was him, wasn't it?"

Eliza laughed. "Yes, and he's mad as a hatter, but is giving me thirty minutes before sending me home. I plan to make the most of it."

The two sat in chairs along the edge of the dance floor near the center and Frederick settled less than a dozen feet from them. At precisely nine, the Mystics of Dardenne members marched in to the ballroom led by the black-clad doorman.

"Welcome, my carnival friends!" the man in black shouted. "We only have one rule to keep in mind. Mystics of Dardenne members pride themselves on their anonymity and we ask that even if you recognize someone's voice, you do not call them by name. Our dances are always 'Double Rush,' so ladies may cut in as well as the men. And anything goes, although we'd rather not have the police raid us this year."

Most in the crowd laughed, but it sent a shiver down Lucy's spine.

"Food is on the second floor, but the third floor is a members' oasis. Only those escorted by us are allowed, no exceptions."

Several whistles and cheers trilled through the air as Lucy's heart sank to her stomach. After reading news briefs about what happened at their previous masquerades, she didn't want to imagine what went on in the top suite.

"To start this party off, we open the dance floor for members and their partner of choice. No rushing from the general guests until the second song, please."

The leader came straight for Lucy and she ducked behind Eliza.

"You can't deny the host, Madame Butterfly."

"Go," Eliza whispered, "Alex can cut in."

Hesitantly, Lucy extended her arm to him. He bowed over it and led her onto the floor as the Vivaldi tune began. Before they were situated, another Dardenne tapped his shoulder.

"You dare interrupt me?"

The man in gray—wearing a mask like Alexander—only shrugged. He took Lucy's right hand and immediately grasped her waist with the other. His shoulder felt different, but it could have been the odd layers of cloth hanging from him. But when he led the first few steps of the dance, Lucy knew it wasn't Alexander. Even drunk he'd be better able to dance than the faltering man.

From behind, another Dardenne approached. Rather than tapping his comrade on the shoulder, he boldly wrapped one arm around Lucy's waist and the other under her arm and round her chest. With a fluid motion he lifted her out of the man's unsuspecting arms and twirled her to an empty spot of the floor where he positioned himself before her. The kneading grasp on her waist and the caressing touch of his fingers as he trailed the length of her gloves revealed his identity.

"Thank you for coming for me."

"I almost didn't after seeing how friendly you and Freddy were at the door. But then you pulled away from him and bravely walked the carpet alone. My heart swelled with pride as the others wanted a piece of you—my queen." His words, though muffled through the mask, calmed her.

"Please don't leave me alone tonight."

"I'll do my best."

Alexander kept them moving quickly across the floor to lessen their chances of being interrupted. His experience afforded him the skills to hold her snug against him while doing so. Lucy clung to the fact that Alexander had chosen her—saved her from the strangers—and held her like everything was fine. She tilted her head back and watched the paper birds swirl as they waltzed around the floor.

"Lucy, you're stunning." Without losing a step, he brought his hand from her waist to her neck, trailing his gray glove down the expanse of her skin all the way to the butterfly emblem at her chest, which he traced before returning his hand to her side. "Curse these gloves and mask. I want to touch and taste you."

"And I want you to as well. Can we leave when Eliza does?"

"I need to stay until midnight, but we'll have some personal time at ten, I promise." When the song ended, most of the dancers clung to each other as more couples and singles came onto the floor. "Let's go before someone tries to take you from me."

Eliza, one of the brave women to chance the Double Rush, strode across the floor to one of the plague masqueraders and the petite partner was sent away. Eliza filled the space before the Dardenne with flare as she sashayed through the box steps while her partner held her low on the back, the other arm straight out in a nod to the tango.

"I hope Eddie behaves himself for a few minutes." Alexander brought Lucy to a nearby alcove and hugged her to him before helping her to one of the chairs. "You're not wearing your ring?"

"I am." She held out her left hand. "It's under the glove."

He laughed as he touched the lump on her finger. "Most women wear a diamond that size over the glove."

"But I wanted to be as nondescript as possible."

"When you walked in the door, all I saw were those bright lips and porcelain skin and I felt guilty for looking upon such a striking figure. When you removed your cape, I recognized the curve of your neck and realized whose lips they belonged to. My guilt turned to longing. It nearly broke my heart when Freddy touched you."

"I think it was the gloves."

"They do beckon to be stroked, but I'm so confined in this costume I can't even caress you properly. I'm glad this is my last masquerade with this society. I'm getting too old to play dress-up."

"You're unnerving looming over me. If it wasn't for your voice, I couldn't stand it."

"Then I promise to always speak to you so you know it's me and not a monster."

"Like that monster that came to my house this evening?"

His hand went to his head covering as though he wanted to run his fingers through his hair. "I don't remember much until this past hour. Was I awful?"

"You had me pinned on the front porch swing but Edmund pulled you off me."

"Lucy, I'm sorry." Alexander dropped to his knees and brought his hands around her waist. "I have no black eye to show for it."

"Edmund was happy I witnessed the side of you he'd warned me about. I offered coffee but he decided leaving was the best option."

"Forgive me, my queen. I did drink coffee once we got to the dressing rooms. I haven't drunk since I left my house hours ago, but I'll need to indulge soon. And I need to find you something tolerable as well."

"How will you drink?"

From under his tattered gray robe he pulled a slim, hollow tube attached to a necklace. "All of us have them."

His voice held the vocal cadence of a smile, causing Lucy to yearn for his handsome face. "Can't you take that off for a few minutes? We're sheltered in here."

"There are strict guidelines to follow. I have to wait until my break at ten for us to have our time." He fingered her décolletage. "Let's take the next dance and then I'll send Eliza home."

When the opening notes of Tchaikovsky's "Swan Lake" sounded, Alexander danced her around the crowded space with fluid grace.

"Did you know they would play this?"

"I may have requested it."

Lucy's smile broadened as they floated through the song. As it came to a close, she rested her head on his shoulder. "I love you."

His glove trailed down her throat. "It won't be long now."

Twenty-Four

Lucy waited in the alcove while Alexander collected Eliza. A minute later, three Mystic of Dardenne members surrounded her. She gripped the arms of her chair and tried to ignore the tightening sensation in her chest.

"Our brother is being neglectful."

"No pretties may be left alone tonight."

"You must pick one or dance with all."

"Excuse me. I'm here for her." Frederick attempted to reach Lucy, but the members closed their ranks.

"Too late," the one in the middle said. "She's ours now. She must pick one or dance with all."

Knowing that Frederick watched over her helped steady her breathing. Lucy glanced at the hideous costumes and took the hand of the one with a mask like Alexander's. The other two blocked Frederick until Lucy and her partner were out of reach.

The man rested his hand on her left hip with a groping touch, and then took her right hand in his. "Did you want to finish our dance from earlier?"

"You're the one who interrupted your leader for the first dance."

"And then you were stolen away before we were able to have any fun." His touch slithered from her hip to her backside.

Lucy jerked away but he held fast to her right hand. He repositioned his hand to the small of her back and tugged her against him.

"Don't play shy with me. I'm all too familiar with the type of women my brother prefers the company of." He wrapped both arms around her and pinned her against him. "You're going upstairs with me so I can spread your wings."

"No!" She loosened an arm and grabbed his beak, the papier-mâché crushed in her grip.

He brought his hands to his mask and Lucy took the opportunity to flee, running into Frederick.

"I've got you, Lucy." He put an arm around her shoulder and walked her toward the alcove. "I saw what happened and won't leave your side until Alex returns."

Lucy choked back a sob. "He said the most horrible things."

Frederick sat with Lucy, his arm still around her. A Dardenne approached, a drink in each hand, and seemed to stare at the two.

Frederick stood. "Lucy needs you."

"It looks like she's doing fine with you, Freddy."

"There were three of them forcing her to dance. Her partner had wandering hands and—"

"Are you implying I neglected my fiancée? I was seeing my sister out of this hell. It's not like I was out cavorting with women or drinking with friends, though I did stop to bring something back with me. Is that a crime?"

"That's not what I meant."

"I know you're here because you don't think I'm good enough for your precious Lucy." He shoved one of the punch glasses at her, then pulled his straw from around his neck and sucked his glass empty in seconds.

"I agreed to come long before you were engaged," Frederick reminded him.

Alexander clasped the glass to his chest. "But every time I turn around, you're at her side, as if those congratulations you gave us the other day were lies."

"I offered comfort at the front door because she was scared to death of the row of plague masks. No man in his right mind would leave someone he loves to that walk of shame. The whole display was insulting to the guests. I came to her side now because one of those same members attempted to take advantage of her. This is no place for a woman you cherish."

"I agree! This is my final year with the lot. Where I once found thrills I now find vulgarity. I'm doing the best I can to fulfill my obligations for the season and care for Lucy, but I'm not perfect. Having Eliza thrown in on top of it all only compounded the situation."

"I understand, and am glad you're back. I told Lucy I'd stay until you returned. I'll take my leave."

Alexander blocked his path with his empty glass. "Be a sport and bring me another so I don't have to leave her again."

Frederick took the cup with a nod, though he looked like he'd rather strike him.

Alexander sat beside Lucy and their gloves intertwined in a pattern of gray and navy. "I'm sorry, Lucy. Do you know who it was?"

"He's dressed like you, the same one you took me from in the first dance. I did manage to crinkle his beak. That might help identify him." She sipped at the punch but didn't care for the strength of the alcohol.

"He didn't force himself on you, did he?"

"His hand roamed to my backside, but it's what he said that was the worst."

Alexander brought their linked hands to his chest. "I'll pound him for touching you when I see him, but what was said?"

"When I flinched away from his advances, he said to stop being shy because he knew the type of women you associate with." She stumbled over the bitterness of the words.

"That's no longer true." He caressed her face with his free hand. "You know that, don't you?"

She nodded and sucked in her breath. "Then he said he was going to bring me upstairs and spread my wings."

"I'm going to kill him!" The swell of the music and laughter built to a crescendo and seemed to enfold Alexander into the lunacy.

"No, Alex! Just stay with me, please! No one will bother me when you're by my side."

Frederick returned with a fresh glass. Alexander snatched the drink and downed it as quickly as he had the first. He turned to Frederick. "I need your help."

"Don't do it, Freddy!" Lucy begged. "Don't let him leave me!"

Alexander's fists were straining against the seams of his gloves. "I'm not sending him off to fight my battle."

"Stay with me. That's all I ask."

The catch in her voice caused Alexander to pause. "Lucy, you know what his intentions were. I can't let him go after saying that to you. I'm sure even Freddy would agree, and your brother. Maybe we should all pay the man a visit."

Alexander motioned Frederick to the entrance of their alcove and told him what had transpired. Even in the shadows Lucy could see Frederick flush with anger.

"There are police all around the building! If you start a riot—"

Alexander gripped her hand. "Lucy, there will be no riot, though they've been started for lesser things than the virtue of a beautiful woman. Freddy is going to make your brother aware of the situation, and should the opportunity arise, we'll each give the wayward man a friendly reminder about how a gentleman is supposed to behave. What better way for Freddy to put his gym time to use?"

Frederick touched Lucy's chin and gazed at her bright lips. "Keep it high. None of this is your fault."

"Thank you. It seems as though I'm forever thanking you for something."

"Think nothing of it." He voice was rich with emotion. "I'm happy to be of service."

After Frederick left, Alexander made short work of Lucy's punch. "Now we can go upstairs and gather some refreshments. I'm sure they have something more to your taste at the bar on the second floor."

Alexander's costume afforded them a clear passage and a certain air of respect among the guests. He helped Lucy fill a plate with a sampling of the food before collecting two glasses of champagne from the bartender.

After giving Lucy her glass, he took the plate. "Take my arm."

They walked to the staircase going to the third floor. Lucy stopped. "Where are we going?"

"The third floor is the only place we're allowed to remove our costumes. That's why no guests are allowed unless accompanied by one of us. Up here we can eat and drink freely, but we have shifts so we don't all crowd in at once and leave our party without hosts downstairs."

"Oh." Lucy tightened her hold on his arm as they ascended.

"Some of us have been known to use the space for more than eating and drinking, but things are usually mellow this early in the night."

"Is this where those women were last year?"

Alexander sighed. "Don't ask questions you don't want to know the answer to."

A man in an executioner's costume stood in the hallway. He opened the door with a nod. "Ain't seen many women up yet. Best keep her close if you don't wish to share."

Alexander paused. "I won't let anything happen to you, Lucy. And Eddie's on the same shift. You'll be well protected."

She nodded and they entered the open room. A few groupings of sofas and dozens of ice buckets filled with bottles of all types were in the center. Along the sides were alcoves partitioned off the same way as in the ballroom—by giant potted plants and palm trees. The first alcove had a chaise wide enough for two people to lounge next to each other filling the bulk of the space. Lucy's stomach tightened as her understanding increased about what sort of merry-making Mystics of Dardenne cherished above all.

"Just in case," Alexander whispered, "close your eyes until we get to our area."

Her heart pounded as she walked blindly the last several feet.

Alexander relieved her of her glass. "You can open them now."

Their food and drinks were on a small table next to a folding chair along the wall of plants. Alexander removed his gloves and hung his cloaked hood from the back of the chair. Then his hideous mask was off. As soon as he dropped it on the seat, Lucy clung to him. Alexander's hair and face were damp with sweat and his mouth tasted of vodka-laced punch. The thought that the three glasses he'd drunk in the last half hour might soon overwhelm him caused a rumble of unease.

He lowered himself onto the edge of the chaise as his hands playfully roamed her waist. With a gentle tug he brought her to his lap. "Your lips feel as good as they look and your dress is a perfect combination of textures."

"I missed your smile and the gleam in your eyes when you say things like that."

As though she'd turned a switch, Alexander's movements increased in intensity. "You like my naughty side?" He kissed his way from her jaw to her plunging neckline.

"And she was mad when I merely took a grab."

All pleasure drained from her body as the harsh words filled the intimate space. With deliberate motion, Alexander's head raised, and when it did, the chill of his icy stare filled Lucy with dread. He shifted her from his lap to the space against the backrest. Alexander stood and faced Rupert Lyons, another young lawyer with family connections in legal and political circles. He smirked at Alexander until he found his neck in the other's clutch.

"Friend or not, if you ever look upon my fiancée with impure thoughts, I'll slit your throat." Alexander's loosened his hold on the other man.

"That's Eddie's little sister?" Rupert stammered. "What the hell, Alex? We never bring legitimate dates to our parties."

"I didn't invite her, but since she's here, she's with me and I'd have it no other way." Alexander shoved Rupert aside. "Now leave us."

"Your contacts from last year's masquerade were happy to hear from us again. They'll be arriving by midnight, and your sweet little Consuela says she's missed you this past month and looks forward to—"

Alexander's fist struck his nose with a sickening *thwack* and Rupert went down. Lucy hid her face against the curve of the chaise but it didn't block the whimpering sounds Rupert made.

"Eddie!" Alexander shouted.

Hurried steps approached.

"That's who I figured it was," Edmund said. "I elbowed him in the welcome line because he'd said the same thing when Lucy entered."

She glanced over in time to see Edmund kick Rupert in the ribs, and then her brother and fiancé helped him stand.

Alexander pulled Rupert's cloak up to his face to catch the blood. "Don't talk in front of my fiancée like that again and we'll be square."

With Rupert's arm draped around Edmund's shoulder, he led him away.

"I'm sorry you had to go through all that." Alexander settled beside her and caressed the triangle of skin her gown exposed on her upper back. "You knew I was lecherous. Now you know more than you probably ever wanted to."

She breathed through a sob stuck in her chest, hoping to calm it before it erupted. It manifested as a heaving catch in her exhalation.

"Lucy, forgive my past, once again." He pulled her to his chest, his chin resting atop her silk turban. "It might be easier for you not to know the details, but they're still there. I've been with no one since the Christmas party—you've been my only desire and will be the rest of my life. I'll take no liberties with my station as my father has. You've changed my destiny with your true heart and gentle eyes."

Her body wracked with the onslaught of tears. Alexander hastily untied her mask to save the leather butterfly from damage.

"Cry, Lucy. I don't blame you. I've often cried over my mistakes. You deserve a man without blemish, but I'm afraid there isn't one to be found." With a tender touch, he removed her gloves. Alexander tossed them onto the chair with all the other accessories. He fingered the engagement ring. "I'm blessed you accept me as I am. My happiness was only skin deep until I met you. Now I'll never achieve joy without you by my side. It wounds me that I cause you such pain."

"I'm crying because I'll never live up to your needs and expectations. I fear you'll not love me if I fail to pleasure you in the ways you're accustomed to."

Alexander shifted with her until they lay back on the chaise, nestling her under his arm. "You, Lucille Amelia Easton, are my everything. There's no contest between you and the past. It's a hollow trail of services rendered, not love."

"No love? Ever?"

He hesitated as though deciding how much to share. "I thought love was the act itself. The sacred act of love making between a man and woman was reduced to a deed of exhibiting dominance and relieving stress. The privilege of manhood my father paid for me to experience before I left for college, and then made sure I had the means to acquire from then on."

"Alex." His name melted into fresh tears.

"It was wrong, but it was easier to go along with it than try to explain my reasoning for not doing so. To my father, church is only another place to find potential clients and appease those who wish to employ the saintly type. I didn't want to appear weak to him because he would have pushed me harder to be the type of man he thinks us Mellings need to be."

Edmund paused in the entry to the alcove, a half-empty bottle of wine dangled from his right hand. "Rupert's with John. Hopefully, his nose will be set straight, but the young doctor's already had too much punch. Do I need to pound you for making my sister cry?"

"That's up to her." Alexander's hand went down her forearm until he laced their fingers together.

"No, Edmund. But thank you for offering, and more especially for not dragging me away from him right now."

"Don't give me any ideas." His gaze locked with Alexander's. "And don't give me any reasons for harming you."

Lucy stayed in Alexander's arms until a bell rung.

"That means five minutes until eleven. We're supposed to leave to allow the next group access, but I'm not in a hurry and we still need to eat."

Alexander brought the glasses and plate to Lucy and they ate together on the chaise. The room quieted for several minutes, then a boisterous group, complete with giggling women, entered. Alexander brought Lucy her mask and she understood he meant to protect her identity. If Rupert—who'd attended many parties with her, including Christmas and New Year's—hadn't recognized her, there was a good chance other acquaintances wouldn't either. Especially drunk ones.

Lucy fed Alexander the last strawberry as a couple stumbled into the next alcove. She immediately paled over the sounds emerging, and then heat struck. "Do I sound like that when we kiss?"

He laughed. "No, my queen. They're drunk and sloppy."

Alexander brought her the navy gloves when she finished her champagne. Just as she pulled the second glove over her ring, a Dardenne stumbled in.

"Melling, weren't you on break last hour?"

"We're running late. Give me a moment to suit up." Alexander pulled his cloak off the chair.

The man crawled onto the chaise behind Lucy. He removed his mask and flopped against the backrest. "The classy girls don't know how to be quick, do they?"

As soon as he touched her glove, Lucy jumped.

"Don't get any ideas, Sean, she's coming with me." Alexander grabbed his mask and took Lucy's arm. "Let's just leave. I see no point in waiting until midnight when things have already turned bawdy."

Alexander paused near the door to put on his mask, momentarily releasing Lucy's arm. She turned to see his face one last time before it disappeared under the hideous cover and witnessed a woman's hands reaching around Alexander's torso in a sinuous hold.

"Alexander the Great, my conqueror."

He dropped his mask and pulled out of the grasp. "I have nothing for you."

Despite her station in life, the woman's painted lips turned down and sadness washed over her dark eyes. Mortified, Lucy stared at the prostitute. Her tousle of dark hair lacked any style other than it was pulled up. It gave her a little height, but she barely reached Alexander's shoulder. Her white blouse was accented with a black corset on the outside, her buttons opened to the top of the binding.

The woman—who must be the Consuela mentioned by Rupert—only had eyes for Alexander. "Did I displease you last time? It's been too long. Maybe you've forgotten my—"

"I'll not need your services ever again." Alex snatched his mask off the ground and secured it. Then he raised the hood and offered Lucy his arm.

The woman's laugh was bitter. "You found one of your own to satisfy you. I hope she's worth the price tag and trouble."

Alexander jerked around, his hand raised to strike.

"Alex, no!" Lucy cried as she grabbed for his arm.

The woman's face contorted in fright for a moment, then she glared at Lucy. "What we had was good, but you've ruined him!"

A growl of rage erupted from Alexander. He yanked Lucy by the arm, ripping one of the cords on the reticule at her wrist in the process. Halfway down the stairs, he dropped his hold and absconded the next flight alone. With vision blurred from tears, Lucy hesitated at the foot of the stairs. She wrapped her trembling arms around herself and leaned against the wall for support.

Frederick came to her side. "Lucy, was that Alex who ran through?"

She nodded, unable to speak.

"Are you okay? He didn't do…anything, did he?"

She shook her head. "Can you help me?"

"Of course." He put an arm around her waist, but she shrugged him off and took only his arm as though they took a casual stroll through the park instead of an emotional journey through the bowels of debauchery.

When they reached the ballroom, he leaned closer. "Where do you wish to go?"

"Home. Unless you see Edmund or Alex."

He scanned the crowd then shook his head. With a quivering hand, she removed her coat check ticket and handed it to Frederick.

Twenty-Five

Reeling from everything she'd learned about Alexander in the last six hours, Lucy didn't speak until she was safely on the front porch of her home.

"Thank you, Frederick. I don't know what I would've done if you weren't there tonight." She clutched the black cape with her satin-covered hands.

"Do you want to talk about what happened?"

"I want to change out of this cursed outfit. You can wait in the parlor, though. All the fireplaces are probably burned out and I could use help lighting them."

"No, Lucy. I promised your father I wouldn't go in this weekend. Light the fire in your room and get yourself comfortable. Maybe boil water for tea or something. I'll be fine out here. I'll get the travel blanket from my automobile if I get cold." He wore lined leather driving gloves and his full-length wool coat buttoned to the top.

Lucy trudged through the empty house, turning on all the gaslights as she went. She returned her mother's cape and gloves. In her room, she placed the reticule that needed mending and the turban on her dressing table before peeling off the leather mask from her tear stained face. With a fire going in her hearth, she ran the bathroom sink tap hot and thoroughly washed her face.

She returned downstairs in a gray wool skirt, shirtwaist, and house slippers with her hair loose around her shoulders. She opened the front door.

"Coffee or tea?" she asked Frederick.

"Whatever you're taking is fine."

While the water heated, she stoked the fire in the parlor. She came to the porch wearing the red cloak and carrying a tray with coffee and cookies. Frederick closed the door behind her and relieved her of the tray.

"You must be tired, Goosy."

Frederick placed the tray on the table between the two rocking chairs in front of the parlor window, tucked his travel blanket around her lap, and pulled the hood of the cloak over her head. Looking into his face illuminated by the gaslights, Lucy noticed the tenderness in his brown eyes and nearly cried because she realized she'd never be alone if Frederick knew she needed him. He poured her coffee and handed her the steaming cup.

Lucy unfolded the story of Alexander, beginning with his behavior when he picked up Edmund and the remarks from the Mellings about the tidbit in *Snitch*. Since she told him about Mrs. Melling's harsh pronouncement on postponing their wedding, she had to tell him about what both his parents said when she and Alexander shared their news about their engagement.

"Your love for him must be extraordinary for you to persevere as you have."

"I ache for him, Freddy." Tears ran down her cheeks. "I fear for what he'll do—what he could have done by now. He's been erratic today. I don't know what to expect when he comes to me or word reaches me of his fate."

He placed a handkerchief into her hand with a loving touch. "What happened on the third floor? I followed you both up to the food area and watched you go with trepidation. When Eddie brought Rupert through, I worried more. And then when Alex fled, I thought the worst."

She told him the details of Rupert and Consuela. "Don't think less of him. I knew he was experienced and it only hurt a little to find out how tight his ties were. But it's his father's doing. He started him on the path."

"He's a grown man and is capable of knowing better. The question is if he's man enough to stand up for what he knows is right. There'll be no future for you with him if he can't stand firm against his parents." Frederick refilled his cup. "Forgive me for speaking out of turn, Lucy. I don't mean to be harsh, I only wish to protect you."

"I know you mean well, and it's true."

"How many times must he wound you before your heart says 'no more'?"

"But it's not him as he is now that causes pain. It's the shadow of his past, his parents, but not him. He's good to me, Freddy. He truly is."

"He's dragged you away when upset at least twice from what you've told me. That's not how a lady is to be treated by the man who loves her."

"But I would have gone with him! It was no hardship on me, except maybe on my wrist."

Frederick set down his cup and reached for her. He lifted her arm into the rectangle of light from the window. "Lucy, he's marred your skin."

"But it wasn't him! It was the demons from his past. He loves me, he truly does! I offered myself to him in the carriage ride home from the Revelry Makers' ball, and he wouldn't allow it because he knew I'd hate myself in the morning."

"Lucy…" Frederick buried his face in his hands.

She sobbed anew. "My God, I'm a wretch! Please don't tell Edmund or my parents. Please!"

Frederick's brown eyes shimmered with moisture.

"Freddy, you hold the fate of my future with all I've told you. Will you safeguard me?"

"I'm afraid what you need protection from is the one aspect I have no control over." He touched her cheek with his gloved hand. "I'm going to stay here until Edmund returns or daybreak, whichever comes first. And don't worry about me. I've slept many times out here. Remember the summer evenings on the second-floor porch, all us kids out there to stay cool during the hot nights."

"But, Frederick—"

He brought the back of her hand to his lips. "You know you can trust me with your pains, Goosy. I'll not share your secrets. I just pray tonight was the worst of what's to come."

The blanket fell to the floor when she stood. Lucy stared at Frederick a moment before she dashed into the house. She collapsed across the settee in the parlor, her body heaving with sobs under the red cloak.

***

In the dark of the three o'clock hour, Alexander's Model B squealed to a stop in the Eastons' front yard. His gloved hand was on the front door before noticing the figure watching from the rocking chair. In the half-light from the window, Frederick's glare was deadly.

"You abandoned her and it's inexcusable!" His burning words escaped with steaming breath.

"But you were there and got her safe—"

"Cut the caring act." Frederick stood. "As usual, you're only concerned with Alexander Melling. If I hadn't been on the second floor waiting for you both to return to the ball, she would have been pulled back up those stairs by the next man."

Alexander shook his head. "Lucy's stronger than that, and you and Eddie—"

"Eddie was plastered and missing by then. He still isn't home. And you ask too much of Lucy. She was shaking and speechless when I found her. How could she defend her own honor in a state like that? How could you walk away from one who laid herself before you and leave her to be found by the next monster that might happen by?"

Alexander pulled at his blond hair in frustration. "You don't understand what happened, what she was subjected to! The pain it caus—"

"She told me everything. Everything, Alex! And you left her to fend for herself! Be grateful I don't strike. She never should have gone to the ball and you shouldn't have brought her to the den."

"Yes, and I never should have kissed her at the Christmas party. But God help me, I did and I haven't been the same since!" Alex fell against the window, resting his forehead on the sleeve of his black coat as he gazed at the figure sleeping on the settee. A bare foot stuck out from the bottom of the red cloak, her slipper having fallen to the floor. "You don't think me changed, but I am. The longing within when I see her radiates from my heart, my very soul. For the first time I feel like there's hope for me. Then remembrance of how unworthy I am rushes back, and I feel the need to run from her lest I damage her beyond repair."

"Your running wounds her more than anything. She feared you were going to injure yourself tonight. She was preparing for the worst. I sat here and watched her cry, though I wanted to find you and ring your neck for leaving her in that hell."

"I've told her myself you'd be a better match. I tried to warn her of the baggage that a relationship with me involves, but it was too late. Our destinies were already entwined. God forgive me, Freddy! We're either going to live a life of redemption or we're going to combust."

They stood side-by-side, staring into the parlor at Lucy.

"The fire's dying and her foot must be half frozen." Alexander turned to Frederick. "I don't suppose you stepped inside, did you?"

"Of course not."

"As you are my witness, I'm going to build up the fire and cover her properly. I'm sure her parents wouldn't want her to be uncomfortable." Alexander went to the door.

"Before you go in, I must know where you went. If you ran to someone's arms for comfort, I'll not let you enter."

"If she told you everything, you'll know I've touched no other woman since the Christmas party. That still holds true." He scuffed his loafers against the floor boards. "I ran home and attempted to scrub the vileness off me in the shower. I dressed, drank coffee, and tried to think how I could repair the damages. I still only know that I have to see her, not what I need to do or say."

Frederick nodded, though he still scowled. "Go."

Alexander went first to the fire and added more kindling. With the blanket from the back of Mrs. Easton's chair in hand, Alexander approached Lucy. He gently lowered it over her legs with a bittersweet smile. He paused to finger her loose fan of hair that spread over the settee and then kissed the top of her head, dimming the gaslights on his way out.

He shut the front door as he exited. "Thanks, Freddy. Maybe I'll be able to sleep now."

Twenty-Six

The first lights of dawn shone through the parlor window. Upon sitting, Lucy gazed at Frederick sleeping in the rocking chair on the porch. She fingered the blanket over her legs before righting her slippers and crept out the front door. Placing a warm hand on Frederick's cold cheek, she believed she could be happy to see his dear face each morning. His eyes blinked open and he smiled.

"Thank you for building the fire and covering me. I wish you'd have stayed inside, though. It's freezing out here."

"I never went in, Goosy."

"Did Edmund come home?"

"No. Alex came by and wouldn't leave until he made sure you were comfortable."

"How was he? Why didn't either of you wake me?"

"It was three in the morning and I didn't think it the best time for a level-headed conversation." Frederick pulled his hand out from under the blanket and touched her arm. "He ran from fear of hurting you. I have no doubt he loves you, but he's unsure how to let go of his old self."

"What did he do?"

"We talked. Then he said I would be his witness as he saw to you. I watched from here as he tended the fire and covered your legs. He thanked me and said he hoped to get some sleep."

"Nothing more? Nothing about when he'd be back?"

"No, sorry." He took her hand. "If you're all right, I think I'll go home now."

Her sigh created a cloud of breath between them. "Can I make you some coffee or breakfast first?"

He stood, the travel blanket bunched in one arm and his other went around her shoulders. "No, but thank you." He kissed her forehead. "You had a trying night and should rest. If you need anything, call or send Eddie for me. Call me midday if Eddie isn't back and I'll go looking for him."

She nodded but didn't meet his eyes.

"And if I don't hear from you, I'll call later this afternoon to see how you're doing."

Lucy rested her head on his shoulder. "Thank you, for everything. Once again you swooped in to rescue me."

"Anytime you need me, I'll be here for you, no matter what."

She hugged Frederick goodbye before locking herself inside. After a warm bath, Lucy dressed in a green wool traveling suit in case Eliza and Alexander came as previously planned. If they went to the Mellings' cottage, it would be the perfect opportunity to talk with Alexander without being overheard or interrupted.

At eight she nervously waited in the parlor. Five minutes later, an open-topped automobile filled with Mystics of Dardenne members pulled onto the lawn. Edmund tried to climb out, but landed face down on the grass. Lucy took pity and rushed to his side while his friends laughed.

"That's a sweet sister you've got there, Easton," one called out.

"Why weren't you at the ball last night with all the other pretties? I would've danced with you again." Sean smiled, showing his chipped tooth.

Lucy clutched her brother's arm. "Those aren't my type of parties, but thank you."

A guy in the backseat, still in his gray cloak and looking green, pointed at her. "I'm sorry to tell you, but your man was there with a striking blue butterfly woman. We don't usually rat out our brethren, but seeing as how you're Easton's kid sister—" He let loose a belch that Lucy could smell ten feet away. "And Alex busted Rupert's nose, he's not sitting well with the group."

"Yeah," the guy in the driver's seat hollered, "but I got his Consuela!"

The remarks went downhill from there and Lucy turned Edmund toward the house. "Do you need coffee?"

"Just help me to bed." Edmund stepped on her feet and fell several times, but he eventually made it to his room.

Returning downstairs, Lucy found Eliza in the foyer looking like royalty in a purple winter suit and cape with a black fur muffler and hat.

"I knocked, but no one answered."

"I was helping Edmund to bed. He made such a racket stumbling around, I didn't hear anything."

Eliza's hand came out of her muffler and went to her chest. "He's in bed, drunk?"

"He was snoring when I shut the door."

"Oh, may I see him? I'd like to know how the muscles on his face relax when he's asleep. People take on such a different countenance while sleeping. It was marvelous dancing with him last night, but I felt slighted since I couldn't study his face or anything beyond what I touched."

"You're not supposed to touch my brother," Lucy's voice was hard.

She shoved her hand back into the fur. "I won't this time. Please, Lucy. And it has to be quick before Alex rushes in because we're taking too long. He's anxious today. He told me you might not be up to going, but you look ready. Are you?"

"Yes, I'm coming. Hurry upstairs."

Edmund—still fully clothed and snoring through his gaping mouth—caused Eliza to giggle. She tilted her head to see him from different angles and then leaned in by his ear.

"Edmund. It's your guardian angel. Can you hear me?"

Lucy covered her mouth as Edmund shifted and mumbled something that sounded like "yes."

"Did you dance with many women last night?"

"Mm-hmm."

"Did you have your way with any of them afterward?"

"Oh, yes." He stretched, half asleep, and started tugging at his buttons.

Eliza licked her lips as he opened the two at his collar. Lucy lunged for her arm, ready to pull her out of the room, but Eliza dodged and went in for another question.

"And what do you think of Eliza Melling?"

He smirked and half-laughed. "Sweet little thing."

"Eliza!" Lucy hissed as she grabbed for her.

"Eeeliiiiizzzzzahhh," Edmund breathed.

She grinned wickedly. "Do you want to kiss her?"

"I'd more than kiss her." He went again for the buttons at his chest.

Eliza giggled. "Do you need help with that?"

"Eliza, no!" Lucy snapped.

Edmund sat up and peered one-eyed at his sister standing at the foot of the bed. "Lucy?"

"Go back to sleep, Edmund." Lucy went for Eliza.

But Eliza took hold of Edmund's shoulder. "Sleep is good but you can get that kiss you wanted from Eliza first."

He squinted toward the voice and then blinked at her gleaming eyes. His hand went clumsily over her face which caused her to giggle. Lucy froze in disbelief.

"It's really me, Edmund. Shall I kiss you?"

"Yes." He grabbed her cape and wasted no time in deepening the kiss. Eliza trailed her fingers through his beard as they went at each other.

When Eliza moved like she was about to climb on the bed, Lucy pulled her back. Only then did she see where Edmund's hands were.

"For the love of all things holy! You two deserve each other!" Lucy ran into Alexander at the base of the stairs. She didn't have a chance to speak, nor did he offer anything more than a steadying hand on her forearm, because Eliza called down to her.

"Lucy, don't be mad. It was just a bit of fun and he's so drunk he won't remember anything." She adjusted her shapewear, a hand under her fitted shirtwaist, as she descended the stairs. "But Edmund sure is thorough for being half asleep. I had no idea a man could be that quick to get—" Eliza came face-to-face with her brother.

"Lucy has every right to be mad, and I the right to be furious!" Alexander's harsh stare was reflected back in Eliza's own. "Should we leave you here so he can have his way with you?"

"He's already snoring but I got what I came for—the kiss of an Easton man—along with an unexpected bonus." She smoothed her hands down her torso to make sure her wool jacket laid flat and a squeal escaped. "I feel great!"

"At least you're happy. Thanks for ruining mine and Lucy's day."

"Lucy said she was coming with us."

"Was that before or after you let her brother grope you?"

Eliza straightened her cape. "It's wasn't like that."

"It was exactly like that!" Lucy rushed to the parlor, pretending to see to the fireplace screen.

"I won't blame you if you decide to stay home today." Alexander placed a hand on her shoulder and she leaned her cheek against it.

"I think we need the day to talk." She gazed at him in the mirror over the mantel.

"That sounds wonderful, Lucy. We should have enough time to make the ferry."

***

After the frigid ride across the bay, the three scrambled into the waiting carriage at the top of the Montrose pier. Alexander gave one of the two blankets to Eliza and tucked the other around Lucy, who kept her nose to the cold glass of the bayside window, which afforded the scenery of forests with an occasional bungalow.

"I can't wait to see the enchanted red cliffs from the top. I often regarded Ecor Rouge with longing when passing it on the ferry, but I've only stopped at Point Clear. Do you think it will be too cold on the beach to ride or picnic?"

Alexander put his arm around her. "We'll do whatever you'd like, but if the wind is too strong, we'll have to skip a bonfire."

"You two can create your own fire."

Eliza's tone and eyes were playful, but a nauseous feeling overwhelmed Lucy as she realized the younger woman had as much of an intimate experience with Edmund in half a minute as Lucy had with Alexander in over a month of courtship.

"Eliza, I'd appreciate it if you keep remarks like that to yourself."

"Yes, Alex. I understand Lucy's more uptight than I originally thought."

"You're the one who started things wrong this morning."

"Fine." Eliza crossed her arms. "I'll keep to the attic or the cliffs. Maybe I'll see you at supper."

The carriage pulled onto a private drive, climbing a hill on the west side of the road.

"It's a bit drab in winter, but it's gorgeous in the spring and summer," Eliza said.

"It's lovely and makes me want to get out of the city more often."

Alexander leaned against Lucy's shoulder. "After we're married, we can come as often as you'd like. Stay for days or weeks even."

"That would be nice." Lucy rested her head against his.

"Where's your passion?" Eliza stared at them. "Don't tell me you've fallen out of love like an old married couple. A few weeks ago, you were practically licking each other's faces off. I haven't seen you kiss today at all."

"We suffered a setback last night. It's completely my fault, so don't blame Lucy."

"Did you make a grab for her in the middle of the dancefloor?"

"Hardly, Sister."

Lucy stared out the window. "Seacliff Cottage is supposed to be quaint but that's—"

"Hideous," Eliza finished for her. "Some sort of Gothic country church gone wrong is what I like to say. We can blame Grandfather Melling for it. Apparently, he didn't have an eye for beauty."

"I'd say it has character, even if it's out of place." Lucy eyed the white washed gate surrounding the pale house as though it tried to keep the forest at bay.

"You're much too kind." Alexander opened the carriage door and helped the ladies out. Eliza immediately ran for the back of the house. "She's going for the cliffs. Do you want to go now too?"

"No, let's use the privacy."

Alexander tucked her arm around his and led the way up the front walk. When they reached the front porch, the door opened and a dark man stepped to the side.

"Welcome back, Master Melling. It's a chilly day for a trip across the bay. May I take your coats?"

"Yes, it is, Watts." Alexander helped Lucy remove her red cloak and passed it and her gloves to the butler before removing his own coat, hat, and gloves. "My fiancée, Miss Easton, didn't want to wait another week to see Seacliff. Could you have coffee sent to the parlor? And if there are fixings for hot chocolate, I'm sure Eliza would enjoy that. She's run to the cliffs, but she'll be back before long."

"We read about the engagement in the paper. Congratulations to you both. I'll get Rosemary started on the drinks right away. Fires are lit in the parlor and dining room. Will you require one elsewhere?"

"No, thank you. I'll see to any others myself." Alexander brought Lucy into the darkest, reddest room she'd ever experienced. "Would you like a shot of brandy or something to help warm you while we wait for coffee?"

"No, but you take one if you'd like." She explored the room, fingering the carved furniture and looking over the photographs on the mantel. "Eliza looks positively startling in this one."

Alexander laughed. "That was her fifteenth birthday. She hated that dress with its ruffles and high collar. I think she wanted to burn a hole in the camera lens with her glare." He pulled one of the wingback chairs closer to the fire. "Will you sit with me?"

She nodded and he tugged her onto his lap, nestling her into the warm space along his side.

"You're the first lady I've brought here." He kissed her cheek. "This whole side of the bay is a clean slate for me. Us."

"Alex…" She tucked her head into the curve of his shoulder.

"Do you forgive me, my queen? I should never have abandoned you last night. There's no telling what could have happened if Freddy wasn't standing vigil. It was completely selfish of me and we owe him much for his kindness."

"He does it because he's Frederick, but I thanked him last night and this morning."

Alex trailed his fingers down her arm. "He does it because he loves you and I'm grateful for it. But it's not his behavior that needs discussing, it's mine."

"You were upset over seeing that woman. I understand."

"I was beyond furious when Rupert brought her up, but I suppose it was better that you'd heard of her before she came at me like that. You looked mortified and the embarrassment of my sins overtook me."

"It was somewhat easier having knowledge, but it still smarts to think of the women you know better than me."

"I've known no one as I know you—your soul, your dreams, your heart. What we have is eons bigger, brighter, and more significant than anything else I've had."

"That woman, Consuela, has feelings for you. You shutting her down like that pained her, and when you raised you hand…that's why she lashed out, but I did ruin—"

"You haven't ruined me, Lucy. You've brought me healing."

"Even so, being your regular probably offered her some sort of protection or status in her profession. When Edmund was dropped off by a carload of drunken Dardennes this morning, one of them boasted of having gotten *your* Consuela."

"Oh, Lucy, I'm sorry."

"That was after another had confided in me that you were there with a mystery woman in blue. They were trying to get you in trouble because they didn't like you cheating on Edmund's little sister or breaking Rupert's nose."

"I'm sure I'll get my letter of expulsion soon, and good riddance."

A smiling woman almost as dark as the butler arrived with a tray of coffee and cakes. Lucy shifted to stand. "Don't you worry, Miss Easton. We'll be as informal or formal as you please. I'm sure you're happy to have a few minutes' privacy. I'll just leave this here and be on my way, unless you'd like me to pour for you."

"No, Rosemary," Alexander said, "we're fine. Would you shut the door on your way out, though?"

"Of course."

"Allow me to fix your cup." Lucy perched on the side of the settee to ready the coffee. "What would you like in it?"

"A splash of cream." He sat beside her and placed a hand on her knee.

"Why did people not recognize me last night?"

"When people think of Lucille Easton, they think of your blonde hair. It was ingenious to cover it. You were stunning, though I prefer you with it loose." He pulled a few pins from her hair, causing tendrils to unwind in various places.

She nudged his foot with hers. "Might as well finish it off."

He pulled the last of the hairpins out, dropping them beside the serving tray. Lucy relaxed into the back of the settee as Alexander's fingers raked through her hair and massaged her scalp.

"Lucy, do you still love me?" his voice was breathy in her ear.

"Yes, Alex."

Their lips met for the first time in almost twelve hours. Hands clung to clothing and arms, seeking the familiar. They soon settled back with their own cups of coffee and a shared piece of cinnamon cake.

A quiet knock on the door reminded them they were not alone in the house.

"Come in," Alexander called. He held Lucy's legs over his lap to keep her from moving away.

Eliza smiled. "That's the old Alex and Lucy I remember. Rosemary's fixing hot chocolate for me. Is it okay to wait here so she doesn't have to bring it upstairs?"

"Just be wary of your topics of conversation."

She stuck her tongue out at Alex and grabbed a piece of cake off the tray.

"How were the cliffs?" Lucy asked.

"Absolutely freezing." Eliza plopped into the chair by the fire. "I'd wait until afternoon before venturing outside if I were you. How do you like the old house?"

"This is the only room I've been to but it has an interesting feel. It's completely different from your other house."

"Give her a tour, Alex."

"I will, when we finish." He trailed his fingers over Lucy's skirt, following the lines of her legs. "We're in no hurry."

They waited until Eliza left with her hot chocolate and then kissed more before venturing into the hall, holding hands. The dining room, half bathroom, Mr. Melling's den, and a peek into the large kitchen were shown to Lucy before they ascended the front stairs. The upstairs hall was dreary even though the gas chandeliers were lit.

"It's cold up here."

"We don't need to stay, but if you'd like, I'll light a fire." He brought her hand to his lips.

From the hall they looked into his parents' rooms, though she did not wish to step into their spaces. Then on the opposite side of the hall he showed the guest room, Eliza's room she was transitioning out of in preparation for a move to the attic, and a full bath.

"And what of the door in the middle?"

"That's my bedroom." His hand went to her face and lifted her chin, azure eyes kind but expectant. "Would you like to go in?"

Her slow smile curled at the corners of her lips. She gradually pressed her body against his before she kissed him. Alexander's arms wrapped her waist and hers encircled his neck as their measured movements flowed from chaste to tantalizing. He reached behind her to open his door and then scooped her into his arms.

Twenty-Seven

"My bride, the owner of my heart, welcome to my sanctuary." Alexander set her on the edge of a goose down comforter on his dark canopied bed. "Let me start a fire."

Lucy, mesmerized by everything within the paneled walls, inhaled his sandalwood scent that permeated the room. Alexander locked the door, hung his suit jacket on the coat stand, and knelt before the fireplace. The curve of his back leaning into the hearth as he set the logs beckoned to be touched. It took all her self-control to stay on his bed. The glow of the fire turned Alexander's hair and complexion a warm gold, infusing him with the luster of life.

He shut the curtains and returned to Lucy with a smile. "Do you want to sit by the fire to warm up?"

"No, I just need you, my angel." Her hands followed his waist until her arms were wrapped around him. She rested her face against the front of his shirt and breathed him in.

Alexander's hands shifted through her hair. "I need you as much as I need air to live. May I hold you in my bed, Lucy?"

"I wish you would."

He stepped to the side and brought one of her legs up to remove her boot. "Anything that comes off you today, I want to be the one to do it."

She blushed at his touch but smiled. "Then take the stockings too, please."

"With pleasure, my queen."

Lucy sighed with contentment over Alexander's hands on her bare skin as he removed her thick winter stockings. He had to reach above her knees to get at them, but he did nothing more.

"Anything else?" he asked.

"Not until the room warms."

Alexander shed his cravat, belt, shoes, and socks and climbed beside her on the high bed. She immediately stood.

"What is it?"

"It's your bed. I want to see how you relax, then I'll decide how best to fit with you."

"I don't go to bed with this many clothes on, but I usually spread out in the middle. I'm afraid it's not very accommodating."

"Will you show me? I want to know everything about you."

"You want me to disrobe?" His hand went to her cheek. "I'll gladly do anything for you, Lucy, I just want to make sure you understand where this is leading."

"It's leading us closer to being man and wife. When will it happen? Is there someone we could go to over here who would marry us today?"

"I won't rob your family of seeing you down the aisle. We'll talk to Father Quinn tomorrow and see what date we can have a wedding at the cathedral, even if it isn't Saint Valentine's Day."

"And your parents?"

"They don't have to come if they don't want to. I started looking at rentals and there's a charming duplex that's available on the first. I'll put a deposit on it Monday and it will be ours by next weekend."

She fell on top of him. "Oh, Alex! I was worried about everything after how you were yesterday. You said that article gave you things to consider and I worried you might decide to wait until summer like your parents want."

"There's no question of my love for you, or yours for me. I won't deny you for months just to appease the ones who have wounded you with their words." His hands went up her back, pressing her fully to him.

As their kiss deepened, Lucy shifted her legs to straddle him. The new position excited her instincts and she moved against his length. Alexander seemed to lose himself in pleasure for several seconds before holding her to his chest to still her movements.

"Lucy, we're crossing a line I don't think we're ready for."

"My body's been priming for this since you first kissed me." She opened the top buttons on his shirt and kissed his neck.

"Remember what I told you in the carriage that night?" His hands held her face so she'd look him in the eyes. "We have weeks, maybe even days to wait. We'll know as soon as tomorrow, Lucy. I don't want to lose you over a moment of impatience."

"I wear your ring and we've pledged our love to each other. In my mind, we're already united. It's just a matter of formalities."

"But what of God's? We can't be one in His eyes until we're joined in Holy Matrimony."

"Then why did you bring me here? Why are we in this house—in your bed—if not to consummate our relationship?"

"Part of me wants to, desperately." Alexander kissed her. "But more than that, I just want to hold you without interruption or fear of being caught. I wanted a relaxed day with no societal restrictions."

"Alex, I'm yours."

He ran his fingers over the hair falling around her face. "And it means the world to me. But allow me to share with you what you asked of me for the time being—how I go to bed."

Her smile made the heartache of the last day vanish. Alexander clung to her and rolled them over, taking the dominate position.

"It feels good, doesn't it?" she whispered. "The one you love pressing against the sensitive areas of the body."

He fell upon her figure with wanton passion. Just as she was about to cry out for relief, he stood, offering his hand to help her up. Standing nose to nose, he tilted to the side to kiss the corner of her lips. "Sorry, my queen. I won't be like that when the time comes."

She wrapped her arms around his waist. "You'll be gentle with me?"

His hands roamed the green wool of her skirt over her hips as though he had all weekend to get to know that one area of her body. "Lucy, I'll be so slow and gentle you'll beg for more."

In a show of how soft his touch could be, Alexander kissed both of her eyelids before letting go. He started undoing his shirt but Lucy reached out to help.

"Don't I have the same privilege as you when it comes to undressing?"

He gave her a mischievous smile. "Are you claiming it now?"

"Most definitely." Her hands boldly opened the remaining buttons on his shirt and pulled at his sleeve.

"Cufflinks." He rotated his arm and she unhooked the oval fasteners with his initials engraved on them. "I keep a dish on my dresser to hold them when I take them off."

Lucy removed both and tucked them into the safe spot before removing his shirt. After hanging it by his jacket, she ran her cool hands over his chest and down his torso.

"I'm not a disappointment, too weak for your liking?"

"You're perfect, Alex. You have strength enough to sweep me off my feet and that's all that matters." She leaned against his shoulder, marveling over the feel of his hot skin against her cheek and the fact that his scent was even stronger on his body than his clothes.

He kissed her temple as she continued to nestle against him. "This is what I wanted today. You and me and the quiet of togetherness."

"You must be getting cold," she whispered. She brought her hands to the top button on his waistband and straightened. Holding his smoldering gaze, she blushed as her fingers touched the soft area below his bellybutton. "I don't know if I can do it, Alex."

"You don't have to do anything you're not ready for." He trailed his hands down her arms. "I can easily get in bed like this."

"I want you to be comfortable." She faced the bed to give him privacy and turned down the covers to keep her hands busy in her nervousness.

Lucy had often seen her brothers about in their underdrawers while growing up, making the sight of Alexander in his not as shocking as the act of removing his pants. He jumped onto the bed and collapsed on his back with arms and legs stretched wide on the expanse of white sheets.

"I start like this, but usually end up curled up on my side. What about you?"

"I've never had a bed this big, but I usually sleep on my side too." Lucy pulled the covers over him and then snuggled atop the comforter in the space along his left side, resting her head in the crook of his arm that enfolded her.

"I love you, and I love loving you." Alexander kissed her forehead. "Thank you for forgiving me and coming here today."

"I can't imagine not forgiving you. You're my angel, the very breath of me."

***

Lucy, certain she'd closed her eyes for only a moment, found Alexander looking down at her with a loving smile. He wore his trousers and his shirt was on, though not buttoned.

"There you are, my sleeping beauty." Alexander caressed her cheek and kissed her lips.

"Did I really sleep? I hope I didn't snore. I must be a mess." She sat up and ran her hand over her tousled hair.

"Only for an hour. You didn't snore, though you sighed contentedly many times. As for your appearance, you look good enough to eat." His nibbled the tender place below her right ear until she shied away from the intense sensation. He took her hands and helped her out of bed. "It's still below freezing outside so I decided to bring our picnic here."

Before the blazing fire he'd spread a red blanket over the Oriental rug. A bottle of wine, two glasses and plates, plus a basket overflowing with food sat in the middle of it.

"You shouldn't have gone through all this trouble for me."

"You're worth every effort, but Rosemary prepared it all, I merely brought it here. And before you ask, I left food for Eliza in the dining room so she won't starve."

"And what must the help think with us squirrelled away all day?" She stepped toward the hearth.

"I told you before, they're as loyal as anything. When I collected the food, Rosemary told me you had a radiant smile and she's glad to see me settling with a nice girl." He winked at her. "After you wash up, we'll lock ourselves back in."

Lucy returned from the bathroom and found Eliza perched on the footboard. "Looks like the bed's been used, though you lack that glow I've heard about."

"Where's Alex?"

"He forgot napkins. I suppose that means he doesn't wish to lick your fingers." Eliza sauntered toward her. "Has he worn out his tongue in other locations?"

"I don't even know how to respond to that."

"You shouldn't." Alexander marched into the room. "Eliza, you need to leave. Now. Your luncheon is in the dining room and I made sure there's plenty of dessert to satisfy your cravings."

"I find myself craving more sultry than sweet since my encounter this morning."

"Then have Campbell drive you into town and find yourself a local boy to torment." Alexander's glare matched his sister's and he crushed the napkins in his fist.

"I need a man not a boy. And anyway, most of the locals will be hidden away by their fires in this weather. I suppose I'm resigned to painting for the afternoon." She sighed as she left the room.

"Sorry about that." Alexander locked the door. "She doesn't realize how vulgar she sounds when she talks that way. Here, come sit by the fire."

The space before the hearth felt more summer than winter. After pouring the wine, Alexander seemed to notice Lucy inching away from the hearth.

"I got carried away with the tinder. It'll burn down eventually."

Grateful she'd worn her best underclothes, she stood. "It's too hot in this wool suit. You'll need to remove it for me."

His face was a mix of euphoria and distress as he came to her side. "You're—"

"Certain. Yes. I'm suffocating in this even with my stockings off. I wore my heaviest suit because I thought we'd be outside a lot with the ferry and beach."

"We'll have to come back another time to enjoy the outdoors." Alexander's hands paused at the first button of her wool top. "Tell me if you change your mind."

When his hands came to the button directly on the peak of her bosom, Lucy took a heaving breath, startling him. She broke into laughter and Alexander took her into his arms.

"You're such a joy in my life," he said as he returned to freeing her from the heavy clothes. When he unbuttoned it, she turned her back to him so he could slip it off her arms.

She glanced over her shoulder and caught him studying her. "The button for the skirt is back there. Might as well undo it before I turn around."

A quake in Alexander's hand as he slid the button through the hole forever endeared his efforts to Lucy. When he lowered the skirt to her knee level she stepped out of it and smoothed her petticoat before turning to him.

"You're perfect and innocent." He ran his finger along the ruffle of her cream-colored chemise. "Would you like the corset off too?"

"Yes, please, but it can be tricky."

He took her in his arms and buried his face in the veil of hair hanging over her shoulder. Just when she thought he was about to turn away, his hands moved deftly over the laces. Seconds later, he had the corset loose enough to remove. She tried not to imagine how many times he'd undressed a woman. As soon as it was off, Lucy plopped to the floor cross-legged, her petticoat a poof of layers around her lap. She brought her glass to her lips and set it back half-empty.

"Thank you, Alex. It's better already."

He sat in front of her and stroked her cheek before leaning in for a lingering kiss. "I'm blessed to have you in my life to show me the wonders of pure love."

"And I you." She took a handful of grapes from the basket and ate one. "May I ask you something?"

"Of course." He laid a slice of cheese atop a piece of bread.

"Why do you seem nervous at times? I've felt a tremor in your touch, like you're not sure how to do something when I know that can't be the case."

He took his time chewing as though delaying his response. Then he took a sip of wine from his glass and swallowed hard. "I told you last night my history and weeks ago I told you we'd share many firsts in our relationship, though I come to you with more experience than I'm proud of."

"Yes, and I love that you point out things like you do. It helps me understand you better." She popped another grape into her mouth.

He laughed. "In that case, this is my first courtship picnic—inside or out."

"Mine too." She grinned at him in return.

Alexander leaned in for another kiss and then rested his forehead against hers. "Lucy, you're my first virgin. I'm in uncharted territory and it feels like the first time for me too. That's why I told you I'd be slow and gentle—I'm afraid of hurting you."

"Don't be scared on my account. I know what's coming. Remember my poems?"

"How can I forget?" He wrapped his arms around her and pulled her into his lap.

> "'White and pure
> Until you touched me with your soul
> Now I'm pink with desire
> Cravings for you flooding

As I wait for the red your touch will bring.'

"Lucy, that first intimate touch can be painful, but you expressed it eloquently. Your mind is beautiful, your soul enchanting."

She flushed at his words. "You memorized it?"

"I couldn't help but to with all the times I read your treasured words. They're etched in my heart, all of them." He kissed her firmly on the mouth. "Your gift is amazing. I know you've been busy typing your manuscript, but don't neglect new words for the sake of the old."

"You want another poem?"

"Yes, Lucy. Whenever you find the time, the inspiration."

"Inspire me now, my angel," she said as she fingered down his chest. "Let's explore everything."

The fire in the hearth burned cooler, but the flame inside Alexander's eyes never looked brighter. He raised her from their picnic and carried her to his bed.

***

Lucy stared up at the mahogany canopy and fought back the emptiness that threatened to overpower her if she speculated on the significance of what she'd done. Alexander's head rested on her breast. His breath, deep and even, warmed her skin. If she focused on the absolute nakedness of them in the bed—of the feel of his leg over hers, his relaxed arm draped low across her hips—she'd go mad. But if she relived the passion, the melancholy couldn't take her. The act itself was a trickster because guilt and remorse couldn't simultaneously exist with fervor and desire. She closed her eyes and remembered the sensations from the moment Alexander laid her on his bed. Words flooded her mind. She itched to allow them to flow through her hands, to record them on paper to share with him.

"Alex, are you awake?" She fingered through his hair and his hand on her hip grasped it in a pleasing way. "I need paper, Alex. I have a poem for you."

He clung to her. "Your body is poetry."

"I don't want to lose the moment. I need paper and pen. Tell me where and I'll go."

Alexander pulled on his trousers and rushed out the door. Lucy curled onto her side, pulling the goose down blanket up to her chin in an attempt to hide her vulnerable self.

Half a minute later, Eliza peeked in. "Lucy, are you okay? I heard Alex run downstairs like there was an emergency."

"I'm fine, I just need to write."

Eliza stepped in and surveyed the situation with a smile. "Oh, did you—how was it?"

"Not now, Eliza, please." Lucy didn't like the whining quality in her voice showcasing her fears.

"Just tell me and I'll slip away."

A tear rolled down her cheek. "It was glorious in the moment."

The door clicked shut and Lucy wiped the wetness off her face, hoping Alexander wouldn't notice when he returned. She closed her eyes and called forth the image of his clear eyes marveling over each curve of her body, how he revered her very being as he sought to please her.

Alexander burst through the door. "I'm sorry, Lucy. I should have planned ahead to have supplies at your disposal. I'll be sure to bring a stationery set next time so it will be here for you in our room."

Our room.

She sat up, her hair cascading over her shoulders, and crossed her legs beneath the blankets.

"I grabbed a book for you to use as a desk. May I watch you work?"

"Yes." Lucy smiled at him and settled into position with the book on her lap. She adjusted the papers he must have raided his father's den to retrieve. The pages had an embossed M at the top but were otherwise plain. The gold fountain pen flowed smooth across the page as she wrote the title in practice of holding the new instrument.

Forever

Lucy closed her eyes, tapping into the thoughts that swirled in her head just minutes before. Between the interruptions of asking Alexander for help and sending Eliza away, she knew she'd lost some of it, but what was left poured through the borrowed pen as she relived her time of passion.

We became man and wife by our actions
Before anyone could turn us away

You recited poetry
My words on your lips seduced me
As they had seduced you on paper
The sweat and sounds we created together
Salty and sweet awash in my mouth
Your hands over my skin
Mine on yours
Your scent all around me
In me
Your impassioned words as I cried out
You showed me much
But there is more to learn
Know that I'm forever yours
And I'll need this again soon

Alex cautiously moved her writing things to the side table and lowered her onto the pillows. "Lucy, my queen. Do you wish for more learning?"

Anxious to hold to what appeared to be the good, she ran her hands down his chest and shamelessly unfastened the button on his pants. "Show me more, my angel."

***

Lucy reclined in a warm bath Alexander had drawn for her, exhaustion setting in. It was ten minutes after four. They were expected in the dining room at five to allow time to eat supper before returning to the ferry, but Lucy wasn't in the disposition to hurry.

Alexander slipped into the room wearing only his pants, all her clothes in his arms. He laid them carefully across the wicker chair in the corner before kneeling beside the paneled tub and taking her hand.

"Are you sure you're okay?"

When she nodded, the messy bun her hair was knotted into slid down her neck. "I'm just a little sore in my thighs."

"Your body will get used to the new positions and build muscle in those areas." He kissed her damp cheek. "I didn't want to hurt you."

"You didn't, Alex. You were loving and gentle."

He brought her hand to his lips and with fear in his eyes, kissed her knuckles. "I noticed a little blood on the sheets."

Lucy paled. The discomfort—though brief—still burned fresh in her mind. "Then the maid and everyone—"

"There will be no problem with that. I've messed my sheets with nose bleeds a dozen times over the years. It's only a few spots, think nothing of it. I'm only concerned for you."

But it was all she could think of—the overwhelming flood of physical, mental, and emotional sensations being known to everyone that looked upon her. Her sacred virginity, gone. The option of wearing a white mantilla to church no longer there. Being able to think herself a worthier partner than all the other women Alexander had been with, evaporated.

I'm no better than any of them.

The darkness spread within, but she tried for a brave face. "I'm alive and well, a new woman, though no longer a proper young lady." She bit her lip to keep it from trembling and pulled the plug from the drain. "Do you still love me?"

"More than ever, my queen." He retrieved a thick gold towel and wrapped it around her before lifting her out of the tub. She stretched her arms around his neck and laid her head on his bare shoulder.

"I do believe you're spoiling me, Alexander Melling."

"Pampering, honoring, and loving you. Never spoiling, Lucille Amelia Easton."

He set her near the pile of clothes and lifted her chin for a slow, probing kiss that rekindled desires within her. It replaced the darkness with a flame and she clung to it. Caressing down his back, she heaved against him, the towel falling to her feet. For a minute, his hands roamed her body uninhibited, and then he brought her back into a simple embrace before kissing her forehead.

"It's time to dress. Would you like help?"

"No, thank you. I'll be out in a few minutes." She locked the door behind him and cried.

Twenty-Eight

Eliza's nosy questions throughout dinner and their trip across the bay were incessant. Seeming to understand Lucy's need for a respite, Alexander didn't question his fiancée when she climbed into the backseat of his automobile at the docks.

"Sit with me, Eliza," he said.

"But Lucy should." Eliza adjusted her cape.

He took her elbow and forced his sister into the front passenger seat. "Our time is drawing to a close. You won't see as much of me once I'm married."

Eliza laughed and turned to Lucy. "Thank you for taking my brother off my hands. I'll have quite a bit more freedom without him around, though I'll miss his parade of friends at the house, especially the youngest Mr. Easton."

"Will you shut up about him already?" Alexander's voice grated. "You're to leave him alone, now more than ever after that stunt you pulled this morning."

Eliza brought the fur muffler to her face and rubbed it across her nose. "Trust me, he won't remember a thing."

"What makes you sure?"

She smiled in her cheeky way. "I may have tried it on some of your friends before."

"Eliza, save yourself the trouble I've gone through and settle down quickly."

Lucy was grateful for the drive home. The freezing temperatures meant there were no pedestrians out for pleasure strolls to stare at her, the dark hid her shame, and the quiet left her alone with her thoughts. She huddled under her red cloak and imagined all would be well once at her house, but it only became more tangled.

Frederick's automobile was parked in front and the lights in the parlor were on.

Alexander groaned and turned to Eliza. "I'm counting on you to hold your tongue and keep your promises in regards to me and Lucy."

"I will, just let me in there a moment to glory at the sight of those fine men."

"Whatever you do, don't flirt with Frederick." Lucy's voice came out sharper than expected. The siblings in the front turned to her. "He's not like Edmund and would be most flustered. He's done much to help me. I'd like to return the favor when I can."

"Fair enough." Eliza jumped out of the automobile and dashed to the house.

"God help us all," Alexander muttered.

Edmund and Frederick were on the porch with Eliza when Alexander escorted Lucy there.

"What did you do with my sister?" He stared at Alexander.

"I told him we took her across the bay," Eliza said.

"So we did." Alexander stood before Edmund. "We took the public ferry over to Montrose. We spent the day at Seacliff Cottage, our property on Ecor Rouge, attended by a husband and wife that are the butler and cook at the residence. Since it was freezing, we had to abandon plans of the beach and riding, but we managed to have a pleasant time out of the city and had an indoor picnic before the fire."

Lucy tried to keep a serene smile on her face but buckled under the weight of Frederick's gaze—which she refused to meet.

"Why didn't you tell me?" Edmund asked her.

She gave an honest laugh. "Would you have remembered if I had? You were cockeyed when you rolled in at eight this morning—the whole stinking carful of you wretched Dardennes were! I had to scrape you off the lawn and practically carry you to bed all while those men were telling stories not fit for a lady's ear."

Frederick took a small step forward. "Why didn't you mention the trip to me last night?"

"Because after the events at the masquerade, I didn't know if it would happen." She saw the understanding in his brown eyes and flushed.

"When I called to check on you midday, no one answered. I tried again with the same results at three. I drove over and had to sober Eddie up to try to get information, but he remembered nothing. Then an unmarked letter was delivered for you." Frederick turned to Edmund.

"We were worried," her brother said, "and I thought there might be information about where you were. I opened it."

"You had no right!"

"I know, and I'm sorry." Edmund appeared sheepish. "It was from Kate Stuart, telling you A.R.M.'s mad-dash from the masquerade last night and you being escorted out by F.L.D. was acceptable as your scandal. All you need is one more handkerchief and you'll be on your way to Wragg Swamp and a permanent position at *Snitch*."

Lucy's tense body went slack and Alexander set her in the nearest rocking chair. "I'm done with her! But how did she know it was you running out?"

Alexander raked his hand over his face with a groan. "I couldn't see straight and pulled the mask off in the lobby. Someone must have seen me. I'm sorry for the whole miserable night, Lucy. But we should be married by the time the next edition is out and all this won't matter."

Edmund shook his head. "She'll spin it that Alex caught you with Freddy and ran out with a broken heart or something."

"I'll never be rid of my shame." Her words spoke of more than Kate Stuart's gossip.

"Lucy, my queen." Alexander leaned down and lifted her chin. "Everyone who matters knows the truth."

The silence was uneasy, but no one contradicted Alexander.

"Why are we still standing out here?" Eliza poked Edmund in the stomach with her muffler. "It's freezing and I could use a drink to warm me."

The hint of a smile tugged at the corner of his mouth and he raised his eyebrows at her. "We aren't supposed to entertain this weekend."

"But you already had Frederick inside." Lucy rubbed her arms under her cloak. "We might as well all go in and suffer the consequences if word gets back to Father."

"Agreed." Edmund held the door for Eliza to pass through.

"You could have left me a note," Edmund said as Lucy entered.

"I suppose I could have, but your drunken state put me behind schedule and I didn't think of it."

Alexander helped Lucy remove her outerwear. After he discarded his own things, he stood directly behind her and wrapped his arms around her waist and rested his chin on her shoulder. Pressing behind her, his warm breath on her cheek, Lucy felt him to her soul. She leaned her head against his and tried to keep her heart from beating out of her chest as yearning for more coursed through her veins.

Eliza—fur muffler dangling from one hand—continued to wait for Edmund to offer his help. But he appeared mesmerized by the glow of her violet-blue eyes under the gaslight.

Frederick stepped around Alexander and Lucy with a jabbing look that cleared Lucy's lust-filled mind, and stopped in front of Eliza. "May I help you with your things, Miss Melling?"

Eliza smiled like her face would melt from sweetness. "Why thank you, Mr. Davenport."

He laid her muffler and hat on the bench while Edmund stared on like a simpleton. When Frederick reached to remove her cape, Edmund stuck his arm between them.

"No, allow me." He used the time before her to stare at her full lips as he fumbled with her cape. After hanging it, he offered her his arm to lead her into the parlor. "We danced together last night, didn't we?"

"Yes, Edmund, we surely did." Giddiness dripped from her voice like rain off a magnolia.

Frederick, as though he sensed the electricity between the young woman and his friend, followed close behind, leaving Alexander and Lucy alone.

"I think Eliza's a lost cause, but I feel better knowing Freddy is privy to her schemes. He seems able to read people's intentions like a book." Alexander pressed against her back as he nuzzled her ear. "Did you see that cutting look he gave us?"

"Yes, he's always known me better than I know myself." Lucy needed to distance herself from Alexander, but knowing where the physical sensations led left her body craving to experience them again.

She brought him into the dining room. Alexander pulled Lucy against him and encouraged her arousal while they tasted each other's mouths. She went under his suit jacket and untucked his shirt to get at his middle.

He pressed her against the wall and stroked her cheek. "We can't do this here."

"But I need you. My body aches for you like nothing I ever thought possible." She slid her cold hands up his back, savoring his hot skin as he shivered at her touch.

"Your brother and Freddy are across the hall. They'd kill me, Lucy. You know they would." But even as he said the words his hands roamed down her.

"When can we? I feel myself splintering and fear I'll never be whole without you."

He kissed her lips and rested a hand on her cheek. "First, let's get through Mass and choosing our wedding day. I'll make arrangements if we have to wait long, all right?"

Lucy nodded and tried to absorb the tears welling in her eyes but one slipped out, striking Alexander's palm.

"Lucy…" He spun her to the doorway and studied her in the light. "God forgive me, you're devastated."

When she didn't respond, he kissed her. "Things are different now," he whispered fiercely, "but we'll be joined in matrimony soon and this confusion will be gone."

"Will it?" Her voice cracked.

"Of course." He cupped her face in his hands and wiped her cheeks dry with his thumbs. His eyes shone like sapphires as he focused on her wellbeing. "You're not a ruined woman to be cast aside, you're my bride. What you gave me—what we shared—no one can steal that from us. I'm yours and you're mine. Forever, like you wrote in your poem."

Alexander's smile warmed her soul. They straightened their clothing and Lucy fixed tea, bringing it to the parlor. Edmund, already at the bottle, added brandy to his tea. Eliza giggled and joked in such a tipsy way Lucy feared she would spill the details of their time at Seacliff Cottage. Alexander seemed to worry over the same thing. He forced his sister to drink her tea black then hurried her home.

Frederick motioned to Edmund dosing in the armchair. "Would you like me to help him upstairs before I leave, Lucy?"

"Yes, please. I don't know if I can handle the stress tonight."

"You had a long day." Frederick rested a hand on her knee. "I hope there was more joy than pain for you in these past twenty-four hours."

"It's been a mixed bag, that's for certain, but Alex and I are reconciled. It was good to be away from everyone. Eliza was a bit of a handful, but I'm used to demanding little sisters."

Frederick's laughter brought Edmund back to conscious, but he appeared green.

"Ready to sleep off your drinks, Eddie?"

He held his head. "Why didn't you stop me?"

"I tried," Frederick said, "but it seems like you preferred showing off for Eliza Melling."

A toothy grin split his previously haggard face. "She's a perky little thing."

He reached for his glass but it was empty. Lucy moved down the settee to pour the rest of the tea into his cup and passed it to him. "Your poor body needs a break after last night and then your stint this evening."

"No drinks tomorrow!" He raised a finger to punctuate his declaration but left it there as a forgotten thought. "I think I dreamed about Eliza this morning. Those brilliant eyes and succulent lips. I can almost feel the memory of kissing her."

"You're hammered." Frederick stood. "Let me help you to bed, old friend."

Lucy brought all the dishes to the sink while Frederick helped her brother upstairs. She turned off the lights in the kitchen and Frederick met her in the hallway. Lifting a hand to her shoulder, he gazed down at her with kind eyes.

"You look weary. Is there anything I can do, anything you need to talk about?"

"No, I'll be better tomorrow."

"Let me know if there's anything I can ever do for you."

She lifted his hand off her shoulder and kissed his knuckles. "Thank you, Freddy."

He grabbed his coat and gloves from the foyer and pulled them on while rushing onto the porch. "Lock the door behind me," he called over his shoulder.

Lucy wrestled with sleep until after four in the morning, causing her to regret the plans to attend early Mass with Alexander. He arranged to pick her up at a quarter to six so they would have a better chance of speaking to Father Quinn between the less populated early services. At half-past four she resigned herself to sleeplessness. Upon standing, an aching warmth spread between her legs. Scared she'd injured something with her actions the previous day, she carefully cleaned herself in the shower. She wept in relief as the water ran over her when she realized it was her monthly cycle, not damage from Alexander.

Wearing her red Christmas dress, Lucy sat at her vanity brushing her hair. Since she would need to wear a hat to Mass, she simply braided her hair from the nape of her neck. After a piece of toast and coffee, she added her mother's black velvet cape and hat set to her ensemble, followed by her white lace gloves. She waited on the porch, hoping the cold would bring rosiness to her pale cheeks.

When Alexander pulled in, he rushed over to admonish her. "How many times do I need to remind you that you're not to wait around for me, Lucy?" He removed a hand from his driving glove and touched her face. "My frozen queen, let me warm you."

His mouth was hot and he wrapped his arms around her underneath the cloak. Lucy relaxed into his embrace and sighed. "It was a long night."

"You could come home with me after my family leaves for church." He fingered the lace overlay across her chest and kissed her.

Lucy's hands took his. "Not today, Alex."

An impish smile played across his lips. "Are you a good girl, not wanting to do such actions on the Sabbath?"

"It would make for a lovely Sunday afternoon in my opinion, but I have my monthly."

He leaned away, blue eyes wide. "Last night?"

"Hours ago. I'll be fine in a few days."

Alexander pressed their hands to her lower abdomen. "Last night while lying in bed, I wondered if what we shared would grow into something more. At first the thought terrified me, but then the idea of you and me creating a baby together took my breath away."

His kiss was tender, matching his stirring words and gentle touch.

"It's bound to happen sooner or later," she whispered, "but we must be careful. The child would be part you, so the potential for spoiling will be almost certain."

Alexander glowed with joy as he laughed.

Twenty-Nine

The cathedral that cold morning had parishioners in only a fifth of the pews. Lucy and Alexander sat by themselves near the front. After Mass, they greeted Father Quinn near the doors. Alexander wasted no time in explaining to him their desire to marry within the next few weeks.

"And her parents approve?" the priest asked.

Lucy smiled, grateful he'd not asked about Alexander's parents. "My mother ran our engagement announcement in the paper last week."

"Our preferred day is Saint Valentine's, but as it is short notice, we'll go with another date if needed, preferably sooner."

Father Quinn took his hand to shake it. "I understand, Alexander. I'll speak with the bishop and we'll see what we can work out. In the meantime, you both can prepare for the sacrament of matrimony by attending Mass often and be sure to come to confession Friday afternoon."

"Thank you, Father." Alexander grinned at Lucy.

When the priest took her hand, she forced herself to meet his eye. "Is there a reason you did not come forward for communion today, Miss Easton?"

"Have you ever had a day you didn't feel worthy?" she countered.

"Yes, many times. That's why frequent confession is good for the soul. I cannot recall the last time I have seen you here for confession. Come this week. You need to make sure you are well with God before your marriage."

"Yes, Father."

Once they were around the corner at Alexander's automobile, he took Lucy into his arms. "You're weighted down by our actions, aren't you?"

She studied the massive profile of the cathedral as she determined the right way to express her feelings. "It was beautiful, but after…I'm changed and I don't know if it's for the better."

Alexander looked up and down the empty street then kissed her on the lips. "Do you want to make a full confession or perhaps not have a cathedral wedding? Whatever you decide, I'll stand by. Just tell me before we hear back from Father Quinn so we both relay the same message."

"Allow me to think on it for the day."

"Of course." His hand went to her cheek, his gaze intense. "You asked me to seek marriage yesterday and I denied you on the grounds of robbing your family of seeing you wed. Ask me today and I'll run away with you. As you've said, we're already committed to each other. It's only a formality."

Alexander helped her into the passenger seat to drive her home. On the Eastons' front porch, she didn't want to say goodbye.

"Sit with me on the swing?" she asked.

"Of course, my queen."

Lucy had him sit first and then curled on her side next to him, placing her velvet hat on his legs to use as a pillow. Alexander smoothed her dress and cape to cover her limbs before resting his arm on her.

"Will you be upset if I fall asleep?" she asked.

"Only if you drool on my leg."

"Alex!" She squeezed his knee and he laughed. "Are you warm enough? Do you need anything?"

"I have the most beautiful woman I've ever seen in my lap, what more could I want?"

"A fire and brandy."

"You know me well, but I assure you I'm pleased for the time being."

Lucy dozed until Edmund came out the door a few minutes after ten. "Don't tell me you've been like that all night."

She kept her eyes closed.

"No," Alexander said, "just the last two hours. We went to the first Mass, remember? You gave us permission last night."

"The only thing I remember about last night is your sister and a lot of alcohol."

"I believe I'd be validated if I punched you for that remark."

Edmund laughed but then his face turned hard. "You need to get out of here. I'm not stupid enough to leave you alone with Lucy, even if you're outside. I'm off to see if Mary Margaret will speak to me after that wretched article in *Snitch*."

"Good luck, Eddie."

Lucy sat up and uncurled her legs. "I am sorry, Edmund."

"One of those things." He shrugged. "But I suppose it's only fair after all the men I've chased away from you. The thing is, I really like her. But now I can't get Eliza out of my head."

Alexander stood. "You'd be a terrible match and my parents would never approve. Step closer if you want a beating to go with it."

"I'm besotted, smitten by her shapely form and dancing skills. Is that what happened to you, Lucy?"

"Oh yes." She wrapped her arms about Alexander's waist. "It was his shapely form."

Alexander laughed but Edmund frowned.

"You know what I mean."

"Yes, I do, and it's much more. That part is there, but there's an understanding at a deeper level. Our connection goes to our very souls."

"Disconnect them physically for the next two hours. I need to catch my girl."

***

Monday afternoon, Lucy's parents and Opal were back from their weekend in Grand Bay.

"How was your visit?" Lucy asked as she hugged her mother.

"Very good. Susan is miserable with fatigue, but Opal and I were able to help out with the children, so she rested most of the time. Opal did a great job with her niece and nephews this time around. Perhaps I was too hasty in sending her after Christmas." Mrs. Easton peered across the room to her youngest, who sat at the piano, staring at the keys. "I believe she made amends with the family over her previous actions."

"That's wonderful." Lucy glanced at her sister uncomfortably then turned back to her mother with a bright smile.

"And what of you, Lucy? You have a glow like all is right with the world."

"I met Alex at the Cathedral and we ate breakfast together before he went to work. Father Quinn wants us at Mass as often as possible until we take our vows, to prepare ourselves for the sacrament of matrimony."

Opal pivoted on the piano bench and stared at Lucy with her cutting, emerald eyes. "That's because he knows how sinful you are!"

"Good heavens, Opal! That's no way to talk to your sister. Go to your room at once!" Seeing Lucy's trembling hands, Mrs. Easton took them into her own. "You know how she is."

She stomped back into the room. "How am I, Mother? An angry child not fit for friends or relations?"

Lucy went toward her little sister. "That's enough from you!"

"So says the sinner." Opal shoved Lucy, causing her to stumble against the chair.

"To your room, young lady!" Mrs. Easton pointed the way, and then sighed warily. "Think nothing of it, Lucy. Let's talk of pleasant things. When is your wedding to be?"

"We were just told this morning we're on schedule for the afternoon of the fourteenth."

Mrs. Easton kissed her cheek. "Dear Alex got his choice day, and two weeks is plenty of time. We'll need to get it printed in the paper and see to your dress."

"I already know what dress I want to use, though it might need to be altered for me. It's in the attic."

"Lucy, we can buy you a new one."

"I'd like to try it first. Let me get it."

When she came down in one of her mother's old Christmas dresses, Mrs. Easton was momentarily speechless. Then she dropped her hand to her chest. "Lucille Amelia Easton, under no circumstances is that appropriate!"

Her shout brought Mr. Easton and Opal into the parlor. "Talk some sense into your daughter, James! She'll look like a jezebel if she wears that to her wedding."

"She's fully covered and red is the traditional wedding color," Mr. Easton remarked. "I remember how pretty you looked in that dress…was it eighteen ninety or ninety-one?"

"We're not living in the middle ages, so red is no longer suitable!" Having gotten her frustration out of her system, Mrs. Easton calmed and pulled at the loose waist. "But yes, it was Christmas of ninety-one. Aaron was the youngest that year, God rest his soul. And you, Lucy, are positively swimming in it! What are you thinking picking a dress I wore after birthing eight children?"

"The silk and lace have held up wonderfully." Lucy ran her hand down a sleeve to the four-inch ivory lace detail at the cuffs. "And the arms are perfectly fine. It's only the waist and bust that need adjusting. This is the dress you wore when I remember Christmas for the first time. Alex and I fell in love at his Christmas party, the wedding is Saint Valentine's Day, and red is the color of love, besides what Father said about it being the traditional color of marriage within the church."

"Lucy, you put too much symbolism into this. It isn't a story—"

"But it is, Mother! This is my love story, the most important one I'll ever write."

Mr. Easton put an arm around his wife. "There's no harm, dear. It's Lucy's special day and if she wishes to wear a family dress, I see no problem. The women around town will find something to cluck about no matter what. You only need to concern yourself with calling the seamstress for an appointment for this beautiful dress to be altered. And finding a veil. A red one would look pretty against her hair."

"You two have no idea of the scandal you'll cause!" Mrs. Easton rushed from the room.

Mr. Easton paused to kiss Lucy's cheek. "It's your day, hold your ground."

With their parents gone, Opal circled her sister. "I hope you're happy about dragging this family through more gossip."

Lucy straightened the row of ivory lace on the skirt. "Half of what's said isn't my fault."

"But the other half is." Opal's eyes narrowed. "Even though you're Father's favorite, he knows he's spent too much money on dresses for you lately. He's willing to let you get married looking like a harlot."

Thirty

The best thing for Lucy during the next few days was seeing Alexander for morning Mass. She found him waiting for her at the front gate to kiss her on the cheek and escort her inside. The rest of the day, Lucy spent her hours typing. She made a point to sit with the family for meals and for an hour or more in the evenings, but otherwise she worked at typing *Azalea Blossom* and carrying her guilt like a knapsack.

"Is everything coming along well?" Alexander asked her on Wednesday morning as they left Mass.

"Yes, I have nearly seven chapters typed. I'm getting better each day."

He laughed and brought them between two columns on the portico. "That's great to hear, but I was referring to our wedding plans."

"Oh, sorry." Lucy blushed. "My dress, which Mother hopes I change my mind about, is with the seamstress for alterations and the wedding date will be posted in tomorrow's social column. Mother asks me every time we're at the dining table about flowers, what to serve at the open house afterward, and whatnot. I tell her what I like and she writes it down."

"Lucy, don't you want to be involved?"

"Mother's been through this three times before and is capable of planning grander receptions than this one. I'm not worried, and she knows where to find me if she needs help."

He placed his hands on her arms and stared her straight in the face. "I'd kiss some sense into you right now if I could. As a matter of fact, come back with me to my office. You've never been there, have you?"

"No." She clung to his arm as he hurried down the steps.

"Then it's time you see where your husband works so you may stop in to meet me whenever you wish. I should hear about the duplex tomorrow. We could go once I get the keys. I can't be expected to continue without a proper kiss. It's been three days." Alexander winked.

"We only have thirteen days to go."

"Yes, and in those days, you need to help your poor mother."

"She's been hounding me about a list from you of whom you want invited to our open house. We need to place our invitation order Friday and she needs to know how many to purchase."

"I'll have a list ready tomorrow and have my secretary compile the addresses for you."

Lucy turned to look at Alexander. "Is she pretty?"

"Who?"

"Your secretary."

He laughed. "She's seasoned, Lucy. Old enough to be my mother. When I started working, Father wanted me to have someone he knew I could rely on and gave me his original secretary. He upgraded his own to a fresh-out-of-typing-school brunette with a penchant for dropping things, but he never complains because he likes the view."

"Alex!" She backhanded his chest.

"It's true, and I plan on keeping you well away from Father. As it's Wednesday, he'll not be in yet so you're safe this time." He raised her hand and kissed the back of it. "You've saved me from that hollow life, Lucy. Thank you, a million times, thank you!"

Alexander threw open the door to Melling and Associates. "Everyone, come meet my fiancée!"

A young secretary and clerk that had been milling about the front desk stood at attention. Both sized up Lucy—the clerk with a sly smile and the secretary with a less than pleased look. Alexander removed Lucy's wool cape and hung it and her hat on the coat tree before removing his own. Then a junior law partner—though he had at least five years on Alexander—came in from the back offices. Lucy had introductions to all, and while no one was rude, she felt like a foreigner.

"We have to step into my office to go over a few wedding plans, but it shouldn't take long." Alexander took Lucy's hand and led her to the stairs. His second-floor office had a window overlooking Bienville Square. "Sit at my desk and see how you like it. I can get you a setup like this in our house if it suits you."

The oak armchair swiveled and rolled. Lucy liked the molded wood seat and arm rests. She leaned back and closed her eyes. With her eyes still shut, the chair spun and her knees bumped Alexander.

"I look forward to being with you as you sleep. Even the short times at Seacliff and on your porch Sunday morning were magnificent." He went to his knees before her chair. "Those lips of yours curl into the slightest smile like you're pleased with your dreams."

"I'm pleased with you, Alex."

Their free roaming kisses and touches brought Lucy to the edge of the seat and Alexander, more comfortable than ever with their intimacy. He stood, bringing her with him.

"Do you wish to know a secret?"

"Yes, if it's about you." She smiled as he wrapped his arms around her waist.

"See that bench over there?" He turned her to face the window, an arm still about her middle as one rose to point a finger into the park. "Do you recall sitting there with Grace Anne one Thursday this past June? June sixteenth to be exact." He rested his chin on her shoulder.

"We've sat there often through the years."

"Well, this particular day was humid and gloomy. I sat up here brooding over losing a case in court that morning. I had my flask out, planted myself on the table, and glowered at the world. The bright hair on your hatless head caught my eye. You wore a sky blue walking suit and were the sunniest thing on the horizon as you fed the squirrels."

"Oh, no! I know what day that was! You saw me?" Her hands went to her hot cheeks. "Grace Anne warned me anyone could be watching from the business fronts, but I didn't listen."

He turned her to face him and kissed her hard as he ran his hands down her back. "I'm glad you didn't listen. You were just what I needed that day. The streets cleared of people when the rain came and Grace Anne huddled under her big umbrella on the bench. I watched you pull your boots off. You were without stockings—"

"It was burning hot that day!"

"I don't blame you, but it stunned me to see a society lady that way in the middle of the city. I stood to get a better look and nearly busted my nose tripping over this chair, spilling the rest of my brandy."

Lucy laughed. "You poor thing."

"Then you hopped the fence and started splashing in the fountain without a care in the world. I stood here laughing and knew I had to speak with you because you gave me such hope that dark day." Alexander kissed her again. "I'm sorry it took me six months to approach you. I think of all the time I've missed with you, all the pain I could have avoided if I'd just been brave enough to go up to you when Grace Anne was by your side at a social event or when you were with your family at church. The best I could do was say hello when I'd pick up Eddie."

"I found you the most interesting of Edmund's friends." Lucy smiled as she fingered his collar. "There was always a spark in your eyes."

He held her to him. "The light was a reflection of your glow. I've wanted you since you danced in the fountain and now you're mine, forever."

***

"We saved the paper for you, Lucy," Mr. Easton said as she took her seat at the breakfast table Thursday morning.

Mrs. Easton poured her daughter's coffee. "Yes, but don't take too long. I'm sure your father would like to see the headlines before going to work."

With all eyes on her—including Opal's cutting stare—Lucy spread the paper on the table and rustled through the pages until she found The Social Side page. Her eyes fell upon the marriage announcement, but a second later the words on the next column drew her eyes.

"Did they get everything correct?" Mrs. Easton asked.

"Of all the luck and blessings!" Lucy clutched the paper to her chest for a moment. "He's coming here tomorrow!"

"Are you already pining for someone else?" Edmund teased. "Some actor perhaps?"

"No, even better. Listen to this. 'Mr. Wilson Noble, president of the Noble Publishing House of New York, will be at The Battle House on Friday as part of his tour of the South in pursuit of fresh Southern authors for upcoming publications. Those with literary inclinations will have the pleasure of meeting Mr. Noble at The Battle House before he continues his journey to New Orleans.'"

"That's perfect for you, Lucy. Would you like me to accompany you there?" Edmund asked.

"It gives no times, but the hotel is just around the corner from Alexander's office. Maybe I could wait there and he could walk me over. I'll ask him today. I'll need to type a new copy of chapter one. Or Maybe I should just bring everything I have typed from *Azalea Blossom*. Or—"

"Lucy!" Mrs. Easton cut through her chatter. "The marriage announcement!"

"I think she cares more about that story than she does her rich fiancé," Opal said. "She spends more time with that stupid typewriter than she does the man. I hope she drives him mad with her *clackity-clackity* all day."

Mr. Easton stared over his coffee at his youngest. "Opal, watch your words."

Lucy hid her warm face behind the newspaper as she read over the announcement. "It's perfect, Mother. They got everything just as you sent it to them."

"That's a relief. Now I just need that head count from Alex, then we can finish the invitation order and plan for the menu."

"I'll get it from him today." She passed the newspaper to her father. "Thank you for allowing me to see it first."

"It's not fair Lucy gets to run about town every day. I've been stuck at home since we got back from Susan's," Opal complained.

"Would you like to go to Mass with your sister?" Mrs. Easton asked.

"Yes."

"But her lessons," Lucy stammered.

"I'll ring Miss Candice to postpone until ten thirty," Mrs. Easton said. "I'll even give you spending money to buy something sweet on the way home. Make a time of it, girls."

Opal chugged down the rest of her milk and skipped out of the room with a huge smile.

Edmund smirked. "Have fun with that, Lucy."

"The seamstress called yesterday evening," Mrs. Easton said. "She wants you to try on the dress before she makes the final darts as those are more difficult to undo. I told her you'd stop in this morning."

"Mother, with Opal along? You know she'll complain the whole time."

"She's part of this family too."

"Would you like to come with us?"

"I don't think I can handle the stress of seeing you in the dress. I know everything will work out, but it's still upsetting to me. Just be sure you bring that guest list back with you."

When Lucy and Opal exited the streetcar by the cathedral, Lucy turned to her sister. "Do you wish to hold my hand?"

"I'm not a baby!" Opal shoved her gloved hands into her coat pockets and snarled.

Lucy started up the sidewalk, relieved when her sister came without prodding.

"Good morning, Lucy." Alexander took her hands and kissed her cheek in front of the cathedral gate as he always did.

"Have you no shame before the house of God?"

"Good day to you too, Opal." He straightened his jacket. "Are you here on an errand of the Lord?"

"Yes. He says to make sure you give Lucy that guest list to stay on your mother-in-law's good side."

"Clever girl." His cool gaze didn't leave hers as he retrieved a folded piece of paper from his pocket and handed it to Lucy. "These are the names. Addresses will be ready tomorrow."

"Thank you, Alex." Lucy slipped it into her reticule.

He turned to her with a questioning look. "Aren't you going to read it over?"

"I will. Did you see the announcement in the paper?"

"Yes, and Mother's not pleased we're going on with the plans."

Lucy grabbed his arm. "And did you see what was right next to it, like it was a message for me?"

"No, I only had eyes for our marriage news, which I assume isn't the reason you're excited right now."

"You know I can hardly wait, but this news is what I need! Mr. Noble from Noble Publishing in New York is going to be at The Battle House tomorrow for the express purpose of discovering new writers! He's doing interviews of a sort, but the paper didn't list any time or details beyond those with literary inclinations should come meet him."

"We can stop in the hotel after Mass and enquire."

"You two are going to be seen going into a hotel together?" Opal sounded repulsed.

"Isn't that why you're here, to act as chaperone?" Alexander teased.

She crossed her arms. "I'm here to get out of the house and buy fudge."

Alexander laughed. "I respect your honesty."

"I have an appointment at the seamstress I need to get to," Lucy said. "Would you like to come along?"

"Of course, and then we can stop by the hotel and enquire about tomorrow."

"But I have to get Opal home for her tutoring, I can't be out long."

"If we run late, I'll stop in the hotel myself and then drop by after work to let you know the details." Alexander led them to a pew near the center and situated himself between the sisters, Lucy resting her head on one shoulder and Opal leaning as far away from him as possible on the other side.

Thirty-One

"You took him with you when you tried on the dress?" Mrs. Easton collapsed onto the settee. "Lucy, can you not stick with traditions for a few weeks to spare me the anxiety?"

"I told her it was bad luck for him to see her in it before the wedding, but she didn't listen." Opal twisted the tip of her long braid around her finger as she smiled. "I guess we'll see what happens to wreck her magical love story."

"Opal," Mrs. Easton said, "go wait for Miss Candice on the porch and take your lessons in the breakfast nook. It's warm enough today."

She trudged out but paused in the doorway. Opal looked back at her older sister, a glint of mischievousness in her eyes that chilled Lucy.

"How did it fit?" Mrs. Easton asked. "And did he like it?"

"It's beautiful, Mother. I wish you would have come. Alex adores it. He knew exactly what I was going for by choosing it. He loves to see me in red."

"Is that why you're going about in my mother's old cloak lately?"

Lucy blushed. "It's been a cold winter."

"So it has. And did you get a guest count from him or were you too busy thinking about that publisher?"

Lucy joined her mother on the settee and handed her the paper.

"Only twenty-five, and some of these are already on our list. Do you know if he consulted with his mother?"

"Probably not. He told me this morning she was upset that we're going through with the wedding this month. She wanted us to wait until after Lent."

"I should telephone her, even if it sets her off. Why don't you call Alex at work and invite him to stay for supper so he doesn't have to go home right away?"

"Call him?"

"Yes. The operator will put you through if you don't know the number. They have a directory."

"Mother, I detest the telephone. I never know what to say."

"You're a grown woman now and must get used to doing things you don't care for. Now hurry up, Lucy. I want to get my conversation out of the way too."

Lucy waited until Opal and her tutor were on the back porch before holding the receiver to her ear. "Yes," she spoke in to the mouthpiece mounted on the wood box on the wall, "I need to be connected to Melling and Associates on Saint Francis Street, please."

Static and buzzers sounded in her ear as the call was transferred appropriately.

"Melling and Associates Law Firm," a friendly voice answered.

"I'm trying to get ahold of Alex. I mean, Alexander Melling. *Mr.* Alexander Melling."

"He doesn't take unsolicited calls. Are you a client or seeking an appointment?"

"Neither." She giggled nervously. "It's Lucy. Lucille Easton."

"Oh." The secretary's voice turned brisk. "I'm sure he'll make an exception for you. One moment, please."

Two minutes later, Lucy tried to decide if the secretary had deliberately hung up on her or if the connection might have been lost, when the line crackled. "Lucy?"

"Alex, you sound far away."

"I am miles away." His laughter seemed thin over the wires. "I got the information for you, but I'll not tell you over the telephone and miss my chance to see you this evening."

"I wouldn't want that either. I'm calling to invite you to stay for supper."

"I'd like that, thank you."

"And to warn you my mother is calling yours to ask if there's anyone special they would like to invite to our party."

"I wish she wouldn't, but if anyone can hold her own against Mother, it would be yours. I need to get back to my court preparations. I'll see you about five thirty. I love you, my queen."

She hung up the receiver and stood staring at the telephone. Mrs. Easton stopped beside her. "What did he say?"

"That he loves me. It sounded enchanting over the telephone!" She hugged her mother. "I'm sorry for being neglectful with the wedding planning. I want everything to be wonderful, but marrying Alex will make for the most glorious experience for me no matter what. I'll try to keep my typing to one time of day rather than morning and afternoon so I can help more. Whatever happens with Mr. Noble tomorrow, my family is more important. Besides, it will be good practice in balance and housekeeping skills. Do you think Cook will allow me to help with supper today?"

Mrs. Easton laughed and hugged her. "It's good to see you out of the clouds for a while."

***

Mr. Easton and Edmund dropped Lucy at Melling and Associates on their way to work Friday morning. In a briefcase borrowed from her father, she carried the first seven typed chapters of *Azalea Blossom*, as well as a portfolio of her poems handwritten in calligraphy that she'd compiled the past year. She paused on the sidewalk and smoothed her beige skirt with the embroidered scroll design before entering.

The secretary and clerk she'd met the other day were the only ones there.

"Good morning, Miss Easton," Miss Sawyer said when Lucy came in the front door. "I'm afraid Mr. Melling isn't in. He has a court date at eight thirty. He most likely won't be back until after the lunch hour."

"Alex made me aware. I have a literary appointment at The Battle House later this morning and he said it would be fine for me to wait in his office until then."

"It's not our standard practice to allow anyone into the lawyers' offices, as they could have sensitive documents in them." The secretary took a breath before prattling on with a hand on her hip. "Besides, his office is locked and I don't have a key. It's out of the question."

The young clerk looked from Lucy to Miss Sawyer with an eager smile as if he expected one of the women to attack the other. The front door opened and Lucy turned toward a graying woman in a brown wool suit.

"Miss Easton, isn't it?" She offered her hand. "I was sorry I missed you when you stopped in the other day. I'm Ms. Renna, Alexander's secretary. He telephoned me at home last night to inform me to care for you today. Let me get you settled in his office."

Ms. Renna hung Lucy's capelet on the rack and led her upstairs.

"I hope Miss Sawyer wasn't unkind to you. She can be stabbing at times—extremely jealous of anyone Alexander spends time with. I think she was under the impression when Mr. Melling hired her she'd have an easy in with the younger Mr. Melling, but he's paid her no mind, much to her chagrin." They stopped outside Alexander's office for Ms. Renna to remove a key from her bag.

"Is she Mr. Melling's personal secretary?"

"Heavens no. He keeps his girl tucked away in his rooms up here. Miss Sawyer is just a pleasant face to greet clients, brew coffee, and field phone calls to the appropriate desks." She pointed back to the stairs. "That's my desk at the top of the landing. The door there leads to Mr. Melling's suite. He has a private waiting room with his secretary's desk and a spacious office with a view of the square like Alexander's. Didn't Alexander show you around?"

"He wishes to keep me away from his father," she whispered.

"He's a sharp one. I must confess, it's been a pleasure to work for him since he started courting you." She swung Alexander's office door open and motioned Lucy inside. "He was always prone to brooding, but he's been as cheerful as anything since Christmas, even when his father comes down on him. That's the calming mark of a good woman."

"You're very kind." Lucy laid the briefcase on a chair near the door.

"Shall I bring you coffee or tea?" Ms. Renna asked.

"I'm fine, thank you."

"Make yourself comfortable, but don't hesitate to call out. I'll check on you soon."

Lucy placed her reticule on the desk and observed the park for several minutes before deciding to try her hand at a poem. The wall clock chimed the half hour and she tried to imagine Alexander in the courtroom—his cool disposition sure to convey authority and charm the jury. With a smile, she sat at his desk and opened the top drawer in search of paper.

"Do you make a habit of rifling through people's drawers?" Mr. George Melling stared at Lucy from the doorway.

"I'm sorry, Mr. Melling. I was only looking for some paper." She stood. "I guess it would be better to ask Ms. Renna for help."

"Come now, Miss Easton, I was merely teasing. Alex told me you were invited here this morning and had free range of his office."

She glanced at his face, but had trouble looking in his hard, blue-gray eyes since she learned he'd supplied Alexander with the means for paid companionship for half a decade. Looking away, Lucy didn't notice him moving until he was along the edge of the desk.

"I fear you got the wrong impression from us at your last visit to our home. I'm pleased with Alex choosing you. Ruth will be too as soon as she gets off her high horse. You aren't what she expected for her son and it's a bit of a shock. She wanted a demure doll she can play dress up with, not the headstrong, creative type."

"Miss Easton," Ms. Renna spoke from the door, "are you ready for coffee now?"

Knowing it would bring her back, Lucy didn't hesitate. "Yes, please, Ms. Renna."

As soon as the secretary left, Mr. Melling took a step closer. "Business has increased since Alex settled down with you. His case load is growing, yet he's not buckling under the weight. A few of my long-term clients have even asked to switch to Alex in a show of their support for his upcoming nuptials. I pointed this out to him last night, reminding him that your pretty face and good form are nothing short of a boost to his bank account." He trailed a finger down the side of her cheek. "Yes, you're pure asset to Alex. I don't understand why he got upset at me for saying so."

Lucy stepped backward, her heel striking against one of the chair's casters. She caught her balance with a hand on the edge of the desk, but Mr. Melling took it and kissed the back of it.

"Come now, Miss Easton. There's no need to fret. Make yourself comfortable, we're all family here. What would you like me to call you?"

She sat in Alexander's chair and rolled it until tucked under the desk. "Lucille, please."

Ms. Renna returned with a service for one on a small tray. "Mr. Melling, I believe Alexander would like to know Miss Easton was able to take her coffee hot."

He smiled and straightened his tie. "Of course. Excuse me, Lucille, I have work to do."

"Thank you, Ms. Renna." Lucy breathed a sigh of relief. "I suppose it's awful for me to say about my future father-in-law, but I'm not comfortable around him."

"The only women who are comfortable are the ones blinded by dollar signs." Ms. Renna placed the tray on the desk. "Do you require anything else?"

"Do you know where Alex keeps his paper and maybe an envelope?"

Lucy settled in with the supplies and a strong cup of coffee, but before she could write, there was a knock at the open door.

"Special delivery for the soon-to-be Mrs. Alexander Melling." A delivery boy carried in a vase filled with red and white roses and set it on the desk.

"Why, thank you!" Lucy stared at the gorgeous arrangement and inhaled its scent a moment before pulling the card from it.

> *Lucy,*
> *Blessings to you this day.*
> *Keep writing, no matter what.*
> *All my love, always,*
> *Alex*

A single tear cascaded her cheek, washing away Mr. Melling's vile touch. Lucy pushed aside the coffee and let her words flow with Alexander's pen.

> *Life with You*
>
> *You let me into your sanctuary*
> *At home and work*
> *Both are filled with your smell*
> *Your taste of living*
> *And loving*
> *You shared your secrets*
> *Your skeletons*
> *Without fear*

Because our love is true
I'm not ashamed of what we have
I glory in it more each day
Your kindness
Unconditional love
Burning passion
Every sunrise brings me one day closer
To my life with you

Lucy read it over and then folded it into thirds. Across the front of the sealed envelope she wrote *Alex* and propped it against his marble pen holder. In an impulsive gesture, she pulled one of the red roses from the vase and pinched the stem short with her fingernails. She tucked it behind her right ear to display her devotion to Alexander. With briefcase in hand, she headed for the hotel.

Thirty-Two

Lucy hadn't been to The Battle House Hotel since the New Year's Eve ball. In the month since, her life had become glorious, messy, and magical. A woman now—Alexander Melling's bride—but still herself, and Lucille Easton was a writer. As her fiancé reaped professional benefits from their union, Lucy did as well through the form of confidence and a deeper understanding of life which she infused into her work.

With her capelet left at the coat check, Lucy entered the ballroom. A quarter of the space was arranged as a lecture hall so Mr. Wilson Noble could address the group before conducting personal interviews. Women outnumbered the men, a sea of wool walking suits and big hats with a few business suits sprinkled throughout. Wearing the red rose behind her ear, Lucy took a seat in the center of the front row and folded her hands on top of the briefcase in her lap.

Mr. Noble's speech cemented Lucy's desire to join the publishing world. Afterward, his assistant called each guest one at a time, beginning with the front row. When she entered the small conference room, she was met with a knowing smile from the New York gentleman.

"I've been looking forward to interviewing the Southern rose." He touched the gray at his temple before folding his hands. "In the whole crowd, you stood out as the artist in the group. Your subtle, classic taste allows the viewer to savor the carefully crafted details, such as the red rose and the embroidery on your skirt. If you write half as well as you dress, you'll have a contract in your future. Now, tell me about yourself and your work."

"Thank you, sir. My name is Lucille Easton and I'm a native Mobilian." Without planning to, Lucy spoke with a pronounced

Southern drawl. "My family is in the import business and I've been writing seriously since I was ten. Novels are my favorite, but I dabble in poetry and have had a few published in *The Mobile Register* during the past two years."

"Already published! That's a good step, Miss Easton. Many fail to meet that goal in their lifetime."

"I brought with me my poetry portfolio if you are interested, as well as the first seven typed chapters of my Southern romance, *Azalea Blossom*."

"Typed! It's good to know you embrace the industrialization of the craft."

"I received an Underwood for Christmas and have been slaving away on it daily. I'll finish typing the rest of the manuscript next month."

"Are you willing to leave your chapters with me? I'd like to read them on the train to New Orleans this evening."

"Of course, Mr. Noble."

"My assistant has a contact form to fill out. Let him know I've requested pages and he'll attach it to your partial manuscript. Thank you for coming, Miss Easton. You'll hear from me one way or another within the next month. In the meantime, keep typing."

Lucy couldn't stop grinning while she filled out the form. When she reached the exit, Kate Stuart's towering figure blocked her path, her gold watch glinting from its chain.

"I suppose you think you are the chosen one since Mr. Noble spent more time with you and asked for pages."

"No one is chosen yet, Miss Stuart." Lucy kept her chin high. "But I have decided one thing. I hereby resign from my trial position as a reporter for *Snitch*."

"There's no need to resign, Miss Easton. Your marriage this month nullifies your obligation as I only want unattached ladies on staff since they are my target audience. You can be assured, though, that you will make it into the pages even if not penned by your hand." She fingered her watch and looked at the time as though bored.

"Have fun fictionalizing the truth, Miss Stuart. I prefer to create my stories from scratch rather than at the expense of others."

Kate Stuart's eyes narrowed. "You're no better than me. If one of your novels ever gets published, the truth of your life and everyone's around you will be laid bare between the lines. You give people fresh names while I only abbreviate them, but we are both telling the same stories."

Not wanting to admit the partial truth, Lucy pushed passed Kate. She folded her capelet into the briefcase and rushed across Royal Street, not stopping until she reached her preferred bench in Bienville Square. She relaxed her breathing and actively replaced the memory of Kate Stuart's biting remarks with the kind words she'd heard from Mr. Noble.

"Bag o' peanuts for the squirrels, miss? Only a penny," a peddler in a worn gray coat said.

Lucy raised her face to the man. "I'm sorry, I forgot my coin purse. Next time, I'll purchase two."

From behind her, a hand rested on her shoulder. "Allow me. Two, please." Alexander passed the man two cents and collected the bags as he came around the front of the bench. He sat beside her and studied her with longing. "The white flower of innocence at Christmas turned to red as we approach our special day. How perfect you are, Lucy."

His kiss fell on the corner of her lips as though he couldn't decide between a chaste public peck on the cheek and a full one. She ran her hand over the navy lapel of his three-piece suit. "You look dashing. I'd like to see you at work one day, grilling the witnesses and charming the jury. How did it go this morning?"

Alexander handed Lucy one of the bags and stretched his legs out, causing the gathering squirrels to scatter. "Smooth as anything. I won the case for my client and returned to the office to find a poem penned by the one I love, who I soon spotted from my window. How was your appointment? Is your case lighter than it was?"

"Not really, but that's because my wrap is inside. Thank you for the flowers. It was the rose that caught Mr. Noble's eye. He told me if my style was anything like my writing, I'd have a contract in my future. He took my pages to read and said I would hear from him soon."

"My talented queen! Shall we have a celebratory luncheon?"

"All right, but first we need to feed these poor squirrels."

***

"Are you certain?" Alexander asked as they reached the looming front doors of the cathedral for monthly confession after their midday dinner. "It's been a long, emotional day."

"Yes, even if my faith wavers, I need to clear my conscience."
She placed her hand atop his on her arm. "Thank you for doing this
with me."

"We're man and wife, partners forever."

They approached the confessional booth and Alexander
pulled the heavy tapestry aside on the right alcove for Lucy. "I'll be
on the other side, Lucy."

Her brow moistened with sweat and she retrieved her rosary
from her reticule before the window slid open.

"Bless me Father, for I have sinned. It's been four months
since my last confession," she whispered.

"Yes, my child." Lucy recognized the voice of Father Quinn
and shame colored her cheeks.

"Last Saturday, I committed two acts of fornication with my
fiancé." The tears started. "I didn't take communion this week
because of my wretched state. I wish for penance to set myself right
before God so I can be joined in Holy Matrimony with the one I
love. He's in the other confessional at this time."

"Please wait, my child, as I hear him." The partition slid shut.

Lucy sat back on her heels. Already the paneling and drapes
closed in around her. The minutes ticked by and her thumb rubbed
an indention into the wood of her crucifix. She feared she'd been
forgotten and used the handkerchief to wipe sweat from her face.
Just as she reached for the curtained door, the partition slid open.

"I have heard the confession of the other party involved and
wish to speak with you both together. Your fiancé has already agreed
to it."

Back on her knees, she clasped her hands on the ledge. "Yes,
anything to reach forgiveness and grace."

Grace. Grace Anne. How many times had her friend found
herself in the confessional over Mortal Sins? The other partition slid
open and a wave of sandalwood washed across the confessional to
Lucy's soul in a stirring remembrance of Alexander's embrace.

"Though grieved over your actions," the priest spoke, "God
is pleased that you both see the errors of your ways and wish to seek
reconciliation before you move forward. Being bound together in
Holy Matrimony is what you are called to do in this life, and cleaving
unto each other is an important step. As you have taken things out of
order, you must both set them to rights before you proceed. Here is
the path to redemption for both of you: daily Mass until your vows,
Hail Mary a dozen times morning, noon, and night, and attend a

special confession the day before you wed. I will advise you each separately of more."

"Father," Alexander's voice sounded raw, forcing tears from Lucy's eyes, "is the option of the full marriage vows in the cathedral gone for us?"

He cleared his throat. "Your families are well respected and loved in this parish. You were both baptized as infants and took your first communion here. Both of your parents were married within these walls, and in the case of the young lady, four of her siblings as well. I see no reason to publicly shame you and cause heartache in your families for one day of lustful actions when it is clear all else is well between you. Now let me speak with the young woman a moment, then I'll come back to you."

The window of communication to Alexander shut with a bang.

"I noticed you've already opted out of the white mantilla, which shows you are aware of your sins before God, but I must advise you not to wear white on your wedding day."

"I understand."

"What you tell your family and friends is up to you, but if you do as advised, all will be well between you and God, as well as you and your soon-to-be husband."

"Thank you, Father."

"Avoid situations that might tempt you. Do not seek privacy in the days ahead as you will have plenty of time together after marriage, which can proceed on the fourteenth if you both fulfill your penance."

"Thank you, Father."

"Bless you, child. Now go and sin no more."

The air outside the confessional felt lighter. Lucy knelt in prayer before crossing into the nave. She took a seat along the side aisle near the back.

When Alexander joined her, he slipped his hand around hers and leaned beneath her hat brim. "You're my first shared confession," he whispered. His smile was optimistic though his eyes were rimmed with red.

***

Alexander stopped at the Eastons' home on Saturday morning, seeking permission for Lucy to accompany him to their newly leased duplex after Mass the next day. "Just a quick walk through for Lucy to see what we'll need so we can go shopping next week. I'd have her back home in time for dinner," he assured Mr. and Mrs. Easton.

Mr. Easton stared at Alexander over his newspaper. "Not alone, but if you can get someone to go along with you, I see no problem."

"Could we go now?" Lucy asked. "That is, if you aren't busy today and we can find someone to accompany us."

"I have a fitting for a new suit at two, but I'm otherwise open. Would it be okay if I telephone my sister, Mr. Easton? If we can stop in this morning, we might be able to get some shopping completed today, that way I won't have to miss as much work next week."

"That sounds like a sensible plan." Mr. Easton went back to reading his paper.

Lucy followed Alexander into the hall. He kissed her before picking up the telephone. She continued to the foyer mirror while he spoke to Eliza. Pulling apart her messy braid, Lucy finger combed her locks.

Alexander came up behind her and put his arms about her waist as he kissed her neck. "Whenever I see us in a mirror I'll think of that line I used on you at the Christmas party."

Her smile reflected back tenfold. "When I saw myself standing next to you it was like seeing my future—all my hopes coming true."

His hands migrated—one north and the other south—when Lucy caught movement on the stairs in her peripheral vision. She turned to him with a quickness that nearly sent them off-balance. "Opal's watching us," she whispered.

"Let her watch, I can't resist." One of his hands went to her hair as their lips played. His other hand pressed against the small of her back as his body moved against hers.

"Mother!" Opal shrieked.

Alexander and Lucy relaxed their hold until they were only hugging, Lucy's head resting on his shoulder while she tried to catch her breath.

Mrs. Easton found them as such and laughed. "Opal, they're to be married in a week. There's nothing wrong with them showing some affection."

"But they—"

"That's enough, Opal."

"My sister can accompany us this next hour. We'll see to the house with her before shopping. I'll have Lucy home in time for supper, if that's agreeable."

"Of course, but only after she fixes her hair."

Lucy felt queasy on the way to collect Eliza. She hadn't seen her since the previous weekend and worried over being with Alexander in the new house after what happened while Eliza chaperoned them at Seacliff Cottage.

Eliza breezed out the front door of the mansion and hugged Lucy. "Thank you for inviting me to see the house." She settled in the backseat and Alexander drove them to St. Francis Street, two blocks west of his office.

He parked in front of a several-decades-old red brick Federal style row house ornamented with updated cast iron porch and balcony railings. Lucy noted the two doors—one at sub-street level under the pretty porch, and a second on the middle level, which appeared to include the top two stories.

"Are we in the basement?" she asked.

"Never, my queen. We're in the main apartment, our first home." After unlocking the door, he pushed it open and carried her over the threshold.

Alexander carefully set her on the polished wood of the spacious main room. Eliza ran by, sliding on the floor in her soft-soled shoes on her way to the stairs.

"It's bright and airy!" Lucy turned about, taking in the pale yellow paint and the white woodwork. "And the crown molding is amazing. There's room enough for me to have my writing desk by one of the windows too."

"That's what I thought, but there's a little study near the back if that is more your taste. Wait until you see the rest."

Next was the formal dining room on the left with a half bathroom under the stairs across from it and the cozy study just beyond that on the right. A spacious kitchen with an eat-in nook and modest pantry took the full width of the back of the house.

"I can hire a house keeper and cook as soon as you're ready, Lucy."

"I'd like the first week to be just us."

Alexander brought her into a warm embrace. "I'd like that too. That way, whenever we feel the need…" His kiss was penetrating.

"Even if we need to take a daily meal at a restaurant?"

He kissed along her jaw. "I'd live off bread and honey with you, Lucy. Come see upstairs."

When they reached the landing, Eliza went for the stairs. "Remember, I need to be home at the top of the hour. Otherwise, have fun!"

He started by showing Lucy the modern bathroom with gleaming porcelain fixtures. The back of the house had two small bedrooms, snug enough for a guest or child, and then he brought her to the main bedroom that ran the length of the front of the house. It was painted the color of lavender wisteria with three French doors that opened to a narrow balcony. The room had enough space for a sitting area before a fireplace on one end and a carved, four-poster mahogany bed stood on the left side of the room.

"Alex, it's beautiful!" She ran a hand up the nearest post, feeling the sturdy craftsmanship.

"You're beautiful. The bed is functionally pretty." He caressed her over her blue afternoon dress, hands roaming up her sleeves and down her back. "Lucy, it's been a week. A long week of remembering how wonderful that day was. The feel of you, the taste of your skin, your gasping breath, and the smell of you on the pillow afterward."

Lucy started to pull back. "Maybe we should go downstairs."

"I have control." He kissed her gently. "I'll not put you through the shame of confession ever again. This will be our wedding bed, unless you want to stay at The Battle House our first night."

"Let's stay here, in our home. There could be nothing more romantic."

"Then we must furnish this room and the parlor as soon as possible. Do you like the wall colors? I'll have painters in here Monday if you don't."

"They're lovely, everything is. It's so much more than I expected. We don't have to furnish everything at once if it will be a burden."

"Don't worry about that, Lucy, I've been saving and I earn a comfortable living." He led her to the fireplace on the side wall opposite the bed area. "I thought a big carpet and then a chaise and maybe an armchair, both big enough for the two us to cozy in together if we wish."

"Everything sounds amazing. Do you think we could bring my mother here after Mass tomorrow? I could let her help with ordering the kitchen things or something."

"Bring your whole family if you wish." He pulled a key from his pocket and pressed it into her palm. "This is yours. Come whenever you wish. I'll slowly bring things over next week. You can as well. Don't be shy, this is our home. Let's fill it with all the things we love."

Thirty-Three

The Eastons scrambled up the steps to the portico just as the doors were about to close. Alexander waited for them in his gray suit, standing bold before one of the pale columns. He took Lucy's arm and they trailed behind her family into the cathedral. The family's tardiness afforded her and Alexander the chance to sit together in the back corner because the pew her family entered was full. Lucy's anger over what she perceived as Opal's false claim of not being able to find her Sunday shoes dissipated.

Alexander's arm went around her shoulder and he kissed her ear. "Everything okay?" he whispered.

She leaned closer and touched his blue tie. "Yes, everyone wants to stop by our house on the way home."

After church, they waited on the portico for the Eastons, holding hands.

"Did you read the paper this morning?" he asked.

"No, I rarely do."

"Eliza said a production of *The Wizard of Oz* is coming into town Wednesday, one night only. Tickets go on sale tomorrow and I thought we could invite our sisters along."

"I don't know if I can handle Eliza and Opal at the same time."

Alexander laughed. "Maybe they would calm each other in some odd way."

"Or make our evening twice as horrifying." She kissed the hand she held. "But go ahead. It's sweet of you to want to do that."

Edmund came out the door with Mary Margaret on his arm, but Lucy kept her distance, not wanting to say the wrong thing to the proper young woman. Then the Mellings exited and Eliza set her sights on Edmund.

"Can you stop her?" Lucy asked Alexander.

"I'll try."

Lucy couldn't hear the conversation but read the body language clearly. Mary Margaret angled away from the Melling siblings and looked at Eliza's hand on Edmund's arm with annoyance. Edmund was all smiles but the grin eventually slipped from pleasure to discomfort as he noticed Mary Margaret's mood. Alexander attempted to pull Eliza away from Edmund while he spoke to her. Words were exchanged by all and the two Mellings returned.

"Edmund and Mary Margaret are coming to the show as well, but they're going to meet us there." Alexander took Lucy's hand. "And Eliza is not to sit by Edmund."

"Why not?" Eliza pursed her full lips.

"He doesn't need you distracting him, and I've told you to stop touching him."

"I can't help it," she whined.

"Then stay away. He's not a good match."

"But he's sensual and you said he wasn't."

"I said he isn't romantic. There's a difference." He pointed to the bottom of the steps where one of the Mystics of Dardenne members stood. "Now, Sean there, he'll romance you. Why don't you go talk to him?"

Eliza turned up her nose. "But his hair is the color of wet clay, nearly unbearable to look at."

"He often wears a hat."

A spark brightened her eye and she bounded down the stairs, black hair shiny in the sunlight. Interested in the flirtatious workings of Eliza, Lucy watched the young woman reach a hand out to the unsuspecting Sean.

Alexander stiffened beside her. "Hello, Father, Mother."

Lucy made sure she had a smile on her face when she turned to her future in-laws.

"Is there a reason for you loitering today?" Mr. Melling asked while his wife studied Lucy's pale blue outfit she'd worn often that winter.

"We're waiting to show the Eastons the duplex we've rented."

The way he spoke of them as a real couple—we, not I—
warmed her. She squeezed his hand twice, like her own mother did
with her father.

"Would you like to join us to make it a joint family event?"
Alexander caressed the side of Lucy's palm with his thumb as he
waited for his calculating parents to decide. "It's between here and
the office on St. Francis, not quite two blocks either way. We'll be
able to walk most places and I'll take dinner at home on workdays."

"How convenient for you." Mr. Melling leered at Lucy. "I'm
sure you'll enjoy your dinner hours."

"Let us go see their little nest, George," Mrs. Melling said.
"But I will not take part in a caravan. Give us the address and we will
meet you there."

Alexander gave them the house number and added, "I'll bring
Eliza. We'll see you soon."

When the Mellings were down the steps, Alex tenderly
touched her face. "I'm sorry, Lucy. Father's set on reducing you to a
plaything."

"It's not your fault." Lucy kissed his hand and then leaned to
his ear. "But I do hope to enjoy your dinner hours with you, among
other times."

The blue of his eyes was brighter than ever when he smiled.
"You're a dream, Lucy. An absolute fantasy. If we weren't on the
porch of Heaven—"

"Mother, there's that look! That's how he was yesterday when
they were in the foyer doing what they should not have been doing."

Alexander kissed Lucy's cheek before turning to the youngest
Easton. "Opal, you're an insightful girl. I have a proposition for you.
The stage production of *The Wizard of Oz* is coming to town and I
aim to buy tickets tomorrow. I'm not sure I'll understand the story
because it's so fantastical. Would you come to the show and sit
beside me in case I have any questions?"

Opal's emerald eyes narrowed. "Are you talking good seats?"

"Orchestra center or loge is the only way to see a show."
Alexander met her gaze with an equally challenging one. "What do
you say?"

She glared at Lucy but then softened her stare when she
turned back to Alexander. "I accept, provided I get to sit in the front
of the automobile."

They shook on it and decided with the Eastons to walk to the house. Opal was sent to fetch Edmund and Alexander collected Eliza from an attentive Sean while Lucy waited with her parents.

"Keep your head on straight this week, my girl," Mrs. Easton said.

"Yes, Mother."

The five Eastons and two Mellings made their way a block north and then east. Mr. and Mrs. Melling were sitting in their automobile in front of the duplex when the group arrived. Once inside, Alexander immediately put Edmund to work helping him carry the Oriental rugs to their assigned places and then unrolled them upside down to help them flatten. Eliza followed Edmund wherever he went, asking questions about Mary Margaret or remarking over his strength.

"It's a delightful home, Alex," Mrs. Easton said, "but the plantation shutters in your bedroom are all that you have for privacy. Allow me to coordinate with Lucy and dress the other windows."

Mr. Easton put a hand on Alexander's shoulder. "Come by our warehouse this week. We have unclaimed shipments including furniture that people can't pay cargo on once it gets here. We do a warehouse sale twice a year to clear the stuff, but I think there's a dining set that might be a good fit, maybe more. Test your luck before you purchase anything else."

"Thank you, Mr. Easton. I'll see if Lucy and I can stop by tomorrow."

Determined not to be outdone, Mrs. Melling came forward. "And allow me to get your china and silverware. Has Lucy chosen patterns yet?"

After several minutes chattering about the merits of different silverware, Alexander took pity on Lucy's exasperated mood and urged their guests to leave. The three Mellings left first and then the Eastons, minus Edmund and Lucy, while Alexander locked the door.

"I was wrong about you, Alex." Edmund put his arm around Lucy. "You do love her, but God help you, she's a pain to live with."

She elbowed her brother in the ribs and they both laughed.

"I'll take pain anytime when it looks like this." Alexander took Lucy into his arms for a kiss. "And you appear to be maturing too, Eddie. Are things getting serious between you and Mary Margaret?"

He shrugged as they turned for the stairs. "I think it is and then Eliza comes by and—"

"Ignore her." Alexander's voice was firm. "She's a free spirit all about experiencing life, love, and art. She'll say or do about anything to see a reaction. She's jerking you around, Eddie. Nothing more. She even went after Maxwell when he brought Lucy to tea several weeks back."

"She did?"

"Yes," Lucy said, "and it was quite disturbing to witness."

"Will you help keep her away from Mary Margaret at the show?"

"We'll do our best," Alexander assured him.

***

By Wednesday evening, Alexander and Lucy's home was draped, the kitchen cabinets half-full, and the rooms partially furnished. They stopped in with their sisters before going to *The Wizard of Oz* to give Lucy a chance to see the dining room furniture that was delivered that afternoon. Eliza hurried Opal upstairs on the pretense of showing her the view out the back windows.

Lucy fidgeted with her reticule cords, uneasy about being left alone with Alexander because he'd been increasingly intense as their wedding approached. During services that morning, his arm stayed around her waist, whether sitting, standing, or kneeling. She set her bag on the table and ran her hand over the curved edge of the maple piece.

"It's wonderful. I thought the eight seats would be too big for the space, but it fits perfectly, like you said it would." She kissed Alexander on the cheek.

He nuzzled in for more as his hands went under her cloak. "We'll have plenty of surface area for our dinner dates."

"Alex!" Her shock was short lived as her body slipped into responding to his nearness. She kissed him on the mouth teasingly. "Would you really? Here, in the dining room?"

"Everywhere, Lucy. There'll be no shame when we're married."

He pulled her across the hall to the empty study and quietly locked the door, leaving them in darkness. He had her cloak off in a second and his yearnings were made known by his roaming hands over the white and silver gown she'd worn to the Christmas party.

"I need you, just for a minute, my queen. To touch and taste of you enough to last me a few days." He kissed across her collar bones and the exposed area below. "I haven't seen this skin in so long. May I mark you as mine once again?"

"Always, Alex." She leaned her head back as he nudged her neckline lower while he created the passion mark over her heart.

He straightened her gown and trailed his fingers over her décolletage. "Six more lonely nights and then we'll never be without."

"We better leave for the show."

"This dress, Lucy…do you have any idea what it brings to my mind?"

"Our first kiss?" She reached for the doorknob.

He pressed against her from behind, kissing the back of her neck. "I wanted you desperately that night. When I found you in the garden, I wanted to take you to satisfy my craving. Instead, I listened to you speak of writing, offered you a love affair, and settled for that stirring kiss before Eddie interrupted us. Amid all that, I fell in love with you."

Lucy turned to him. "I'm glad you fell for me. It made it that much easier because I was over the moon for you."

She fingered his face in the darkness to find his lips and then they were hungrily at each other until a knock sounded.

"Opal is on the move," Eliza called.

After a final kiss and lingering touch, Alexander helped her into her cloak before opening the door. They crossed Opal's path at the foot of the stairs.

She looked them over with an astute gaze. "I think it's improper that the first room you furnished was the bedroom. When you brought the families here Sunday to see the house, there was your giant bed for all to see with nothing else to remark upon except the lightbulbs."

Eliza giggled. "She has a point."

"Have you ever eaten on the ground, like during a picnic?" Alexander asked Opal.

"Of course."

"And have you played a game or read a book on the floor?"

She rolled her eyes but turned her focus back to him without hesitation.

"All those things are quite easy to accomplish while sitting on the floor with maybe a blanket or pillow for comfort." Alexander held her stare as he spoke. "But try to get a decent night's sleep on the floor and you'll come to appreciate a soft bed."

Eliza rested her long fingers on Opal's shoulders, both of them staring at Alexander with their sharp eyes. Lucy shivered and tucked the cloak around her as the two girls silently conspired to take apart Alexander's carefully laid explanation.

"What it really comes down to, Opal," Eliza said in a soft tone, "is there's a symbolism between marriage and beds that you will one day understand. Alex is just too much a gentleman these days to mention it."

Lucy's cheeks flushed the color of her cloak and Alexander cleared his throat.

"I think we'd better get to the theater, girls," he said. "Edmund will be waiting for his tickets."

Thirty-Four

On Saturday morning, Edmund brought Lucy and a carload of her things to the duplex. She carried the first armful of clothes to the bedroom. Between the leather wing-back chair and the green velvet chaise facing the fireplace was a new, two-tiered revolving bookcase. She dropped the clothing on the bed and ran to the top of the stairs.

"Forget about leaving the books down there," she called to her brother. "There's a place for them up here."

Lucy hurriedly hung her clothes on the right side of the walk-in closet. Then she planted herself on the handwoven rug and gingerly spun the square bookcase. A book sat on the bottom shelf—a handsome, leather bound collection of poetry titled *The Great Romantics*, complete with gold leafing and embossed cover. Inside was inscribed:

February 1905
For Lucy, my first and last love affair.
All my love, always,
Alex

Edmund found her on the floor with tears in her eyes. "Did you fall or something?"

"No. I'm fine. Thank you for bringing them."

"They all come up?" he asked.

"Yes, please."

"I'll get the other two crates but you'll have to manage the dresses on your own. You need to move them off the sofa so I'll have a place to rest when I'm done with all this grunt work."

After everything was upstairs, Edmund walked to the nearest newsstand to buy a paper to keep occupied while Lucy unpacked. She sat cross-legged on the rug before the bookcase, carefully selecting her favorite titles from a crate, when the front door opened below her.

"I'm still working, but it won't be much longer!"

Alexander had her in his arms and on the chaise within seconds. He climbed upon her as though he had insatiable needs. "What if I want a long work session with you?"

"Alex!" Startled for the second time that week by his words and actions, she tried to remain in control of her own heightened emotions.

"I won't hurt you, Lucy." He rested atop her and kissed her mouth. "I need to share physical space with you for a moment."

"Edmund went to get a paper and will be back any minute." She couldn't help but arch into him and kiss him in return.

"Come to me this afternoon on Government Street. Father will be out and Mother and Eliza will be at the D.A.R. meeting at three. It'll be our last chance to be together before Tuesday. I feel that there's still much for us to talk about." His gaze was steely as he stood and reached a hand to her. "Will you come to me?"

"You know I'll do whatever you ask, Alex." She kissed him once more. "Thank you for the poetry book."

His eyes softened. "I knew you'd bring enough books to fill the case, but I wanted there to be something new, something that you didn't carry over from childhood. Of course there will be bookshelves in the front room too. I have some being delivered next hour. Whatever doesn't fit here can go down there."

"I'm sure Edmund will love lugging the crates back down."

Alexander's hand went to her cheek. "I'm here and there will be no complaints from me. Go through your boxes. I'd like to see what you choose for your bedroom reading."

She laughed. "When you put it that way, I think I'll need to write a book of our love to shelf in here."

"You could start by putting your poems for me in it." The smolder in his eyes returned. "Our love affair will be never ending, immortalized through your words."

If there was ever a doubt in her mind, it took flight in that moment. "I love you, Alex."

Their kissing grew heated and Lucy nudged him toward the bed as she went for his buttons. "No, Lucy, not now. Edmund would kill us both. Get your books put away."

Half the shelves were filled with Austen, Brontë, Alcott, and Hawthorne when Edmund returned.

"Alex, I see your automobile out there. Your pants better be on when I find you! I have reinforcements!"

Alexander winked at Lucy from where he sat on the opposite side of the bookcase. Edmund stumbled into the room with the newspaper rolled like a bat, arm raised. He looked first to the bed and then turned toward the couple.

"You should have stayed downstairs until I got back, Alex." He lowered the paper. "Nobody was downstairs and I thought the worst."

"This is our house and I'm capable of behaving like a rational adult from time to time."

"Sorry," Edmund backed toward the door.

"Besides," Alexander's face shone as he spoke, "Lucy is positively stimulating while fondling her books. I'm happy just to watch."

"You're an insufferable wretch," Edmund said as he stalked from the room. "Freddy, it's okay. Nothing happened."

"Freddy?" Lucy raced for the door.

Edmund stopped at the top of the stairs. "I ran across him at the store. That's what took me so long. I hope it's okay I invited him over."

"Yes!" She took the stairs two at a time and ran straight to Frederick standing awkwardly in the front room. She threw her arms around him. "I haven't seen you in weeks!"

"I hear you've been busy with daily Mass and meeting with publishers." He limply put a hand on her back as her embrace continued.

"And typing, lots of typing!" She laughed and finally released him. "I'm glad you came. Did you receive the invitation to the open house? Can you come to the wedding?"

"I'll do my best on both accounts."

She turned to Alex and caught her arm around his middle. "Can you give him a tour while I finish up with the books?"

"Of course, Lucy." He placed his hands on her waist and kissed her on the lips—as though proving she was his before their audience. Then Alexander turned to Frederick with a welcoming handshake.

When he brought Frederick to the bedroom, their friend stayed near the door, refusing to look toward the bed. Alexander stood beside Lucy, still on the floor by the bookcase.

"It's a great home, Lucy, and you looked pleased with everything," Frederick said.

"I am." She clutched Alexander's leg. "Alex is taking good care of me."

"I'm just a few blocks north on State Street if you ever need anything. I'll see myself down and wait with Eddie."

When Lucy finished filling the small bookcase, Alexander stacked the extra books into one crate and set it by the door.

"What's in the other?" He pointed to the third crate.

"Odds and ends, including some unmentionables." Lucy's cheeks turned pink.

"Nothing should be unmentionable to your husband." He lifted it to the bed and removed the lid. He took the top pair of underdrawers from the box and folded them respectfully with a twinkle in his eye.

"I was going to ask you which part of the dresser you wanted before unpacking them."

He followed her to the mahogany dresser they'd gotten from the Eastons' warehouse. "I'll take the bottom two, you take the top. Do you sort your underclothes by type?" he asked.

"Yes, but why do you need to know? You'll never put laundry away."

"Ah, but if I've tired you out in bed and you want help dressing, I'll need to know where to fetch your things."

She pulled opened the third drawer. "You're saying the naughtiest things this week, Alexander Melling."

He carefully placed them in and turned to Lucy with the Melling gaze. "Maybe I'm preparing you for what to expect with me once we're married, Lucille Easton. There's much more for you to learn."

***

When Lucy and Edmund returned home, there was a letter for her in behalf of Mr. Noble. He'd enjoyed her opening chapters and looked forward to reading the remainder of the manuscript upon his return to New York. His assistant included the address of where to ship the completed pages.

"I'll have to work double time after the wedding to make up for my slacking this week," she told her mother as she danced around the parlor. "And, Father, the typewriter has proven to be the best Christmas present ever! I don't think he'd have asked for more if I'd handed him my scrawling handwriting."

"But your penmanship is lovely, Lucy. Remember that award you won in school for it?" Mrs. Easton asked.

Lucy continued dancing until Opal screamed in annoyance. Then she retreated to her room to type out a few more pages.

By midafternoon it had warmed to sixty degrees—a temperature they hadn't seen in weeks. Since Lucy couldn't hide herself under her cloak, she borrowed one of her mother's large sun hats and took leave of the house under the pretense of a walk to clear her head. She felt nondescript in the black skirt, not someone who would draw attention from those driving by, especially with her signature locks covered.

As she walked the mile to the Mellings' house, she smiled at remembering how Alexander had chosen to place the two bookcases delivered to the duplex exactly where she would have—between the front and side parlor windows. Either way she turned, her eyes would be filled with sunlight and books. She was only able to fill half of one bookcase in the main room, but Alexander told her to buy more books because writers needed to be readers. He thought taking one day a week to haunt the local bookshop in search of the next great novel or biography would be a great tradition, and Lucy agreed.

She reached the Mellings' mansion a few minutes after three. Halfway up the front walk, the door opened. Alexander stood in the foyer barefooted, his shirt untucked and top buttons opened.

"To my room." He kept her hand gripped in his own as they climbed the stairs.

They paused simultaneously in front of the mirror in the upper hall, Lucy with a smile and Alexander with a haunted gaze.

"This is where it all began." He pulled her against him.

He tasted of brandy as much as he had tasted of rum that night in December. "Do you regret it?" she asked.

"Not for a minute."

She found herself being carried down the hall. "You'll never guess what I had waiting for me when I got home today."

"What?"

"A letter from Mr. Noble's assistant requesting the rest of *Azalea Blossom*."

"That's wonderful, Lucy." He kissed her. "I always said you're talented. I'll get you a desk for our house first thing Monday."

"Right after our confession appointment?"

"Yes, we'll already be together." His smile was distant.

The door at the end of the hall opened to a huge suite with walls the color of Alexander's frosty eyes. A massive bed stood in front of the curving bay windows, curtains drawn. He sat her carefully in the upholstered wingback chair beside the fireplace. After he locked the door, he fell before her and removed her boots while she laid her hat and reticule to the side of the chair.

"Alex, what's bothering you? You've been off all week." She ran her hand over his disheveled hair.

"It's Father. Ever since he went to the duplex he's been on my case. I'm doing everything wrong. I've messed with the system in a way he doesn't approve of. I'm weak, a failure."

Lucy slipped to the floor beside him, wrapping her arms around his shoulders. "But you aren't! You mustn't believe that!"

"According to him, I've gone soft. I'm attending Mass too often and am supposed to pick a mistress near the office, not plant my wife there. Going home for dinner each day is unacceptable and he didn't appreciate Mother having those ideas placed in her head as he's never bothered to go home until after office hours."

"He doesn't understand our relationship." She took his hand into hers and tried to reach him with her love but he looked right through her.

"When I got home today, he confronted me about the whorehouse money, asked if I needed an increase. I thought if I told him I no longer went that he'd finally understand my feelings for you." His hands tremored. "'How dare you be cowed by a woman?' he yelled, and then slapped my face."

"Alex, you must go from here! Don't wait for me, move into the duplex now."

He finally focused his eyes on her. "I'd go mad without you there, Lucy. I set it up for us. It would be too lonely."

"It's only three more nights."

"That's an eternity without you." He took her face in his hands and kissed her, gently at first. Then the force increased and Lucy laid back on the Oriental rug under Alexander's control. "All his badgering this week stirred my old appetites, reminding me that yes, dominating is good, empowering. Mutual pleasure can be tricky, so I need to see to my own needs."

Lucy stared up at him as compassion and fear battled within her. "I'll do my best to be everything you need."

"And you are, Lucy, you are." His hand went down the front of her white blouse as tears welled in his eyes. "You're my everything."

Thirty-Five

Lucy knew what would happen when she accepted Alexander's invitation to his house, but she hadn't expected the baggage he laid at her feet. He smiled now, lying in his bed next to her, but his peace would be temporary—as was her own. She'd pushed aside her guilt in an attempt to help the one she desperately loved and now paid the price.

"We have time to bring a load of things to the house before evening Mass," she whispered.

"That might be best." His hands were hot on her skin. He pulled her to him, kissing her as he stroked her back. "Thank you for coming. I need you, and if that makes me weak, so be it."

"You're far from weak, Alex. Recklessly brave at times, but stronger than you realize. And I love you. Never forget that."

"Are you okay this time?" he asked as she gathered her clothes from the floor.

"Yes." *Physically.*

"Take the bathroom to dress if you'd like. It's that door there."

She stood in the marbled room in only her underclothes, when a faint knocking came from the other room. Instinct had her shut the lights and crack the bathroom door.

"Alex," Mr. Melling said when the bedroom door opened, "have you come to your senses yet?"

"My feelings for Lucy won't change."

"She's a pretty face with a firm figure, I'll give you that, but those things fade and you don't need to feel obligated to her for anything. She doesn't own you, you own her."

"I love her and she has my heart."

"And that's all well and good. I love your mother too, but that doesn't mean I'm going to throw away my desires to sit around and knit with her every waking hour. You're the man, Alexander. Be the type I raised you to become."

"I'll never be able to live like that. Not after loving her and being right before God."

Mr. Melling guffawed. "Such sentiment! What did you do with that allowance I've been giving you if you've not spent any since Christmas?"

"I bought our wedding bed with the funds." Alexander punctuated each syllable through gritted teeth.

"Alex, my boy, I'm sure you've romanced the poor girl good and well, but you know she'll never fully satisfy you. No one woman can—you're a Melling!"

Lucy placed a hand to her mouth to keep from crying out.

"Here, take this. It's more than enough to see that you and a few friends have plenty of satisfaction and drink tonight. No matter how self-righteous you've been these past weeks, indulge before your vows. If you want to be a dutiful husband to the little wife, there'll be time for that as well."

"No, Father."

"Take it!" It sounded as though he stepped closer. "Take it or I'll take the partnership from you!"

"Get out! Get out of my room! Get out of my head!"

"Now there's some spine! Are you going to fight me, Alex? Fight me for what you believe is right when you know my way is superior to anything that little Easton girl could offer you? She's liable to break the first time you drive her."

"Don't speak of her—ever! I'll not have you defile her name."

"Defile!" Mr. Melling's laugh was empty of joy. "My boy, it appears you've done that yourself. Whose hat and boots are those there by the chair? Are you playing pious while bringing your playthings into my house?"

There was a scuffle and Lucy cowered in the far corner. Her bare feet on the marble floor half numb, body shivering. The door shoved open and Mr. Melling blocked a half-dressed Alexander from entering.

With a leer, Mr. Melling appraised Lucy from her bare legs to the passion mark peeking over her chemise.

"Don't touch her! Don't even look upon her!" Alex beat at his father's back, but he was unmovable.

"You stupid boy! For all your self-righteous chatter, you've gone and ruined your fiancée. If I've taught you anything in your life, it should have been that you never marry the ones you spoil. Lucille's ruined soul will own you."

"She's not ruined!" Alexander's strikes increased. "The only one ruined here is me, and it was by your upbringing!"

Mr. Melling went red and with a single blow struck Alexander across his jaw, crumbling his son to the floor. "You'll never marry her now." The voice was cold.

Final.

Before Mr. Melling slammed his way out of the room, Lucy was at Alexander's side. "You have to get out of here, Alex. I'll go with you if you want, but you can't stay here."

"Lucy, I…" He pulled her to his chest and sobbed.

An hour later, Lucy sat in Alexander's automobile as he carried another pile of clothing out the backdoor. He threw the armful on top of the rest of his things in the backseat.

"I'll still get you to Mass in time," he promised before running inside. He came back with a full bottle of brandy tucked under his arm and he nestled it carefully in the back.

"Aren't you coming with me?"

He pulled onto Government Street. "No. I need to get my things to the duplex."

"Then let me help."

"I don't want anyone to see you there with me. I'll meet you on the portico after the service." He idled the automobile on the far side of Cathedral Square and rested his hand on her knee. "I'll come back for you, Lucy."

His vacant eyes were despondent. She kissed him hard on the lips. "I trust that you will." *And pray that you do.*

With twilight, the temperature dropped quickly. Lucy shivered in her thin shirtwaist as she crossed the open lawn and held the hat on her head to keep it from blowing away. By the time she reached the cathedral steps, the organ droned out the first notes that resonated to her core.

He cares more what his father thinks than you.
You've lost him forever.
He'll kill himself before the day is done.

She entered the side door with tears in her eyes, completed the Station of the Cross, and stumbled to the nearest empty pew, hoping the demonic voices would quiet. Retrieving the house key from her reticule, she prayed over it throughout the service, begging in the name of every saint she could think of for God to keep Alexander safe. When the last note of the final hymn filled the cathedral, she raced out the door.

The portico was empty.

The parishioners filed out. Cold to the bone, Lucy huddle in the alcove by the doors, pressing against the wall to avoid being jostled. Edmund and Mary Margaret exited amidst a throng of their friends, but Lucy hid her face, afraid to ask her brother for help in front of the others. As their laughter and chatter died away, Lucy prepared for a cold walk home.

After two blocks up Dauphin Street, Alexander pulled to a stop.

"Lucy!" He jumped out of the automobile and ran to her. "Why didn't you wait for me?"

"You told me never to wait for you." Her tears fell like pine needles in October, erratic and subject to external winds.

He stopped her with one hand and pulled her to him in the dark spot between street lamps. "You're freezing." He pulled off his suit jacket and buttoned it around her. "I'm sorry I'm late. I put my things away properly rather than tossing them in the front door."

"I thought you were gone forever."

"I'm still here." Alexander removed her hat and tossed it into the automobile. He smoothed the top of her hair, tucking a few strands into the low bun at the base of her neck.

"Am I coming home with you?" she whispered.

"No, Lucy. I don't need another father after me today."

"What if your father told my—"

"He wouldn't. It would make me look bad in someone's eyes, and therefore reflect on him." He kissed her forehead. "He won't tell anyone, you can be sure. He'll just use it to control me, but I won't let him hurt you."

"Don't go near him, Alex. If you need help, go to Frederick."

"Yes, Lucy. Now let me get you home." Alexander slouched over the wheel rather than drove with his shoulders back and head high. His profile held furrowed brows and a sulky mouth.

"I'm worried about you," Lucy said when he stopped in the Eastons' driveway, but he didn't have a chance to reply.

Mrs. Easton hurried out the door, the screen slamming shut behind her. "Lucille Amelia Easton, never in all my life have I been scared over you! You've been gone hours for what appeared to be a short walk! Where have you been?"

"I came across her at the cathedral. I loaned her my jacket and brought her home after Mass." Alexander put Lucy's hands into her mother's.

"Lucy, my stars! You look upset. Don't tell me you're getting cold feet about the wedding."

"Never, Mother. It was just such a nice afternoon, and I've been inside far too much with all my typing. Time got away from me."

"Thank you for getting her home, Alex. Would you like to come in for a drink or bite to eat?"

"No, thank you, but Lucy must be famished." He kissed Lucy's cheek. "Eat, take a warm bath, and rest. I'll see you at the cathedral tomorrow."

Mrs. Easton turned to go inside but Lucy ran to Alexander, the hat flying off her head halfway across the lawn. She caught him before he climbed into his automobile.

"Alex, whatever you do, think of me. Think of what we have." She buried her head on his shoulder. "Don't do anything rash. I love you and I'll come to you whenever you need me."

His melancholy face held the hint of a smile for a moment. "I can't help but think of you, Lucy. Everything I've been doing is for you, but it's not always enough."

"It's enough for me, what we have right now."

He kissed the tear from her cheek and brushed his thumb over her trembling lips. "I have to give you what you deserve, and this broken man before you isn't it. Go to your mother, Lucy. She'll care for you tonight."

"But who will care for you?"

His smile shone bittersweet. "I have a bottle for that."

Lucy clung to him a moment, then removed his jacket. She helped him into it and kissed him as though tomorrow was a lifetime away. "I love you."

"I'll try to be worthy, my queen."

Lucy ate enough to keep her mother from nagging. Then she avoided her parents and Opal by taking a shower and waiting in her room until she heard them all retire. Edmund still wasn't home. She slipped down to the telephone and asked the operator to be connected to the Davenport residence.

"Frederick," she whispered, breathless, "I need your help."

"Lucy?"

"I'm worried about Alex. He had a terrible falling out with his father and moved into the duplex this evening. He's erratic, like he was the night of the masquerade. I'm afraid he'll do something terrible. I'd ask Edmund to bring me over, but he's not home and I don't know when he will be. Could you check on Alex for me?"

"Of course, Lucy. How do I get word to you?"

"I'll wait in the parlor and leave the front door unlocked. Come for me if you think he needs me, but give me word either way."

"Don't wait up, Lucy. Try to sleep."

"I will. Thank you, Freddy."

She pulled her robe around her and huddled on the settee. Lying in the dark, she couldn't look away from the memories of the day running through her head. The joy of arranging her books on the new bookcases, the moments of passion with Alexander in their bedroom before Edmund returned wielding his newspaper. Happiness in their home, but heartache at the Mellings' house. She loved being with Alexander, but the regret afterward reached her toenails, dragging her through the muck to be among other filthy things. He'd promised he wouldn't allow them to cross that line again, but in the moment—in his hour of need—it felt like the proper way to succor him. He was used to it, and she'd be lying if she said she didn't enjoy their time as well.

You're no better than his whores.

If you were righteous, his father wouldn't have caught you in his room.

He didn't want you tonight, he's returning to his old ways, using that money his father offered him.

She whimpered, then lay still when Edmund returned home. The water rushing through the pipes in the walls while her brother showered was deafening in the dark. She went to the liquor cabinet, grabbed a tumbler and the nearest bottle, first pouring and then draining without thinking. Without tasting. But then it burned. As the warmth spread, she collapsed onto the sofa and prayed for relief.

Thirty-Six

"Lucy, wake up. It's almost morning."

She tried to sit up but grabbed her head and moaned.

"Your breath's as bad as Alex's. What did you do, Goosy?"

"Freddy, I think I made my nightcap too big." His strong arms pulled her upright and tucked the pillow against her side. "How is he? Tell me everything."

"He'll be about as bad off as you, if not worse, when he wakes. He'd drunk half a bottle of brandy before I got there. I forced bread and coffee into him. He was doing better until his father showed up around midnight with…an unwelcomed gift."

"A gift?" The hard look on Frederick's face spelled out what he refused to speak. "He brought that woman to our home?"

She stumbled to the half-bath and retched into the toilet until her stomach emptied. Frederick dampened a hand towel in the sink and sat beside her on the tile floor, wiping her face.

"Alex didn't let them in, but with all his yelling, the police were called. Mr. Melling smoothed things over with them before leaving."

"But now she knows where Alex is. She'll come back to try to win him! What if she goes to him tonight or tomorrow? What will he do if he's alone and upset?"

"Do you trust him?" Frederick placed a hand on her shoulder. "Do you trust him with your heart and happiness?"

"Yes, except when he's tormented by his past. Then it seems his actions are beyond his control."

"It's worse when he's been drinking. Promise me you'll telephone me if you ever think he's beyond feeling. It won't be safe, even for you."

"I will, Frederick."

"He's sleeping now. I'll check on him this afternoon and again tonight." He helped Lucy up and paused, his hands on her arms. "You have two days to decide if Alex is worth all this trouble before your life gets even more complicated."

"Everything will settle down once we're married. Didn't your life become clearer once you married Harriet?"

He shook his head. "Everything left undone became fully exposed. Marriage isn't a destination, it's a journey all its own. Don't think it will solve all your problems, it only magnifies them."

"But we love each other like nothing either of us thought possible." She broke free of Frederick's hold and leaned against the doorframe as tears ran anew.

"I know you do, but you deserve peace and joy."

"What if I'm all wrong for him, Freddy? What if I'm making things worse?"

Frederick pulled her into a hug. "Goosy, you're the only thing holding him together."

***

For the first time in two months, Alexander wasn't waiting for Lucy on the portico when she arrived at the cathedral. She begged Edmund to run with her to the duplex. He asked Mary Margaret to save them space on a back pew and hurried down the steps with his sister. Lucy's capelet fluttered behind her green dress, and her hat stayed on her head only because she'd pinned it on that morning.

Without speaking, Edmund pulled her to a stop at the bottom of the porch stairs. "Let me go first, Lucy."

Reluctantly, she handed him the key. He stopped at the second window, looked through the sheers, and then returned to the top of the stairs.

"He's passed out on the sofa."

Lucy pushed around him to see for herself. Alex was shirtless, one leg hanging off the blue sofa and an arm covering his eyes. She watched for nearly a minute before she noted movement in his chest and a twitch of his arm.

"The fire's out. He must be cold." She snatched the key from Edmund's hand.

Lucy crossed to the sofa as quiet as her old boots would allow. Alexander's pale jaw held the shadow of a bruise from the strike his father dealt. She wanted to fall upon his turned-down lips with kisses, but restrained herself.

"I love you," she whispered as she placed her capelet over Alexander's torso.

A smile hinted at the corner of his mouth, allowing Lucy to leave with some sense of peace. Once she and Edmund were on the sidewalk, she turned to him.

"If he doesn't show up after Mass, will you come back with me?"

"Yes, but let's get to church."

He took his sister's arm and hurried her down the street. They piled in next to Mary Margaret in the back row as the service began. Edmund whispered his thanks as he took her hand. On the other side of him, Lucy fidgeted. She flipped between praying for Alexander and being convinced that she'd lost him. Afterward, Lucy dashed out and waited for Edmund in the square to keep from being smothered in the exiting crowd.

"I'm lucky Mary Margaret is an understanding girl." Edmund took Lucy's arm and started up the sidewalk.

"You spoke to Father too?"

"I told him we'd be back in an hour or two, but not to hold dinner for us."

"Thank you, Edmund. I'd go alone, but it would make things worse."

"No kidding. What exactly happened yesterday?"

"He got into a fight with his father. I told Alex it would be best if he moved into our house, but now I'm not sure. He's alone there, and he drinks when he's upset. Frederick said—"

"Freddy? How'd he get involved in all this?"

Lucy stopped at the bottom of the front steps. "I was scared last night and you weren't home, so I called Frederick. He went to check Alex and stayed with him until early this morning. Then he stopped by to let me know."

"Freddy came to you this morning? Lucy, this is getting out of hand! He'll do whatever you ask him, but don't involve him in your martial issues. You know full well what Alex is like when he's drunk and that he's no saint. Why start fussing about it now?"

"We'll be fine after we're married. I'll be able to be there with him, so I won't worry—"

Edmund laughed. "You really think he's going to run home to you every night? You think there'll be no sleepless nights waiting for him to come home from the Aethelwulf Club or some other place he's run off to for drinks and fun?"

Tears swelled in her eyes. "You're no better than his father! Alex has changed, and he loves me! If people would leave him alone about his past mistakes, he'd be able to move forward."

"Lucy, I don't mean to hurt you."

She crossed her arms and turned away. "Anyone who hurts Alex, hurts me as well."

"I know he's changed for the better, but you witnessed him the day of the Mystics of Dardenne ball. He's still a man—and a Melling."

Lucy stomped up the stairs and shoved the key in the lock. The parlor was empty, her caplet folded over the back of the armchair. She pulled her hat pins out and set everything on the side table.

"Alex!" She ran through the downstairs rooms that smelled of stale cigarettes, then held her skirt to her knees and mounted the stairs two at a time. "Alex!"

The bathroom door opened and a roomful of steam escaped into the hall as Lucy reached the top. Alexander stepped through the sandalwood-scented fog, a white towel wrapped around his slim waist and his face half covered in shaving cream.

"Lucy, is it after Mass already? I'm sorry I slept late." He opened his arms to her and grinned. "Still wearing old boots to church, I see."

She dropped her skirt and rushed to his embrace. Shaving cream smeared on her shoulder and humidity marked the front of her dress where she pressed against him.

"What do you think you're doing?" Edmund pulled Lucy out of Alexander's arms. "I don't care if you'll be married in forty-eight hours, you need to get some clothes on!"

Lucy wanted to cry out that she'd seen Alexander in less than a towel, but instead bit her lip. Alexander appeared to think the same thing and winked at her.

"Let me finish my shave and dress. I'll be out in a minute."

Lucy disappeared into their bedroom.

"Where do you think you're going?" Edmund called after her.

"To my room."

Edmund threw his hands in the air and retreated downstairs.

The bed was still crisply made and Alexander's clothes were put away as he'd claimed the previous night. Seeing nothing to tidy,

Lucy relaxed on the chaise and imagined what it would be like to share the space with her husband. Behind her, the door lock clicked.

"Do you still have that shaving cream on your dress?" Alexander asked.

Lucy looked down and laughed. "I do."

"I brought a damp washcloth to clean it." Alexander came around the front of the chaise, face smooth and towel-clad body still glistening from his shower. He sat next to her and wiped the majority of the cream with one swipe, then folded the cloth and went back to the marks with smaller strokes. "You tended me this morning, didn't you?"

"Yes." Lucy brought her hand up his bare arm. "I was worried when you weren't waiting for me at the cathedral. Edmund ran here with me. I saw you in the window and slipped in to cover you before we went back."

"You can cover me now." He shifted toward her. "Or allow me to cover you."

Lucy wrapped her arms around him and fingered the towel still tied to his waist. "Cover me with kisses and maybe I'll forgive you for scaring me."

"I think in my current state it would be easier for you to cover me with kisses." Alexander teased her mouth. "I didn't mean for you to worry, but thank you for sending Freddy last night. He helped me sober up and it was good to have someone here when—it was good not to be alone when I was besieged."

"I wish I could have come myself."

"Last night was a drunken ugliness I'm glad you didn't witness. But you make everything right in my world."

"Two more nights" she whispered. "But I'll come to you if you need me."

"I always need you." His minty kiss was deep, and then he sprang off the chaise. "I have to get dressed before Eddie comes looking for us."

He retrieved a pair of underdrawers from the dresser and pulled them on before disappearing into the closet. Lucy smoothed her rumpled dress and closed her eyes, fantasizing about everything she'd feel free to do with Alexander after their marriage ceremony.

"There's that sexy smile." Alexander bent down for a kiss.

"I was thinking about you—what I want to do with you Tuesday night and beyond." She reached out and buttoned the waist of his black pants over his sky blue shirt. "It's going to be glorious not having the guilt hanging over our moments. And there's our confession appointment in the morning to find solace for what we've done this weekend."

"And what we still might do." He kissed her hand and she leaned back with her eyes closed. "My sweet Lucy."

He went to hang his towel in the bathroom and ran into Frederick.

"You look a hundred times improved," Frederick said.

"Thanks for your support last night. I hope I wasn't a complete barbarian."

"No worse than usual." There was a pause. "Where's Lucy?"

"In our bedroom."

Frederick found her on the chaise. "Lucy, have you not been home after church?"

"Edmund and I came straight here."

"You need your rest after the night you had and how you started your day."

Alexander strode into the room. "And how do you know how she was this morning?"

Frederick shifted his weight. "Because I woke her. She begged me to see to you last night and tell her your situation as soon as I could. Because of your state, I stayed with you until almost daybreak, thereby being the one to find Lucy hungover in the parlor."

The light left Alexander's eyes. "Whatever did you do last night, my queen?"

"Ate a little and readied for bed. Then I called Frederick and waited for his report in the parlor. I couldn't sleep so I grabbed a bottle in the dark, poured a glass, and drank it all at once."

Alexander collapsed on the chaise beside her. "And now I'm driving you to the bottle. Will my cycle of destruction ever end?"

"It was a stupid mistake on my part. One I'll not make again. Retching into the toilet at four thirty in the morning isn't how I prefer to start my day."

"Oh, Lucy." Alexander draped himself over her. "I do need to cover you with kisses to make up for the pain I caused you."

Frederick cleared his throat. "Do you think we could move this conversation downstairs?"

"Of course." Alexander stood and took her hand. "Come, my bride. We have guests to see to."

When they got to the door, Lucy stopped Alexander. "Why didn't you sleep in here last night?"

"That's our bed. I'll not use it until it's with you, my queen."

Thirty-Seven

Lucy secured supper invitations for both Frederick and Alexander to join the Easton family and the men arrived together in Frederick's automobile at six o'clock that evening.

After Mr. Easton led the prayer over the meal, Opal's cold stare bore into Lucy. "Something awful is going to happen tonight."

"Really, Opal," Lucy said, "you and your predictions are growing tiresome."

"You're still upset over my pronouncement of something spoiling your wedding because you let Alexander see your dress."

"It's a cathedral wedding. Superstitions have no power over the church," Lucy countered.

"They do when you've not been righteous." Opal continued to stare across the table.

"I admire your imagination, Opal." Alexander speared a broccoli floret with his fork and turned his charm on Mrs. Easton. "Are all the Easton girls as creative as these two?"

Edmund snorted. "The twins are as dense as it comes. The only imaginings they have are fancying what they'll wear the next day."

"Eddie, really." Mrs. Easton sighed. "Opal and Lucy are the brightest. Maybe more than their brothers."

Opal glared at Edmund beside her, and then turned to Frederick on her other side. Seeing the wheels of intrigue revolving in her sister's mind, Lucy's stomach fluttered over what Opal might say. Miraculously, she kept her peace.

When they all gathered in the parlor for post-dinner drinks, Opal settled on the floor next to Frederick's armchair and lifted her sharp eyes to him. "Are you over losing Lucy or does it still smart?"

Edmund kicked his foot toward Opal to nudge her away. Alexander, who a month ago would have smirked to see someone take a jab at the other man, frowned and tightened his arm around Lucy's shoulder.

"You can't lose something you never had." Frederick's voice held the precision of someone well-versed in answering pointed questions.

"But you did. I remember how you were before I was school-aged. If Lucy was around, your eyes never left her. You two were often off talking when Eddie was otherwise engaged. Lucy was never like that with his other friends."

"That's quite enough, Opal." Mrs. Easton went around the group with a tray of drinks.

Lucy declined, but Alexander, Edmund, and Frederick eagerly took theirs.

"With devotion like you showed her," Opal persisted, "it has to sting at least a little."

Edmund slammed his half-drained glass onto the side table. "Mother said to stop."

"Opal, I think it's time for you to get ready for bed," Mrs. Easton said.

"There's no room for me in this family! Even with the others out of the way I don't fit."

Lucy gasped. "The others" referred to their deceased siblings, but everyone else must have taken it to mean the brother and sisters who were married. Opal stared at Lucy on her way out of the room, her gaze seeming to convey that yes, Lucy was right in her assumptions of the siblings she referred to.

***

The ringing telephone roused Lucy from bed. She stumbled to the hallway and listened to her father's side of a conversation at the bottom of the stairs, Edmund joining her. Mr. Easton's face was grim when he came upstairs.

"What is it, Father?" Edmund asked.

"The Battle House is on fire. Sounds like half the city residents are already watching though it's close to freezing out there."

"May I go? It might be good if one of us is there in case the fire spreads to the office or warehouse district."

"That's just a block from Alex's office too."

Mr. Easton nodded. "Stay together and be safe."

Lucy slipped off her nightgown and pulled on a black skirt and the first shirtwaist she grabbed. Wearing her old boots, she slid her reticule to her wrist and tied her red cloak over her braided hair.

An odd glow domed the city at eleven thirty as they drove downtown. The air smelled of charred wood and the sound of alarms echoed down the streets. They had to park beside the cathedral, five blocks before Royal Street. Another automobile pulled up behind them and Sean jumped out.

"Eddie! Have you come to cheer the biggest bonfire in recent history?"

They slapped each other on the back and headed east.

"Keep up, Lucy," Edmund called over his shoulder.

Lucy had no desire to watch the building burn. The ballroom where she and Alexander first danced in public. The alcove where he opened her to a new world of sensations. The location where Mr. Noble requested her first chapters. Lucy wanted nothing more than to go home—home to Alexander.

When they approached Bienville Square, the sidewalks and roads were shoulder to shoulder people and the air thick with smoke.

"Edmund, I'm going to wait here," she called to him.

He half-turned around and raised his hand to her before plunging into the throng with Sean. Lucy counted to five and then turned back, heading north on Joachim Street. Approaching the house from the back alley, she climbed the wooden stairs to the kitchen door.

Lucy locked the door behind her and left her reticule on the kitchen table beside a full ashtray. She removed her boots and cloak and pushed noiselessly through the swinging door. All was dark except the ambient light coming through the sheers over the windows and the open front door.

"You need to leave and never come back," Alexander said.

Lucy crept forward, hugging the wall along the stairs until she had a view of the entryway. Alexander stood in a pair of striped sleep pants before her greatest fear in the world.

"I didn't wish to return after the scene you made with the police last night. You wound me like no other, Alexander the Great."

His hand went to her upper arm with a comforting touch as Lucy's knees weakened. "Consuela, you did nothing wrong. I have to be true to my new self and my wife."

"I see no ring on your finger." She took a step toward the threshold and moved his hand from her arm to the breast of her shirt. "But there is yearning in your eyes. Allow me to remind you of the passion we shared. Your father as already paid for the services."

Alexander lowered his hand and shifted to the side, blocking the doorway more. "It was carnal sin, nothing more."

"Pleasure. Lots of pleasure." The words swirled heavy in the ashy air as she ran her hands down Alexander's torso.

Tears stung Lucy's eyes as Alexander shifted back a step.

"My bride—"

"You have no ring of commitment, and even if you did, it needn't stop us." Her pointy boot stepped onto the hardwood floor.

Alexander's shoulders slumped and he inched back.

But Lucy was ready.

In three silent steps she was behind Alexander, her right hand creeping around his bare waist and her left around his chest, much like Consuela had done at the masquerade. "But there is a ring on this hand. He's chosen me."

All the air left Alexander in a *whoosh*. He leaned against Lucy and she held her position supporting him. After a moment, Alexander raised Lucy's left hand to his lips and kissed the engagement ring.

"She's all I'll ever need." His voice sounded as firm as his father's.

Consuela's dark eyes betrayed her pain for a brief second before darting down the stairs.

Alexander pushed the door closed and locked the bolt. "Lucy, I—"

She leaned her cheek on his shoulder, cold skin against her heated face. "You don't need to speak."

"How did you know I needed you?"

"You told me this afternoon."

He hung his head. "If you hadn't have come to me when you did, I would have—"

"Don't speak it." She kissed him.

"Not saying it doesn't change the facts!" He pushed away from her. "My father knows how to manipulate me to prey upon my weaknesses. By controlling me, he's hurting you, and I can't allow that. You must go from me, Lucy, for your own sake."

"I didn't cross the city on this hellish night to be turned away!" She pulled the drapes shut. "Blocks away, there's fire and brimstone, but what we have together here is heaven. You said it yourself—I'm all you'll ever need."

With the parlor windows all closed, she unbuttoned her shirt and dropped it on the floor.

"Lucy, I don't deserve you."

She stepped out of her skirt and stood before him in her underclothes. "Are you going to tell me after nearly allowing a whore to step into our home that you're not going to touch me? You deny me after what I just witnessed? Well then, maybe you're right!" She raced for the stairs.

"Lucy!"

The bedroom door slammed behind her and she collapsed on the chaise, sobbing.

Alexander let himself in twenty minutes later, smelling of cigarettes and brandy.

"Lucy, my queen. I'm sorry." He wrapped his arms around her shivering body. "You're the best thing to happen in my life and I can't see straight when I've caused you pain. Forgive me, once again, for my selfishness and the hurtful words. I owe you a lifetime of happiness for coming here tonight. You saved me from myself. Saved me from the vile actions of my father. Saved us both a world of hurt."

She shifted until she faced him. "I'd do anything for you, Alex, just don't ask me to leave."

"I'd be nothing short of a broken man without your love." Alexander kissed each cheek, her forehead, and, finally, her lips. Then he situated her before him and undid her braid, running his fingers through the length of her flaxen hair. Outside, an increase of bells and sirens blared. He nuzzled into the curve of her neck. "What's going on out there?"

"I told you, fire and brimstone. The Battle House is burning."

Alexander scrambled off the chaise and ran down the hall. Lucy followed him to the first unfurnished back room and he pulled open the curtains. The skyline, ablaze in red and orange, glowed between the smoke and the high-rises.

"Dear God!" he exclaimed. "Why did you come here in this mess?"

"Father got a telephone call about it and sent Edmund in case it should spread so he could watch out for the business. I was allowed to come on the stipulation that I would stay with Edmund."

"Lucy, he'll be worried!"

"I told him I was staying in Bienville Square and he hurried away with Sean for a closer look."

"And what happens when he comes back for you and you aren't there?" Alexander voice rose higher with each word. He gripped her arms and shook her. "He'll know you came here and will break down the door!"

"Alex, please. You're hurting me." She fought to free herself, but he held fast.

"It'll be hell in here as much as that fire is out there! Opal was right about something awful happening tonight. You caught me in my folly and then trapped me in our den of sin. Do you want your brother to kill me? Is that what this is about? Your revenge for my weak moment on the doorstep with Consuela?"

"No, Alex, never! This isn't about what happened when I got here, this is about you and me. Our love! I came here because I wanted to share myself with you and remind you how deeply I love you one last time before our confession tomorrow."

He shoved her and she cowered against the wall. "You think you can walk away from sin, but it's still there long after confession. With every wrong step it looms higher, shadowing you with your mistakes until you live in the darkness of everything wrong, walled away from all that's beautiful. Unable to feel worthy of touching the one you love!"

"Alex, I'm here because I love you," she whispered. "If you want me in bed or just to hold you on the sofa, that's up to you. I'll do whatever brings you peace."

For a moment his gaze softened, the tender look of utmost love brightened his face as he fingered a lock of hair that fell over her shoulder. Then it washed off like dust in a rainstorm, replaced by a sneer sevenfold more sinister than Mr. Melling ever showed.

"Control will bring me peace, Lucy. I will dominate our bed though the world falls apart around us." Alexander grabbed her by the wrist and led her down the hall.

Thirty-Eight

Pain.

Hot, searing agony radiated from where she used to have a heart. Lucy pondered the words she'd overheard Mr. Melling say: *She's liable to break the first time you drive her.* While she didn't understand the words Saturday, she now knew all too well what he'd meant.

Fear of not knowing where Alexander went kept her still for several minutes. When the terror of him coming back overruled what she'd already been through, she forced her sore body to action. She rolled to the edge of the bed and eased her feet to the floor. Wincing, she reached for the post at the end of the bed for support. But she didn't cry. She didn't think she would ever cry again.

The bedroom door swung open, the light from the hall spilling onto the bed.

"What are you doing up, my queen? I would have thought you'd be exhausted. If you're looking for more, your stamina rivals mine." His arms snaked around her in a caressing movement, but the only feeling it aroused in Lucy was nausea.

She spoke slowly to keep the quiver out of her voice. "I'm looking for my clothes."

"There's no hurry. We have all night and can walk to Mass together in the morning. That's what you wanted, isn't it?" He turned her to face him. His breath was heavy with alcohol and his pajama pants barely covered his pelvis. "I'm giving you everything you want, Lucy."

"You promised you'd never hurt me."

"And I won't, my queen." He kissed her mouth but she didn't return the affection.

"Don't you remember what you did this last hour? How much have you drunk tonight?"

"So this is my fault for indulging in a few glasses after a taxing evening?" He staggered backward. "If I remember correctly, it was you who snuck in the backdoor looking for sex."

"For love! I came because I love you!"

"You wanted to help me feel better, and I'm sure you'll be pleased to know that yes, you can fulfill my every desire. You're very accommodating." He kissed around her neck and lowered her to the bed.

"Please, Alex, think of what you've already done and have mercy on me."

"Are you scared?" He stroked her hair and studied her eyes. The moment her deep-rooted fear reflected on his countenance, he jumped off the bed. "May God strike me down, Lucy! I didn't mean it! Something must have taken hold in me! I'd never—"

"But you did," she whispered. "I can barely stand."

"Will you ever forgive me?"

"Can I trust you to help me now or will that monster resurface?"

His luminous eyes were round with fright. "I don't know, but let me try. I pray to God you'll let me try to make this right!"

"It's ten times worse than our first time, but the warm bath helped me then."

Alexander rushed to the bathroom and the sound of running water soon filled the upstairs. He flipped on the lights when he got back to the bedroom and choked at the sight of Lucy on the soiled bed. "I'm not fit to live. When Eddie gets here, let him at me."

"Edmund mustn't find out!"

"He'll get here eventually."

"I need to be gone by then," she said. "Get me in the bath and go find Frederick."

"Freddy will kill me too!"

"He already knows," she whispered. "Unless I'm mistaken, he's known how far our relationship has gone since we got back from Seacliff Cottage. He can read my heart, remember? There are no secrets between us."

"But this"—he motioned to the bed and the various stains seeping into the new linens—"isn't a mutual romp in the hay."

"Carry me to the bath, please. I need some relief and you need to find Frederick. We'll sort this out later."

He shut off the taps and then returned with a resolute face. "Are you sure you want me touching you?"

"Don't second-guess yourself now."

As gentle as a hummingbird drinking nectar, he lifted her into his arms and carried her to the waiting bath. He cried when she grimaced at the water touching her body, but Lucy took everything matter-of-factly, her mind focused on the present with firm convictions of dealing with her disappointment and fear.

Alexander stopped in after he dressed and stared mournfully at her before rushing downstairs. She soaked for several minutes before touching certain areas to check for damage. Finger marks were beginning to appear on her hips from his gripping her in the act. She was sure her pelvic bone was bruised and it felt as if her insides would fall out, so open and raw it was between her legs. Lucy emptied half the water and refilled it with hot to continue soaking.

"Lucy, we're here!" Alexander thundered up the stairs and came to an abrupt halt. "I guess I need to get you out of there first."

"No, I need to stay in longer. Hand me a towel."

With a saturated bath towel settled over her, she motioned for Alexander to let Frederick in. He stepped just inside the door and kept his gaze on her face.

"I'm really not sure why I'm here, Lucy. Alex was incoherent when he pounded on my door."

"I've hurt her!" Alexander raked his hands through his hair. "I drank too much and turned to that vile place I'm prone to wallow in, dragging her with me. Our wedding bed's in shambles and I need to be locked away!"

Frederick sank to the floor, cross-legged, a mournful expression on his face. Alexander paced behind him.

"It wasn't our first time, Freddy," Lucy said, "but you knew that."

He rubbed a hand over his forehead as he exhaled. "Yes."

"I came here willingly. I left Edmund in the sea of fire spectators and let myself in the backdoor."

Alexander took over, telling about his father sending Consuela. Frederick's knuckles were a constant white in his lap and he refused to make eye contact with him.

"I can't be here when Edmund comes looking for me," Lucy said in closing. "But I can't go home. Will you help me?"

"There's no question of that. What do you need me to do?"

"I need to leave here as soon as possible and then be at the cathedral for seven o'clock." She leaned forward to reach for the plug, but Alexander rushed over to do it for her. "I need my clothes, Alex."

"Of course." He came back from the bedroom with her underthings, looking dazed. "Should I get a dress from the closet?"

"I need what I came in. It's—"

"On the parlor floor." Frederick stared at Alexander as though he deserved to be thrashed while he stood to his full height.

"Belt me, Freddy. I know you want to and I deserve it. At the very least, put your hands around my neck and give it a firm squeeze."

"Alex, you need to focus," Lucy said. "Help me out."

"I'll get your clothes." Frederick closed the door behind him.

Alexander lifted Lucy out of the bath and gently toweled her dry. As he pulled her drawers up, he tentatively placed his fingers alongside the marks on her hips. He looked up at her with sorrow in his blood-shot eyes.

"We'll get through this." But even as she said the words, she didn't believe them. Trying to convince herself, she hugged him to her.

He ran his hand down the length of her hair and leaned his forehead against hers. "I'm my father's son and can't be trusted. I'd rather die than cause you pain or be unfaithful to our vows. I'll remember you always, Lucy—my first and last love affair."

With her neck cradled in his hand, he brought their lips together. For a moment, Lucy forgot her pain and focused on the kiss she'd craved every hour for weeks on end. She held nothing back because she didn't want it to stop. When he walked away, she would be alone—a ruined woman spurned the day before her wedding—but for now, she was the future Mrs. Alexander Melling.

"Freddy will care for you. I tried to tell you at the beginning he was a better choice. I'm sorry for failing you, my queen."

In the hall, he shouldered passed Frederick and descended the stairs.

Frederick helped her into her shirtwaist and skirt without speaking, and then carried her to the sofa. He pulled his automobile by the backdoor and lifted the cloaked figure into the passenger seat. When he came back from locking the door, he offered the key but Lucy refused.

"I can't go back there."

He nodded. "I'll see to your things."

Frederick brought her coffee and a sandwich in the parlor of his two-story Greek revival home. The house—every bit as square and impressive as the man—was classic and functional, completely comfortable. Lucy sat with a blanket over her on the sofa while Frederick kept watch from the leather armchair.

At four in the morning, a frantic knock struck the front door. Frederick paused to lay a hand on Lucy's shoulder to calm her.

"Freddy, I need—"

"Come in, Eddie. She's here. I found her and brought her home with me to keep her out of harm's way."

Smoke permeated Edmund's clothes. He leaned over and kissed Lucy's forehead. "I thought you'd gone to the duplex. I pounded on the door, but no one answered. I was close to breaking a window but thought to enlist Freddy's help before doing anything rash."

"I'm sorry, but the crowds were too much for me," Lucy said.

"It was awful," Edmund agreed, "but the firefighters kept it from spreading. You should have seen it when the roof collapsed. Spectacular! Let's go home now."

"I need to be at the cathedral in a couple hours. Why don't I stay here? I'm sure Frederick will see me there."

"And Alex will see you home or to the streetcar after that?"

She gave a half-shrug, not wanting to verbally commit to one thing or another.

"But how would he like for his bride to leave the house of another man unchaperoned the day before his wedding?"

"It's Freddy," Lucy whispered. "He's innocent beyond a shadow of a doubt because he's never done anything to merit suspicion."

Edmund smirked. "But that cad Alex—"

"I'll see her to Mass, Eddie. You can be sure."

She waited until Edmund was gone before she lowered her guard. Frederick held her through the wracking sobs for half an hour, and then another hour while she slept, exhausted, in his arms.

"Lucy, it's time to get ready for church." He fingered her blotchy cheeks. "You need to wash, and I'll make fresh coffee."

Frederick slipped out from under her and offered his hand as she stood, wobbly-legged. He held her elbow all the way to the half-bath. After washing up, she opened the door and Frederick helped her to the table for a silent breakfast.

Afterward, he drove them to Cathedral Square and found the closest parking spot. Lucy held his arm the whole way to the portico, then let him go, resting a hand on one of the columns. She gazed at the smoky haze over the town, her eyes falling to a lone figure in the park with a black derby over his eyes. She raised her hand in a disjointed greeting—or farewell. In return, he tipped his hat and turned away. Frederick ran down the steps and Lucy continued alone.

As the service finished, Lucy waited until everyone else left before she pulled herself up. When she reached the center aisle, her eyes fell on Frederick and Alexander in the back corner. Father Quinn entered the center door of the confessional and Alexander wasted no time disappearing behind the first curtain.

Frederick came to Lucy's side. "I didn't force him, he wanted to come. He just needed the moral support to make those last few steps across the street." He walked with her to the confessional and held the drape open for her.

A few minutes later, the priest's window slid open.

"Bless me Father, for I have sinned. It has been ten days since my last confession."

After Father Quinn went through confession and penance with Lucy, he asked if he could speak to them both. Lucy agreed, though she didn't expect Alexander to still be waiting.

"I've already told her goodbye, Father." Alexander's voice trembled. "I'd only keep hurting her. She deserves better than me."

His shoes striking the marble floor as he rushed out rang through the cathedral like solemn bells.

"I'll pray for you, child," the priest said as he closed the confessional window.

***

On the drive to the Eastons' house, Frederick spoke calmly. "You need to tell your mother, Lucy. It would be better that she knows in case you turn up in the family way."

Remembering the words Alexander's spoke to her just two weeks ago brought a lump to her throat. *At first, the thought terrified me, but then the idea of you and me creating a baby together took my breath away.* Would a baby bring him back to her? Did she still want him after experiencing what he was capable of doing?

Lucy found her mother in the parlor with a basket of mending. She waved Frederick in and closed the pocket doors behind them.

"Lucy, dear, I didn't expect you until later this morning. And, Freddy, what a surprise. Shall I ring for coffee or tea?"

"No, thank you, Mrs. E." Frederick waited until Lucy sat beside her mother and then took the closest armchair.

"I've come straight from Mass and confession. Alex and I…we've parted ways. The wedding is cancelled."

"What could have possibly happened? He doted on you like nothing I've ever seen! Is it your writing? Did he get cold feet just as you're finding success?"

"No, Mother. He's supported me to the end with that. He was to buy me a desk this morning for my typewriter." Her lower lip trembled. "It's as you said, we loved each other, too much it seems. Our passion flared and—"

"Lucille Amelia Easton! We have a guest in the room!"

"He knows, Mother. Frederick is the one we went to when things went too far."

"The scoundrel! He has to marry you now!"

"It's probably better that he doesn't. He's dealing with a lot, and with his drinking…we're better off apart, even though it hurts."

"Out of all my daughters, you're the one I worried about the least! How long has this been going on?"

Lucy took a breath and clasped her hands together. "Twice this weekend, and two weekends ago, while you were in Grand Bay."

Mrs. Easton sniffed back a tear. "Did you bring him to your room, young lady?"

"No, Mother. Never here."

She shook her head and covered her eyes. "Over a two-week span? There's no telling what will become of this, Lucy! It might be best to send you off for a few months. If needed, do you think he would have you back? Support you financially, at least?"

"I don't know, Mother. He's upset with himself right now and I don't wish to burden him more over something that might not come to fruition."

"I'll telephone Susan and see if she'd like your help for the next few months. And you being there when her baby is born might help you see the responsibility associated with unbridled passion. Now, if you will excuse me, I'm going to lie down for a while. I feel a headache coming on."

Lucy and Frederick sat in silence as the minutes ticked by. Finally, Lucy made eye contact with him. "Thank you for seeing me home. You don't need to stay."

"I'll see to your things."

"My clothes are on the right side of the closet and the top three drawers of the dresser. Otherwise, it's just my books and a few odds and ends. They should be easy to spot as there isn't much else. There are crates in the back bedroom you can use."

"You should get some rest, Goosy." Frederick helped her stand. "You look pale, and I'm sure you're still hurting."

"Thank you for everything, Freddy." Without thinking, she kissed him on the cheek to show her gratitude.

"You whore!" Opal stomped into the room and grabbed the Chinese vase from the nearest side table and hurled it at the fireplace, shattering it into a thousand pearly fragments. "You absolute harlot! You've ruined yourself and the rest of the family!"

"None of this is your concern." Lucy stepped toward her.

"You shame the whole family by your lustful actions, and now you have your sights on the one who's loved you the longest." Opal grabbed the candy dish off the table and threw it at her sister.

Lucy dodged it and advanced. "You know nothing!"

Frederick moved to step in front of Lucy, but he wasn't fast enough. Opal tackled her around the legs, taking her down. Lucy's head struck the corner of the coffee table and then Opal was upon her lifeless body, scratching her face like a bobcat.

Thirty-Nine

Alexander waited in the doctor's breakroom at the hospital for the signal from his Mystics of Dardenne brother that the hall was clear of the Easton family. The doctor-in-training slipped in, a cigarette dangling from his lips, and offered Alexander a smoke.

"They're still here and it doesn't look good." John Woodslow said as he lit the cigarette for Alexander. "She's still unconscious. I heard the mother pull the doctor aside and asked him if they found injuries on other parts of her body. He said she had bruising on her hips and pelvis but it could have been from the girl climbing over her, though he said it looked slightly older than her other marks. You think that crazy kid did that or is the sister's attack a cover-up for something else?"

Alexander took a long drag before blowing out the smoke. "It's two different things. Two horrible, unfortunate things for her to go through within a day's time. Where do they have Opal?"

"The kid sister? Sedated and tied to a bed upstairs. There's talk of getting her into an asylum. You might want to think twice about marrying that one if there's lunacy in the family."

"Can't be any worse than what runs through mine," he muttered. "Go on and check again, will you?"

Alexander collapsed in an armchair, remembering the sight of Lucy struggling to climb the cathedral's stairs on Freddy's arm that morning, and wiped a tear from his eye. He'd taken out his frustration over his father, his weakness for pleasure, and the fear of losing her with each brutal thrust, and it only proved that he didn't deserve her. Out of all his liaisons, the ones known to her or not, his actions against her proved once and for all that he was the man his father molded him to become—a barbarian unfit for a devoted wife.

He saw the finality in her eyes when he'd kissed her goodbye in the bathroom, yet the look on her face when she raised a hand to him from the portico showed a wistfulness he wasn't quite sure of. *Would she have taken me back after confession if I hadn't run away? Is there still a chance? Dare I find out?*

The door swung open. "Come on, Melling. I'll bring you to her room but you're on your own from there."

The lights were off, the blinds drawn, and the second bed empty. Cold and lifeless—the opposite of his beloved Lucy. Her alabaster face was marred with scratches and a swollen lip. She lay motionless on the pillow. Her head, wrapped with gauze, reminded Alexander of the silk turban she'd worn to his ball the night everyone had envied him his trophy. But he'd run out on her because he was scared of his past.

Now he feared his future.

Alexander slumped into the chair adjacent her and took her chilled hand into his, rubbing gently to warm it as he hung his head.

"Lucy, forgive me. Forgive me a million times over. I want it to work for us, but I don't see how it can."

"It could work if you truly repented and let go of your sins once and for all."

"Freddy." Alexander kept his head down. "I was told all the visitors were upstairs."

"All the family is, but the two of us are still outsiders."

Alexander raised his tear-streaked face. "What happened? I got a call at the office from a friend working that she was brought in. When I got here, he said Opal attacked her."

"She went mad. Came in screaming at Lucy, threw the Chinese vase at the fireplace, and tackled her. Her head hit the table on the way down and then Opal pummeled her. I had to restrain Opal until help came." He motioned to his own bandaged hand.

"But why?"

Frederick paced the room. "Opal must have been listening when Lucy told Mrs. Easton about the two of you."

"I'll never be able to look at the family again. If they catch me here—"

"She only told her mother, and it was at my suggestion. If she turns up pregnant, it would be more difficult to explain the truth. Mrs. Easton planned to send her to Susan on the pretense of Lucy helping her during her pregnancy and the weeks after while they waited to see if she might be pregnant herself."

"Her mother must hate me now."

"The first thing Mrs. Easton said was that you needed to marry her. When Lucy said it wasn't to be, she asked if you would care for her should she be carrying your child. She might be put out by you, but she'll not deny you Lucy's hand should you two change your minds."

"And what did Lucy say to all that?"

"That she didn't want to burden you by asking about something that might not be an issue because you're too cumbered with your own troubles. The drinking is her biggest fear, Alex. Stop drinking and the problematic behaviors will lessen."

He shook his head. "Mrs. Easton will think differently now. She asked the doctor if Lucy had any other injuries and they told her about the bruising. Her mother has to know it's from me."

"Haven't you confessed? Make proper amends with Lucy, repair what you can, and forsake the behavior that caused you to act that way."

"It's not that simple, Freddy. All that I've done—"

"You've stood on the highest peak of love with this amazing woman and you jumped from the mountain because of a shadow from your past."

Alexander hung his head.

"This is your second chance, Alex. Forsake the alcohol, women, and that wretched father of yours. Be here when she wakes up, show her family how much you care, and ask her to have you back. The wedding guests will think things were postponed because of this. They needn't know it had been called off before Lucy ended up here."

"You make it sound easy, but you don't know how it feels to live with it all! You don't know how long the nights are alone with your thoughts."

"You forget I've lived alone nearly two years. Why do you think I go to the gym so often? It's not for my health, but for my sanity. I avoided the men's clubs in part because I didn't want to turn to drinks for comfort. And I've stayed the hell out of the red-light district though it's just five blocks from me. I've made concrete decisions to try to keep myself afloat amid my worries and loneliness. Isn't Lucy worth the effort?"

Alexander ran his hands through his hair. "She is, but she might not think me worth the trouble."

"Let her decide."

When the Eastons returned, Alexander stood to leave, but Frederick motioned him to stay and took Mrs. Easton into the hall where he told her what he'd prearranged with Alexander—that he was wrong to call off the wedding and he wanted to make amends with Lucy when she woke. Mrs. Easton returned looking less putout than before, but she kept her contact with Alexander to a minimum.

Mr. Easton, Maxwell, and Eddie didn't appear surprised at seeing Alexander. He assumed the commotion of the attack and having two daughters in the hospital left no time for a minor complaint like a broken wedding date. But seeing the two Easton brothers and Freddy together brought back the memories of the threats each of them had given him since his intentions for Lucy were known. One phrase from Freddy—*he had his way with her*—would bring the righteous indignation of the Easton brothers upon his errant self. He could only assume Freddy held his peace and wished to help him mend his relationship with Lucy for her sake.

"Please," Alexander said to the Eastons, "allow me to sit with her tonight. You'll need your rest for the days ahead. I'll call if there's any change."

Twenty-four hours after he'd broken her trust, Alexander found himself alone, staring at Lucy's unconscious form on the white hospital sheets. After the nurse checked her pulse and breathing— which were stronger—he curled on the narrow bed beside her.

"Lucy, my queen, come back to me. I love you."

He kissed her neck because her face was too damaged, and snuggled closer until he felt secure enough to sleep.

***

"Mr. Melling, I'll have to ask you to leave if you cannot abide by simple rules of decorum!" He opened his eyes, taking a moment for his vision to adjust to the light spilling into the room from the hall, backlighting the nurse. "And you should have told us she's awake. The doctor needs to see her."

He was off the bed in a second, leaning over Lucy. "Thank God!" He raised her hand to his lips.

The nurse pushed between them to check Lucy's vitals before sending for the doctor.

Alexander knelt on the chair and clasped her hands in his. "How long have you been awake?"

"I don't know. It was dark, but I felt you breathing beside me. I tried to understand why you were here when I remembered you leaving me. Was that a dream?"

"Yesterday was a living nightmare. I left you, my queen, because I feared I'd hurt you again." He kissed her forehead on an unblemished spot near her head wrap. "But I was wrong. If I'm going to become a better man, it'll only be while at your side."

The doctor had Alexander leave while Lucy was examined. He used the time to call the Eastons and Freddy, as well as beg for a cup of coffee from the nurses' station. Alexander paced the hall with a cigarette in one hand and the coffee in the other until the doctor emerged from her room.

"You are her fiancé?" the doctor asked.

"Yes, we were to be married today. Her parents are on their way."

"You'll need to postpone things, as you probably realize, but I expect her to make a complete recovery. She has memory of her sister's attack and her reflexes and vitals are all in order, but we'll keep her a few days to be sure."

"Thank you, Doctor." Alexander snuffed out his cigarette and rushed back to Lucy.

Propped with pillows, she sat in bed, her head unwrapped and hair braided at an odd angle to display the stitches amid the shaved area at the base of her head.

"The nurse is coming to redress it," Lucy said. "If it looks as bad as it hurts, I'm sure it's unpleasant to see."

"Your family is on their way, and Freddy. He was here all day with everyone." Alexander moved the chair back beside the bed and held out his hands. Fortunately for him, she accepted them. "This is my fault, Lucy. Will you forgive me?"

"I don't recall you striking me down." Her green eyes—how he missed her gaze in only one day was a wonder—didn't need to be harsh to pierce his soul.

"If I hadn't behaved the way I did last night, we would have gone shopping after Mass and you wouldn't have needed to go home to tell your mother about my mistakes."

"Our mistakes, not yours alone. And Opal's been on the verge of madness for months. She might have overheard my conversation with Mother, but she came screaming at me, calling me a whore because she saw me kiss Frederick."

Alexander's eyebrows narrowed.

"I didn't mean anything more than to thank him, a kiss like I might give my family—on the cheek. But I knew in the instant I heard that word from Opal that all of Edmund's warnings about me stringing poor Freddy along were true. I've asked too much of him and given him just enough to keep him hopeful while I loved you. And now I see the pain in your eyes."

"Pain because you blame yourself." He kissed her ear. "The connection you have with Freddy is nothing like what plagues me. He won't go hunting you on the whim of a payday. Your father won't send him to our home to tempt you. And he doesn't see things like you've painted them. He spoke with your mother and let her know of my regrets and full responsibility over our fractured wedding. Freddy told her I want to work this out and in all this madness she hadn't told anyone else about our parting. Freddy supports us, so long as it's what you want. Lucy, my heart is yours to do with as you wish."

She squeezed his hands. "Keep loving me and we'll see what happens when I get out of here. Is that too much to ask?"

"No, my queen, it's more than I deserve."

***

Friday afternoon found Alexander at Lucy's bedside in the Eastons' home. The scratches on her face were thin, scabby lines, her lip was healed, and the head wound only required one bandage, though the doctor wanted her on bedrest a full week. Much to her mother's distraction, she often snuck to the typewriter when no one watched her. Alexander agreed to sit with her, allowing Mrs. Easton to see Opal before the hospital transferred her to a children's asylum several hours north.

"Now," Mrs. Easton said as she adjusted her gloves, "the door stays open. Naomi is under instructions to check in frequently, and Cook is downstairs and wields a mean wooden spoon. Don't let her up unless she needs to use the facilities, and in that case, call for Naomi. You know how chilly it is out there today, Alex. She needs to be covered."

Grateful for the chance to prove he could be trustworthy, he looked at Mrs. Easton and grinned. "Yes, ma'am. I'll be on my best behavior."

"And don't try to charm your way out of anything with those blue eyes and that smile of yours. Oh, how can I fault Lucy for falling under your spell?"

"Mother!"

Mrs. Easton adjusted her hat and prattled on. "Lucy's supper is to be served at five, and if I'm not back by then, the men will be home soon after. Have Eddie relieve you if you need to leave before I return."

"Yes, ma'am."

"Taxi's here, Mrs. Easton," Naomi said from the hallway.

She kissed her daughter on the forehead and hurried out.

"I'll have my eye on you two." Naomi pointed to her dark brown eye and winked shut her faded, blind one. "If you're good, I'll share a story with you, Mr. Melling."

He straightened. "About my lovely bride?"

She nodded and Lucy groaned.

He laughed. "Then hurry back."

Lucy sat upright and threw off the covers. Alexander's hands went to her shoulders, surprise striking him at how thin they were. *Did five days in bed atrophy her, or had she always been this frail? She always seems larger than life in my mind—vivacious and lusty.*

"Where do you think you're going?"

"To get some air. Mother's suffocating me under all these blankets and not allowing me to open my windows. I'm used to sleeping with at least one open. The cold air invigorates me."

"It was down to twenty-five last night, and since you're unable to tend your own fire, I think it's wise to keep it closed."

"But you're here now and Mother told you to care for me." The way she tilted her head and raised one corner of her mouth never failed to provoke his desires.

His right hand moved to her neck, above the ruffled edge of her nightgown, his thumb tracing the curve of her bottom lip. "Lucy, it's been five days since I mistakenly kissed you goodbye. Might I—"

Lucy leaned into him, her kiss as hungry as his own. It took all his self-control to keep his hands above her shoulders. He wanted to feel her, to bring pleasure to them both, but also out of curiosity to know if the rest of her felt weakened too.

He wrapped his arms around her and breathed in her lavender scent. "How did I ever think I could live without you?"

"You were scared," she whispered, and hugged him back.

"And I'm still scared." With gentleness his hands went down her back to her waist. "Did they not feed you in the hospital? It feels like you're wasting away."

"I've been too upset to eat. With Opal, seeing my parents distraught, and thinking about what happened with you…"

He tucked a loose strand of hair behind her ear. "Does it still hurt?"

Holding his gaze, she removed his hands from her waist. "Not physically."

"Lucy, my queen. What can I do to help you heal and prove I'll never do that to you again?"

"Show me through your actions how you're changing." She lay back on her pillows, her hair fanning out behind her in glittering blonde waves.

Naomi stopped in the doorway. "Ready for that story, Mr. Melling?"

"Yes, please, Naomi."

"A few days before Christmas, Miss Lucy left something under her pillow one morning and came in frantic that it might be sent to out with the laundry. Seems like she'd been sleeping with it every night, but as the wash day was different with the holiday, she'd left it in place by mistake."

"And what was it?"

"I'll leave that for her to tell you." She retreated to the stairs.

"How cryptic." He turned to Lucy. "Do you care to explain?"

"No, but you may see for yourself." She leaned forward.

Alexander reached under her pillow until he found a different texture of fabric and pulled it out—the handkerchief he'd given her in the camellia garden. "You've kept it with you all this time?"

"It's not every day a woman is kissed for the first time by the man she's fallen in love with. Now how about some fresh air?"

He opened her window four inches and turned his attention to the fireplace.

"Don't do what you did at Seacliff Cottage."

Alexander turned—eyes wide, cheeks pink. "I'd never try— not here, not now!"

Her familiar laugh, like silver bells, filled the room. "Not *that*. I meant over-fueling the fire. You got it so hot in there I had to ask you to—"

"I remember well." His words tumbled over themselves as his face grew hotter.

"Why, Alex, I don't recall seeing you blush. That could be a good sign. Come back to me. And my mother told you not to use that charming grin."

"It's good to see you happy. We haven't had time to talk since the night you woke, but there are a few things I'd like to tell you. The first one is I met with Father Quinn Tuesday morning and told him we're trying to work things out and would keep him posted."

She closed her eyes and smiled. "And?"

"He said he'd pray for us to have clarity—as if we'd been blind until now."

"We have." Lucy opened her vivid eyes. "Blinded by love. Blinded by desires. Blinded by—"

"I've missed our conversations, Lucy." He linked their fingers together. "I hope it feels as good for you as it does me."

She gave him a curling smile. "Yes. Tell me more."

"I haven't touched alcohol since that night, and to keep myself from going crazy after work and visiting with you, I've been staying in one of Freddy's guest rooms at his invitation. We play chess after supper and drink too much tea. Now I'm officially an old man."

Lucy's twinkling laughter filled him with light. "It's absolutely perfect of him to do that. But try not to beat him too often. He takes it seriously and might throw you out if you're a better player."

"I'll keep that in mind." He kissed below her ear. "I love you."

Her eyes lowered to their hands. "I love you too, but I'm still nervous."

Alexander kissed her hand. "Take as long as you need, Lucy. I'll wait for you."

Forty

On Monday, Mrs. Easton gave up on keeping Lucy in bed. She allowed her half an hour at a time on the typewriter and Lucy spent all of her allotted minutes that day practicing the nursery rhymes to get back into the rhythm of typing. On Wednesday, a week after coming home, she was released from the doctor's care—pending her stitches being removed the following week. She spent all morning working to get caught up on the pages of *Azalea Blossom*, but her mother couldn't complain because she had her appetite back.

"Remember," Mrs. Easton called to her as she left the dinner table, "Alex and Freddy will be here for supper. Try to make an effort to be dressed appropriately by five."

Lucy glanced down at her kimono. "I need to stop dressing like an invalid."

But she wasn't dressed when callers came at one o'clock.

"Lucy!" Eliza breezed into the bedroom in a lovely red dress with a blue capelet and white boots. "I've been calling Alex at the office every day to ask about you, but he's kept me away. I had to threaten him to let me stop by for a few minutes on my way to the boring D.A.R. tea for Washington's birthday."

"You look very festive," Lucy said as she accepted a hug from her. Eliza fingered Lucy's silk kimono with an appreciative gaze.

"I'd rather be here typing in a silk robe of my own." Eliza threw herself onto the bed.

Alexander took the opportunity to greet Lucy by pulling her to her feet and embracing her. He nuzzled into the curve of her neck on the left side—away from her unbandaged stiches—and kissed above her collar.

"Alex." The pleading tone in her voice let him know fright found its way in—again. Alexander did all he could to bridle his passion, but at times like that, it slipped through with a tender touch.

Eliza sat up and studied Lucy with her bright eyes. "Are you still in pain?"

"Some." Lucy referred to the type in her heart.

"I thought you must be with the way you said his name. Looks like you'll have a nasty scar back there, but at least your hair will cover it."

Lucy took a seat on the bed by Eliza, leaving the chair free for Alexander should he chose to sit.

"Do you have a new date yet? I could start on that engagement portrait Alex always talked about. It would be a nice exhibit at the reception."

"No, not yet." Alex ran his hand through his hair.

"We should be able to narrow it down next week," Lucy offered. "I'll telephone you with news."

"Oh, good!" Eliza stood. "Is your brother hiding somewhere?"

"Afraid he's out on a picnic for the holiday."

"I keep seeing him with that bore Mary Margaret and fear he'll settle down with her."

"It would be good for him," Lucy said.

"Yes, he's been running wilder than me lately." Alexander kissed Lucy's forehead. "I'll be back after I get Eliza to her tea."

"But she's disproportionate!" Eliza continued. "Her nose is too big for the rest of her facial features. I could never stand to draw her."

"And you shan't need to, Sister. Say goodbye to Lucy and let's be on our way."

When they were gone, Lucy dressed in her white and blue tea gown that she wore when hosting the Melling siblings last month, though it seemed like years. She carefully brushed through her hair and twisted it into a simple up-do. Then she was back to typing.

"I rather enjoy having access to your room," Alexander said when he returned half an hour later, "but I'll miss seeing you in your nightgowns and robes. They're quite alluring. Promise me you'll write in them often when we're husband and wife."

"You'd have me refuse convention by staying in loungewear all day?"

"Are you worried about convention now, my queen? It's rather late for that." His teasing smile brought her to her feet. "I remember that dress. Do you have any notes for me?" He tucked two fingers into her sash.

"Not today, Alex." She stepped away but he took her hand.

"Please, let me try something." Alexander stood behind her, wrapped his arms loose around her middle, and rested his chin on her shoulder like he often did over their weeks together. "Stay with me for as long as you can."

"But Mother could come."

"She's seen us like this before and knows we've been closer." He gave her a gentle squeeze. "I've missed holding you."

Lucy turned to him and rested her head on his shoulder. "I've missed it too," she whispered. "Sometimes I lie in bed at night and imagine you holding me. The vision is so clear I can smell sandalwood."

She kissed along his jaw and up to his lips. He reciprocated her kisses with tenderness and she slowly opened her mouth to him as her hands played through his hair.

"I think it's time you return to taking callers in the parlor, Lucy."

Alexander turned to the door with a sheepish grin. "Sorry, Mrs. Easton."

"Never you mind, Alex. I'm glad to see you two making amends, but your courting needs to return to the first floor." Mrs. Easton left them with a sharp stare.

"How would you like to take a walk or sit in the gazebo?" Alexander asked Lucy. "Fill your lungs with that crisp air your creative side loves."

"The gazebo." Lucy returned to her desk chair. "Would you bring me my shoes?"

He knelt before her to slip them on her feet.

"Mrs. Easton sent me to see what's holding you up," Naomi looked in from the door and smiled. "I don't think she'll believe me."

"You just tell her Alex is charming his way into my heart."

"Yes, Miss Lucy."

Alexander stood and pulled her into his arms. "I think Naomi understands us."

"When you mentioned hiring help for our house, I immediately thought of her. She's capable of doing more than they allow her here. Her aunt shelters her and my mother practically waits on her when she's working."

"I'd be happy to see to that when the time comes, my queen." He offered his arm and Lucy stole a kiss before accepting it. "You give me much to hope for."

They spent the hour before tea cozied together on a bench in the gazebo, hidden away from the world by the green azalea bushes a month shy of blooming. After tea, Alexander read the newspaper in the parlor while Lucy typed upstairs. Mrs. Easton allowed him to fetch her just before five so she would be downstairs when the others arrived.

Mr. Easton returned first, after an afternoon of golfing with Maxwell. He started into a conversation with Alexander about the horrors happening in St. Petersburg with the royal families and the socialist revolutionaries.

"Terrorism, plain and simple. What they did to Grand Duke Sergei was unforgiveable." Mr. Easton turned to the liquor cabinet. "What will you have today, Alex?"

"Nothing, thank you, Mr. Easton. I've been dry for over a week." Alexander rested his hand on Lucy's knee.

Mrs. Easton smiled her approval. "And it shows, Alex. You've had a healthy glow this week, as has Lucy. Everyone's on the mend and the weather is finally warming toward spring."

Frederick let himself in the front door and joined the others in the parlor. He shook Mr. Easton's hand but declined a pre-dinner drink and moved along to kiss Mrs. Easton on the cheek.

"Were you off today, Freddy?" she asked.

"I went in for the morning, like Alex did at his office. I finally caught up with what I was behind on from missing those days last week." He nodded a greeting to Alexander and rounded the coffee table to greet Lucy.

"Sit with us," she said as he took her hand in his and quickly kissed the back of it.

"Gladly." He unbuttoned his suit jacket and settled next to Lucy. "You look well today."

"She's dressed and spent a lovely hour outside." Alexander's smile displayed his own enjoyment.

"Yes," Lucy said, "I'm cleared of bed rest."

Frederick laughed. "Like that's stopped you."

"It put a damper on things."

"Don't get me started, Lucy." Mrs. Easton shook her head. "I'm just glad you're doing better, in spite of not following the doctor's orders."

"Family and distinguished friends, it's time for a toast!" Edmund raced into the room. "Champagne with supper, Father. You're looking at an engaged man!"

Mr. Easton stood and clapped his son on the back. "Looks like I'll be playing golf more often than on holidays!"

"You haven't even brought her over here yet!" Mrs. Easton cried.

"May she come to supper tomorrow?" Edmund asked.

"Of course, Eddie."

Alexander and Frederick shook his hand and Lucy stood for a hug. "I'm happy for you, Edmund."

"I figured with everything that's gone on in the last few weeks, I might as well find out if Mary Margaret was up to joining this circus." He turned to his mother. "Her parents are going to want to do it up big, just to warn you. They only have three daughters and she's the first to get married. It'll probably be May, so don't rush out to buy a new dress."

At the supper table, Mr. Easton sent a bottle of champagne around in preparation for a toast, but Lucy, Frederick, and Alexander passed it along without pouring any.

"What's this? Do you not approve of my fiancée?"

"It's not that at all," Lucy said.

"It's my fault." Alexander met Edmund's eye. "These bleeding hearts are refraining to show their solidarity to me. I haven't had a drink in nine days."

"What? How can you look well? I thought you had the glow of a pre-dinner buzz." Edmund laughed at his own joke.

"That sallow complexion of his is finally improving," Frederick told Edmund. "We can raise our glasses of sweet tea in toast as well as anything."

Edmund sulked, but perked up after Mr. Easton offered him a refill since there were only three people drinking from the bottle. After supper, his animation returned when his parents retired for the night. He looked between Alexander and Frederick.

"Friday night, I'm going to live it up in a final hurrah. I know Mary Margaret will expect me to dote on her frequently and there are several balls to attend with her in the two weeks before Lent. Friday night is my time out with the boys. I expect you both there to help me send out my bachelorhood in style. I drop my parents at the station that morning for their trip to see Opal's new home, so there'll be no issues in me coming home late or even at all."

Alexander crossed his arms. "Sorry, Eddie. I'm practically a married man."

"Lucy has you cowed and she isn't even your wife yet."

"You should know by now I don't do anything I don't want to. Right now, I don't want to get drunk and behave like an ass. I've done…too many things I'm ashamed of afterward to wish to go back to that."

Edmund rolled his eyes and stroked his short beard into more of a point, making him appear devilish. "Just one more bash, for old time's sake. I'm inviting all the Dardenne brothers, though some will probably be at the ball that night, even if it's a snore."

"And what of Lucy being here alone?" Frederick asked.

"You've proven a good protector. If you don't wish to come along, I'm sure you can employ your time here."

Frederick stood. "It's getting late and I have an early day tomorrow. Congratulations again, Eddie. Lucy, it's good to see you looking well. Alex, I'll see you at the house."

"Goodbye, Frederick." Lucy smiled, hoping he knew she appreciated his concern.

When he was gone, Edmund turned to Alexander. "See you at the house?"

"I've been staying at Freddy's place." Alexander twisted Lucy's engagement ring around her finger.

"Since when? You have the duplex to yourself."

"Since Lucy was hospitalized. The house is too lonely without her."

Edmund snorted out a laugh. "It's not like she was there before that."

Alexander turned to Lucy, then back to her brother. "She would have been, but we missed our wedding."

"And because you *might* have been married you aren't going out on the town with me? What are you and Freddy doing if you aren't drinking, stitching samplers?"

"Playing chess when we aren't over here, if you must know."

"You two are the sorriest bachelors in the city." Edmund stood. "I suppose I needn't worry over my sister's virtue since you're sober. Good night, both of you."

Lucy put her head on Alexander's shoulder.

"You've been quiet," he whispered. "Are you okay?"

"I didn't know what to say without yelling or spilling things better left unsaid. Sometimes he's insufferable."

"As am I." He brought a hand to her face. "We can't all be as pleasant as you, my queen."

She laughed. "Tell that to my mother."

"She needed someone to fuss over this week. We've been good today, haven't we? Holding and kissing without fear."

"Yes, very good. So good we both have a healthy glow, as Mother said. Are we lit by the fires of passion?" Lucy shifted to face Alexander, their knees touching.

"I would say we are. Do you need to be warmed, my queen?"

"Only for a minute, then you should go before we get carried away."

Forty-One

Alexander telephoned at four Friday afternoon. Lucy, pulled away from her typewriter by Naomi, hurried down the stairs to take the call.

"Alex, is everything well?"

"Well as can be. I went to morning Mass and told Father Quinn afterward we wanted to speak to him about a marriage date Sunday. He said we could go to his office after final Mass. Shall I pick you up at ten Sunday?"

"Yes, I don't think I'll be able to rely on Edmund for anything this weekend."

"And that's why I'm calling. It won't be wise for me to come over this evening with him going out. Things are going well between us and I'd hate for an issue of overzealousness to set us back."

"Can you stop by after work for a good night kiss?"

"I'd love to, but I don't see how that would satisfy either of us." His voice dropped lower. "I'm craving much more than a kiss, my queen."

Her arms broke out in gooseflesh. "You know where to find me, Alex."

"That's what I'm afraid of."

Lucy went back to typing until supper was ready at six. She and Edmund ate in their regular spots across from each other.

"What's really going on with you and Alex? Why isn't there a new wedding date?"

"I just came off bedrest two days ago, but we're speaking to Father Quinn Sunday about scheduling the new day."

"You've never been a teetotaler, why are you holding him back from drinking?"

Lucy gazed across the table at Edmund. "I'm not, though I appreciate him for doing it. He's not trustworthy when he drinks. He's done some despicable things."

"Have you heard stories about him, Lucy?" His voice was cold. "Are you now enlightened to all his vices?"

"Stories or not, he broke Rupert's nose."

"He had that coming to him. Even Freddy would have done it." His hazel eyes narrowed. "And speaking of Freddy, he keeps coming here for you and now has your fiancé in his house. I might as well write both of them off as friends given in martyrdom to Lucy."

"Just because Alex and Frederick are growing out of your boyish whims doesn't mean they aren't your friends. There's a thing called maturity. You might want to try it sometime, especially as you stand to inherit a partnership in the business. Father and Maxwell won't take kindly to you squandering profits on parties."

Edmund stood and threw the napkin on the table. "You've ruined my friends, you ruined my engagement toast, and now you want to ruin my fun."

"You sound like Opal, blaming everything on me when you're too smug to look at yourself."

Edmund smirked. "Well, maybe Opal was right. Too bad she wasn't able to knock some sense into you."

As soon as Edmund left, Lucy packed her reticule and donned her red cloak. It wasn't cold enough for the cloak to be necessary, but it helped her feel safer as she headed into the night. She caught the streetcar and walked five blocks north to Frederick's house. Before she could knock, the door flew open.

"Lucy! What are you doing here?" Frederick's brown eyes were huge and he gripped her shoulders.

"I had a fight with Edmund and I didn't want to be alone after he left. I thought I could stay here with you and Alex until I grew tired."

"Alex isn't here. They took him!"

"Who?"

"Half a dozen Dardenne members in skeleton suits."

Lucy collapsed into Frederick. "Why didn't you stop them?"

"I was cleaning up the supper dishes when I heard the racket. By the time I exited the kitchen, they were already out the front door. They had a sack over his head, shoved him into an automobile, and sped off."

"Edmund's going to ruin all Alex and I have worked toward for one stupid evening!" Bitter tears spilled down her face.

Frederick offered his handkerchief and put a hand on her arm. "Maybe we should have told him what's happened between the two of you."

"No!" She brushed him aside. "Edmund deserves no explanation."

"Let me get you home, and then I'll search for Alex."

"Bring me to the duplex. Alex said there's phone service there now. You can telephone or stop by easier since you'll be looking on this side of town. You still have my key, don't you?"

"Yes." Frederick rushed into the house to retrieve it and then hurried Lucy to his automobile.

At the duplex, he escorted her inside and paused, holding her gaze. "I'll do my best to bring him home to you, for both your sakes."

Lucy walked the rooms she hadn't seen for almost two weeks, arms wrapped around herself in want of Alexander's touch. A thin layer of dust coated the furniture and floors. She retrieved a cloth, broom, and dustpan from the kitchen and cleaned the downstairs. Her arms and back were sore when she was done, but it was a helpful exhaustion. Frederick called before ten o'clock to let her know he'd just missed the group when he reached Aethelwulf Club.

"They were kicked out for unruly behavior and it sounds like Alex is as drunk as the others."

Lucy cried in the parlor for several minutes, and then set to cleaning the kitchen. She started by emptying the ashtray on the table, still filled with the cigarette butts from Alexander's rough weekend that ended with Lucy in the hospital. Raw pain seared through her heart at the memory, but the ache in her soul for Alexander was more pronounced.

When the telephone rang next it was close to midnight. "It's like they disappeared. I even checked the whorehouses, Lucy. I'm not sure where to look now."

"Freddy, you're going through hell as much as me." Lucy rested her head on the phone box and sighed.

"I'll go back everywhere and check Monroe Park too."

Upstairs, Lucy dusted the bedroom furniture and mantle. The care in which Alex had chosen each piece for their home was heartwarming all over again—beginning with the gorgeous carved bed. She changed the soiled sheets and made it with fresh linens.

Finished with cleaning, Lucy craved the role of missus over maid. She collected a nightgown from the dresser still stocked with her items and readied a bath. Lathering herself with Alexander's soap, she fantasized he had joined her so she could give him her all once again.

"Lucy!" Frederick's voice called from the hall, followed by a knock on the bathroom door. "Are you in there?"

"Yes. I decided to wash and dress for bed. I'm going to try to sleep." Wrapped in a towel, she opened the door. "Is there any word?"

"Lucy!" Frederick immediately turned away. "Shut the door!"

"We had a conversation while I was in the bath two weeks ago."

"You goose, you were hurt and things were a mess, but Alex was with you. Now it's just us, and though your heart is heavy, you aren't in physical need of someone tending you." He took another step away, arms crossed. "You may think of me as just a friend—a brother even—but I'm still a man."

Lucy pushed the door until it was within an inch of being closed. "I'm sorry, Freddy. You're dear to me, though not like a brother. You're much too good for that."

He faced the cracked door. "I'm going to check the smaller saloons and ask around more. I'm glad you're going to try to sleep. I'll check on you when I get back."

"Wake me, even if you don't have news."

"Of course, Lucy."

She dressed in a mossy green summer nightgown, styled like a knee-length chemise with its simple, silky lines and no underthings. Then she brushed through her hair, careful of her stitches. After tidying the bathroom, she retrieved the book of poetry from the revolving bookcase, turned on the bedside lamp, and climbed into the bed.

Sometime later, she woke to loud voices. Disoriented, she clutched the book to her chest and listened to the hoopla.

"It's the perfect party house, why have you kept it from us?"

"He means to make it his special love nest with my kid sister." *Edmund!*

"Your sister has a lot going for her. Rupert told us she was Alex's date at our ball when we thought he'd hired a high-class companion. She's a looker when she wants to be. Man, I'd—"

"Enough!" Alexander's voice nearly shook the house. "Help yourselves to anything in the kitchen, but none of you are welcome upstairs. Stay as long as you wish, I'm sleeping this off."

"Poker at the dining table!" someone shouted.

Heavy footsteps climbed the stairs. Lucy tucked the book on the bedside table and clicked off the lamp. She listened as Alexander stumbled to the bathroom to relieve himself. Then the bedroom door locked behind him, the odor of cigarettes and alcohol crowding Lucy's nostrils while he shed his clothing. The thud of him striking the floor almost moved her to action, but it was immediately followed by pleading.

"God, forgive this sinner. I didn't ask to go, but I didn't leave once I was freed. Help Lucy forgive me, and help me forgive myself."

Alexander fell onto the bed, catching a tendril of Lucy's hair on the pillow. He felt to the far side with blundering hands, catching her cheek with one, her hip with the other. His hands moved across her body until they met at her chest.

"Am I hallucinating, or is this my sweet Lucy in our bed after all the pain I've caused?"

"It's me, Alex." She pulled him to her side, wrapping a leg over the top of his. "I've been waiting for you to come home."

He caressed her leg and leaned over her for a kiss, the brandy heavy on his tongue.

"Lucy." He breathed her name with anguish. "Forgive me. I brought them here. It was either here or they were going to—"

"You're back. You're with me and not out running around." She kissed down his neck to his bare chest, causing him to shudder and clutch her in response. "May I help you heal?"

"I might hate myself even more come morning light, but yes. I need you more than ever."

***

Lucy rested beside Alexander, their bodies damp with sweat in the chill air while he trailed his fingers down the back of her nightgown. Below them, the front door banged open, followed by rowdy shouts and whistles.

"The scoundrels!" Alexander scrambled out of bed and searched through his pile of clothing on the floor. "Keep the door locked. I'll rid the house of every last one of them."

"But what—"

A knock sounded on their door. "Alexander the Great, your wait is over."

His hands froze at the button on his waistband. "Lucy, I swear to you I don't want her. This whole night has been a setup at Eddie's command. I didn't ask for any of this!"

Lucy ran her fingers across his chest as she turned on the light switch. They both blinked to adjust to the brightness and then stared at each other. Alexander's eyes traveled the length of the body he'd only felt in the dark and seemed to admire how the green nightgown clung to her glistening skin in all the right places. Her fair locks were a waterfall of tousled waves, every bit as sensual as the rest of her, while he was imposing in only his black trousers.

"Alexander, I know you're awake," Consuela's voice called through the door, but they both ignored it.

"You're breathtaking, Lucy. Everything I'll ever need." He kissed her and moved to the side because he recognized her determination.

She put her left hand on her hip in just the spot to accentuate every feminine curve and opened the door. "You've been misinformed. Alex lacks nothing and you are never to step foot in our home again."

Lucy—focused on Consuela—didn't see Rupert standing in the hall until the woman turned to the stairs with a scowl. His smirk turned to a hungry stare.

"Hey, fellas! Alex beat us at our own game. He's already had his way with a woman tonight!" Rupert leaned toward the doorway to catch Alexander's eye. "But careful, Alex. She won't be as easy to dispose of as Twila proved to be."

Alexander tore out of the room. "Everyone out of here, now!"

Lucy went to the stairs and listened as Alexander cursed and yelled at the men and the companions they invited. When the front door finally slammed shut, she descended the stairs. He hugged her on the bottom step, resting his head on her chest.

"I'm sorry about all this."

"It could have been worse," Lucy said.

"Wait until I get a hold of Eddie!"

"You didn't kick him out with the others?"

He narrowed his eyes in thought. "No."

Giggles rippled through the air followed by a squeal of delight.

They turned toward the study, staring at the closed door. When the familiar giggle erupted again, there was no doubt what sordid thing happened and with whom.

"Lucy," Alexander's voice was hard, "please lock yourself in the bedroom until I come for you."

Lucy climbed the stairs but sat down on the top step to listen. The study door opened and disgruntled noises followed, probably from the light being flicked on.

"Get your clothes in order and get out, both of you!"

"But, Alex, it's only fair Eddie gets to try me out when you and Lucy—"

She could picture Eliza covering her mouth.

"You and Lucy what?" Edmund demanded.

"What are you even doing here, Eliza?" Alexander asked.

"Mother's driver dropped me off over an hour ago. You haven't telephoned in days and I worried. Eddie was kind enough to let me in. He said you were sleeping so I played a couple rounds of poker with the boys, drank a few shots of whiskey, and came in here for a little fun."

"Did Eddie mention to you that he's engaged now? That's what this whole stupid night was supposed to be about, his final drunken shenanigans with the guys, to which I repeatedly told him I didn't want to be a part of. But he kidnapped me, ruins eleven days of sobriety, invites whores into my home because I refused to go to the red-light district, and beds my little sister!" He took a few deep breaths. "Now I want both of you miserable people out of my house!"

"Aren't you going to hit me? Break my nose like you did Rupert's?"

"What, so you can do the same or worse to me? Do you want to know why I didn't toast your engagement with champagne, why I haven't been going to the Aethelwulf Club, and why I didn't want to go out on your drunken trip through town? I'll tell you why. My drinking nearly cost me Lucy's hand!"

While he explained each dreadful action he'd inflicted on her the night of the fire, Lucy clutched her knees to her chest and cried. Halfway through Alexander's horror story, Frederick let himself in the door. He stood behind Alexander, poised to fight or support—whichever was needed.

"Yes, wanting to keep your sister safe from men like me was smart, because you know how easily predators like us hide in plain sight. Yes, like *us*, Eddie. Even if the stories about you aren't as numerous, you're no better than me. You want to jump me with Maxwell or have Freddy team up with you, go ahead. Just remember that it'll all heap upon you when your sins catch up with your smooth, Easton ways."

"You wretch!" Edmund yelled.

"Eddie, no!" Eliza shrieked.

Lucy scrambled to the bottom of the stairs as Edmund's rage exploded on her fiancé. Alexander stood stoic, taking strikes to his face and middle but Frederick took Edmund from behind. The two took their sparing stances and circled each other in the entry to the dining room.

Lucy guided Alexander to the bathroom to stop the blood seeping from his nose. She held a wet cloth to his eye, hoping to reduce swelling from the hit.

"I'm sorry, Lucy. I had to make him understand the destruction this behavior can do to a good relationship." He smoothed her hair back as she wiped the blood from his face.

Eliza pushed into the bathroom. "Lucy, you have to stop them!"

Worried for Frederick's well-being, Lucy rushed to his aid. But it was Edmund who needed tending.

"You've gone soft, old friend," Frederick told him as Edmund doubled over, holding his ribs with one arm and his bloody nose with the other hand. "Sure, you can win against a man who's not fighting back, but you're no match for me anymore. Hurting Alex hurts Lucy, and I can't allow that."

"Freddy," Lucy whispered as she placed a hand on his taunt arm, "thank you, but it's enough. There is no honor left in me for you to fight for."

"You're still that golden maiden, Lucy, always worth defending." The fierce conviction in his voice almost persuaded her. His eyes roamed the green silk and she found herself wanting to be worth defending.

No longer bleeding, Alexander offered Edmund a towel for his nose before stepping between Lucy and Frederick to block his appreciative gaze. "I'm sure you were out searching for me, Freddy, but could I ask one more favor? Would you see these two home?"

Frederick agreed.

Eliza fawned over Edmund as they prepared to leave. "I'm sorry, Alex," she said on her way out. Then to Lucy, "You're the best thing to ever happen to him. I'm sorry for spoiling it."

"Stay safe," Frederick told Lucy. "I'll check in with you in the morning."

"Come see us, Freddy." Alexander locked the door behind the others and rubbed Lucy's bare arm. "You're freezing, my queen. Let me tuck you in."

Lucy climbed into the bed and he pulled the blankets up to her chin, kissing her cheek.

"Aren't you getting in?"

"I figured I'd sleep on the chaise." He pulled a pair of sleep pants out of the bottom dresser drawer and switched to them.

"Alex, will you not hold me after all we've been through? We've lain together but have yet to wake in the morning as one." She reached an arm out from the blanket to him, hoping she didn't appear as desperate as she felt.

"I was expecting that pleasure the day after our wedding." He came to the edge of the bed and kissed her hand.

She fingered under his blackening eye. "We've used the bed as though married. After all we've done, it can't hurt to hold one another while we sleep."

He turned off the light and spooned in beside her, whispering in her ear.

> "'My love for you is constant
> Through the storms
> And the waves
> I sail on
> Your arms around me
> Your lips upon mine
> Our bodies cleaving ever closer
> Until the break of day.'"

Forty-Two

Sun shone through the cracks in the plantation shutters as Alexander held Lucy with complete possession and ease, but she knew there would never be peace in a life dominated by secret societies and alcohol. Not wishing to leave their beautiful bed or lose his touch, she shifted further against him. But the drunken passion and fights the night before clashing within her head showed her life with Alexander Melling was anything but serene.

At least we slept together in our bed once. Hot tears dripped onto the pillow before her agony trembled into wracking sobs.

"Lucy!" Alexander rolled her to face him and wiped her tears with the edge of the sheet. "What is it, my queen?"

His arms around her were both comforting and heartbreaking. Everything she ever wanted, but what she needed to leave behind. Her kiss was hot and wet, masking the stale taste of the remnants of his drinking. She devoted all her attention to its execution in an attempt to clear her mind.

Stepping out of bed, she opened the shutters. He looked upon her with such devotion that it pained her to speak the words.

"I love you, but I can't live like this."

"We talk to Father Quinn tomorrow, but I'll run find a justice of the peace right now, Lucy." He scooped her into his arms and kissed her in the rectangle of light. "I'll make it right, I swear."

"I don't see how the cycle will ever end, and I need security. I'll always be afraid you'll slip into your old ways or that your father will send women to you. Your friends will eye me as someone you bedded and had to marry to make peace with my family."

"I don't need to associate with that sorry lot of Dardenne brothers anymore. I don't care what they think. I marry you because I love you. You're all I need, Lucy. You're all that's good in my life."

She placed her hands on his chest, noting his right eye rimmed with bruising from one of Edmund's strikes. "You're more than you give yourself credit for, Alex."

"I need you, my queen." His hands went to her waist with a kneading grasp she couldn't ignore.

She pressed her lips to his and backed him toward the bed. "You have me today."

"And I'll do my best to change your mind."

They spent hours exploring their desires, but Lucy wasn't sure if what she clung to was Alexander himself or the fantasy of an epic love affair. Midday, she curled into the crook of his arm.

"Each moment we spend together makes it more difficult to leave."

"Stay with me, Lucy. You needn't face the cruel world, the judging faces. Let this be your tower and I'll provide everything you could want. Satisfy all your cravings." He ran his fingers through her hair and down her back.

"But what would I do up here beside worry about you when you're gone?"

"Write. A desk by one of the windows looking down on the street should give you a good perspective. I'll bring your meals and bathe you each night in perfumed water."

"Food and a bath sound good."

She stretched and Alexander trailed his finger down the length of her body.

"I'll remember the sight of you always, but will you not allow me to gaze upon you all the days of my life?"

"I don't wish to live under the power of those with malicious tendencies."

"Then let's run away together." He went to his knees, clasping her hands to his heart. "Let's start fresh in a new city where no one knows us."

"We can't hide from ourselves." She stared at his earnest face with the memory of Rupert's words. "Who's Twila?"

He glared. "Where'd you hear that name?"

"Last night, before you chased them out, Rupert said I wouldn't be as easily disposed of as Twila."

Confusion followed by rage pained his face. "That was a lifetime ago."

"You've been my greatest temptation. You molded me into a woman who's willing to go against everything she's been taught for moments of pleasure. You're an amazing lover, Alex, but I don't see how this can work if you aren't honest with me. If you treated a woman as disposable, I need to—"

Alexander shoved her and jumped off the bed. "They've all been disposable! Every last one of them was to use and walk away, as Rupert well knows."

"Then why did he bring up that particular name? He's no fool. Just as he did with Consuela's name at the masquerade, he used Twila's name with a purpose."

"The purpose was to grate me! She's the only other woman I've had that I didn't pay for." A vein pulsed violently in his neck. "He's a jealous cad and wanted to wound you to stab at me because you're beyond his touch. I've told you I was no good and you were warned by others. You didn't run when you found out about the whorehouses, so why bother now? The rest of my past is just as seedy, but we can keep this goodness and beauty—have this every day—if you grant me your hand! You said we were already joined in action, that marriage was just a formality."

"I was wrong." She slipped his ring off as a tear rolled down her cheek. "We turned what we had into a love affair when it could have been everlasting."

"You asked for a love affair!" He clutched the ring in his fist. "I gave you what you wanted, Lucy, now it's my turn!"

"What did I know? I'd never been kissed."

He threw the ring on the floor and grabbed her neck. His icy stare traveled the length of her body in a way that caused Lucy to fear her safety. "You knew how to entice me, how to be so seductively innocent that I craved nothing more than a taste of your virgin skin."

"Alex, please let me go." She couldn't mask the tremor in her voice.

"You said I have you today. I claim that privilege over you until midnight." His left hand groped across her nightgown. "Is my drunken behavior part of the shadow of fear you don't wish to live under? Shall I prove you right by showing you how loathsome I can be while sober?"

"No, please, Alex. You'll taint everything we had together if you force yourself on me now."

He gripped her shoulders with both hands. "But if I make you hate me, it will be easier for you to run away."

"I love you too much, Alex. I'll never hate you or resent the time we've shared. Kiss me once more and let me go, please."

His smile was laced with malevolence, his penetrating gaze hard, but he released his hold. "I'll let you go, but just from our bedroom. I'll take you in every room of this Godforsaken house! It's nothing to me without you in it!"

"But you can live here to keep away from your father."

Alexander laughed. "If your love can't cure me, nothing can. I am who I am—another Melling who cares more for himself than those around him. I'll go back to my whoring and binge drinking like these two months never happened because that's the only way I know how to get through this heartache."

"Alex, you're not yourself."

"I'm a drunk who has his way with women, that's what I am! You want to know about Twila, I'll tell you. She was a sweet blonde who worked in the saloon in Tuscaloosa my fraternity brothers frequented. It was her first year away from the farm and she had her heart set on capturing one of the university fellows, no matter the cost. After our winter exams in '03, we drew lots for who would get a go with her before we took the train home for Christmas. I won." He licked his lips and thrust against Lucy.

Trembling, she closed her eyes.

"Don't you like my stories, Lucy? You always said I had a way with words." He rubbed against her in a mockery of lovemaking. "Sweet little Twila had a reputation by then, and it didn't take much to coax her into the storage room. Unfortunately, I'd drunk too much and passed out after I got what I wanted. Then I woke to the sound of moaning and found Rupert having a go with her. He was always a sore loser."

She leaned away. "He's despicable."

"And so am I, yet you love me." He trailed a finger down her cheek. "After Christmas and opening the Mardi Gras season, I'd quite forgotten Twila after returning to school. She approached us one night at the bar that spring and told us she was in the family way. Rupert argued it could have been any number of guys she'd been seen with, but she assured him the timing pointed to the two of us and expected one to marry her or she'd go to the police. She didn't know better than to confront law students with an ultimatum."

Alexander held her tighter and kissed Lucy with probing tongue.

"We believed she singled us out as potential fathers to her unfortunate bastard as we were from the wealthiest families. Rupert immediately offered her fifty dollars and the pay to be rid of the problem because he feared it would have been him she went after because there were witnesses who saw Twila go with me willingly." He gently kissed her cheek. "Like you, Consuela, and all the others, she wanted me."

Lucy's pounded his chest, hoping he'd let her go as the tears cascaded her face.

"Not until I'm done with my story, darling. We drew lots again for who would take her for the procedure. I lost that time and had to hire a wagon to haul her to some ramshackle barn where a man in a butcher's apron set about undoing a night of pleasure. I waited for it to be done so I could bring her back to town, but she didn't survive the experience."

Lucy gasped and he tightened his hold.

"That, my queen, was the old me. The one you will push me back to by leaving."

"You can't put this on me! I told you in the beginning you'd have to be responsible for your own actions! You're better than this. I've seen the good in you. You're capable of love and respect!"

"Don't try to shower me with trifling words. I can't trust you with my heart if you're willing to let one night of drinking draw a wedge between us." He shoved her away. "Storytime's over. I'll count to five, and then I'm coming to take you wherever I catch you, Lucy. One. Two…"

She stumbled from the room, first thinking to lock herself in the bathroom, but she went for the front door instead. Before she reached the bottom of the stairs, he ran the upper hall. Her plan switched to reach the kitchen because it would be less of a spectacle to run through the alley than down St. Francis Street. Lucy slammed through the swinging kitchen door just as Alexander jumped off the stairs. Instead of clear shot to the back door, Lucy ran into Frederick, who reflexively put his arm around her to keep her from falling backward from the force of their collision.

"What's—"

"In the kitchen it is!" Alexander shoved the door open. "Please return my wife, Freddy."

"She's not your wife."

"Some people would consider us married with all we've done together, even if she returned my ring after making love to me."

"Alex, you need—"

"No, Freddy, *you* need to go! What are you doing here anyway? Did Lucy plan for you to meet her after she stomped on my heart?"

"I'm here because you invited me. I've been here the last hour, cleaning up after your friends so Lucy wouldn't be subjected to it. I know she spent several hours cleaning while I was out combing the town for you last night."

"I wish you would have found me, then they all wouldn't have ended up here." Alexander's voice sounded like a boy who'd lost his best friend, but the sad face soon turned to the hard mask he'd inherited from his father. "But you failed me, just as Lucy has! You've both failed me because I failed myself! After the second tavern, I accepted Lucy was out of my reach for the night and cozied with the bottle."

"Don't talk of her breaking your heart when you've given her enough reasons to walk away."

"But she keeps coming back for more!" Alexander spread his arms wide. "I may not be a fighter or as muscular as you, but there's no complaint over my stamina and prowess in bed. I can give you a list of women who'll swear to it."

"Please don't be crass," Lucy pled. "You make me sound like another conquest."

"That's what you're making yourself into by walking away when what we have is worth saving!" His blue eyes burned like flames.

"We've both tried." Lucy reached her hand to his arm and he snatched her wrist.

"We were doing well and it was heavenly to hold you in my arms and wake up with you in our bed. But I guess that proves that Consuela was right. You have ruined me."

Lucy's free hand struck his face with an infuriated slap. In his shock, Alexander let go of her arm and she fled through the swinging door. Seconds later, he pinned her on the settee.

Frederick threw him into the nearest armchair. "Get dressed, Lucy. I'll bring you home."

Blinded by tears, she managed to feel her way up the stairs. At the top, she erupted into noisy sobs.

"Lucy," Alexander's voice cracked, "I'm sorry!"

The ride across town was over too quickly and facing Edmund was almost as difficult as leaving Alexander. Lucy's brother sat in a rocker on the front porch with a cup of coffee, two black eyes, and a swollen lip. She wished Frederick's hands were free in case Edmund tried to attack, but he carried a crate of her favorite books she insisted on bringing home with her. The other things would be a later trip.

The Easton siblings stared at each other. Edmund motioned to Frederick and the crate. "Does that mean the wedding's off?"

Lucy nodded.

"Is it my fault?"

"The chain of events starting with your friends kidnapping him didn't help our situation, but I can't blame it entirely on you." She opened the door for Frederick. "And don't feel like you have to defend my honor anymore. Rupert saw me come out of the bedroom and I'm sure he told everyone."

"I've fielded several calls about that today."

Frederick returned and stood beside Lucy with a watchful eye.

"I love him. It wasn't some cheap affair, though I'm sure it will be reduced to one in the minds of others. Don't feel you need to erase him from your life. He could use a few friends that know what he battles."

Edmund scoffed. "And what would that be? Insatiable desires?"

"Demons." Lucy clutched Frederick's arm. "His father, alcohol, and women are the worst. Alex has a generous heart and could soar if it wasn't for those chains holding him to his past. I tried to free him, but it wasn't enough. Maybe someone will be able to reach him one day."

Epilogue

Alexander woke with a headache, the light too bright to comfortably open his eyes. He tried to move his arm to shade the sun, but it was pinned under something.

Someone.

He yanked his limb free, groaning from the effort.

"Alexander the Great, are you ready for more?" Consuela's warm hands caressed his bare chest when he would have given anything for Lucy's cool touch.

"No." He flung his arm across his face, flinching from the contact against his blackened eye, complements from Eddie's beating nearly a week ago.

But Consuela never listened. Her hand went lower. "I'll have you ready to conquer in no time."

"I said no." He shoved her arm and rolled away.

She huffed. "I'm only doing what you pay me to."

"I'll give you an extra five to leave me alone."

"I don't neglect my clients, especially my favorite one." Her nails playfully scratched down his back. "It's been a pleasure to have you in my bed all week, but I'm afraid Madame Case will expect you to start paying rent if you stay any longer. Bring me to your house the Dardennes celebrated in last Friday."

"The duplex was for Lucy." He pulled the blanket to his chin, trying to keep the chill off, though it was more than on the surface. "I'll have no other woman there."

"But she's left you."

"I never deserved her."

"She didn't deserve *you*, Alexander the Great." Consuela's hands roamed as she heaped him with flattery. Despite his guilt, his eyes closed from her soothing administrations. "You need more than a spoiled society chippie to keep you satisfied."

He was off the bed in an instant. "Lucy's not spoiled! She's nothing like the other ladies, nothing! If she's ruined now, it's because of me, not something she did."

Consuela shifted on the bed to better display herself in her flimsy undergarments. "You don't need her. I can satisfy you better than anyone in your set."

Alexander laughed and looked at her with disgust. "I might have agreed with you last year, but no longer. Lucy fulfilled everything and more. She touched me in ways I didn't know were possible because we loved each other. Not only did she give me her innocence, we shared dreams, our very souls. Nothing will ever be that magical, that satiating. Lucy is my everything."

"I could love you and share your life." Her smile was more greed than devotion.

He took his pants from the chair beside the bed and pulled them on. "Get over yourself, Consuela."

"We've shared much pleasure."

He closed the button on his trousers, his head aching as much as his heart. "You're nothing but a whore."

"Then get out of my room!" Consuela threw a pillow at him.

"I've paid to be here, though I think you'd accept me otherwise."

"Then I'll give it back, Mister High and Mighty!" She snatched a wad of bills out of her side drawer before marching to him.

He looked down at her annoyed face and smirked when she shoved the money at him.

"Are you paying me for the pleasure now, Consuela? I'll let you touch me if you ask nicely."

Alexander took her free hand and trailed his fingers the length of her arm until he squeezed her bare shoulder. Her dark eyes sparked much like Twila's had that night. *Curse Rupert for dragging that to the light. It was part of my confession to Father Quinn at Christmas. I don't need that guilt—it's over!*

Seeking to prove his worth, he flirted. "Do you want to touch me?"

"Perhaps." She licked her lips and lowered the money.

His head spun with a delayed buzz from the night before, but he turned it into a sultry motion with his hips while he tugged her closer. "Do you want me to touch you?"

"Always, my conqueror." She tucked the cash into his waistband. "You may do whatever you wish to me."

His gaze lowered from her face to her heaving chest. Seeing the passion marks he'd left made his stomach churn. *She's not my Lucy!* For a fleeting second, the desire to treat Consuela as he had Lucy burned through him like fire. *At least I wouldn't be able to say I treated a whore better than my beloved queen.* But remembering what pain and dishonor he'd done the times he was drunken caused bile to rise in his throat.

Grasping Consuela's backside, he forced his mouth to hers. She angled back from his unshaved face but he waited until her tongue masked the stale taste in his mouth before releasing her.

"I wish to leave you." Before she could speak, he continued. "You're no longer satisfying."

Her face fell into an ugly sneer. "If you're going to let a few nights with that chit ruin what we have, then I don't want to see you in my room! She's no better than me!"

"Lucille Easton is a thousand times better than you."

Consuela threw another pillow at him. "Then get out!"

Alexander stood his ground until she grabbed his empty brandy bottle off the table. He opened the door to escape but paused to look back at his temporary home.

"I said get out!"

Several other women peered from their rooms at the disturbance as the bottle shattered on the doorframe beside him. One of his shoes struck his back as he walked down the hall. Prudie motioned him into her room at the top of the stairs. The buxom blonde was another favorite with him—Consuela's stand-in during her monthlies.

She closed the door behind him. "She's been irritable the past few weeks, but you're always welcome here, Alexander."

Smiling, he ran his hand over Prudie's loose hair—the closest to Lucy's he'd ever seen. "Would you be a dear and collect my clothing and shoes?"

"Happily." A minute later, she returned with his things in her ample arms. "She's still on a rampage, but I got everything. May I help you dress?"

Her brown eyes were bright compared to Consuela's dark ones, but it was her hair he couldn't stop looking at. "Turn around, please."

She set his things on her bed and obeyed. Alexander helped himself to her brush on the dressing table to care for her golden hair. Once it was smoothed, he dropped the brush and wrapped his arms around her, burying his head in the silken strands.

"I know you loved your fiancée and it hurts," Prudie whispered. "I saw her at your masquerade last month. She's very beautiful and elegant. It'll be difficult for you to find a replacement, whether for a night or a lifetime."

Alexander turned her to him. "You always understood me best, darling Prudie. May I kiss you in gratitude for your kind words?"

Prudie's warmth and softness beckoned him to continue to indulge, but he needed to get away. He dressed without shame, enjoying her quiet attention.

"Thank you for your help, Prudie." He handed her the money that had fallen from his clothes. "This was technically Consuela's but she gave it back. You can have it."

"I couldn't, Alexander. Once she calms down, she'll accept it. I'll return it later."

He kissed her cheek. "As you wish."

"Come anytime, even if you only need a listening ear." She straightened his cravat and smoothed the lapel of his suit jacket.

"I appreciate it."

Alexander drove the half-dozen blocks to the duplex, remembering the pain of his last night there anew. After Frederick took Lucy home, he went to the whorehouse to find solace, spending the remainder of the weekend indulging in old behaviors to numb his pain. His nights were too full of drinks and debauchery for him to be much use in the office, but his father patted him on the back and told him to leave early if he wanted. And he did, returning to Consuela each afternoon.

He stayed in the duplex long enough to shower and shave, and then went to the office, asking Miss Renna to telegram the Watts family to prepare for him on the afternoon ferry. A weekend of solitude and riding Janus were what he desired. When he headed for the docks that afternoon, the spires of the cathedral caught his eye. He needed confession more than anything but he wasn't ready to drag himself before Father Quinn.

Shoving his fists into the pocket of his coat at the docks, he sought warmth against the wintry wind as much from the feeling that the world was closing in on him. The seats on the boat were more than half empty but he found himself drawn to a priestly looking fellow on a side bench, two ragged suitcases at his feet.

"Do you mind if I join you?" Alexander asked.

"You may sit as you like, *signore*." The man's voice was thick with an Italian accent but his smile was large, putting Alexander immediately at ease. "It appears you had some troubles."

He motioned to his bruised eye and Alexander laughed.

"Yes, a rough weekend last time around. I hope this one will be quieter." Alexander pointed to the man's cassock. "Are you a priest at the Italian parish in Daphne?"

"I hope to be in the days ahead, but for now, I am a deacon. Father Angelo is expecting me for training. Are you a believer?"

"Born and raised in The Cathedral of the Immaculate Conception, though I feel unworthy to enter at the moment. I'm Alexander Melling." He offered his hand.

The man's olive hand was strong. "Deacon De Fiore, recent immigrant from Florence. I decided to come to America while seeking the priesthood. I feel my destiny is here."

Alexander studied the deacon's Romanesque face and found openness in his soul. "It's not even the close of February, but I've done awful things this year, Deacon De Fiore. Many have been confessed, but with my latest infractions, I feel completely at odds with myself. I cannot return to Father Quinn nor can I face the ones I love. Would you help me find consolation?"

"I am not yet a priest, but speaking of troubles helps one improve. If you would like to talk with me, I am at your service, *Signore* Melling."

"Mr. Melling is my father, Deacon De Fiore. Please call me Alexander."

"And you may call me Claudio."

As the steamboat pulled into the bay, Alexander unfolded the story of his lost love. The deacon listened raptly, smiling over the descriptions of Lucy's beauty and his face showing concern when told about the violence against her. In closing, Alexander confessed how he'd spent the last six days.

"My indulgences this week have compounded my guilt and made me realize I treat strangers better than the one I desperately love." He looked to the deacon, tears in his eyes. "What can I do?"

"You are correct to be concerned, Alexander. Knowing you are in the wrong is the first step. You will need confession and proper reconciliation with the Lord, but you may begin by promising yourself to change. Forsake the women, for a start. Those establishments will only bring heartache and disease."

Alexander nodded, though he couldn't imagine either Consuela or Prudie harboring filth. "God knows my weaknesses. He knows finding release has been habitual for years."

"Did you not refrain for more than a month after you started courting Lucy?"

"Yes, but—"

"If you want to improve yourself so you can feel worthy of Lucy or a woman like her, it must be done."

"Do you think she would have me back?" Alexander asked as the Daphne shore grew closer.

"That is up to her, but it sounds as though she truly loves you. Even so, her trust will be hard won." Claudio looked at the approaching dock. "This is my location, no?"

Alexander nodded.

"Since you are staying for the weekend, would you like to come to the parish Sunday? I believe you need someone to check in with you, to hold you accountable until you are back with your priest and right with the Lord."

"All right, Claudio. I'll come for Mass Sunday morning. Ask Father Angelo if you can come back to Seacliff with me to share Sunday dinner."

"*Sí*, I will request the time off. It is good to make your acquaintance, Alexander Melling."

***

On Saturday morning, Alexander rode Janus up the beach, traveling all the way to the Civil War lookout in Spanish Fort before turning south. As he galloped along the Montrose beach, a familiar figure rode toward him from Seacliff. He spurred Janus faster, passing Eliza on Flora with a rush of air.

"Alex, stop!"

But he rode all the harder, knowing his steed was quicker.

In the yard, he jumped off his horse and threw the reins at Mr. Campbell. "I'll ride again later, so keep things at the ready."

Alexander was on the back porch when his sister arrived, but he didn't turn at the sound of Flora whinnying or Eliza calling. He grabbed a muffin off the counter in the kitchen, nodding to Rosemary as he passed through. A minute later, he was locked in his room, muffin and bottle of brandy in his lap before the fireplace.

Eliza pounded on his door. "Alex, please talk to me! I want to say I'm sorry."

"You just did!"

The banging returned. "I'll not leave until I see you!"

He drank straight from the bottle between bites and managed to ignore the incessant knocking until he was done. Knowing how stubborn Eliza was, he stomped to the door and flung it open.

"Alex!" She threw her arms about him. "You look better than I expected. I ran into Sean in Bienville Square Thursday afternoon when I tried to catch you at the office. He said you looked haggard all week."

"Your approval means nothing to me."

"Does it bother you I'm now on friendly terms with your Dardenne brothers?"

"They're no longer my brothers and I've washed my hands of you. If you can't listen to what I tell you, I'll tell you nothing."

"I'm sorry, Alex." She took his arm, periwinkle eyes pleading. "I should have listened about Eddie. He's been nothing but a headache and not worth much beyond his kissing abilities."

"Woe is you, Eliza Rose." He crossed back to his chair and took another swig from the bottle.

"I'm sick about you losing Lucy. You two are perfect for each other."

"Tell me something I don't know."

"I miss you, big brother." Eliza folded her arms across her chest. "Why aren't you staying at the duplex?"

He shook his head and turned away. "I can't stay without Lucy. Everywhere I look, she's there, haunting me. I see the bed I ravaged her on, the empty bookcases, her clothes missing from the closet. It's too damn painful."

"Then come home to Government Street."

"I don't wish to put up with Father any more than I have to."

"Home has to be better than where you've been hiding this week." She raised an eyebrow at him. "You were in the red-light district, weren't you? Sharing a filthy bed with one of those women you swore you were done with after finding Lucy."

"I tried to forget her." He raked his fingers through his hair. "But she's in my soul."

"You're meant for each other." Eliza's dark hair, half-undone from her ride, made her look younger, innocent—the little sister he used to harass. "Her essence is a part of you now."

"She'll never accept me back, especially after what I've done this week. I walked away from our home and straight to another's bed."

"You need to try, Alex. You owe that much to yourself and her. She knew you weren't perfect and looked past that for months."

"I had her trust before. I'll need to prove that I've changed before ever trying to win her back." He sighed. "But she has the noble Frederick Lionel Davenport comforting her now. I'll never measure up to him."

"He's a fine specimen, maybe the finest in the city, but she doesn't love him like she loves you. She admires him and respects him, but her eyes don't burn with passion like they do when you're together. Dancing or talking, you two are pure fire."

"That I dowsed with cold water when I hurt my queen."

"Don't be too hard on yourself, Alex." She squeezed his hand. "Let's stop talking about it and make plans to ride together like old times. How about one after dinner and then another in the morning? You're staying the weekend, aren't you?"

"I take the ferry Monday morning, but I already have plans tomorrow."

"What could be more important than spending time with family?"

"Attending Mass. I met a deacon on the ferry yesterday and he invited me to attend Church of the Assumption. I hope to bring him back here for dinner afterward."

"Church of the Assumption?" she questioned. "Is he Italian?"

"From Florence. He's doing his priesthood training here."

Her eyes widened. "I've always admired the bone structure of Italian men. Is he handsome?"

Alexander narrowed his eyes. "You're to leave him alone, Eliza!"

"So he is!" She clapped her hands and squealed. "An Easton chin will be nothing compared to the lines of a full-blooded Italian."

"I forbid it! He's training to become a priest and doesn't need you as a distraction."

"I'll be on my best behavior, Alex. What time do we leave for Mass?"

THE END

Bonus

"Masked Flaws"

A prequel short story to

The Possession Chronicles

Edmund Easton spent the minutes before his lunch hour scowling at his brother's office. Maxwell flaunted his full partnership with Easton and Sons by leaving his door ajar—thereby providing a clear view for his only living brother to witness him indulging in cigarettes and cigars whenever he felt like it. Cramped in his corner desk in the main room with the secretaries, Edmund wasn't allowed to smoke. Though it was 1903 and women were ready for voting rights, his father, James Easton, deemed it ungentlemanly for him to light up in the same room as the ladies.

I'm nothing but a secretary in pants to those two. Easton and Sons be damned! The sign might as well read Easton and Eldest *Son.*

Stomping out of the building as soon as the clock struck noon, Edmund paused long enough to light a cigarette before making his way through the lunchtime crowd.

"Eddie!" Maxwell called from behind. "Wait up!"

He exhaled a cloud of smoke and turned, hazel eyes glaring. "What do you want?"

Maxwell clapped his shoulder, giving it a squeeze. "You're wasting away, little brother. I ran across Freddy the other day and had to take a swing at him to test his burgeoning strength. You two used to box together as often as you could. Why'd you stop?"

"He got married." Edmund smirked to hide the bitterness over his childhood best friend inheriting an accounting firm. Sure, Frederick Davenport had lost his father and new bride within half a year, but he didn't have to answer to anyone for his choices.

"Father always said he'll make you a partner when you settle down."

"I'm not in the least ready to settle in with a wife. And it didn't do Freddy a lick of good either as he's stuck in mourning bands for carnival season." Edmund elbowed around Maxwell. "I'll see you after lunch."

He finished his cigarette as he neared Bienville Square. A group of lawyers were congregated before the bandstand, men he'd gone to grade school with who were settling into roles as important fixtures in the legal scene about town. Alexander Melling turned his icy blue eyes on Edmund and smiled with a dark glint amid his fair complexion.

"Easton!" Alexander, the third generation and only son at Melling and Associates Law Firm, waved him over. "Where have you been hiding yourself? I only see you at Mass these days."

Rupert Lyons, long face as serious as ever, gave a sardonic laugh. "He's hiding in that dusty warehouse by the river, counting cargo."

Some of the others smirked and turned away from the newcomer, but Alexander shook his hand. "I'm glad to see you. How are things looking for your carnival season?"

Edmund shoved his hands in his pockets. "Order of Mayhem with my family on New Year's Eve. No other invitations yet, but they'll come along. I attended five balls last year."

"Poor sop," Rupert muttered.

"What do you expect for a guy who grew up amid so many sisters?" Sean joked.

"The sisters are his only saving grace," Rupert replied.

"Is sweet little Lucy coming out this season?" Sean asked with a leer.

"Get your facts right," Rupert said. "Lucille Easton was presented last New Year's Eve, though she failed to make another appearance all season." He moved his hands in an hourglass shape. "Believe me, I've kept my eyes out for that filly, but she keeps eluding me."

Edmund fisted Rupert's suit jacket, his other arm moving back to strike. "You better keep your hands off my sister!"

Alexander took Edmund's elbow. "I'd be careful if I were you, Rupert. Eddie was a champion boxer in school, and I've heard he's taken out a few guys who looked not even two seconds at his sister's assets. I think his legendary strength is what we need. How would you like to join a society for yourself rather than rely on your family's meager social connections, Easton?"

Bristling with indignation—his family was as well-off as any of theirs, but his father would rather spend his downtime playing golf than hobnobbing around at parties—Edmund controlled his anger enough to force a smile.

"What, you think you have a monopoly on Mardi Gras?"

Alexander threw an arm around him and whispered from his several-inch disadvantage. "As a matter of fact, we do. Mystics of Dardenne members tend to rule the revelry." He mussed Edmund's brown hair. "We'll save a spot for you, Easton. Let me know by midnight Mass."

***

Edmund held the sleeve of Lucy's pale green dress as they climbed the steps to the portico of the cathedral for Christmas Mass. Her nineteen-year-old figure—two years his junior—was displayed to its best advantage in the flared ensemble. Her blonde hair was skillfully wrapped high on her head, adorned with holly sprigs and her white mantilla. Edmund followed the path his parents and youngest sister took until he spied Rupert and Sean nearby. Hoping to steer Lucy from their hungry eyes, he angled her toward the far door.

"Easton!" Sean called.

Lucy elbowed him. "I think your friends are trying to get your attention. I don't mind if you say hello."

Giving an inward groan, Edmund brought them to the column the men leaned against.

"Eddie," Sean said as his grin flashed his chipped tooth, "how about an introduction to your lovely sister since it's been so long since we've spoken?"

"Lucy, this is Sean Spunner and Rupert Lyons. I'm sure you've seen both of them around since those days Sean was running around our yard in short pants. *Gentlemen*"—he stressed the word, as if willing them to behave—"my closest sister, Lucille Easton."

Her smile was tight, her offered hand stiff as they each took it. Edmund wanted to knock the smirk off Rupert's face as he visually took Lucy's measurements.

Rupert brazenly kissed the back of her hand. "The pleasure is mine, Miss Easton."

Alexander made a show of brushing against Lucy as he maneuvered into the group. "After making the acquaintance of a charming young woman, you can't say it was a wasted evening at Mass."

Rather than shying away, Lucy's green eyes appeared to brighten as she took in the sight of the Alexander as he shamelessly pressed against her before settling beside Rupert. She smiled and managed a hello before Edmund had her by the elbow.

"We must join our family," he said. "Please excuse us."

"A moment of your time, Eddie." Alexander leaned across Lucy. "What's your response to my question from the other week?"

He narrowed his eyes, inclining his head toward Alexander's hand hovering near Lucy's backside. "Yes, though it must be understood that some things are forever off limits."

Alexander grinned. "You'll hear from me this week, Easton."

"Melling, you dog." Sean's voice snaked through the boisterous chatter of the parishioners as Edmund took his sister inside. "You nearly pinched her seat under Eddie's nose!"

Edmund carried the taint of the encounter with him over Christmas. He'd heard the stories—both from the guys themselves and others—of the conquests made by Alexander and Rupert, but to think of anything happening to his naïve sister was too much to fathom. Lucy spent the better part of her life with her nose in a book, though in their youth she was just as eager as the neighborhood boys to join in games of knights and castles. She and Frederick had been the best players, but Edmund no longer wished for his friends to play with her. Not at their present games.

***

On Thursday, two days before New Year's Eve, the doorbell rang after supper. Edmund heard Alexander's smooth voice coupled with Lucy's tinkling laughter and nearly spilt his brandy in his rush to the foyer.

"Alex," Edmund said as he came around the corner, "what brings you here?"

"I require your advice. Would you step out with me a moment?"

"Of course." He turned to his sister. "Thanks for getting the door, Lucy."

She glanced at Alexander and bowed her head as though embarrassed before returning to the parlor where she'd been reading. Alexander eyed her departing figure with open appreciation.

"Stop looking." Edmund collected a coat, still holding his drink in the other hand.

Alexander relieved him of his brandy. "To chase away the unrighteous thoughts. You owe me that much for parading her around." He swallowed the rest in one gulp and set the empty glass on the credenza.

Edmund yanked him to the porch. "Like hell I parade her! I've been shielding her for years from cads like you."

"And for good reason." Alexander jumped off the steps and removed his cigarette case from his pocket, holding it out for Edmund. They both lit up and after the first few puffs, Alexander gazed at the parlor window where Lucy sat in profile under the lamp, head bent over a book. "I never noticed how perfectly formed she is."

Edmund swung but Alexander dodged the punch. "If you ever touch her, I'll—"

Alexander laughed. "I'm not in the habit of deflowering debutantes. I prefer my women experienced—something you'll learn in the days ahead if you complete your initiation. There's a wide world of pleasures to be had, and Mystics of Dardenne members are the ones that gather them with gusto. Don't you want in?"

Edmund nodded. "But like I said Christmas Eve, Lucy's off limits to all of you."

"We tease. Well, maybe not Rupert." Alexander removed an envelope from his breast pocket. "Your instructions. Look for me at the Mayhem ball when you're ready to embark."

***

Edmund adjusted his black tuxedo jacket and scanned the ballroom at the Battle House Hotel. With his blond hair, Alexander stood out amid the masked crowd at Order of Mayhem's ball. Combined with his metallic Columbina mask and bowtie, he proved to be the golden boy of the night, from his practiced moves on the dancefloor with a variety of women, to his infectious laughter among the men. Edmund would be lying if he said he didn't envy the notoriety of the young lawyer, not to mention his confidence. He did whatever he wanted and others followed.

Unable to cut in while he danced, an hour passed before Edmund had the opportunity to join Alexander. Without speaking, Alexander nodded toward the punch bowls and slipped Edmund a flask when he came alongside him. With the first of his three-part initiation complete, Edmund helped himself to a glass of the spiked punch.

Alexander laughed. "Easy there, Easton. You'll need all your faculties for your next exhibition. Meet me in the alley in twenty minutes."

Throat burning from the whiskey-laced drink, Edmund watched Rupert carry a glass toward Lucy. She stood with Maxwell and his wife on the edge of the dancefloor. After rushing to her side, Edmund took Lucy's arm by the silk of her long gloves.

"How about a dance, sister?"

Without waiting for a response, he began a waltz. Rupert stopped a few feet away, shaking his head before drinking the punch himself. When the song ended, Edmund escorted Lucy to their parents' table.

"Be careful tonight, Lucy," he whispered as he kissed her cheek.

Maxwell followed Edmund into the lobby. Taking him by the shoulder, he shoved Edmund into a corner behind a potted palm. "What's got you on edge tonight?"

"Nothing." Edmund pushed him out of the way, but Maxwell blocked his escape.

"Tell big brother Max all about your troubles, Eddie."

"There's no trouble. I've been invited to join a society, and I need to be somewhere."

Maxwell crossed his arms, his broad-shoulders intimidating. "Does it have anything to do with your yanking Lucy about?"

"Some of the guys keep insinuating that they'd like a go with her. Please watch her while I'm gone."

Maxwell laughed. "You have *one* sister to defend. I had to keep tabs on Susan, Cora, *and* Emma when they were all out at the same time. But don't worry. Lucy's too reserved to get swept away by any revelry makers."

"Even debonair Dardennes?"

He scoffed. "Those types aren't interested in deep thinkers. They want ones who don't wish to philosophize."

"They're interested when she's built the way Lucy is. I've heard more than enough from several of them."

"Mystics of Dardenne members?" Maxwell looked skeptical. "I find it hard to believe those guys would ever announce themselves to you. You're not their type."

"Shows how much you know!" Edmund charged past in his anger, heading for the exit.

Maxwell caught him on the sidewalk and nudged him against the stone wall. "I know more than you think, Eddie. It can't have changed that much since I was a bachelor. I was a member before I married, and as recent as last decade they only invited the highest on the social ladder from influential families."

Shame burned his clean-shaven face. "I'll prove I'm just as worthy of membership as the next guy! Especially you, since you're only the son of an import salesman, same as me."

"The *eldest* son who was given full partnership upon graduation." His mask shadowed his hazel eyes, but Edmund knew they were as challenging as ever—just as his own. "Go ahead, Eddie. You won't last a night with those animals."

Minutes later, Alexander stood lookout while Edmund crawled under all the carriages and automobiles belonging to the city council members to disconnect the axles and then leave Mystics of Dardenne calling cards on their seats. Afterward, Edmund followed his friend back into the ballroom.

"Which young woman will be blessed with your attentions tonight, Easton? Kate Stuart?"

Edmund gave a nervous laugh at the mention of the sharp-eyed ruler of the debutantes. "Hardly."

Alexander's pale eyes flashed with mischief within his gold mask. "I get the feeling she'd skin you alive and run you up the flagpole in front of the courthouse. You need a meek soul who won't spread gossip. Too bad you can't use your sister."

Edmund scowled. "No one touches Lucy!"

"I swear to you we haven't. A sweet conquest like her wouldn't pass without bragging." Alexander's gaze roamed the ballroom. "What about Grace Anne Marley? I hear she gives and takes a bit with each of her escorts without playing pious."

His stomach soured at the mention of Lucy's best friend. *She'd better not teach my sister her tricks!* "No, she'd be sure to tell Lucy if something happened between us."

Alexander slung an arm about his shoulders. "Judith McGowan?"

"But she's friends with Kate," Edmund protested. *Who would have thought feeling up a woman would be the most difficult initiation to pass?*

"Yes, but unlike frigid Kate, she'd welcome the attention. I'll ask her to dance and you cut in. And remember, it doesn't count unless you've got her whole buttocks or breast in your hand. I'll be watching. Do this and I've got a special celebration planned for you."

Edmund slunk to a nearby chair, keeping his gaze on Alexander's arrogant stride. Judith smiled at his invitation, and he set them around the dancefloor in a lavish display of fluidity and charm, to the strains of the string quartet. Where most men would shy away from taller women, Alexander didn't allow his average build to be a disadvantage. He'd danced with women of all shapes and sizes, and Judith was no exception.

After a minute, Edmund took his chance. "May I cut in?" he asked Alexander.

"Miss McGowan, you know Edmund Easton, don't you? His family owns the largest import company in the city."

Her smile widened. "Why, yes, Mr. Easton. I'd be happy to dance with you."

Edmund's right hand set comfortably on her jutting hip beside her abnormally tiny waist. Her brunette hair, piled in a pompadour, almost reached his own height, but he kept his eyes on her face— plain but pleasant. Judith's hand traced the definition of his shoulder as she angled closer, giving him a clear view of her cleavage that proved to be as shapely as her lower half.

"You're a fine dancer, Mr. Easton. Why have we never shared one before?"

Taking the opportunity, his gaze lingered at her chest several seconds as he tugged her closer. "It appears I'm finally outgrowing my shyness around beautiful women."

"I admire a man who knows what he likes."

"Your warmth puts me at ease, Miss McGowan." He gave her his best smile and chanced another look at her front.

"It's Carnival, Mr. Easton. You needn't be bashful if there's something you'd like to try."

Wondering if Alexander had set him up, Edmund raised his brows.

"Don't go telling your friends I offered," she whispered. "I'd only do so for someone as respectable as you. I've never heard gossip about your exploits, unlike Alexander Melling. Unless he changes his ways, he'll have to find a wife out of state because no respectable young lady in Mobile would accept a cad like him, with or without his father's fortune."

"Is that so?"

She nodded. "Keep us moving briskly and bring your hand up from my waist. No one will notice."

I hope at least one person does. But for all your chatter against Alexander, I do believe you've done this before, Judith. How unladylike.

Edmund did as requested, feeling her corset seams through the blue gown until he reached the softness of her left breast. Judith gasped with pleasure and clutched his shoulder. Fingers spreading to palm her generous mound, he squeezed as they reached above her décolletage, gently nudging the ruffle lower.

"So soft and feminine," he whispered.

"Mr. Easton." She was near breathless.

"Call me Edmund." He smiled as his hand snaked back to her waist and then around her hip to grasp her buttocks.

The song came to a close and she stood before him with dewy eyes. "Will you ask me for another dance?"

"Sometime this season, if not tonight, Miss McGowan." He kissed the back of her gloved hand. "It's been a pleasure."

***

"Rupert didn't think you had it in you, but I knew you did!" Alexander slapped Edmund's back as soon as they were outside the ballroom. "You had her all worked up and then scored a bonus point! Does she feel as good as she looks?"

"She does, though I don't see how she can breathe all bound up in that corset."

"All the more fun to undress when things come spilling out." Alexander laughed and led him to a waiting carriage. He glanced at the driver. "You know where to."

"Yes, Master Melling."

"How did Judith compare to others you've handled?" Alexander asked once they were underway, hands cupping his own non-existent breasts.

Edmund fiddled with the coat in his lap. "She was soft…"

"Easton, have you no experience? For the love of all that's holy, don't let the others guys know!" He patted his knee. "It's a good thing I've whisked you away. By the time the others arrive, you'll know plenty."

Arrive? Edmund looked out the carriage window and saw they were entering the red light district. *Maxwell was right. I'm in over my head, but I can't back out now.*

Swallowing his fear, he managed a smile. "I appreciate this, Alex."

"Here." Alexander pulled a bottle of medicinal tooth ache drops from his jacket. "Take a swig or two. It makes for an amazing experience where we're going."

The liquid cocaine was meant to be taken in tiny doses not mouthfuls, but Edmund needed the courage, so he took a swig as directed. By the time they climbed the steps of the brothel, Edmund's head was buzzing with energy that couldn't escape.

"Happy New Year's, ladies!" Alexander called as he let himself in the front door.

Several women lounging in the front room looked to him with smiles. A petite brunette tucked herself under his arm, and he immediately cupped a breast possessively as he claimed her mouth with a kiss.

Edmund stood awkwardly before the display while the women watched with perceived jealousy. *He has it all, even the envy of the other harlots.*

When they came up for air, the woman had a hand tucked in the waistband of Alexander's tuxedo. "Consuela, I need your help."

"Anything, Alexander the Great."

His impish smile doubled as he pulled an envelope from his jacket. "I need you and as many of your friends to attend the Mystics of Dardenne masquerade in a few weeks. Arrive together and this will provide entrance for you."

She clutched the invitation. "A real masquerade rather than waiting for you to stumble here in the middle of the night?"

"Yes, Consuela. I want you to come to us this time. There's no reason our revelry can't handle more indulgences, especially with new blood in our group." He nodded to Edmund. "Meet our finest newbie. He had a deb gasping under his touch in the middle of the ballroom."

She giggled and looked to an older woman who'd followed the conversation. "You hear that, Hazel? We're going to a masquerade, and there's a fresh crop of men to delight!"

The willowy woman nodded and sucked on her cigarette. "The Dardennes never disappoint."

"Come on, Eddie." Alexander steered Consuela toward the stairs as Edmund followed. "I'm going to need Prudie's assistance tonight. Is she busy?"

Consuela crossed her arms.

"For my friend." Alexander groped her backside. "You know I need your ministrations more than anything. Go ready yourself for me."

He knocked at the first door on the landing. A voluptuous blonde with a surprisingly innocent face opened the door. The smile she gave Alexander was wanting, and she did nothing to cover her scanty nightgown beneath the open robe.

"Good evening, Alexander."

"Prudie, my dear." He claimed her mouth much like he'd done with Consuela, hands splayed over her broad hips. "May we come in?"

Her eyes widened as she seemed to notice Edmund for the first time. "Both of you?"

"Yes," Alexander said with a wink, "but nothing too naughty this time."

Prudie flushed and looked up at Edmund when he followed Alexander into the room. Closing the door behind them, she crossed to the bed where Alexander motioned to her. She settled on the tidy bedspread where he sat beside her, a hand going to her bare knee.

"I've got an important job for you," Alexander said with a seductive tone, pointing to Edmund where he stood before the dressing table. "My friend, Eddie Easton, is the newest Mystics of Dardenne member this season. He has a little secret I need you to confidentially address."

Face heating, Edmund studied the gold carpet.

"I've brought him to you, dear Prudie, because I know how sweet you are and that you won't talk about this to anyone. Can you believe this handsome fellow is inexperienced? We need to remedy that, don't you think?"

"Yes, Alexander. I can help."

He kissed her and ran a finger down her neck. "He needs a gentle hand to guide him, but look at that shoulder span! He was a championship boxer a few years back. In his exuberance, he'll likely require a sturdy partner. I'm sure you'll work him into a frenzy at some point tonight, but I know you can take whatever he delivers. What do you say?"

"Anything for you, Alexander the Great. But he won't be a hardship." She looked to Edmund and smiled. "You're very attractive, Mr. Easton, and I'm honored to be your first."

Alexander pulled her to the mattress with a dominant stance. "Don't get too comfortable with him, darling Prudie. You know I relish our monthly exchanges. I won't let him take that from us."

Hands roaming, they necked and touched, exchanging whispers. Edmund tried not to follow every movement and moan.

A minute later, Alexander stood and grinned at Edmund. "Do you need me to demonstrate any positions or techniques?"

Wanting Alexander to leave so the woman's appreciative gaze would focus on him, Edmund shook his head. "I'm sure Prudie's a capable teacher."

Alexander laughed and took him in a brotherly embrace. "Do whatever you want within this house, but Consuela is mine."

Prudie watched him leave from her perch on the now rumpled bed, but smiled warmly at Edmund once they were alone. "Would you care for a glass of brandy?"

Head still buzzing from the shot in the carriage, Edmund declined. "Maybe later."

She nodded and patted the spot beside here, blonde hair shifting across her shoulder with the movement. "Then join me, Mr. Easton."

"Call me Eddie."

***

Edmund woke with a splitting headache. Groaning, he rolled facedown to hide from the ambient light through the curtains.

Prudie's soft hands massaged his back. "Eddie, may I get you some coffee?"

"Mmm, please."

The mattress shifted when she left him and he tried to remember the details of the night. He recalled Prudie's guidance the first time. Though he knew Alexander would take credit for arranging things, it was Prudie who deserved the praise. At some point, Rupert's loud voice sounded in the hall. Doors slammed but no one disturbed them, so Edmund had indulged again and again—both with Prudie and alcohol.

By the time Prudie returned with a tray, he sat on the bed in his underdrawers. Bumping the door closed with a magnificent hip, her smile brightened the room.

"Please don't tell anyone about this. We aren't supposed to serve men in our rooms, except a shot of whiskey or brandy during their paid time."

He blanched as he took his first sip. "I'm sorry, Prudie. I wasn't expecting to come here. I don't know if I have enough in my billfold to cover—"

She laughed and settled beside him. "Don't worry about it. Alex told me he would see to the payment when he's around later today."

Trying to understand how much of the night was pre-planned, he questioned her. "When did he decide that?"

Her cheeks turned pink and she tucked her hair behind her ear. "While he had me on the bed before he left. But I'd have stayed with you without payment, Eddie. It was an honor to share that with you."

Edmund grinned and straightened his posture. "Would I be as sought after as Alex if I make a habit of coming here?"

"The young handsome clients are always fussed over, but Alex most of all. He's good to us girls, those of us lucky enough to be chosen. But he doesn't disrespect the others. He's a gentleman to all while most of the men leer at us like we're ham hocks in a butcher's window."

"I'd never treat you that way, Prudie." His finger caressed her lip as he leaned in, plundering her mouth to seal himself as worthy a lover as Alexander Melling.

"We're advised not to kiss," she whispered.

"But Alex does, and I aim to indulge you even better than him."

"I'll look forward to your return."

True to her obliging nature, she helped him dress. He tucked his bowtie into the pocket of his tuxedo before leaving. It was nine in the morning, but the streets were near empty after a night of partying. Edmund walked to the safety of Dauphin Street before encountering anyone he knew.

"Eddie!" Frederick Davenport called to him from across the road. He jogged over, hair slightly damp as though he'd just showered. He shook Edmund's hand with a firm grip. "I haven't seen you in months."

Edmund grinned and thumped him on the back. "How do you look so alert this morning?"

He nodded over his broad shoulder. "I just finished at the gym. I didn't have a partner for the ring, so I had to take extra time on the rowing machine and punching bag." He did a few arm rotations then took a sparring stance. "Join me sometime, Eddie. I'd like another go at you."

Edmund ran a hand through his tousled hair and laughed. "After the night I just had, you'd knock me flat. And I haven't been in the ring for over a year."

"It's never too late to get back to it, and it'd be good to see you on a regular basis again." Frederick motioned to his tuxedo. "You've been out since the ball?"

Edmund nodded with a grin. "I now understand what a man like you enjoys."

"What do you mean by *like me?*" Frederick crossed his arms.

"You know. Having been married."

Frederick cleared his throat.

"Have the months been rough?" Edmund asked. "We haven't talked since the funeral."

"I'm getting along."

"It's a shame you have to miss the balls this year. Lucy was there last night. I always fancied you two together, but instead I'm stuck chasing the cads away because you had to go to Pennsylvania and marry a stranger last winter. Why didn't you bring Harriet over to meet us?"

Frederick's fists tightened. "It never seemed like the right time, and she was sick much of her time here. How are your parents?"

"Well as anything. Opal's with a private tutor now but is still giving Mother trouble with her moods. Father's hinting to me about settling down so he can retire."

"And Lucy? Is she still writing?"

Edmund noted the emotion in his friend's voice. "She's forever scribbling and watching the mail for word from publishing companies when she doesn't have her nose in a book. Come over and see her sometime. I'm sure she'd appreciate the visit. The only caller she ever has is Grace Anne Marley."

"It wouldn't be proper." Frederick pointed to the black band around his upper arm that set him apart as being in mourning. The Davenports were all about honor and tradition.

Edmund guffawed. "You're family to us, Freddy. No one would mind, and I'm sure Lucy would be a sympathetic listener to your woes. You two always got along splendidly."

A bittersweet smile found his clean-shaven face. "I've always had a soft spot for Goosy. We three had fun together with our battles when we were kids. It'd be nice to escape reality and return to those carefree years."

Rubbing the stubble on his jaw, Edmund nodded. "Those were the days."

"We can relive our games in the boxing ring at least. Find me in the gym any day after work or Saturday mornings."

"I'll let you know. It's good talking to you, but I need to get home and sleep this off."

"You shouldn't need to sleep off a pleasant night. Take care of yourself, Easton."

He looked to his scuffed dress shoes. "You too, Freddy."

***

Ever since meeting Frederick New Year's morning, Edmund's soul grew heavy with guilt. Seeing his oldest friend morally and physically fit despite life's upsets cast a shadow on the choices he'd made since Alexander had offered him camaraderie. To hide from himself and to help him feel more distinction amid his peers, Edmund decided to grow a beard like the European royalty wore.

In the weeks leading up to the masquerade, he attended four planning meetings with Alexander where he met the full Mystics of Dardenne society and felt the rush of being among the wealthy bachelors he used to run about with as a boy. A chasm had grown between them as they had gone away to universities and oversea adventures after graduation, while Edmund was stuck in the family business. But now they were equals. The meetings were followed by visits to the brothel, where Edmund furthered his liaisons with Prudie on his own dime.

The Friday afternoon of the event, he met Alexander after work. They were one of the first to arrive at Temperance Hall, and Alexander showed Edmund the layout of their party. The main room was decorated as a cemetery, complete with false headstones and monuments. A mausoleum erected in one corner added to the atmosphere, and potted trees throughout the space gave the appearance of the outdoors. The second floor offered a full bar and facilities for guests, the third story a private oasis for members to indulge in whatever they saw fit.

On the top floor, Alexander and Edmund relaxed with a few drinks as the others arrived. An hour before the doors opened to their guests, they all dressed in matching costumes—full-body skeleton suits on black material. The hooded skull masks were the last things to be pulled on. Then the Mystics of Dardenne members lined the red carpet in the foyer like a gauntlet of death for guests to pass between as they entered the ballroom.

The thrill of being in a position of dominance over the captive arrivals brought Edmund to a new high. Following the other members' leads, he began touching women as they passed before him. A caressing hand down an arm. A pinching touch on a backside. When Consuela and her friends arrived, the skeletons increased their boldness. Many broke rank and absconded into the ballroom with the women.

For the members-only first dance, Edmund chose a striking brunette dressed in all black whose escort gave him a frown as he led her onto the floor. Her feathered Venetian mask offset her porcelain skin, and the cut of her gown showed much of what she had to offer.

His hand migrated from her waist to her hip. "Do you mind?"

Her painted lips parted into a smile, and she shook her head. "But my cousin might."

"Why would a man bring a cherished family member to a ball like this?"

She giggled. "He's visiting from Birmingham and didn't know better."

Edmund took her merriment as invitation for more and did what he'd done to Judith at the New Year's Eve masquerade. By the end of the waltz, he wished to take the woman to the third floor den and explore her further, but it wasn't his break time.

"May I find you later?" he asked as his gloved hands lowered.

"Please do."

Knowing there were willing women that didn't need to be paid delighted Edmund. He settled near a punch bowl with a glass and drinking tube that allowed him to partake of the laced punch through his mask. Head woozy, he almost fell when someone knocked his shoulder. A skeleton leaned next to his ear.

"I know that's you, Easton," Alexander whispered. "Don't disappoint me by loafing around on our night. Go up to the den and see Lyons. He's got something that will get you going. And take a guest with you."

Under the lights of the ballroom, Prudie didn't shine as she did in her bedroom, her fleshy form not as comely as the others and her blonde hair too reminiscent of his sister's. Scanning the crowd for someone new, Edmund noticed Hazel coming out of the mausoleum with a guest, the man's tuxedo in disarray. Understanding it was a place for the non-members to indulge as they weren't allowed on the third floor, he felt himself heat beneath the mask.

Complete debauchery! But I can't blame them.

He went for the stairs and found Consuela pushing away a man who couldn't keep his hands off the black corset she wore on the outside of her red gown.

Edmund shoved the guest to the ground and took Consuela's hand. "Come with me."

"Thank you." She clutched his arm and climbed to the third floor with him.

With a nod to Edmund's skeleton costume, the man dressed as The Grim Reaper standing guard allowed them into the Mystics of Dardenne den. Consuela squealed in delight over the ice buckets full of bottles and the couples in various positions on the settees about the sitting area.

"Welcome, brother!" Rupert, unmasked, waved him over to a table in the corner. "Bring that sweet little woman over here so both of you can get a hit."

Consuela tugged Edmund's hand until he followed her to the offering of white powder displayed on a flat tray. As he stood beside her, Rupert studied him.

When she'd snorted her fill, Rupert took her by the neck. "That's not Alex."

"I don't know who he is, but he was nice enough to defend my honor."

"Like you have any." He sneered and shoved her before turning on Edmund. "Who do you think you are, bringing Alex's whore up here?"

Edmund pulled his mask off and slapped Rupert across the face with it. "I'm a Dardenne! Who do you think *you* are handling Alex's girl like that?"

Rupert's face went from shock to humor as he laughed. "Easton, you've proved me wrong. I thought Melling had lost all sense when he invited you because I believed you were like saintly Davenport since you were such friends with him. How wrong I was!" He emptied another metal case of cocaine onto the tray. "Load up, Eddie. Then you can unload in Consuela. I'll get Alex high to keep him from interfering. He doesn't like to share and sometimes needs to be reminded that Dardenne brothers need to sacrifice for each other."

Edmund did as Rupert suggested and brought Consuela to one of the chaises in the partitioned-off space in the rear of the room. By the time they emerged, Edmund felt the effects of his binging and Alexander was face down in the middle of the room. Consuela laughed and went to Rupert for another fix.

The guard burst through the door. "There's a raid! Get out the back!"

Edmund immediately sobered. Rupert grabbed his supplies and led the way to the fire escape out a back window. Consuela went with the throng.

Feeling guilty for being the reason Alexander was plastered, Edmund hauled him by his armpits. "Come on, Alex!"

He moaned and started twitching.

"Police are coming, Melling. We've got to scat."

As he pulled him through the window, Alexander went limp as though he'd passed out. Edmund slung him over his shoulder, wishing he'd spent time at the gym the past few weeks so that carrying him wouldn't be as taxing. When they got to the alley, he realized their only means of escape was on foot. Edmund toted Alexander through the night to the closest safe place he could think of—Frederick Davenport's house.

***

The first Friday in February, Edmund forced himself to The Cathedral of the Immaculate Conception for confession. Thanks to the look on Frederick's face when he'd opened the door to Edmund and Alexander on the night of the masquerade, Edmund had managed to stay sober and away from the red light district the previous week. Disappointment and disgust were what his old friend had conveyed without words, and the feeling still loomed over him.

Edmund went so far as to go to the gym once—he was sore for two days afterward—and had spent one evening at Frederick's house playing chess as a means to pacify the upset in their friendship. At Easton and Sons, he worked harder and volunteered to go every time something was needed from the warehouse. But it was all for naught, because after the fast times with Alexander and his crowd, nothing was fulfilling.

Then the invitation came that morning.

Edmund Albert Easton
Of Mobile, Alabama,
Is hereby invited to join Aethelwulf Club
Please arrive on the evening of…

The premier men's club of the city! Within those smoking rooms, political deals were made, business partnerships were forged, and the downfall of lesser men was plotted. The Melling and Lyons men had all been members for generations. Edmund's father and Maxwell were members but obviously had given no thought to mentoring him into their folds, because Alexander Melling was listed as his benefactor—probably because he'd saved him from being arrested at the masquerade.

But no matter the reason, Edmund wasn't going to let the opportunity slip away. He promised himself he'd start fresh after confessing his indulgences since New Year's Eve and would be free to mature into a position of respectability among his peers without the aid of Mystics of Dardenne mischief.

He paced the marble floor as he waited in the rear of the nave for an opening in the confessional booth. When the curtain finally parted, a contrite Alexander stepped out. Catching Edmund's gaze, his typical puckish grin returned. Nodding to greet him, Edmund stepped into the enclosure as Alexander held the curtain for him.

Falling to his knees, Edmund's heart raced as he crossed himself and waited for the window to open. Going through a watered-down version of his sins, Edmund promised to carry out his penance when prompted with how to make amends.

Breathing a sigh of relief when he exited the cathedral, Edmund faltered at Alexander's mirthful expression as he leaned against one of the portico columns.

"Feel better, Easton?"

He shrugged. "Better than I felt last Friday."

Alexander laughed. "Thanks for helping me out of that mess. I assume you've received your invitation."

"It was most unexpected. Thank you."

"You deserve it. It'll be another place we can drink and cavort. For now, let's go celebrate our lightened souls. There's never a wait in the district on confession day." Alexander started down the steps.

Edmund hovered at the edge of the portico two whole seconds before following Alexander back to the indulgent revelry of carnival season.

THE END

Author's Note

Though written after what is now books two and three in The Possession Chronicles, *Perilous Confessions* wouldn't be here without Sean Connell urging me to try writing horror. Thanks for your support and kind words over the course of the journey. What started with an idea for a basic Gothic tale set in a creepy house on a cliff, in the vein of *Jane Eyre* and mid-twentieth-century Gothic romances, morphed into a multi-generation family saga of epic Southern Gothic proportions. Within these pages you'll find the catalyst for the joy and pain of Alexander Melling, Lucy Easton, their families, friends, and enemies.

My literary sanity (what little I have) is due in large part to my critique group—both those officially still participating and otherwise. MeLeesa Swann, Candice Marley Conner, Joyce Scarbrough, Lee Ann Ward, and Stephanie Thompson were the first to meet these characters. Thanks for being there for me to bounce ideas around, bringing me back to reality when I drifted too far, cheering me on, and putting up with my McAvoys.

Special thanks, as always, to my family for tolerating my possession by these characters while writing/editing this saga. I love you all.

I spent many hours in research: online, in books, on location, and also at Mobile Public Library's Local History and Genealogy special collection using their extensive files, maps, books, and newspaper archives. Thank you, librarians! As a visual learner, I found inspiration through the social media posts featuring postcards and photographs of the area and people from the early 1900s from The Doy Leale McCall Rare Book and Manuscript Library at the University of South Alabama. (That being said, I took a few liberties in the series to suit my purpose, the biggest being the use of Cathedral Square, which was not in existence at the time.)

Another source of information was Andrew BeauChamp. Thanks for your help with questions regarding period clothing and sharing your reference books with me over the years. Not to mention feeding me when I'm in your neck of the woods. Cookies and guacamole are some of the best writing foods!

The Mobile Bay Area is blessed with an awesome literary and arts community. Thanks to the membership of Mobile Writers Guild as well as the other local groups who've hosted me for presentations over the years. I've met some great people through MWG and have honed my writing and speaking skills in the process. And kudos to Sean and Amanda Herman and their labor of love, The Serpents of Bienville, for keeping local folklore, history, arts, and the distinct Mobile vibe alive and well: "All power to the imagination."

Last—but not least—a shout out to Alisha Vincent. Thank you for being supportive of me and this series.

About the Author

While experiencing the typical adventures of growing up, Carrie Dalby called several places in California home, but she's lived on the Alabama Gulf Coast since 1996. Serving two terms as president of Mobile Writers' Guild and five years as the Mobile area Local Liaison for the Society of Children's Book Writers and Illustrators are two of the writing-related volunteer positions she's held. When Carrie isn't reading, writing, browsing bookstores/libraries, or homeschooling her children, she can often be found knitting or attending concerts.

Carrie writes for both teens and adults. *Fortitude* is listed as a Best History Book for Kids by Grateful American Foundation. She has also published *Corroded*, a contemporary teen novel about friendship and autism, several short stories that can be found in different anthologies, as well as a multitude of Southern Gothic novels for adults.

For more information, visit Carrie Dalby's website:

carriedalby.com